AOPATO
By
Margaret Afseth

Amazon/kindle Edition

ISBN: 978-0-9917562-9-2

Publisher's note: This novel is a work of fiction.
Names, characters, places and incidents are either
products of the author's imagination or used
fictitiously. All characters are fictional, and
similarity to people living or dead purely
coincidental.

This book is dedicated to my brother David, whom
we lost during the preparation of this book.

1

TABLE OF CONTENTS

Prologue:

1902 Northern Canada

The settlement consisted of the lumber office, a trading post and the row of connecting log houses everyone called the motel. It was in the cabin, third from the left, that the man and the boy had spent the night.

Inside, the room smelled of alcohol, stale cigarette smoke, dirty socks and urine, which emanated from the chamber pot in the far west corner. Littering a small table, three feet from the dingy bed, were two dirty aluminium plates, two tin cups, one still half full, and pages of newsprint scattered across the top.

It was dim, the window shades drawn.

Sprawled upon the tousled cot was a tall, extremely thin man; his salt and pepper hair matted, his unwashed red chequered shirt ragged, and the coveralls worn. He was shoe less.

In his right hand he held a half empty bottle of cheap whiskey. Near his left hip, a small loaded pistol waited for his courage to be fortified enough that its owner might actually carry out the purpose for which the weapon had been purchased.

The man wondered *how did I come to this place?*

He lifted the bottle to his lips drawing deeply. The amber liquid burned as it travelled down his throat.

First, he had killed his favourite son while working in the bush, the tree falling with such finality, ending the child's life before it began. He had felt that last breath leave his slight frame, and

4

as he grieved his loss beside the mounded earth they had come.

The man had seemed just like any other, but it was hard to make out features for the light that shown behind him. In his arms he carried a sleeping boy near the age of Jake's lost son. He offered to give the child to Jake...said that one could take the place of his treasure.

Would Jake take the small one, raise him as his own; keep him safe from something that hunted the child?

Jake had agreed, too numb from his sorrow to think ahead to the consequences such an action would bring.

A night bird called from outside the window. Darkness was closing in.

That child would never replace his own, though he had so resembled his son in face and features. The new one acted strange, different somehow, peculiar.

Jake had given the new boy his son's name. *Avery.*

The outside door rattled in the wind.

Is it here? Has it found us at last?

But though he listened hard, only distant sounds of revelry came from outside in the night.

They had travelled together, he and the child, moving from place to place, the man always feeling hunted, though by what he could not tell. They had just kept running.

The bottle found his lips once again, but it did not drown his fear.

I am tired of running; I can do this no longer; I will flee no more. This is over. Finished. Let someone else protect the boy...

He had sent Avery to the store.

"We need supplies," Jake told Avery, handing him money. "Go to the post. Pick up some grub... spend time looking around."

Jake raised the bottle, draining its contents.

The smell of the room was becoming overpowering; added to the usual stench was now the odour of sulphur, rotting flesh; the metallic taste of blood.

The air filled with overwhelming anger, rage; utter viciousness.

It is here! I can feel it!

He could not see anything; never could, only felt the presence of something so evil his heart threatened to stop with the fear.

I will face it this time.

A hollow voice, as though someone breathed through a tube, sounded about him.

Too loud! It was more inside his mind than around him.

"What have you done with him?"

"He's gone," the man answered. "Go find him yourself."

A hard-derisive snort, and Jake began to tremble.

"I will kill you first, so you can no longer hide him."

Jake did not care anymore.

Let the creature have its way. I am tired of running; I am ready to die.

Trying to wear him down, drawing out the minutes, the being meant to torture him.

Silence dragged in the room.

Suddenly, without Jake's will or control, his hand released the bottle, and picked up the gun. He raised it to his head, pointed to his temple, pulled back the trigger…and fired.

Simultaneous with the loud report, a blinding flash occurred, flooding the cabin in light. On either side of the room, two small bright star-like orbs appeared in mid-air.

Beside the bed, a huge grotesque shape shimmered to visibility, a reptilian creature, reeking of hatred and revenge.

"You will not stop me!" it thundered.

A beam of red light zapped from the reptilian to the star shape on the right, while at the same moment another of blue went from the star at the left to the monster.

The first star object exploded with such force the room went almost dim.

Beside the bed, the ugly being began to melt slowly, as a hot candle melts in extreme heat, turning to dark vapour, then at last fading from sight.

As the outside door began to open, the second star vanished. All went still…and dark.

A slight boy of seven entered, a bag of groceries in his arm.

Avery pondered the darkened room; set his burden in the chair by the door. He made his way to the bedside; fumbled to light the lamp. His hands came away sticky, and wondering why; he turned up the wick.

The scene accosting his senses stunned him. The man upon the bed had only half a face; the pillow beneath him was covered with chunks of brain matter; the faded blue blanket was spattered with bright red blood, as was the yellowing walls. The lamp dripped with dead tissue and gore.

At first, he did not comprehend. He raised his hands and pondered them. He looked up, gazing about the room.

It sure stinks in here, he observed.

He looked again at the man he knew, sprawled upon the bed. Realization finally hit him; what had just happened in this room; why he had been sent away.

The young boy screamed.

From then on, he entered a world of numbness from which he would never quite recover. As from a distance, his screams continued…on…and on…and on.

Outside alarmed voices called to one another. The door was rammed in hard; it banged against the wall.

Finally, someone was leading him away.

Outside. Fresh air. Someone folded him in comforting arms…

But forever, that memory would visit him in dreams.

CHAPTER 1

Present Day

The day was as pleasant as any Labour Day could be, sunny, mild and warm, the last long weekend of summer, just after the children all filed back to school. But instead of spending it by the lake, they were all working.

Though only seventy-five, grandma Sonia was moving into Senior Housing. She was coming from small town to city, hoping to be closer to family.

Her son-in-law Ivan, short and compact at five-six, weighing well over three-twenty, was his usual controlling personage, commanding all: his wife Rhea, their two sons Tyler and Shawn, Jessica his daughter and his own son-in-law Wade.

Granddaughter Kara, he could not control. She moped and sat at the sidelines annoyed at being forced to come at all.

All were conditioned to Ivan; he always assumed he was in charge, booking no argument.

The consensus had been that for Sonia's migration a paid mover was too costly. So, each family member was using their own vehicle: a mini-van, two small trucks and a number of cars…so many as to necessitate some of them be parked in the vacant lot across from the building.

The complex stood five stories high, housing some eighty-five residents. It was of brick, flat roofed, at the edge of a very unsafe neighbourhood, but Sonia had been told it was secure.

Inside the entrance, the other inhabitants sat together in the foyer like penguins seeking warmth together from the cold winter wind.

As the crew moved back and forth unloading, many inmates introduced themselves to Sonia, but being weary already from packing and sorting her belongings, her memory lacking clarity when exhausted, she forgot their names soon after they declared it.

She met ninety-five-year-old emaciated Lena, whom she would later call 'the puzzle lady', because of her apparent rule over the games room, plump eighty-year old Ellie, who had trouble with her feet, and rail-thin Laura who used a walker. The last, only sixty-five, had just lost her husband recently.

It would not take Sonia long to realize this was the core group of the building. They knew most of what transpired within its walls for they gathered every day in the common room for coffee to catch up or gossip, as the feeling moved them.

Later, also, Sonia would quickly learn these women had no concept of the meaning of the word confidence.

Sonia's family was not a quiet bunch. As they unloaded their matriarch, they visited loudly, tramping noisily down halls bumping into people, banging the walls with furniture, making such a racket when setting up in the small rooms, you would think they were out at an old farm house in the middle of nowhere. It never entered their minds, this was a quiet, less private facility and walls being thin, they might be disturbing others.

While the family arranged furniture within her new apartment, emptied boxes on to shelves, a constant stream of new neighbours came through the open door to see what was transpiring.

Sonia felt friendship had its place, but having just been uprooted, she needed things to settle down.

She was polite...

All she really wanted was for everyone to go away so she could be quiet and relax again.

She begged silently, *Please, just leave me alone.*

She was so tired. She almost wished, now, she was back in her village home again.

At last, her family finished. They shooed out the visitors, suggested going out for supper for chicken and fries, and carted Sonia away with them.

****

It was four days later, before Sonia finally felt organized and settled enough to descend to the lower levels of the building to explore.

CHAPTER 2

Sonia was unpacking groceries when the telephone rang. Call display said it was Myron.

Sonia sighed.

Her middle brother was not always easy to talk with. Myron could go on and on, or get miffed at the slightest thing and hang up abruptly. He could wait three weeks or call three times a day, mostly at meal times or late at night, and you were expected to give him his time, whether it was convenient or not.

Mostly, Sonia chose to ignore his inconsiderate behaviour, but at times, when she was already weary, as was the case today, the thought of his unpredictability made her cringe. Self-control would take more effort than she was capable of at present.

Reaching for the phone, she dropped into the recliner.

"Hi, Myron."

"Hey there, beautiful. What you up to?"

"Just putting away my groceries; I just got back from shopping."

"Oh?" Myron paused for effect. "I thought you were five, four."

"What?" puzzled Sonia.

He's certainly upbeat today.

Suddenly, she realized what he was talking about.

"Oh! How tall, you mean?"

"Yaaa…"

"Fun…ny! So, how are you?"

"I'm not doing so good."

"Why's that?" Their conversations always started this way. It was Myron's way of getting attention.

"I don't know what's the matter. I'm losing weight; lost so much that when I put on this old pair of jeans I haven't worn in years, I fit into them. They fit like a glove."

"Isn't that good?"

"No! Not for me, it isn't."

Sonia thought of her brother's appearance. He was built like a boxer, all imposing five-nine, three hundred pounds of him. Usually unkempt, unwashed, he had the annoying habit of chewing his tongue because he refused to wear his false teeth.

"Have you been eating, Myron?"

"I go across to the 'dub' once in a while; get a burger."

He isn't eating regularly, again.

"Myron! You're a diabetic! You have to eat even spaced meals. Don't you have food in the house?"

"Just went to the food bank; got all kinds of stuff."

"Everything you shouldn't eat, right? Do you ever tell them you can't have sweets?"

"I trade; get things I like…"

"So, you could make yourself something to eat?"

14

"I just can't make myself get off the couch to do it. I hate cooking."

Sonia made an exasperated sound.

"I sleep a lot. Can't sleep at night, so when I do get to sleep, I don't wake up until three in the afternoon."

"No wonder you can't sleep at night, you've slept all day! Did you eat today?"

"Just got up."

Sometimes, she wondered if he would ever change. He seemed to enjoy getting her riled.

"Make yourself something! I mean it!"

"Yes, mommy."

"I'm not your mommy; I'm your sister!"

"You're the Matriarch of this family."

"No! I'm not meant to think for you. You're a grown man! Your seventy!"

There was a pause, but only for a minute, while Myron thought of a comeback.

"I made myself a steak yesterday…"

"And did you put your dentures in to eat it?"

"Nope!"

"What do you do, just swallow it whole?"

"I masticate it with my gums." He laughed, delight by the fact his sister was reacting.

"Right." Frustrated, Sonia gave up.

Finding the silence too long, Myron declared, "I threw out my bed."

"Why?" Sonia came back as calmly as she could.

"It was covered in red spots underneath."

"Was it bed bugs or just mould?"

"Didn't see any bugs…"

"So, what are you sleeping on now?"

"My chesterfield…my colour TV quit on me, too," he added. "But I still got a black and white to watch."

"Oh Myron," Sonia moaned in exasperation. "What are we going to do with you?"

He chuckled. "So, how do you like your new place?"

By now, Sonia was ready to vent.

"I don't!" Without taking a breath, she launched into all that annoyed her. "My neighbour baby-sits her grand kids. They bang on the wall between us, and I can hear her scolding them. When they are not there, I hear this squawking; both she and the couple across the hall have birds.

"Then there is 'lady banger' down the hall. She slams her door every ten minutes, over and over and over.

"And at three in the morning, the guy above me gets up to go to the bathroom, bangs down the lid after and flushes; wakes me from a sound sleep every time."

Sonia took a breath, but continued on again.

"The building smells constantly like rotten potatoes in a root cellar, and I smell smoke, and gasoline fumes from the lawn mower when they mow the lawn. It comes in my window, even though it's closed.

"The puzzle lady, Lena is mean to me, calls me all kinds of names…and would you believe it? One old geezer actually propositioned me; said he'd like to climb in my window."

Myron laughed outright.

"It's not funny!"

"Just tell me his name and I'll pound the living shit out of him."

"No, you won't! Just you stay out of it."

"So, you don't like your apartment?"

"I like the apartment. It's lovely. I just don't like the situation. I thought when I moved in here it was like any other high-rise building except it was for seniors, but they act like we are all supposed to live in the common room during the day…like a family in a house.

"I'm claustrophobic in crowds. I never signed on for a community. If I had wanted that, I'd have gone to a care facility. I like privacy."

"Well, it was your idea to sell your house and leave your nice yard."

"Because I couldn't manage any more, and my family is always too busy to come help me.

"I'm not ready to sit by the entrance doors and vegetate, waiting to die," Sonia added. "Do you know, they took away three of these 'inmates' to the hospital, in my first week here alone?"

For some reason, Myron found no sympathy for her. "Looks like you're stuck there."

"Ya, I know. I'll never get out of here again. I can't afford another house. Prices have gone too high."

"Kind of like a prison sentence…"

"Ya…a sentence to 'senior's prison'; only way out is by stretcher."

Sonia suddenly realized what a tirade she had gone on.

"Sorry, I've been dumping on you. But you're the first one to ask…"

"You're entitled to one tantrum in a life time."

Sonia laughed, chagrined. *And this was from the brother I only half listened to most of the time.*

Finding it hard to let go, she added one last complaint.

"You know we have a thief in the building as well? People have put up decorations at Christmas and they disappear right at the front entrance where the security cameras are monitoring. They put this clock up in the puzzle room; somebody took it, so they put up another real nice one, with butterflies on it and everything. Two days later, it too went missing. People hang ornaments on their doors. They disappear within hours."

"They are always stealing from me here too," Myron admitted. "They come in my bedroom window and take stuff while I'm sleeping on the couch. I can hear them, but I just can't wake up to stop them."

"You know, you can put a stick in the slider between the panels. Then, they couldn't get in."

"Ya, guess I'll have to try that. I swear they've been fooling around in my computer…"

Myron sighed in a dreamy, distant way, his thoughts drifting away.

Uh oh, I've lost him, Sonia thought.

"I remember one time when I was on Joel's computer. I got into this CIA site. They told me, 'get off right now!"

Ya, right Myron.

Myron was given to telling stories when a conversation went too long for his mind to remain focused. Some were factual, others pure fantasy.

"You know, Joel was a spy for the American military. I saw the scanner right there on his work bench…"

Sonia knew it was time to side track him.

"Say Myron, if you could go anywhere; do anything you wanted to, what would you do? Where would you go?"

"Me? I think I'd like a cabin by a lake, up north in the bush, with just a dock and my fishing rod…" Myron's mind went away with that thought.

Sonia brought him back to real-time. "No one to bother you?"

"Ya, I wouldn't have to answer to anyone…could do what I want to."

"Would you have a dog?"

"Ya."

"What kind?"

"Something like one of those greyhounds…a Russian wolfhound…you know…I had horses once, when I worked on the rigs. Those royal white horses…"

Oh, man! It's time to end this conversation.

"It cost me an arm and a leg to board them…"

"Myron, I really need to put the rest of my groceries away…"

"Fine!"

The line abruptly went dead, and Sonia felt guilty.

Somehow, he always has the last word…even when he doesn't say a thing.

CHAPTER 3

Sonia would be the first to admit her brothers were opposites: Myron rebellious, often aggressive, and lacking any respect for women, Joel caring, gentle, appreciative of all.

If she were to choose between them, Joel would be the favourite. Youngest of the three, only sixty-five, he seemed the more intelligent, the best educated, and the most sympathetic. He had always been there for her; her anchor; their leader; the one they always turned to.

When Sonia picked up the phone, she looked forward to talking to Joel.

She dropped into her favourite chair, getting comfortable for a long conversation.

"Hi Joel."

"So…what are you doing?'

The tease rose to the surface in Sonia at his cheerful voice. "Talking to you."

Joel on the other end chuckled. "That's usually my line."

Satisfied at her accomplishment, Sonia smiled to herself. "Just thought, for once, I'd beat you to it. So, what's up?"

Joel at one time had been a teacher of a beginner's class in a registered Computer training school. Now retired, he still fixed computers out of his own home. He spent a lot of time surfing the Internet;

computers had been his love, and would always be his life.

"I needed a break," Joel admitted. "Thought I'd call you."

Curious, Sonia prompted. "What were you working on?"

"Our genealogy...mom's side."

He's been working on that for a long time.

"Anything of interest I should know about?"

"Humm...other than mom being middle child; the odd girl between six male and six female siblings; the most sickly of thirteen strapping farm kids...oh, yes, and the one forced to do all the menial tasks...or so she always said."

Sonia laughed. "Sounds like we have a Cinderella story here."

"Who knows?" Joel lowered his voice in jest to a husky, haunting timber. "Maybe, like an ugly duckling, she was spirited in and they never realized she wasn't born to them."

"Joel! What an awful thing to say."

Joel chuckled deep down in his chest, a mischievous, hearty laugh Sonia loved about her brother. "Then, there is dad," he added. "If I could just find out where he was...there is a gap in his history from the age of seven until he was twenty-three."

"No records at all?"

"Nothing...zilch! He just drops off the face of the earth after his father committed suicide..."

"Dad was with him when he did that?"

"He found him!"

Shock flooded Sonia. "Oh, my. I never knew that! Where was his mom?"

"Dad's mom and dad separated when he was five. His father took dad; his mother got the rest of the kids."

"Why?"

"That's what his father wanted. Back then they didn't settle things in court. Nobody aired their dirty laundry in public…differences were kept private."

"So, any idea why dad's father killed himself?"

"I don't know any details…he was an alcoholic…just that dad found him shot."

"He was what…seven?'

"Yep!"

"Man! A memory like that must have been hard to carry through life. No wonder dad drank…"

Sonia went down memory lane, remembering the man himself as she grew up.

"I remember how he used to say he could hear the police radio on his fillings…said he heard voices in his head."

"Back then, they didn't have the medical knowledge we have today. Dad was schizophrenic," Joel observed. "But they never picked up on it. He was a great one for telling stories."

Sonia laughed to herself, thinking how much Myron was like their father.

"Myron sure can make up the stories, too."

"Well, he's schizophrenic like dad," Joel agreed. "Have you talked to him lately?'

"A few days ago. I'm worried about him, Joel. He's not eating right again; says he's losing weight..."

"You know, he just tells you he's sick to get your attention?"

"He's depressed, Joel, sleeps all the time, then goes for fast food..."

"That man! I wish he'd take better care of himself."

"If he doesn't, he'll be the first we put under the ground. I'm not supposed to bury my younger brothers."

"Tell me about it! Mind you, you'll outlive us anyway. The females on mom's side have the longevity. Look at mom's oldest sister. She's ninety-seven...and another is ninety-two."

"Seems all her family were long lived...except mom. Why was that? How come she had a heart condition when everyone else was robust and strong?'

"I don't understand what happened there...she must have gotten all the bad genes..."

"And we inherited them," Sonia agreed.

"I always say, no use getting married, wouldn't want to visit our genome on anyone else."

"But that makes life very solitary..."

Joel sighed. "Ya, well, it was better that way, better where Myron's concerned, too.

"And I do have my friends, not that Myron can be classed in that category...I shocked him the last time I talked to him, told him...I have to love him...because he's my brother...I'd still love him no matter what he did...but, we are not friends! Friends care about each other, and he never cares about anyone but himself."

"Joel," Sonia admonished, not liking the fact that her brothers were warring. "Do you realize how lonely he is? How many holidays has he spent alone?" It occurred to her she was lax in this area also, and she immediately put in a defence. "I couldn't include him until now, because I didn't live in the city..."

"I don't include him because he cuts up!" Joel rejoined vehemently. "He embarrasses me; he says inappropriate comments to my lady friends, even made one cry. I never know what he'll do next..."

"He's never learned how to act around people..."

"So? Why not? What makes him such a misfit?"

"Maybe things that happened in our childhood?"

Joel huffed in disagreement.

"We all had a rough upbringing!"

Sonia wanted to defend. "I remember when Myron was five, you were just born. The neighbour kids put him down this big hole because they didn't want him tagging along. I think they were putting up telephone or power lines through the school yard across from our house."

Sonia visualized the deep round pit that had been in the ground, and shuddered.

"Myron was down there for six hours before anyone found him; all alone; he'd been screaming his heart out for hours until he was too hoarse to yell any more. When mom found him, he was rigid with terror because of the lizards down there with him. He was too small to climb out by himself."

"That's why he's so terrified of anything reptilian! Snakes, lizards, even spiders, and he's out of the room like a shot."

"Ya…now you understand. And he doesn't trust people for the same reason. Mom didn't help either. I remember her chasing Myron with a switch for blocks trying to catch him because he refused to do something. It embarrassed mom…and him before the entire world."

Joel laughed ruefully. "Man, our family must have been a sideshow. I guess we all were a handful, but Myron…he was a real character.'

Drifting on memory lane, Joel's thoughts went to their father.

"I remember once when dad hit you with a 2x4; he knocked you out cold…I think you'd been sassing him. You were fourteen or fifteen, and thought you were smarter then he about something."

Mortified, Sonia remembered another time. "I got back at him unintentionally…that's when I decided violence was counterproductive. I've never forgotten how bad he made me feel…

"He was mad at Myron for something, broke a chair over his head. Well, I picked up this glass bowl from the supper table, and smashed it over his head.

"The neighbours must have heard all the ruckus, because someone called the cops…

"But the part that stays with me, is when the cop asked dad who had done it. Dad looked up at me with sad eyes, and told them he had just tripped.

"I could have gone to jail that day, Joel. I would now be a criminal…my life would have been way different…"

Somehow, Joel found no sympathy toward their violent father; he related more to the frustration with the man's behaviour.

"Once, I took the shot gun and pointed it at dad to stop his beating on Myron. It was never loaded, and he probably knew that, but my very act, made him realize we were fed up with his behaviour."

"It was like dad couldn't handle life…"

"And mom couldn't handle us, so she expected him to discipline…"

"And he'd only known violence, so he didn't know how…we sure grew up in a dysfunctional family," Sonia mused. "I think, though our parents are dead, we still are one…"

"Yet, you can't say we didn't love one another," Joel countered. "I always say, you pick your friends, but family…we've been placed together; you stick by each other. Who else do you have?"

"It was us against the world," Sonia laughingly agreed. "Do you remember, when you were little, how you'd get stuck in the mud, and I'd pull you out? Our yard was a slue every spring, because it was built over an artesian well…"

"I remember," Joel agreed. "We always had to leave my boots behind. They stayed out there too, until the ground dried up."

"I had to get to you on old boards placed across the mud..."

"Yes, those were the days...well," Joel broke off. "I have to go. I can smell my pot roast, and the bread maker's finished making my sour dough bread...I haven't had lunch yet."

"What do you mean? It's almost three P. M.!"

"Ya, I know. By the time I get to it it'll be 'lupper'."

Sonia laughed. "Love you."

"You too."

When Joel cut the connection, Sonia went away thinking how different, yet alike, her brothers were.

Joel, with his heart of gold and love of cooking, had the body to go with it: five-six and tipping the scale at four-fifty. While Myron ate the junk food and fast food, but gained just as badly.

Sometimes, she wondered if these two had not been placed in bodies too small for them. If they had been given the height in proportion to their weight, they would have made powerful protectors, a force to be reckoned with.

CHAPTER 4

It was Sunday evening. Sonia always made her favourite meal on Sunday evenings: a garden salad; two fried eggs, the yokes good and runny with just a film of white over the top, and two pieces of toast slathered with a generous portion of margarine…oh, yes, and a large mug of hot chocolate with marshmallows and cinnamon on top.

She had been eating this same meal each Sunday since her husband had passed away. Before that, they had eaten it together for years longer than Sonia wished to recall, the same thing, on the same day, seated together before the television to watch a movie while they ate their supper. It was their special time together, his favourite meal…

Sonia still missed his companionship.

She turned up the television. In a moment the nightly news would be on. Sonia sat down in the recliner, pulled the TV tray toward her, and began eating.

The news broadcaster had only just begun when the screen went blank. The lights remained on, so Sonia waited.

The station must be having difficulty. It would correct itself directly.

The screen filled with snow and static-like sound, then was replaced by a breathy, hollow voice, which came not just through the speakers, but seemed to emanate around her in the room. It felt as if it was even inside her head.

How do they do that? She wondered. Was this a movie commercial?

"Beings, all! Hear us! We will not harm you.

Upon your planet an enemy has hidden our children…"

Sonia's insides went tense.

"We grieve for these young, and beg your permission to search among you for them."

It seemed so real; Sonia could picture the creatures living in their midst.

"They can not be distinguished from your own kind."

They look like us!

"But we are able to identify them with a simple eye scan."

Thank goodness this isn't for real! The thought is frightening.

"Please ask your leaders to meet us at the following coordinates."

A series of numbers moved across the screen. Then the message followed by the numbers repeated itself…over and over. After the fifth time, Sonia grew impatient.

Enough already!

Picking up the channel changer, she pointed, but whatever station she flips to, the same message was playing.

Finally, exasperated, she shut down the TV.

"Guess I'll just read!"

****

The next morning being Monday, Sonia went downstairs to do her washing. Usually, the laundry room was empty at 8:30am, and she had her pick of the six free washers and dryers, though the sign on the wall asked people to be courteous enough to use no more than two each, and to remove said clothing as soon as the cycle was finished so that others might have a turn.

Today someone had gotten there ahead of Sonia. Beside the back machines a frail elderly woman in a wheel chair was loading wet wash into a dryer.

Sonia opened a front-loading washing machine to use it, but found it still contained small wet cloths pasted to the sides. Assuming they belonged to the other party, she took them to the woman.

"Are these yours?"

"No!" was the curt reply. So, Sonia, holding them aloft, sought for a place to leave them.

"Put them on top," the other woman ordered, pointing to the dryer she worked at.

Sonia obeyed.

As she loaded her two loads of laundry, the handicapped woman was attempting to turn about with her wheel chair.

"Can I be of help to you?"

"No! I'm fine."

Apparently, she was, for when Sonia looked again, the lady had her chair facing back toward Sonia.

Her task completed, Sonia went to park the wheeled cart, which had held her laundry, in an empty space by the dryers.

"Don't put it there," yelled dryer lady. "I put my wheelchair there."

Okay, thought Sonia. *Best not to argue.*

She went to park the cart back closer toward the entrance.

"Stupid! Don't leave it there either."

Sonia decided to ignore this order.

"Shouldn't use such a big cart in here, anyway," grumbled her adversary.

Fine, thought Sonia. *I don't need to fight.* But even as she decided it, her annoyance was getting the better of her.

"I didn't know you owned the building," she fired back.

Vacating the room hurriedly, so as not to hear further argument, Sonia left the conveyance where she had placed it.

****

She always worked on the current puzzle in the games room across the hall while she waited for the washing machine buzzer to tell her the loads were finished. Other residents had warned Sonia articles were stolen if left unattended.

She sat down at the table, getting down very close to the pieces, because Sonia could only see detail near at hand. Today the picture had small figures of intricate houses, people, dogs and birds, a puzzle of substance. As it was still only half finished, there were hours more of entertaining work ahead, which Sonia enjoyed.

A half hour later, sixty-five-year-old, rail-thin Laura, pushing her walker, ambled in. Laura never sat down while in the puzzle room; even though she used the walker everywhere she went. She simply stood at the side looking on. Perhaps, once a half hour, she would pick out a piece and try it. Usually, it failed to fit, but Laura tried anyway.

A few minutes passed. Then Lena, commander of the games room, rushed in scolding.

"What's that stupid woman yelling about? Who's she bad mouthing today?"

"You mean the woman in the washing area?" asked Sonia.

"Ya. She's yelling about somebody being a real mean person…"

Sonia chuckled. "Guess it's me she's talking about. Who is she?"

"That's Roseanne from fifth floor. She's always yelling and ordering people around…thinks she owns the place. Says you're a real bad woman…"

"She doesn't even know me! I never met her before today."

"Don't let it bother you. She's got it in for everybody."

The room grew silent again, as Lena went to working the puzzle. After a few successful placements, the next piece she sought eluded her eye.

"Where is that white dinky?" Lena wondered aloud. "Laura, find my white hooker; that one there!"

When Lena pointed to the empty area, Laura, at the other end of the table, reached over, picked up a piece, moved to where Lena had indicated and deftly placed it where needed.

Lena grinned. "That one has eyes like a hawk, can always find what I need."

Laura smiled self-consciously.

Once again silence took over.

After a time, Sonia made an attempt to make conversation. "So, Lena, are you going for the flu shot?'

"Me? Not on your life! I've always been healthy as a horse, and never had a shot in my life."

Sonia had all she could do not to laugh. Lena was the most emaciated woman she had ever laid eyes on. Next to her, even Laura looked normal.

"It used to be," ventured Laura. "They'd come into this building to give us the Flu shots. Now we got to go to the distribution centres…"

"Well, they ain't getting me there," declared Lena.

Sonia was grinning to herself, as she headed for the laundry room. The buzzer on her load was calling.

These two are quite the pair, she thought. "Got to go guys."

"Oh ya," Lena fired back. "Go desert us now, you lazy witch!"

By now, Sonia had realized, Lena said whatever entered her head, no connection between mouth and brain.

****

That night Sonia was tired, but she felt she had accomplished much. All the wash was put away, dishes were done; she had even paid bills on line.

When supper came, she was ready to relax. But she had no sooner pulled up her tray to eat when, again just as the news was coming on...

The screen went black, and that stupid advertising came on.

"Beings all...

Maybe it is some sort of prank? It isn't funny!

"Boy, somebody's going to jail!"

"...An enemy has hidden our children..."

"Ya right! You would think that a mother would know if one of her children were not her own," Sonia mumbled, turning off the television for the second night in a row.

"Mind you," and she laughed at the thought. "Joel would say, our whole family is weird, so why not?"

****

This interruption was only a blip on the screen of humanity, to most...a mere annoyance.

But...

It would change some lives...FOREVER.

CHAPTER 5

Today, Rhea was way over working in the paying work force; retirement could not come soon enough. But she feared, for her, it would never come at all.

Every day she fielded phone calls from irate cable customers; people too poor to afford the amenities of life but who considered the boob tube a need: single parent families; the welfare crowd; seniors. Any disruption; any extra charges; even when they failed to understand the how and why of the channel changer, Rhea was the scapegoat, yelled at, sworn at, called unspeakable names…And, after last night, she was ready to throw in the towel.

To add to this, on her day off she was juggling meals and cleaning, with little help from her two men. Actually, from way back, Rhea had always maintained she had four kids, the fourth being her irresponsible, immature, dominating husband.

It was not that Rhea did not love Ivan. He had wooed her, romanced her, swept her off her feet…and, he was a great lover. She covered for him; defended him; claimed people did not understand him, and would never, ever confess to anyone how hard life with him really was. But after thirty-two years of marriage, her stamina was running out of steam.

Life with Ivan had never been dull. To put it bluntly, the man was a workaholic who expected the same ability from everyone else. He was an unfulfilled entrepreneur, an opportunist constantly looking to make a fast buck. Good at persuasion and manipulation, Ivan could talk any price down, yet stayed inflexible when he was the seller.

From the first day of marriage, he perused want adds, car magazines, and yard sales for ancient restorable wrecks. Ivan was not content to tinker one at a time; three or four was his norm.

It was the same in regard to furniture. He frequented auctions, garage sales and flea markets, all for that ultimate bargain, and called it refurbishing antiques.

Then there was housing. First it was a fixer-upper mobile home, then an old farm, complete with dilapidated house and barn, and finally, at long last, a remodel of a twenty-year-old house on the edge of the city.

The excuse for the turnover was always the same: renovate to increase revenue. But in all honesty, they always put more in, were they to count their labour, then they ever got back.

There was always a lack of ready cash flow; a dependable vehicle was a dream, and the family scraped by on hand outs and gift certificates.

When ever Ivan had over extended himself, his reasoning was, "I've got to get rid of something; the bank won't okay another loan."

Though she had worked extremely hard for her keep: framing, dry-walling, painting, shingling or landscaping with Ivan, until the children reached their teens, Rhea had remained an unpaid, stay-at-home mom. When Ivan was let go from one of the three jobs he juggled, she was forced into the legitimate work place.

In Ivan's mind there was only one solution to their financial difficulty: everyone in the family had to carry their own weight. The children each had part time jobs, but that was not enough. Therefore, Rhea could no longer stay at home doing nothing.

But Rhea had no training or experience for a high paying professional position. So, babysitting it was.

Her position as a nanny had Rhea raising six preschoolers in the home of one of two teaching moms, who had combined their children of six months to five years, calling it a Day Care.

Rhea worked for a monthly wage; the mothers planned all activities and meals out beforehand. When time came to report to government these ladies pocketed the savings such status afforded, but failed to inform Rhea she was reported as running a pre-school facility.

For two years Rhea endured uncooperative victims of potty training, fussy appetites, sick children and unappeasable moms. Then she discovered what her employers had been doing behind the scenes.

When she confronted them, Rhea was laughed at and told she could do nothing about it. There was no proof they were scamming the government and cheating their employee.

To their utter amazement, normally docile Rhea up and quit, putting an end to her headaches, and leaving the resulting financial debacle for the dishonest women to deal with. In the process, she reported them to the government for misrepresentation.

At home, Ivan was supportive at first, but soon became impatient. Rhea could not find a replacement position rapidly enough.

After much searching, fortunately for all, Rhea happened upon a cable company willing to train her on the job. The position was to change her life drastically.

The perks were excellent: the health plan covered all family members for medication, dental and optical; they now had full cable, all channels, free, and best of all, in Ivan's eyes, the burdens had been taken from his shoulders, placed on Rhea's, and he was free to do as he pleased. It was a dream come true; Ivan could continue to trade, loan, buy and sell uninhibited.

It was now eleven years later; Rhea was still at the same job and could not afford to quit. Jessica, her oldest, had left home and married; Tyler, second in line, had gone to train as a RCMP constable, moving away also; leaving Shawn, the youngest, still at home.

Though their youngest was twenty-six, he had been trained in the shadow of his father, and saw the situation was to his advantage. As far as he was concerned, the benefits of home could not be equalled elsewhere. So, he remained.

When Jessica had moved away, Rhea found life more burdensome. She missed the long girl chats, enjoyable nights watching chick flicks, and shopping with her daughter. Their phone conversations and texts became shorter, further apart, then almost non-existent, as Jessica found other interests.

Rhea was left alone with the guys; the boys and their father retreated into maleness. More and more, TV shows were of violence and humour with questionable innuendo…always Ivan's choice, his favourites. After Tyler was no longer there to object, Ivan and Shawn became totally oblivious to the woman in the house. It was all about them.

Rhea felt alone…abandoned, at the end of her rope…a female human slave amongst Orang-utans.

In all this, Sonia had been her one constant…but now, her mother was getting too old to do many of the things Rhea enjoyed, such as staying up late; shopping; a fast walk in the park; she simply could not keep up.

With the thought of her parent, Rhea realized she had not called Sonia in over three weeks. Abruptly, she stopped what she was doing; swallowing down the anger she was feeling at life, Rhea punched in the number.

"Hi honey. You must have the day off."

Sonia always was the cheerful one.

"Yes, but I can't talk for long, have laundry to do."

"I did mine Monday. So, how's everyone?"

"Shawn and Ivan are both working." Rhea sighed heavily. "It seems we are always on opposite shifts. And when Shawn is off, he spends all his time with friends…"

"Well, that should be good; you and Ivan get time alone."

If Ivan would stop long enough for that to happen, Rhea thought.

"Maybe Shawn is finally looking for a place of his own?"

Rhea made a rude, discouraged sound. "Not likely. Anyway, if he did move out, I probably would never see him or hear from him again."

"Ah, honey. You are feeling down. You okay?"

Rhea forced back tears, bringing her voice to a lighter note.

I have to get my positive back.

"It'll all work out. It always does."

At least someday, I hope it will.

"Hang in there, honey. Have you heard from Tyler lately?"

Rhea thought about her middle child, Tyler the quiet, gentle one. He had shot up past six feet in his late teens; at twenty-eight, he was now almost a foot taller than his father. Ivan had always been hardest on Tyler, but he had been her good boy.

"I think he's still in exams...or were they finished last week? I forget. The days fly by...don't have time for a life anymore. I could use a vacation, mom...a real vacation."

"Tyler loves you, Rhea; he'll call when he's not busy. Maybe he's found himself a girl?"

"Oh, wouldn't that be nice! But I doubt that. He avoids that recreation like the plague. Ever since that girl Darla dumped him at seventeen, he won't trust his heart to any other. I often wonder what really happened there; sometimes I think it was Ivan who scared her away...they were so in love; she really hurt him..."

"I thought it would be permanent, too. He fell pretty hard that first time; he's a loyal, one-woman guy. But...he sure would be a nice catch for the right girl."

Rhea had to get away from this subject or she would definitely be in tears.

"So, what have you been doing?"

Evasively, her mother chose a different topic.

"Say, did you see that stupid alien commercial?'

Why does my mother always do that since the move? She changes the subject every time she is asked about her own activities. Is she hiding her real feelings...maybe unhappy where we put her? Is she upset that Ivan insisted she move?

Today, Rhea had no patience to deal with that subject.

I have enough on my mind. She chose to react to Sonia's question instead.

"That commercial has been the curse of my nights." Rhea laughed ruefully. "We never heard the end of it...just swamped with calls, all three nights."

Rhea let the annoyance she felt stay in her voice. "There was absolutely nothing we could do about it, you know, but people sure got mad at us about it. They'd lost their precious mind-numbing, hypnotic!"

"Was it an advertisement for a movie?"

"Nobody knows. Honestly! Every station, all across the continent...some say it was worldwide...but, I really doubt that."

"Strange. I hope it has stopped now; it scares me."

"Me, too. I've had enough crabby customers for a life time!" Rhea hesitated, reluctant to break off so soon. "Well, mom, I hate to make this so short, but I really have to get a move on. Ivan said he'll be off work at noon...that's in fifteen minutes, and I haven't even got dinner started..."

"Okay honey. Cheer up. I love you."

"Love you too, mom."

Somehow, the very act of talking to her mother had cheered Rhea, helped her to let off steam, and given her the will to go on. The sun outside seemed to shine brighter. And maybe...now that Ivan was off work...they might spend some alone time together.

CHAPTER 6

"They failed to take our message seriously," Net observed.

Egar grunted in disgust. "We will do it without them, then."

"How will we find the dormant if we can not openly walk the planet?"

"To be sure, it would have made it easier," agreed Egar. "But humans have never been aware of us before. We used to observe without their knowledge and learned much about them."

Egar pondered the problem at hand.

"This vaccine they plan to give to the population…we could use it to our advantage."

"What are you thinking?"

"When ever the needle is placed in their arm the recipient turns away from the one administering the injection. They seek comfort by conversation; they are uncomfortable with the procedure. A scanner placed at just the right angle…"

"And we would be able to see directly into their eyes! An excellent idea!"

Egar agreed, priding himself that he had come up with the thought.

"You will place hidden scanners at each distribution centre."

Net made to leave, but quickly turned back, when his leader spoke again.

"While we are at it, we could tamper with the vaccine itself. Something to make a dormant violently ill, even kill it…"

"You have an idea?"

"Over the centuries our blood has become toxic to the other side. If we were to mix some into the next batch of serum…"

"At the very least, every dormant who receives it will become very, very sick."

But Net knew he was present to point out what might go wrong, to come up with all possible negatives.

"What if they notice the vaccine causes sickness, or…too many deaths occur as a result? They will think the dead dormant were humans. Then, they will stop administering the vaccine…"

"How many dormant do you think are hidden here?"

"Fifty?"

"I am certain there is even less. And these would be scattered throughout the entire planet's population! So few dormant dying; I doubt anyone will equate that to the use of the vaccine. And…as for humans being affected by blood-dosed vaccine…about all it will do to them is turn some homicidal, or at the very least, rebellious."

"They are already lawless," chortled Net.

"Yes, they are more like us than they realized."

They chuckled together at such a joke on the beings of Earth; humans prided themselves on their moral fibre.

"But master," Net objected. "Most of the population receiving these injections are the infirm or elderly...or, it is administered to the very young."

"Stupid! Do you not understand? A dormant becomes just that! They are unable to survive this environment, so they become malformed, susceptible to every disease known to man. Besides...the first dormant who were placed here are long dead. These are their descendants we look for. They will be first, second, even third generation removed, and after that long a time, the blood line will be so badly corrupted with human DNA ...they will be sickly, elderly...helpless!"

Net thought of the beautiful opposite beings...*History alleged 'Pure' females were of unequalled beauty, and when conquered, were the ultimate satisfaction.*

"What should we do if we find a female?"

"There will not be surviving females! They are too fragile; are usually lost in child birth."

"But just suppose one did survive..."

"Never!"

But, after a moment, Egar decided to entertain this thought.

"Add a large dose of Tansy oil to the serum. This will cause immediate abortion should they carry young, and...it will kill a female dormant within six to twelve hours."

"Would that not do the same to a human?"

"Why do you care if we lose a few dozen humans? But...you are right. Too many deaths could point to us and cause trouble."

For several minutes, Egar silently worried this problem.

"Make two versions: the one will be the general, for the young, the physically impaired and the elderly. It will contain just the extra blood ingredient; the second will be for pregnant females. It will contain both the blood element and the Tansy oil. And...just to keep our interference a secret and the humans unaware, that last will be given only to dormant females."

"And how will we determine beforehand whom are our dormant?"

"We will be in control of the humans involved. Have them depend on a computer to judge when the regular vaccine is supposedly unsafe. It will scan their eyes when it searches the data bank to screen the patient. If the pregnant female is a dormant, the computer will signal to use the Tansy oil sample; if she is merely human, she will get the vaccine containing only the blood additive. If the subject is only part human...she will get sick; completely human...maybe only with some...they will become violent, or temporally mad, but...not much harmed."

"What if we are unable to control some of these providers, or centres fail to use a computer?'

"Only dormant can resist suggestion; even sometimes those mostly human, with a fraction of 'Pure' blood, can still be made to see things. Those who can not be controlled will be our dormant...the ones who disobey commands are to immediately be given the lethal vaccine."

"Would a dormant be aware of us...what we are doing?"

"It might possibly sense something is wrong. But we will scan and require workers to be immunized before they begin to administer the vaccine to others. Without an injection, they may not proceed. They will be informed, it is for their own protection."

"But when a dormant is given vaccine it might take hours before the effects are felt."

"The chances of a dormant in their health field is minimal. Besides, if one is, it will be forced to take its inoculation first. By the time it is scheduled to work, it will be too unwell to go."

"If one is hardy...it might slip through..."

"Not likely!"

"It is a brilliant concept, master," praised Net. "Flawless!"

"Of course," Egar acceded without modesty. "That is why I gained commander, and you did not."

Net ignored the implied insult, but queried timidly. "Might I suggest one more course of action, master?"

"I am listening."

"Well...a dormant might be among those travelling from country to country...The full body scanners..."

"Of course!" agreed Egar, finishing the thought. "If we were to connect to them, it would be another means at our disposal. When a dormant is scanned, we would see inside its shell to the luminescence beneath...we would see what they should be."

"Even though the dormant is incomplete, the inner being is still bright..."

"The human sight range is too limited to pick this out...they can not even see us unless we change to lesser form..."

"So of course, they can not see the million times brighter..."

"Do not dare to name the creatures we seek!"

Net cringed. Trembling, he awaited the blow he expected.

But Egar had gone to thoughts of capture and elimination.

"Such a marvellous plan! We will initiate it!"

Encouraged, Net suggested. "Should I order Ruof and Epar to begin working on these matters? If that be your will, master?"

Egar waved his second away. "Of course. I command it!"

When he was alone, Egar travelled in thought, anticipating gruesome results enthusiastically.

CHAPTER 7

"Hi mom."

"Zane!" cried Sonia excitedly. "I haven't heard from you in it seems like…forever."

Sheepishly, he excused his lapse. "I've been kinda busy."

Sonia chuckled. "Yes, I can see that by your on-line site."

Zane had been preparing an un-roadworthy wreck for dirt racing. He had been posting pictures as he progressed.

"Your car is developing into quite something."

"Do you like it?"

It did not matter how old someone was, they still sought approval from their parent…even at fifty-two. Zane was Sonia's youngest.

"I love it!" Sonia enthused. "The body paint is beautiful. I particularly like that little star at the top left corner of the number."

Zane laughed with delight. "You like my special touch, do you?"

"It is just perfect! Very you. But…all this must be costing a fortune."

"Not really. You'd be surprised how far a can of spray paint can go."

"But surely, engine parts are expensive?"

"I frequent the wrecking yards. And I surf the web sites for cheap replacement parts…also, I trade ones I don't need for others."

In her youth, Sonia had worked at a dealership selling car parts, but her interest in cars did not go much beyond that.

'So, how are you doing otherwise?"

"Oh…it's been raining so much here, I've been going fishing on my days off."

Usually, on the east coast by the great lakes where Zane lived, the weather was more pleasant, but this summer had been a wet one.

"As for work," Zane went on. "A mechanic's work is never done; it's work, sleep, eat…no rest for the wicked, you know."

"You should get a girlfriend," Sonia teased.

"No, mom," he reprimanded firmly. "It's too late for that."

Zane had never married; he had always put career first.

"How about you? What have you been doing?"

"You did know, I moved?"

"Yes, Jade mentioned it."

He must have contacted his oldest sister first this time.

When Zane did call, he made the rounds.

"So…how do you like retirement?"

Sonia harrumphed. "The life of a senior is boring! You wash your dishes, clean the bathroom, do the laundry, and…watch a lot of TV."

"Aren't you making new friends?"

"Oh, ya…"

"Mom," Zane chided. "You're just as much a loner as I am."

"Well, life has a way of making us that."

Zane had spent most of his adult life in the military, living in close quarters with little privacy, under strict discipline. He had done three tours overseas in battle zones, as a paratrooper dropping supplies to the troops. After twenty-five years, he had retired due to an injury, received when his parachute had failed to open on a jump. Now he greatly treasured freedom to do what he wished.

"I was wondering, Zane," Sonia probed cautiously. "A little over a week ago… was your television viewing interrupted?"

"You mean, by what everyone's calling 'the Alien commercial'?"

"Yes! That's what I'm talking about. So, it happened out there, too?"

"Oh, yes!"

"Do you know what that was? It wasn't very funny, if that was a movie advertising."

Zane went very quiet, and that began to worry Sonia.

"Was it some sort of prank?"

Her son finally answered, very quietly.

"Mom…that was no hoax."

Sonia went cold inside. The dread she had been feeling ever since the first broadcast, her premonition of danger, was warranted.

"I probably shouldn't be telling you this, but..." Zane hesitated a moment longer. "I was talking with a buddy of mine who is still in the service...he was speaking to his friend down at NASA...apparently, just about the time of the first message, they picked up a space ship on radar. It left our atmosphere heading toward the moon, but...get this, there were no launches scheduled. They watched it approach the moon, move behind it, and...as far as they can tell, that's where it is still hidden."

"It's for real!" squealed Sonia.

"You are not to tell anyone about this, mom. Do you understand?"

Sonia gulped, nodding even though she knew he could not see her.

"Most of the world powers are on full alert..."

"Our government, too?" Sonia whispered.

"Yes."

"But, why wouldn't they tell us?"

"Can you imagine the panic that would result?"

"Then that was a real message from aliens...do they really think we have some of their children? That's terrifying!"

"Well, I know this much," Zane declared emphatically. No one is letting them anywhere near the children of earth!"

"Good grief! It sounds just like that movie they made about aliens controlling the children."

Zane laughed ruefully. "Sometimes, Science Fiction comes dangerously close to reality…

"But mom, remember…you can not tell this to anyone. They could put us in jail…for treason, mom. We are not supposed to know government secrets."

"Oh, that's stupid! If this is the truth, why would they prosecute us for warning people?"

"They prefer to handle things…"

"And, are they?"

"Well, as far as I know, they have never met with the aliens…but then, I'm not in the loop."

"Thank goodness, my children are all grown…but, there is still little Kara. She's only ten."

"My buddy tells me, the government here in Ontario have the schools under constant surveillance. I imagine it will be the same on the west coast, or the prairies where you are."

"At least that's reassuring."

After Zane had disconnected, a great foreboding weighed upon Sonia.

Is my family in danger from these beings?

Contact with real honest to goodness aliens!

What did they look like? Are they benevolent…or do they mean us harm?

Everything would change because of this…the way they viewed space; their very lives. The possibilities were mind-boggling!

What if these things want little Kara?

Kara may be a wilful child, but her great granddaughter was her pride and joy. Sonia would give her life to keep her safe.

Let's just hope it will never come to that.

CHAPTER 8

Sonia really did not want to go for this flu shot; everything in her rebelled against it. But they had declared this time it was very important; the flu would be of pandemic proportions this year.

Already, it had killed an infant, and a number of young people. They said, protect yourself or die.

The mobile health unit would be parked nine blocks away at a service station parking lot between one and four PM today. But there was no direct bus service to that area.

It was a good thing the weather was as nice as it was. Mid November usually had snow on the ground by now, but this year it was still above zero. Sonia wore a toke and a heavier winter jacket, just to be safe.

The walk would do her good, but it would take her through the most rundown, unsafe section of the city.

Sonia was not afraid. It was daylight, and it would still be mid-afternoon when she returned.

It took concentration walking with her cane. The blocks were long. Not many people were out, and when she did meet someone, they hurried on by without seeing her.

The cars zoomed past, their tires shushing noisily. Birds called from the trees; the sun shone brightly overhead. It was a beautiful day for a walk.

When she arrived at the mobile camper, it was just past one. Already, there was a line of three: a native couple and their son, a big over weight preteen.

They engaged Sonia in small talk, while behind them the line grew.

The vehicle door opened, and a young man stepped down to the pavement.

"I am Chris," he announced. "We can only take three people at a time inside. The others will need to wait out here."

Motioning Sonia to go first, the native couple stood debating which one of them would accompany their son. The decision made, mother and boy followed, while father held back.

Sonia stopped at the three steps leading up into the unit; she had not realized there would be stairs. She could pull herself up going in, but without help, getting back down would be difficult.

As she entered the truck camper, Sonia gazed around delighted. The interior was beautiful, something she had not expected. It was carpet and lino; beside the sink, to the left of the door, was a table spread with papers, a computer at its centre. Boxes of vials and packaged needles were set on the far side, as well.

To the right of the door, the table and one bench had been removed from the breakfast nook, leaving one remaining long seat for the patients. Across from the bench, the empty wall retained just one picture.

All new patients were asked to sit down, remove outer garments, and wait their turn.

Sylvia was the nurse giving injections. All morning she had been feeling ill, but she had come to work this afternoon, anyway; very little prevented Sylvia from working. This was what she lived for...helping people.

With interest, she watched as the elderly woman opened her jacket and slipped out one arm for her injection. As they talked, she learned Sonia had walked all the way here.

How many blocks would that be? And she used a cane, yet. That took stamina... determination.

Something about this fragile senior made Sylvia wish to protect her. She was special; alert...not one to just give up on living.

That stupid computer was acting strange again...like it had when she herself had been processed this morning. It flashed and beeped; then it had said the general was unsafe to be given to her.

Why? I never reacted to a shot before.

Now the machine told Chris to prepare that different vaccine for Sonia.

Is this version really safe for the older woman?

Sylvia had been feeling lousy ever since she had received hers. In fact, she was not sure she could continue working much longer.

Just these three...then I will need to go home.

Sonia turned when the woman came with the needle. Before she was noticed, she observed Sylvia slowly shooting a long stream of liquid into the air. The nurse looked up, as she made for her arm.

"Oh, no, sweetie! Don't watch," Sylvia cautioned.

Almost childishly obedient, Sonia turned away.

Why not? she wondered.

"All done!"

Sonia had felt only a sharp prick; never noticed the needle sliding in, nor had she experienced that sensation of moisture as it passed beneath the skin.

"We would like you to wait around outside for about ten minutes before you start out for home…just to make sure you have no adverse reaction."

Replacing her sleeve, and zipping up her jacket, Sonia felt puzzled.

Did she actually give me a shot?

But nature called; her bladder was screaming loudly…empty me!

There was no time to consider what had just happened.

Not bothering to wait, once young Chris had helped her descend, Sonia went inside the service station in search of the washroom.

After relief, Sonia reasoned: *My arm doesn't even hurt!*

CHAPTER 9

Egar was not pleased; nothing had gone as he hoped.

He stood before the observation room window, pondering the inky darkness of space and the planet below. Stars winked behind the earth, like mighty beings blessing those upon it; mocking him. The idea made him angry.

What right do these dormant have to live, to inter-breed with the bestial beings of this sphere? How does that make them better than me?

At one time they had all been 'Bright Beings'!

Their physicians and scholars had warned them first: if they persisted in negative behaviours, their base inner selfishness could develop an outer shell of evil. Their rebellion would lead to actual physical change.

Such thoughts were met by ridicule and rejected by most. Yet, over time, this prophecy had proven true.

First to be lost were their special abilities: telepathy; precognition; psycho kinesis, and teleportation. The population was forced to duplicate these powers by whatever means possible...mechanical, or technical.

Not that they ever gained back all...never again would they be an intimate community, nor would they hear the thoughts of their companions.

When violence, greed and resistance became the norm, twisting once handsome features into an outer husk of hate, they turned from creatures of beauty and brightness to something saurian and demonic.

They were not yet Wyvern, for if this had been so, they at least would have formed wings, thereby retaining the power of flight. Now, they were land-bound, dependent upon machines.

Wrath ruled to such a point their lack of self-control caused difficulty breathing, the labouring and rasping actually requiring ventilators.

Yet those who chose love, kindness and mercy remained unaffected, 'Pure'… beings of elegance, radiant and beautiful, no longer visible except to each other…and those with ability to read from a scanner their image.

Soon 'Opposite' outnumbered 'Pure', and their difference brought blows. A final battle was fought, won by the unprincipled 'Outer Enemy', and the 'Pure' were annihilated.

Not that the 'Pure' had ever fought back; they would merely defend, refusing to injure or kill.

But just before the last 'Leader female' was eliminated, the remaining males hid their younger offspring…a last-ditch effort to save the original species. The 'Pure' lost their lives doing it, leaving the children in dormant camouflage, alone.

Egar had hated all dormant since his birth. Jealous of their legendary honour, and fearing the power they could develop if once they awoke, he had pledged himself to hunting them down. It was his greatest pleasure to torture those he caught, putting an end to their bent toward benevolence.

Only recently, with his rise to the most powerful position, had this last planet stronghold come within his reach. Now, he could hunt the half-ones also. Nothing stood in his way!

I will make these cowardly ones pay, Egar promised. *They will fight or die!*

Behind him, his second crept timidly into the chamber. Egar paid him no mind; he remained facing the ebony regions of space, lost in thoughts of conquest; purposely requiring Net to wait him out.

At last, without turning, Egar spoke.

"You have something to report?"

Reluctant to enrage his superior, Net hesitated.

"Well?" Egar ordered impatiently. "Out with it!"

Net replied in a near inaudible voice. "They have found... a 'Pure'."

Egar spun with such force the other stepped back in fear.

"What!" he bellowed. "There are no more 'Pure' living!"

"Yet..." his second persisted. "We have found one."

"It is a mistake!" Egar, as if talking to a deficient mind, attempted to reason away such possibility. "In order for another generation of 'Pure' to be brought forth, two 'Pure dormant' must find each other. The chances of that happening are a million to one. Also, they would need to be of mature age when they paired, which is also impossible, because most were killed before...we missed none!" He said this last, more to convince his own mind than Net. "Your instruments are faulty!"

Rather than argue, Net pretended to agree. "Yes, master."

He remained, quietly waiting; yet not backing down.

"It is a female," he ventured.

"Not possible!" Females were to be feared the most. "A dormant female is too weak to survive alone; she would need a companion...we have driven 'Pure' females mad by depriving them of fellowship...and a light source." Egar laughed as he remembered. "We almost made the males fight us; they are intensely protective, especially of a' leader female'...at least they were when they were not dormant."

Even as Egar realized the potential of this particular dormant, he rejected it.

"She can not be 'Pure'...I was here when they killed the last original dormant; watched that last female die. She had become extremely ill; was starving; helpless; alone ...surely, she had no offspring. That was fifty earth years ago..."

Egar hissed to himself, further deluding himself. "This one must be a mix, a half human...and we will eliminate all bi-Pure!"

Net was not convinced. "If this one is 'Pure'...females are all powerful..."

"Only leader females! Besides, that is a myth. If she is 'Pure'...she is alone with no males to protect her!"

"It is said," persisted Net. "You can only kill a 'Leader Pure' when dormant..."

"Not so! How do you think we were successful in the war?"

"She sacrificed herself?" ventured Net.

"But they can be killed when left alone!"

Thoughts like this disturbed Egar.

What if he is right?

"Why do you insist this one is a 'Pure' anyway? Tell me of this dormant."

Net had been waiting for just such a chance. "She was discovered by a scanner from a mobile unit," he disclosed. "Each of her eyes contains cataract strips covering the entire iris centre. Her pupils open only to pin head size."

"Hummm, definitely a 'Pure'" Egar agreed reluctantly. "But how?" Realization hit him suddenly. "She can not see in the light then?"

"I doubt she is able to see much at any time."

"Indeed?" The thought pleased Egar; she would be easy prey. "Without protection, she will never be anything but a dormant."

"A leader 'female Pure' could break dormancy by herself..." disagreed Net. "And, help any others to do the same..."

"She first must be aware of what she is!" thundered Egar. "And...we will make certain she remains in ignorance!"

Egar felt immense anticipation as his thoughts went to the many methods of torture available to him. "Bring her to me!" he ordered.

Net began to tremble. "We can not, master."

"Why not?"

"We have...lost her."

Egar went livid. "How?" he spat. "How could you have lost...something...so ...important?"

Net cowed. "She...she was protected," he fumbled.

"By what? By whom?"

"A ... a 'Keeper'," whispered Net.

"We destroyed all 'Keepers' with the last "Pure'!"

"We...we missed one."

Egar growled, a deep in his throat fury.

"It hid her as soon as she left the vehicle."

"Do not humans have records of where beings reside?"

We have searched the data base; they failed to record her residence...or the 'Keeper' erased it."

"How convenient!" Egar hissed sarcastically. "Someone was lax. Why were these humans not better controlled? She should have gotten the lethal dose."

"We discovered too late, the one who processed her was also a dormant..."

"And you were going to tell me all this, when?" Egar asked, now coldly calm.

Net tried to shrink smaller before his superior.

"Imbecile! Incompetent idiot!" screamed Egar. "If you value your life," he hissed menacingly. "You will find her!"

His second slunk away, backing rapidly from the chamber.

"And do not return to me without her!" Egar yelled at his retreating back.

Alone once more, Egar took his frustration out on the walls of the ship, slamming them repeatedly with full body aggression.

Why is everything against me? What is this mighty force that thwarts my every plan?

CHAPTER 10

Sonia's second oldest, Jade, was one year older than Rhea. She lived with her daughter Nadia, twenty-one, who during the day was at university classes.

As Sonia arrived at the south side mall, Jade text her asking for help. It was just past one.

Help me, mom, the message read. I am in storage room B, north end. Jade.

It was not unusual for her daughter to ask; Jade was disabled, and sometimes got into situations where she needed assistance.

That they had not discussed this beforehand was unusual, for Sonia would have gone with her had she known about it.

Why hadn't someone been with Jade if she was picking something up?

And how had she even known Sonia would be at the mall at this time? Sonia had only just decided to go on spur-of-the-moment.

Upon arriving at storage room B, she found the door open, but the room inside was dark.

"Jade?" Sonia called, reaching inside to the right of the door for a switch. "Jade, are you in here?"

The room flooded with light with the flip of the switch, and Sonia stepped in. The door closed behind her.

Turning quickly, she attempted to turn the knob, only to find it had locked when it slammed shut.

Now I am the one trapped inside! I will have to wait to be rescued, and what a time I will have, trying to explain why I was here at all.

Looking around, Sonia found the room to be empty, except for a bench against the far wall.

Perhaps, I came to the wrong place? I will be of no help to my daughter now.

Taking a seat, Sonia prepared to wait it out.

Her cell had no reception, when she tried calling out.

As she waited, her heart took up a rapid rhythm all its own, yet Sonia could not have told you what she feared.

Perhaps, it is because I am shut up in here all alone?

Five minutes passed, then ten.

A soft whisper came out of nowhere.

"Do not be afraid." Sonia started. "I will not harm you."

Panic rising, she scanned the room. "Where are you?"

The same soft voice came again. "If I choose to become visible, please...will you be calm?"

But Sonia's heart had become a trip hammer. Drawing a deep breath, she made an effort to steady it.

As if sensing her attempt, a small glowing sphere appeared six feet in front of the old woman's face.

It presented as both globular yet stellate: a rotating, multi-pointed, rainbow-coloured star with beams of ever-changing hues flashing from it in pulses.

It is beautiful!

Yet, her intuition termed it deadly, and rightly so.

"What are you?" Sonia enquired somewhat breathlessly. "Are you one of those aliens?'

It hesitated, as if processing her challenge.

"To answer your first question: I am a 'Keeper', meant for protection. To the second query: No…the Aliens you speak of, mean you harm."

This information certainly did nothing to comfort Sonia.

"Why? Have I done something to offend them?" she asked. "What do they want with me? I'm not one of them. I'm not an alien!"

"You are not a human."

Sonia shivered. "I'm not?"

Somehow, all along, I knew this was all about me. From the first TV broadcast, my mind shouted "Not real!" but my heart told me otherwise.

The object was speaking again, defending as if on trial.

"The 'Outer Enemy' has found you, and I must follow the emergency procedure. I would have kept you safely until others of your species returned, but the situation has become urgent."

"Are you an artificial intelligence? A machine?"

"Yes. I serve as a guardian, a cloaking device, a receptacle of all past knowledge pertaining to your race…this last I wish to transfer to you before it is lost forever…and, I am a weapon."

Sonia began to tremble.

"Do not fear; I may never be used against you. I have undertaken to protect you."

That fact reassured her…just a little.

"Will you…tell me…are there…others like me? Do I have…relatives? Are those creatures who search…my kind?"

At first, it seemed to be processing again, or confused by the many questions, but finally, it chose to reply to the last one. "The beings who search for the dormant are no longer of your species. They are a mutated form, the opposite. Never trust them."

My instincts warned me without being told that.

"If you wish," the device offered. "I may give you a brief overview of your history?'

Sonia nodded, assuming somehow it could view her.

"There was a great battle between both sides." It began like a recording. "When it was apparent your species could not survive, Leader caused a distraction while the remaining males hid the small children…your father and mother were among these. The men concealed each child in dormant form with a 'Safe Keeper' to guard it.

"Over the years, as each 'Keeper' was discovered and destroyed, their charges were caught, tortured and killed, or…as some, who escaped unnoticed tried to survive alone, they died of exposure in the harsher environs of this world."

It recites this history with such lack of feeling...but then it is a machine.

"Eventually only three 'Keepers' remained. When I lost my charge in a battle, I joined with the last two: one protected your father, the other your mother.

"When your father was discovered, his 'Keeper' fought valiantly. I joined him and we kept your father safe, but in the battle the other 'Keeper' was lost. It passed its records to me just before destruction, and I took its place guarding your father. Years later your father became diseased and died...I was never programmed for healing...

"Originally, I was programmed to protect a 'Leader Female', so as you were the only other 'Pure' female, I attached myself to you."

What does it mean by 'Pure'? wondered Sonia.

"Your mother's 'Keeper' was destroyed soon after your father passed away; once again its records were transferred to me, which left me as the sole receptacle of data for your species, and also the lone protector of those hidden here. I attempted to guard both 'Pure' females, as they seemed the most important by my programming, but my range is limited to a distance of mere yards. As my priority pledged was to protect you for your life cycle, the enemy discovered your mother when I was not present.

"Because of this...she was poisoned, which inevitably caused her to stroke..."

"We were under the impression it was her pacer caused clotting, and that was what caused her stroke."

71

"That is incorrect. The poison given to her has the effect of paralysing the throat muscles so the victim can not swallow…in effect, results are the same as with a stroke."

"She refused to accept a feeding tube, so we watched her starve to death…it took three weeks! We came every day…"

How could Sonia ever forget that long painful vigil?

"I watched as you all grieved. What you did not know then was how often the enemy came near to discovering you."

"You protected us…hid us?"

"Yes. I am sorry I was unable to save your mother also."

"Thank you…for what you did do."

The machine carried on its recitation, much like an unfinished recording.

"Because I was the only 'Keeper', I chose not to battle the enemy; I remained passive and hidden, cloaking those at the bedside. It was important to preserve the species; my data was also irreplaceable. Without it, when you broke dormancy, you would be required to learn everything over, much as a new infant. If you were discovered before fully prepared, escape would have been impossible. I therefore remained only shielding. Perhaps, I have erred in my choices, for the 'Outer Enemy' has now returned. I am unsure…did I do wrong?"

It appeared to want assurance from Sonia, as if she had some say in the matter.

"I'm sure you performed the right action…I'm certain you did your best."

Exonerated, it resumed.

"I have watched you do the impossible: pairing with a human male, producing two bi-pure females, and raising them to maturity when most females in dormant form either die at birth or in child birth. Then even your daughters brought forth females safely also raising them to adulthood. Your genes are strong with love…"

As if it were not a machine, but a living being, it was praising her.

What kind of device is this? How long has it been functioning anyway? Does it need to be maintained?

Almost as if it had read her thoughts, and realized it approached its end, the "Keeper' began to ramble.

"I thought perhaps the 'Originals' would return for you, but I have gathered information from computers aboard the 'Opposite's' ship, and I find none of the original 'Pure' species have survived.

"The 'Outer Enemy' has won; they have come to the final hold out…the enemy has discovered all 'Keepers' were not destroyed…they are aware I exist! I fight alone!

"I can no longer guarantee your safety…what am I to do?'

The small glowing, flashing thing grew agitated, moving from side to side, like a man pacing, undecided of his course of action.

"I must not let the original species die; it is too valuable…you are all too valuable! And I am certain there are others who are dormant as well...offspring of those left behind in other parts on this world. I have lost track of them all...lost touch...too many for one 'Keeper' to protect. I am at fault..."

If Sonia ever doubted all of this was real, more than anything, the words the 'Keeper' spoke now, its obvious objective, convinced her it had her best interests at heart. The device was confused, breaking down...but it was the only help available.

It was like a man in anguish, regretful of its failure and inadequacy. She wanted to comfort, to reassure it.

Can I help it? Can I direct it to its original purpose?

"What was the 'Emergency directive' you spoke about at the beginning? What are you supposed to do in an emergency?"

The object stilled; the flashing slowed. It was silent for minutes.

"I had forgotten." It agreed. "You are my mistress, the last of the kind that programmed me. I must save and protect this species...therefore, I must do everything in my power to save you."

It still seemed to be reasoning with itself.

"You are the last 'Pure' female. I can not break your dormancy...but a 'Pure Leader' female can do it on her own...if she knows what she is, and...desires that change.

"You are the key, the last hope...but, first I must transfer my data to you, or it will be lost forever."

"How will you do that?"

"I must touch you. Will you permit it?"

"Okay?" Sonia agreed hesitantly.

Still, she was unprepared for what happened next.

The 'Keeper' zoomed forward rapidly, colliding with the centre of her forehead.

Sonia gave an involuntary squeal; for a second in time the room went black; then the sphere was back at a distance.

She had hardly felt the contact, only a slight sensation of a caress, almost gentle... and lovingly given.

After a moment of silence, the 'Keeper' resumed speaking. Its confidence was back; it was whole again, and certain of its direction.

"You will be unable to access the information until you break dormancy... become what you should be."

It seemed so sure she would be able to accomplish the task, but Sonia did not feel that conviction.

What will Joel say to all this? How will I tell my family? They will never believe any of this!

"How do I break...dormancy, you called it?"

"Fear prevents you. It has to do with sacrificial love, child..."

Sonia was no wiser.

"I have set up protection in your home. The enemy will not be able to see you when you are there. But the cover will cease working one week after I am destroyed.

"At that time, your safety…and those of all your kind, will be in your hands."

Sonia wondered how she would even protect herself.

"But now you must go," it ordered. "Flee back to your building residence immediately. I will draw them away, distract the enemy."

"The door is locked." Sonia stated the obvious, like a child who failed to comprehend the full impact of what was happening.

The click of the locking mechanism drawing back sounded in the quiet room. Then 'Keeper' was gone.

Sonia felt…abandoned, left to her fate.

****

The senior who fled the mall so rapidly, and paced back and forth nervously the ten minutes she waited for a bus, in no way resembled unflappable Sonia. She trembled in her seat the whole ride home, appeared frightened of her shadow, unable to speak, and ran pell-mell into the empty lobby when she reached her housing complex…her sanctuary!

It was ironic she had once called it her prison.

Had anyone noticed, they would never have considered her out of the ordinary, let alone having the survival of a species riding on her small shoulders.

Truth be told, Sonia had never been so terrified of the future in her life.

****

Without realization, the evening passed. About midnight, Sonia was stricken by a sudden overwhelming feeling of loss, as if someone who had been with her all her life was abruptly gone...an emptiness so profound you would have thought it due to the passing of a friend. Without being told, she knew...the protective device called 'Keeper' had met a violent end. It was like it had said goodbye just before its end.

And Sonia cried.

CHAPTER 11

When Sonia finally lay down to rest that night, her thoughts went into overdrive.

Maybe I have simply hallucinated it all? Or...I suffered some sort of stroke?

Perhaps, I have been poisoned...like my mother?

Or maybe, that woman never gave me the shot, and now, I am suffering with the pandemic flu...mad with fever?

It had all seemed so real! Sonia knew it was real!

'Keeper' had been solid! It had touched her! Even though the contact had been gentle, she had felt it.

All the things the machine had told her chased through her brain.

Am I a leader, the only hope for these survivors? Not me! Never! There must be some other way!

She almost wished 'Keeper' had kept silent, never told her, just left her to die in oblivion. And then again, she was glad it had not...was not her family in danger, as well?

Only safe for one week 'Keeper' had said.

And that would be, if she never left her apartment.

This is all very, very real!

And what of the other things that had not been revealed? What is locked deep inside my subconscious?

Terrifying images filled her imagination. Her body tensed with her thinking, cramping muscles tight, into bands of steel. Panic filled her spirit, making it difficult to breathe. To sleep was impossible.

She wished she could go back to the way it was before, when she was just an old lady watching life go by, safe, secure, even though it had been boring.

At least so many lives did not depend on her actions.

It continually came back to the same realization: she could hide away in her safe sanctuary, but these creatures would constantly be hunting...and she would always be their prey.

Who would protect her family, if she did not take up this challenge? What would happen to her brothers, her sons, and daughters...what would become of Jessica, Tyler, Shawn? And what of Nadia...even Kara? And were there others dependent for their lives on her, as well?

I have no way to save any of them! Unless...

From panic she went to desire, her longing so encompassing it filled her with hopelessness. Desperation created a yearning to make that change, that she might conquer this unknown, predatory enemy.

To be sure, the reason she must transform was to protect the species, but most of all, she needed to do it to safe guard those she loved.

There is only one answer, but how to do it? There is the real puzzle.

How did one go about this? Did it just happen, maybe...when you wanted it so badly you could taste it, as she did right now? Or was there a process you must follow? Were there special conditions to be met? If so, what were they?

Her speculation only brought back the anxiety.

Anyone with useful information: her parents, grandparents…all of her species were dead. There was no one to help! Sonia did not know what to do, but never the less, she must solve this on her own.

They had destroyed all 'Keepers', and the knowledge that could help was inside her mind, inaccessible.

Oh God! I'm only a weak woman…a lost old lady. What power could I possibly have?

The monsters were out there…eventually they would get her!

Far into the wee hours of the morning, she worried the problem.

"Fear prevents you," 'Keeper' had said. I must stop this fearful tirade! I need to make a plan!

'Keeper' had also mentioned sacrificial love. If that was the key, Sonia was willing. Whatever it took!

If I were a soldier…the only weapon against the enemy, what would I do? Would I turn myself in? Or lay a trap…

Over and over her thoughts churned…until at last, exhaustion took over.

Slowly, her body relaxed. Sleep slipped in…and the mind went on without her, solving the problem much like a computer still on diagnostics behind the scenes when the screen-saver turns on.

And Sonia dreamed…

****

She was flying far above the earth; in skies so dark and thick you felt you could touch them. Sonia was light, pushing away at all that was evil...a streak of luminescence cutting, cutting like a knife.

With glee, she twirled in mid-air, spinning and turning, zooming and rolling, excited by newfound freedom. Her hands together below her head, she dove down like an Olympic swimmer, toward the land mapped below: trees and buildings; tiny lights and moving streaks that were cars; rivers and mountains fled past rapidly.

Studying her hands, she realized she could see through them.

Am I transparent? Am I visible to those on the earth below?

She rose, soaring toward the moon, and then...

There was the enemy ship, tucked away behind that celestial body!

****

And Sonia was back once more in her own bedroom, the light streaming in from behind her blue window shade into her safe nest. The digital read out on the clock radio read ten AM.

I have not slept this late in years!

Somehow, the worrisome problems of the night before seemed minor now that she was rested. It was not that she had forgotten, merely that peace was now her mantle.

Sonia went placidly through the motions of her toilet. Not until she looked up into the bathroom mirror, and saw an unfamiliar face, did the woman realize she had changed in the night.

Memories flooded forward from a deep reservoir: stories and records of times long forgotten, details so vivid it was like she had been there, knowledge, methods and instructions, the how-to-do manual for a new generation.

Sonia knew now exactly what she must do...

But first...she needed to feed her new body; she had not eaten since yesterday noon, and she was famished!

After, she would find...the others.

CHAPTER 12

Sonia stood before the full-length mirror amazed by the changes that had occurred during her transformation. Most remarkable was that she could see from this distance. Gone were the cataracts that had restricted her sight, the abnormalities hiding the true windows to her soul.

Now, staring back at her were the most unusual eyes: the outer membrane was amethyst in colour, a definite light plum purple, with vertical black slit down the centre.

With the wisdom now available to her, she knew her race a master of disguise. By changing at will the colour of their iris and shape of the pupils, they could appear more human-like. It would be easy to hide among mankind; all she required was practice.

Her reflection also showed a decrease in her age; by appearance, she was only mid-thirties...half her actual earth years. Their species matured more gradually, lived substantially longer.

The mirror showed unblemished cream-pink skin with a healthy rose flush to the cheeks.

No need any longer to use make-up, she decided.

Pearl white teeth had re-formed.

The dentures can be thrown away. Good riddance!

The glasses can go, hearing aid, too...and, the cane.

Perhaps, that last could be retained...it would be a definite benefit for deception, if I need it.

Height also had increased, distributing that extra poundage to places more desirable, creating curves that would be most delightful to a male observer.

Sonia estimated she now stood about six foot four.

Her gold-blond hair was short with a soft curl.

Will it keep that wisp if I let it grow long, or will it just turn to frizz?

Desire to see such a result made it so, and the image in the mirror changed. Her hair grew long, to below her hips, wavy with a slight up-sweep at the ends.

Resembling a teen with a newfound talent, Sonia altered her style once again. This time her tresses were auburn, like Rhea's, only with spiral curls caught up with a clasp behind her head, descending in a curtain of ringlets halfway down her back.

This is fun! Nadia's hair looks like this, only it is jet black.

Nadia's father, Isaiah, had been Eritrean, and being bi-racial, she had the colouring to go with her dark hair.

Jade is cream; Isaiah was chocolate, and together they made caramel... Nadia: A taste of delightful love.

Sonia had always loved her granddaughter's hair, but Jade complained it was hard to care for because of its tight curl and tendency to tangle and mat.

Returning her hair back to short, flaxen and curly, Sonia admitted, *that matches my colouring better.*

Absently, she wondered, *will it be as easy to manipulate clothing?*

Then she chided herself.

Enough of this! There is no time for play; lives hang in the balance!

****

She decided: To teleport would be unwise. One of the residents might see me.

So, Sonia descended down in the elevator…as her old lady self.

****

"Why does that stupid door keep opening when no one is on the elevator?" grumbled petulant Laura, as Sonia stepped out into the lobby.

Oh, right! Sonia realized. *They can't see me unless I allow them to.*

But just for amusement, she remained invisible.

Laura stood leaning on her walker, as always, visiting with three other seated individuals.

Without detecting Sonia, Colleen, the most recent addition to the building, rushed past from the hallway.

"Were any of you down here early in the evening last night?" she asked. "Did you see the drug bust? I saw it all from my window upstairs."

Sonia entered her mind without effort, as if it were reflex, before she caught herself. Shocked, Sonia realized this was the building's thief. Colleen had only months to live. Her reasoning for her behaviour was, she could not work; she was unable to buy nice things, so when she saw the things she liked, she just took them. After all, as she saw it, others had plenty of time to replace what she stole.

Out of empathy, as Sonia left the woman's mind, she also reached out and touched her failing heart, healing the damaged left side, to give her a new lease on life.

It was not her place to control Colleen, Sonia decided, so the woman would have to change her own attitude.

Sonia tuned in once again to the conversation.

"The cops were here for hours," confirmed Stan, the lone male of the group. Sonia knew, he lived in one of the suites on the ground floor, and was always involved in any gossip or action that took place.

"I was the one that called it in," revealed eighty-year-old Ellie. "A native drug addict was shooting up in the patio area."

Anxious to be part of the disclosure, Lena added her contribution. "An unmarked car was the first to come..."

Ellie took up the narrative again. "It sat on the street to just watch for a while. Then the other cars and paddy-wagon came..."

"They wrestled him down," skinny Lena cut in gleefully. "Boy, did he fight! Then they cuffed him and dragged him to the police van, and took him down town."

Stan laughed. "We all sat here and watched the whole time. Most excitement we've had in a long time."

"Man! What kind of neighbourhood is this anyway?" Colleen demanded. "It's not safe!"

"Not after dark, it isn't," agreed Stan.

"But this began in broad daylight!"

Stan simply shrugged, as if it were all quite normal.

"Did you hear about Belinda?" Ellie asked to change the topic. "They found her dead at the mall in the washroom."

"Who found her?" Lena demanded. "When did it happen?"

"Yesterday."

What is this? wondered Sonia. *I was at the mall at the same time...with 'Keeper'. Was my encounter two-fold, to protect me against enemy in the building, as well?*

"I found her," Colleen proudly admitted. "I was there to use the washroom. She was lying in the middle of the room jerking, eyes rolled back. She'd wet herself, and was frothing at the mouth...lips were all blue..."

"She died there?"

"I guess so." Colleen shrugged. "She was alive when I saw her. I told the cleaning lady, and she called the paramedics, but after a while the police came and closed off the restroom with yellow tape and placed a guard there...wouldn't let anyone back in for hours."

"She died in there?" Ellie demanded a second time.

"Yes."

"Ug!" Laura proclaimed in disgust. "Don't think I want to use that washroom again."

Sonia went cold in realization.

Belinda was a dormant! 'Keeper' once again protected me first...but it was already too late for Belinda...if she was poisoned.

Only once had Sonia met Belinda. At the time, she had been impressed by how much like Myron she was, always going without her dentures.

She lived right here in the building with me!

The enemy got to Belinda. What prevented me from being poisoned, as well? How did they get to Belinda?

Through the flu shot! 'Keeper' couldn't prevent that!

Sylvia! Somehow, she protected me! Why? She must be a dormant, as well!

Sonia reached out with her mind, searching to find her nurse benefactor… only to find her dead, also.

I am too late for both of them, grieved Sonia. *They would have been like sisters…*

They would have made excellent partners for my brothers. Our own kind...even if half human...

But, it's too late! There must be other dormant nearby? Maybe right here in this building?

Sonia turned to the minds beside her; she would know if anyone were like her. Delving into the first mind beside her hopefully, she was shocked by what she found.

In Lena's mind, she found an angry woman. She said whatever she thought, not caring if her words wounded others, because of their past treatment of her. One night the former building manager had used his master key to gain entry to her suite; the man had raped Lena. Even though he had been let go, to this day, Lena was considered a liar, because no one believed what she claimed. She felt hurt by others; this was the only way to get even.

Sonia gently eased the hurtful memory, and left her mind. That was all she could do for Lena.

Ellie's mind, when she entered it, was filled with complaints: incompetent doctors; medical procedures gone awry; the suffering of others was never as great as her own. And Ellie was not a dormant.

Sonia's gift to her was to touch Ellie's feet, straightening the misshapen toes. Maybe with the removal of her pain, she would become less self-centred.

Saddened, finding no pleasure in her search, Sonia went on to the fourth woman.

Maybe Laura is a dormant...a sister?

But she found Laura scarred beyond help. Abused by her husband, then abandoned by his family at his death, she had been left destitute. Her relationship with him had been common-law, and as Laura had no kin of her own, nor any means to prevent it, his relatives felt free to take all the money and possessions. Unaware her husband had been cashing her pension each month without her knowledge, with the help of a social worker, she was now applying for the benefits she should have

89

received years before. Because she did not comprehend business matters, and her husband had also handled their finances, Laura tended to turn to her fellow building inmates to manage her affairs. This also left her open to further exploitation.

Sonia sighed.

What human kind did to each other made her sad. She touched Laura's brain, correcting blockages preventing comprehension, allowing her to better reason and fend for herself. It was up to Laura to break her dependency of relying on others, if she was to better her life.

Discouraged, Sonia wondered if she should even search the last mind. Because this was a male, she feared what she might find there. She decided to wait.

It was time to move forward with her goal, time to leave this building, and challenge her enemy. Now that she was whole, new knowledge available to her, she could create protection just as easily as 'Keeper' had. She was no longer helpless.

However, it would require going visible, and it was better to do that inside this protected space than outside in the street.

Sonia materialized beside the hall entryway, just to be safe. Stan was the first to notice her.

"Well, look who's here! The Fashionista."

Even though she had appeared in 'old lady' form, the man was undressing her. That annoyed Sonia.

She had never encouraged sexual overtures; never been seductive. Her cleavage was never visible;

skirts were always below the knees. She had always dressed well, but modestly.

But this was Stan...the one who had wanted to climb in her window the first week after she had arrived.

She slid into his mind to see why.

And retreated as quickly.

Unfortunately, that short encounter had given much too much vivid detail. Raised solely by a womanizing uncle, Stan had been taught all women were only good for one thing...and that was to be delivered with considerable aggression.

Sonia shivered.

For a moment, she allowed her anger to simmer; entertained the thought of retaliation.

The perverted, lecherous old fart! she fumed. *Maybe, I should scare that lust out of him? I could appear as an 'Opposite'...*

But Sonia chose instead to forgive.

All human males were not the same. There were some with kind, gentle, compassionate natures. Sonia had married one. He had been a sharing individual, discussing his every thought with her, but...she had never been inside his mind.

Perhaps, he too, would have been different beneath the surface?

Sonia shook away that betraying thought.

Ignoring Stan completely, she voiced a greeting to the group in general, as if she had not been there the whole time listening to every word, and escaped calmly through the front doors.

Sonia knew the enemy ship's sensors would spot her the minute she was in the open. Still, she waited, walking six blocks before vanishing under her mental-formed shield.

She wanted her adversary to know she existed. But not to see where she was headed.

****

"There!" Net gestured at the viewing screen. "We have you now! No!" He yelled in anger, when the small glowing dot disappeared. "No! How did she do that?"

Net paced in agitation, turned back to the consol.

"Did you record where we first sighted her?"

Rab, the operator, checked the log, and shook its head. "She has fooled the system, created an illusion of being in a dozen different locations."

Enraged, Net hit the wall with a small useless fist.

"This one has broken dormancy," Rab observed.

"Then she is a 'Leader Female'!"

"Yes," the operator agreed. "Our worst fears have been realized."

The chamber went silent, except for the beeping of the monitors.

"Will you be telling the master?" ventured Rab.

"He has forbidden me to approach him. Would you invite his vengeance?"

"Not I. Never!"

CHAPTER 13

Behind Joel's back, near the ceiling in the corner of his living room, small glittering pieces of metal materialized one at a time, formed into a 'Keeper', which attached itself to the roof, then vanished from sight. Had the man known his sister had willed it into existence, he would have freaked out and fled his home in terror, rather than open the door to her.

"Well, this is a pleasant surprise," Joel commented when he answered his doorbell. "How come you didn't tell me you were coming?"

Sonia stepped across the high floorboard of the doorframe. Setting her cane in the corner, she moved into the room.

"I needed to tell you something. If I told you beforehand, I thought it might alarm you unnecessarily."

Joel closed the door. Bear like, he shuffled past his sister, heading for his wide, leather lift-chair. The effort brought his breathing to a laboured wheeze.

"Well, come sit down, then." He plopped heavily into the forward-tilted black chair, and then using the attached remote, eased the recliner to normal sitting position. "Oh, do you want something to drink," he added, as an afterthought.

"No, thank you. I just had my breakfast."

Joel found her manner decidedly preoccupied.

"Got up kinda late, eh?"

"Something like that."

Sonia took up a position directly in front of Joel, refusing to be seated.

What's got her so uptight? wondered Joel.

"So, what's up?"

"I don't know how to do this any other way, Joel. I'm sorry. I could tell you, but …you need to see it; and you won't like what I'm going to do."

"Okay. So, show me, and let me be the judge."

Sonia took a step back. "Please, please don't freak out on me."

What can she show me that is that bad?

"Watch close…don't take your eyes off me, okay?"

He would forever remember this as the turning point of his life. Even though she had warned him, he was totally unprepared for what happened next.

His sister began to fade before his very eyes, like a picture out of focus, the edges wavy and distorted. Short, grey-haired, elderly Sonia metamorphed to a younger, taller, curvaceous blond…

With purple cat-like eyes?

Joel almost screamed aloud. If he could have risen from his chair, he would have run, but he could not easily get up without the mechanical lift of the chair.

She had planned it that way, he realized.

That is not my sister! That is not my sister! He told himself, as he gave way to panic. *Those aliens are real! One is in my living room!*

The face on the creature turned unhappy.

"You're freaking out," Sonia grieved. "Please, please, don't be afraid of me, Joel."

Were those tears forming in those extraordinarily beautiful eyes?"

"I love you...you're my brother. If you can't accept me, who can?"

That tore at his will power, leaving him weak.

"I would never purposely hurt you, Joel"

But there was just no way he could believe this was his sister.

"Oh Joel, please." She dropped to her knees, put the most exquisite hands he had ever seen on his thighs. He tried to dissolve into the back of the chair.

"Oh, I knew this would happen," she cried out in her distress. "Am I such a freak, Joel, that you can't believe it's me?"

A crystal, wet tear escaped one mesmerizing eye, coursed down a smooth, dusty-rose cheek. "Won't you please accept what you see?"

No way! Oh, this one is good!

Joel took a deep breath, steeling his resolve.

"You are not my sister! I will not be fooled by you!"

With a resigned sigh, it sat back against its legs, placed its hands against the flat stomach, and placidly prepared to wait him out.

"Mom and dad were beings from another world," she stated with confident calm. She encouraged no argument.

"Right. If that's true, prove it."

"All these years, cataracts hid my eyes. They hide yours still."

Maybe it is true? Only recently, his ophthalmologist had told him of the cataract strips, like extended pupils that failed to open, growing on his irises. The man had declared the condition un-correctable. *Sonia does have a similar problem.*

"I don't believe you," he declared rebelliously.

She persisted, as if knowing she was making progress.

"You have to change…like I did."

"And how do I do that?"

"I can help you…"

Over my dead body! Aloud, he said, "Ya right! I let you touch me, and who knows what you'll do?"

The argument failed to silence her.

"I've already touched you. Did it do you harm?"

He shook his head in annoyance.

"Prove to me you're my sister. Tell me something only she would know."

Without hesitation, she took up his dare.

"When you were five, we went to the movies. You got lost in the crowd, separated from Myron and me. You thought we were the ones lost."

Joel laughed, remembering. *I told her that story, using those exact words. But I mustn't be fooled.*

As if knowing she had failed to totally convince him, she came up with another memory.

"Mom used to make soup from a large can of spaghetti in tomato sauce and another of vegetable soup. She always baked baking powder biscuits to serve with it."

"It was my favourite meal..." He stopped short, not wanting to give her any help.

"Mine was the chicken and dumplings she made every Sunday night."

How does it know so much about us?

"Because, I am Sonia!"

"Whoa! I didn't say that aloud, did I?"

"No, you didn't! I can read your thoughts!"

He cringed, but recovered quickly.

"Then whatever you tell me, you get from my mind."

"No, from my memory! Here's one I bet you don't even remember...

"You had a great love of spaghetti, from the time you were very young. One afternoon, you were so hungry mom gave you the leftovers from the night before. I came home from school, and you were perched on this bar stool at the counter of the cupboard with a white dishtowel tied behind your neck. It draped over your belly, and was covered with pieces of spaghetti that had missed your mouth. You were only three."

"I remember that! But…that could have come from my mind."

"Have it your way…I don't know how to convince you if what I've said won't."

He almost felt guilty.

She let the time drag, watching him with those slitted eyes…like a cat with a mouse.

"What did they do to you?"

"I did it myself."

"Why? How?"

"I could show you…let you inside my mind."

He shook his head; he did not want to do that.

"You can let me see inside your head?"

"Yes."

"And, I bet you'd only show me what you wanted me to see, right?"

"Maybe."

At least she is honest about it.

"Take my hand, Joel."

He wanted to refuse, but somehow his excuses were all stymied. Reaching out his hand, he thought, *if this isn't my sister, I'm screwed.*

The doubts disappeared immediately. It was like looking into a big kaleidoscope: scenes flew by; records of life in another place; images of dad when he was born, mom as a little girl, and always a 'Keeper' close by.

They were definitely not her memories!

He now had knowledge he had never experienced or learned, and...suddenly, he was changing.

****

Sonia broke contact, rose to her feet and stepped back. "Stand up so I can see you better."

Joel obeyed, like a compliant child, rising more easily and quickly than he had in a long time.

Sonia laughed, delighted. "So, this is what a male of our species looks like. Impressive!"

"I'm sorry," Joel apologized, sheepishly. "I can be difficult sometimes."

Sonia shrugged and grinned teasingly. "Only sometimes?"

"Sorry," he repeated.

He was a handsome giant: thirty-three once more, seven and a half feet tall, muscular, proportionate and fit...with eyes of sparkling silver, like polished coin, the slits a rust brown. He was every inch the protector Sonia had thought he would be, though right now, he was embarrassed by all her attention.

"Definitely impressive...my baby brother is a 'lady killer'."

Joel always had been quick on the comeback. "I would never kill a lady," he teased back.

But it was time to move forward. No use in delay.

"Now...you need to do Myron."

It was always better that a male attend a male; Sonia had only done Joel because there had been no one else.

"Ouch! What will we be unleashing?"

"I will act in the guardian position," offered Sonia.

Joel nodded in agreement.

Taking her brother by the hand, they prepared to 'jump' to Myron's suite.

****

"Hey! What the hell!"

Even for delusional Myron the sudden appearance of his sister and brother out of thin air was shocking. He backed away in fright, his eyes feeling like they would escape his skull.

"Where'd you come from? Crap! You can't be real!"

Frantic, he searched the room for a weapon, his eyes lighting on the frying pan still on the table. He picked it up, swung it toward the mirage that looked like his sister, but the one resembling Joel made a hand movement. The skillet vanished from Myron's hand.

He continued forward with the momentum of his unfinished swing, felt some unseen force prevent his fall, and steady his balance again.

Not sure how he knew, Myron was certain the one with the appearance of his sister had stopped his plunge without even touching him.

Myron dropped to his knees in utter terror at this realization. He covered his head like a small boy being punished, and started to whine.

"Oh, Myron," Sonia whispered sympathetically. "Joel, don't be a tease!"

"He would do the same to us," Joel countered. "If the roles were reversed, he'd manipulate us. He's been doing it all our lives."

"It doesn't mean we should get even. Right now, what makes you any different?'

"Sorry. Didn't think of it that way. Sorry Myron." The one that looked like Joel was apologizing. "But you've got to admit, he sure was funny."

Myron looked up, anger flooding his spirit. They sounded just like his brother and sister, acted like them, too. He failed to understand how it was possible for them to be here, but decided to accept their presence.

Dropping his hands, Myron stood up. "Nearly made me shit my pants. How'd you do that anyway? Joel, you buy some new gadget?"

"Why don't we all sit down and talk?" Sonia suggested.

But Myron was ready to take Joel on. "Thought you were funny, eh?"

Joel backed away, raising his hands in the appeal of a non-combative, with palms outward. Myron turned to Sonia.

"Why should I do anything you say, after what you just did to me?"

"What did we do, Myron?" Joel asked. "Seems to me you were going to hit Sonia."

It was all still a puzzle to Myron. "How'd you get in here, anyway? Was I asleep, and you gave me something so I'd hallucinate?"

Joel seemed about to retort, but Sonia spoke first.

"Let's just talk civil, okay?" She pushed away a pile of newspapers on the chesterfield, and sat down.

"Fine!" Myron dropped into his easy chair.

Joel moved to stand in front of him.

"Since when are you so limber? Any other time you'd be the first to lower that fat ass of yours."

"Be polite in the presence of a lady!"

"Easy guys. Please, don't fight. Just do it, Joel!"

"Do what?" Suddenly, Myron was afraid again. *She doesn't mean for Joel to sit down.*

The image of his brother shifted; as he dropped to his knees, Joel transformed to a younger, taller version, and took Myron's hand. It was then that Myron noticed.

Steel-grey cat eyes stared back at him.

"Stop that!" Myron yelled, pulling at his hand, but Joel had become extremely strong. "How the hell do you do that?"

"Stop teasing him, Joel!" It was the last thing Myron heard.

The room went spinning, like he was on some sort of a bender; images chased through his consciousness so fast he could not comprehend it all. Again, Myron heard himself whining like a wounded animal.

This hurts! It hurts!

"Joel that's too fast! You're being rough, causing him pain."

"I'm not doing it on purpose," answered Joel. "I can't do it as well as you. I don't have your gentleness."

"It has to do with love. You can't heal and be angry at him at the same time."

Their words were no longer speech, more like thoughts in his head. He was beginning to understand what was happening, to feel whole for the first time in his life.

"He's coming back to us," Sonia observed.

Myron opened his eyes.

"Whoa! Who's the classy babe?"

Sonia was no longer in disguise. She was sexy...hot! He could get it on with her.

"I'm your sister! Behave yourself!"

She backed up so he could stand. Towering over her, his legs still shaky, he took in a deep lungful of air; something he had not been able to do for a long time because of his smoking.

"You should just see yourself," Sonia enthused. "No more sickness, Myron! No more mental confusion."

Isn't she taller than she used to be?

"Go! Look at yourself!" Sonia offered.

Obediently, Myron strode to the bedroom to look into the dresser mirror. He had to stoop to get through the door, almost banged his head. Amazed, his jaw dropped.

That's me? Man! I'm a handsome dude! I'm shorter than Joel...but that's okay. Silver eyes, just like him, too.

"So, what are we anyway?" But the answer was there in his head, almost before he had asked the question.

****

Some time later, they were no longer communicating aloud; they conversed mind to mind as they would from now on, but Sonia kept all but surface thoughts veiled, as did Joel. Myron, on the other hand, remained an open book, which both she and Joel wished would close. The man had never worried about offending others.

As a precaution, Sonia had deemed it wise to give both men only the information relevant to males of the species. She shared some history, but basically an overview, much as 'Keeper' had first done with her.

She reasoned all survivors of the race would be human raised. They would need the alternative to follow their own conditioning rather than using traditions agreed upon by ancestors, light years away. She was willing to give them that choice. But such decisions were for the future.

She promised herself, no matter what others elected to do, whether they helped and supported her or not, she would use the talents bestowed upon her, to protect all, no matter at what cost.

"I for one, need rest," she admitted. "It's been quite a day. Perhaps, we should each go back to our own places and take a break."

"Good idea," Joel agreed. "We'll meet back at my place tomorrow at noon. And that means you too, Myron," he ordered.

"Ya! Ya!"

Sonia had known Joel would assume leadership; it had been drilled into him, that it was his function. Physical and mental transformation would not nullify that.

She also figured, as soon as they left, Myron would crash again. Old habits also died hard, and his habit was to sleep most of the time.

The full impact of what had just happened would hit them both tomorrow.

To ensure Myron's safety, she had placed another 'Keeper' in his home; both 'Keepers' would stay with the men wherever they went, but as with the one left on her, they each only had a life span of a week.

By then, Sonia hoped her brothers would realize their danger and protect themselves.

Sonia made the 'jump' home; her work was finished…for today.

CHAPTER 14

Promptly at noon Sonia appeared in Joel's sitting room to find all the furniture had been moved back against the wall and the kitchen table moved into the centre. It was set for a meal, and Myron, already present was eating with Joel.

They made peace!

"Sit down and have some fish. Rainbow trout, "Joel offered. "Myron caught them; they're fresh."

"Fried over a campfire in the great outdoors," Myron added. "I found me a spot up north next to a river. Made a cabin; even got a dog. Russian wolfhound. Do you know, animals can see us when humans can't?"

Sonia pulled out a chair and sat down. Joel slid the platter toward her, and she helped herself to a small portion. The men were eating with their hands, so she went with the flow.

We have not eaten together in years. And this fish...is mouth-watering.

"You've been out and about, Myron," Sonia quizzed.

"I'm not going back to that apartment dump again. The landlord can sell my stuff for the last month's rent."

"You don't want something as a keepsake?"

"Nope."

"And you were always such a hoarder."

Myron laughed with her.

"The way I see it, all I have to do now is think, and I can have anything I want."

"You do realize, when you wish something into existence, it actually comes from somewhere?"

"So?"

"Isn't that sort of like stealing?"

Joel laughed at that, and waded into the discussion. "When you manipulated your cabin into being, Myron, did the logs you made it with come from the lumber yard or the trees beside your place?"

"I used the trees at the site."

"Okay." Joel turned to Sonia. "Then, he's not stealing, is he?"

"Where did you get the lamps, chairs…you dog?" questioned Sonia.

"I got him from a kennel. Only the best for me!"

"Did you pay for him?"

"No. It was a pup; one of a litter. No one will miss him. Besides, I couldn't be seen…"

"And you didn't intend to pay, so you didn't show yourself, right?"

Myron shrugged.

"Fine line here," Joel observed quietly.

"Exactly," agreed Sonia.

"We can't pay for everything we use," objected Myron.

"No, but I don't think we should use Earth as our own personal super mart either. We should be honest…someone will be out hard-earned proceeds."

"Who's going to care?" Myron retorted angrily. "It's not like the human race ever gave us a break."

"And we should just follow their example like blind rats?" stated Sonia. "We have a chance at a new beginning here…we are of a different species. We could start out dishonest, but what will that make us? What will we be like in the future, if we follow that course?"

Myron made a rude noise. "No different from the human race."

"Exactly. And I happen to think we have the potential to be better."

While Joel cleared the table using thought control, instantly cleaning and returning his dishes to the cupboard, Myron brooded over what Sonia had suggested.

Sometimes Sonia had to agree with Myron; life living among humans had not been easy. Yet this same human species had been their protection up until now. Though some had been difficult, and others were presently degenerating even farther, there were those who were gentle, generous and self-sacrificing.

Myron who had been listening to her thoughts, answered her, before she realized he was deeper into her mind than she wished.

"They were never nice to me," he objected. "Always gave me the short end of the stick, no matter what."

"But what does it benefit us to be bitter, Myron?" asked Sonia. "That's how we become the 'Opposite'."

Myron frowned, puzzled. "What do you mean? What's an...'Opposite'?"

She showed him in her mind that an 'Opposite' was the enemy, what they looked like, and how they had developed over the centuries.

He let out a frightened yell, stood abruptly; backing from the table so rapidly his chair went flying.

"No way! Those lizards are hunting us? We can become like that!"

"It happened because they chose corruption, failed to restrain their carnal, malicious tendencies...they became the evil they perpetrated..."

Joel had remained quiet though this disclosure; he was appalled. "How come you know about this, and we don't? Is there more we don't know?"

"When 'Keeper' came to me, it was afraid the records and knowledge of our species would be lost when it was destroyed. Usually, according to its programming, the oldest female of the race is the record keeper...it passed what it contained to me."

"Why a female? Wouldn't a male serve just as well?" Joel challenged. "Is there some specific reason they used the female?"

Sonia knew she would have to be careful with her answer or egos would be bruised. "Each of us has abilities; the females have some the males do not. That is why our enemy seeks to kill off the females first...I have the ability to retain vast memory... much more than both of you combined..."

But Joel had picked up on something vital, and he was not about to let it slip by.

"Why does the enemy see a female as such a threat? What harm can there be to them in holding records?"

Sonia did not want her brothers to fear her; she was most reluctant to give them the whole picture, so she chose the limited version.

"How could you be more dangerous than Myron or me?" demanded Joel.

"The female has the power to protect...multiple subjects at once..."

"A male can not?"

"He protects differently...like in a battle...like a weapon. He can only defend one on one...A 'Leader Female' can blanket the entire species...in a cloak."

"But you're not a leader female, are you? What is that anyway?"

"A 'Leader Female' is one born with abilities beyond that of other females..." Sonia was not about to tell her brothers she had that capacity.

Joel went silent, as if sensing she hid something from him, suspicious she might in fact be one, but not willing to accept the answer. He had suddenly become aware his sister had potential beyond his comprehension; that perhaps here was counsel he would be wise to listen to, and for the first time, he also realized, who was the most at risk here. The protection instinct of the males in his species had just kicked in.

Myron, on the other hand, viewed things quite differently. He up-righted the chair he had knocked over, and sat down.

"That thing…'Keeper'? Let me understand this? It gave you more power than you gave us?"

"I didn't give you your powers; it didn't give me my powers! It was just a machine!" Sonia defended. "We were each born with what we have. It was hidden beneath our dormant shell, all this time."

"That's crap! Women can never be smarter or stronger than men! Why the hell did it give the knowledge to you, anyway? It should have been given to a man!"

He's taking this as a personal affront, a threat to his masculinity.

Sonia had always known Myron regarded women as inferior, treated them in contempt, but she had never bargained on his being this malicious. The fact she was better equipped would always rankle him, but she could do nothing about that.

He has one huge ego…or is that an inferiority complex instead?

"Does it really matter, Myron?" Joel broke in. "I think, by the sounds of it, we have more serious concerns on our plate at the moment."

But Myron would not be side tracked.

"I want to carry the records, Sonia," he declared, forcefully. "So, you give them to me, you hear!"

Joel went on the defensive; he knew Myron was a risky receptacle. "Sorry, you can't have them! If the 'Keeper' judged Sonia as the best choice, then leave it be."

But Myron was in no mood to listen. He had never liked it when they paired off against him, and today it only added fuel to the fire.

"Give me the records, Sonia. I know the power goes with them," he asserted. "Better still...I'll just take them from you!"

Without warning, Myron dove into her memories.

Sonia's defence was instinctive, automatic, beyond her control. The minute Myron entered her mind, he also touched her hand...a mistake many males of the species regretfully had learned from before him: never touch the unprepared 'Leader Female'.

The air sizzled with an electrifying zap, much like the sound of a taser, only more amplified, exceedingly more deadly.

Myron screamed; rebounded forcefully against the back of the chair that supported him. Trembling violently from the contact, his breathing rapid, his eyes watering, he placed his hands on either side of his temples, and moaned plaintively.

Joel actually laughed, not realizing the seriousness of what had just happened. "That'll teach you to mess with her. Guess that's why our enemy doesn't like our females."

His callous remark brought tears to Sonia's eyes. "I am not some monster to be avoided, Joel!" She turned to her other brother with contrition on her face. "I'm sorry, Myron. That was my reflex; I can't help it."

Myron simply growled at her like some wild, wounded animal, not forgiving. Until now, his sister had always been helpless in his hands.

He took to brooding over the injustice of the encounter.

After long minutes, Joel broke the silence.

"So…seeing we have this enemy out there, and it's after us, guess we'd better plan some strategy…you know, for our defence, and such…"

Sonia came back from her own contemplations reluctantly.

"We also need to begin a search for others…"

"There are more like us?" Joel exclaimed, amazed.

She nodded. "I hope so. 'Keeper' said the parent race back on home planet had been annihilated; we are all that remain. Our parents, and others, were hidden here to protect them. As our parents did, those others may have reproduced. There might possibly be other dormant born here still surviving in different areas across Earth. The device lost track when it became the only one in existence; it had too many to protect."

"Why would they only leave one 'Keeper' to guard?"

Opening her memories so he could see, Sonia showed Joel more in detail how it had come about. She included this time all the gruesome details of torture and the massacres.

"Oh! Man! "cringed Joel. "This enemy is vicious! How are we ever going to protect everyone against such a malicious opponent?"

"I have placed 'Keepers' guarding each of my family members...except those that are entirely human. That is the one flaw in my plan: when the men are away from their families they will be unprotected, but...I think, the enemy seek the bi-pure, so maybe they will overlook the human partners when they are off alone."

"Why didn't you put a 'Keeper' on Ivan and Wade?"

"I haven't yet figured out how to programme one for a human. I've gone according to specs on our species; the machines work if the subject is part our race, but not if fully human. The 'Keeper' refuses to acknowledge it must protect them."

"I guess, we have our limits, after all," Joel observed. "And, obviously the enemy is also capable of destroying those 'Keepers'."

Sonia nodded regretfully. "We need to set up a safe place for everyone... if we found others to join us, they might help us protect."

"I say, why bother about the others at all," Myron broke in. "We just look after our family...Nobody ever helped us."

"'Keeper' helped us, Myron. It has watched over us all our lives."

"Didn't watch over me! Where was it when I was down that telephone pole hole with the lizards when I was only five?"

"At that time, it was still attached to dad; his original 'Keeper' was lost. There were only two 'Keepers' to watch over all of us. Mom had the other one."

"How come these 'Keepers' were wasted on girls; they should have been watching males only... they are more important."

Annoyed by his constant put-down, Sonia tried to explain the reasoning of their ancestors. "The 'Keepers' were given the task of protecting only original dormant. Our race never expected their children would have to grow up here...never even bargained on offspring. They intended to return when the battle was over."

"Figures! They're not much different than humans, are they? Always breaking promises ...and these creatures made 'Keepers'?" he chided sarcastically. "No wonder they don't work properly."

Sonia was stunned. "I'll have you know, if it wasn't for that guardian device protecting us...when it wasn't even programmed to do that, our enemy would have found us at mom's dying bedside...we would have been dead along with her, and...our death wouldn't have been so pleasant either!"

Non-pulsed, Myron continued as if he had never heard an explanation. "I still say, no one looked out for me, so why should others get treated like they're special. Let the other dormant find their own way...no skin off my back."

Sonia shook her head. *There is no use arguing with Myron. He will never let go of his eye for an eye perspective. It is so sad.*

Turning instead to Joel, she changed the subject.

"I was thinking, if we were to pool our savings...we each have about twenty-five thousand..."

"I don't!" Myron objected quickly.

Sonia took a deep breath in frustration. She was finding it increasingly difficult to maintain self-control with this constant augmentative attitude of his.

"You can't hide things from us now, Myron," she stated with irate disapproval. "So, stop lying! Do you know, if I want, I can force myself deep into your mind and find out anything I want. I could wipe your memory clean and make you start over. You'd never even know I did it...not that I'd want to go that deep into your mind, unless it was absolutely necessary..."

Sonia stopped, appalled by her own tirade, suddenly realizing too late, she had revealed more than she wanted. Joel's reaction to her statements was to close his mind to her instantly; Myron on the other hand, finding all this amusing, widen his access to show every degenerate detail of his imaginings, deliberately taunting her.

Sonia felt like crying, regretting immensely what had just happened. Never would she tamper with their minds. She mentally withdrew from them both, giving them and herself time to regroup.

I do not want my brothers to fear me. Myron never will. But Joel... I needed him to be level headed, trusting.

"You are not taking my money!" Myron exploded returning to the original topic.

Sonia just wanted peace. Steeling herself, she let him back into her mind so they could converse.

"Okay. I believe everyone should have freedom of choice. If you don't want to share, that's fine. We'll use only my money."

Joel came around also at her gentler approach.

"I'll pool my savings with yours," he offered. "What was it you propose to do with all this money?"

At long last, someone is willing to listen!

Sonia opened her thoughts to Joel so as to plead her case.

"As a group, we'll need food. If we grew it ourselves, it would by-pass the usual middlemen. I thought if we were to buy a fertile field...with our ability to manipulate nature, we could produce product far faster than normal. We would eventually stop being reliant on human grown with all the harmful bi-products they contain...there would no longer be a chance of cheating anyone out of their proceeds, and..."

"If we found a good water source nearby, as..."

Joel was making no objection, so Sonia continued forming her ideas.

"I think our enemy will concentrate in the populated areas when looking for us. If we could set up a safe place somewhere in a mountain range…the mining companies don't own the whole mountain, do they?"

Joel shook his head. Sonia went on expounding.

"If we could find a cavern of marble or granite, they wouldn't be able to detect us as easily through the harder rock. It would also be hotter in such an area…that would mask our heat signature from them…"

"You want us to live in a cave," interrupted Myron. "With all the crawly things?"

"Ah, Myron! Cut it out!" Joel ordered impatiently. "Can't you work with us for a change? This is a good idea!"

Myron grunted, and withdrew into his own thoughts.

Joel had caught the vision. "I'll need my monthly income to stay here while we search for and set up this place," he resolved. "I should be able to find one easily. We can travel the world in a blink now… and while I'm at it, I'll be watching for the other dormant, as well."

"You look for the males," Sonia suggested. "I'll try to find females. Don't be out at night, Joel. We are visible to the enemy in the darkness. Stay in lighted buildings…

"And Joel, when you seek the dormant, look inside the body for their luminescence; peering into their minds gets pretty ugly…painful. Don't use that method."

"'Kay. Can you look after your family here, while I'm gone?" Sonia agreed that she could. "How will you ever protect everyone? They are all over the place."

"I'll protect Jade and Nadia," Myron volunteered, relishing thoughts of watching two women undetected.

"You will not!" Sonia objected violently. Such invasion to their privacy was appalling; she knew he would not give her girls the privacy they deserved. "I will be the one to watch over them!"

Joel, disgusted also by his brother's imaginings, joined the admonition. "It's better a woman watches over a woman."

"'Keepers' aren't female."

"Never mind, Myron," Joel ordered angrily. "We don't have time for any more of your mind games."

Myron retreated behind his mental shield, finally realizing to have others see his visions was most uncomfortable; it was wiser to keep them private.

"I think my best course is to remain in the building where I now reside," Sonia decided. "I'll keep this all secret from my kids until we have a safe place ready for everyone. In dormant form they are easier to protect anyway."

"Will 'Keeper' watch be enough?"

"For now, it will have to be…when we have found and changed others, perhaps they will be willing to help protect my family. But, give them a choice, Joel…if they do not wish to join us…"

Joel nodded in agreement. "Free will always makes for better co-operation… we work together best that way."

"I was wondering…is there any way to make our money grow?"

"We could always multiply it by manipulation," Joel joked. "But you already explained how that works, so it nixes that. With the ability to see the future…my vision is limited to a day ahead, but…I could play the markets…"

"Don't see why we don't just take what we want," objected Myron, joining into the conversation once again. "Isn't seeing ahead the same thing as what you were riding me about?"

"He's right there, Joel," agreed Sonia. "Better not do that either. We'll go as far as we can with what we have."

"Maybe some of the dormant have money and will be willing to pool finances," suggested Joel.

"And help us defend ourselves," Sonia agreed.

But Myron was still chewing a grievance bone. "We've got the superior intelligence here," he expounded. "We could rule this planet if we wanted to, make these creatures our slaves…we'd then have all the money and the biggest work force we could ever want."

"We will not make humans our servants," Joel shot back. "They are not ours to command! Why are you constantly bent on getting even?"

"Maybe, because I've been the underdog all my life?"

"I would rather be suppressed by another race," Sonia quietly observed. "Then to dominate…anyone."

What has gotten into Myron today? It is like he had decided to become an 'Opposite'. He is always dwelling on past unfairness.

Myron answered, though he should not have heard her deeper personal thought query at all.

"I never wanted to be a part of all this in the first place. I just would like to enjoy my life now that I have it back. What's so wrong about that?"

He invaded too deep into my mind...again! I need to guard better against him. Myron does not need to accidentally be enlightened in the species' destructive powers!

"We all would like to be safe and just enjoy life, Myron," Sonia agreed. "I wish I had that liberty...and I know you've had it pretty hard..."

"Darn right I have! And I deserve a break."

"But it just isn't safe to do that right now," Joel countered. "We all have to be on the same page here; we can't each be doing our own thing."

Annoyed, Myron retorted. "Well, you've always made your decisions without me before. I won't be missed."

"You would too," Sonia objected. "And going off alone is the surest way to die."

Myron laughed derisively. "You're going to do it! Besides, you said, they're looking for females. They won't kill me!"

"Want to bet on that?" Joel challenged.

At Joel's aggression, Myron made an attempt to compromise. "Somebody ought to check out this enemy, put them out of commission. I can do that."

121

Sonia and Joel both countered at the same time.

"We don't kill!" Sonia declared, but the thought was by passed by both brothers.

"You can't go by yourself," warned Joel.

"Fine then!" Myron stood up. "I'm out of here! You guys can go on planning the future. I'm off to see the world."

"Myron!" Joel yelled verbally in his frustration. "Stay here! It's not safe..." He switched back to thought communication, adding. "You can come with me."

But Myron had vanished, and would not respond.

Sonia sighed. "Let him go. It won't help to control him. I've put a 'Keeper' on him."

"Really?" Joel grinned appreciatively. "Always one step ahead, aren't you? You're just full of surprises today. I suppose you've got one on me, as well?"

Sonia grinned. "Since before you changed. One more thing..."

Joel raised a questioning brow.

"It's not wise to remain on this planet for long. Could you check star charts... for a safe off-world site? Someday...it would be nice to have a world of our own."

From there, the two went to planning again, strategizing long into the night. After all, they had a whole species to look after now.

The wee hours of the morning had already come when Sonia finally made the jump to her own warm bed, and some much-needed rest.

CHAPTER 15

A welcome respite came when her granddaughter Jessica asked Sonia to stay with great granddaughter Kara. Jessica and Wade had won a promotional get away to a hot springs motel. Because it was only for a weekend, two days, Great-Gran came to them.

Three generations separated Great-Gran from Kara, and Sonia's generation was used to children doing their share. Ivan and Rhea, Jessica's parents, had drilled the same principle into their offspring, but Jessica and Wade deviated from tradition.

Jessica catered meals from her home; Wade ran a small welding business. When Kara was a baby, as her mother prepared the delicacies she was so noted for, she paced herself doing housework between baking, cooking, etc. Always available, Wade served as her gofer, between his customer bookings.

But as their daughter grew older, the task of training and overseeing this wilful offspring became an added chore, and finding this too daunting, they gave in to her, realizing it much easier to carry on as they always had.

Now at ten, Kara was a manipulative, self-absorbed pre-teen indulged by her parents who organized their schedules around her needs: transportation to school, dance lessons, music practice or soccer games. Jessica cleaned up after her; Wade gave her money whenever she asked. Make-up, clothing and shoes were the girl's main focus; girl friends were still more important than boys. But responsibility was not a concept Kara was familiar with, and her boat was seldom rocked.

On most weekends Kara went mall surfing with friends, moving from store to store shopping. Usually, Wade, Jessica or another parent functioned in the capacity of chauffeur.

However, when Great-gran came to spend the weekend with Kara, the girl's imperial reign met with an immovable entity...Sonia.

****

"I don't know what you said to her grandma," Jessica marvelled, when she called two days after Sonia had returned home. "She's a different girl. She tells me where she is going, no longer demands rides, even cleans her room. I've never seen her so respectful and helpful; she hasn't lipped me once since we got back."

"I'm glad." Sonia chuckled, as her mind went back. "We had a bit of an encounter ...someday, when she's ready, we'll tell you all about it."

"Well, from the bottom of my heart I thank you, whatever you did. She was getting to be more than we could handle."

"You are most welcome, dear. If you ever need someone again, call on me any time."

As Sonia replaced the receiver, a smile played at her lips. Her thoughts returned to the incident in question.

****

Kara's stance was rigid with suppressed anger. Her Great-gran had just told her she had chores to do before she could go to meet her friends.

"I don't do chores!" she declared with distain.

Sonia laughed. "Well, while I'm here, you do."

"I will not!" Kara stamped a small, high-heeled, booted foot for emphasis. "I'm going to the mall! I won't listen to some stupid, ugly old hag!"

"What was that?" Sonia demanded, appalled.

Kara blew out her exasperation with a frustrated burst of air. "Senile old women have no idea how young people should be treated. You are totally clueless! You think we should all live the way you did back in the dark ages."

Sonia's jaw dropped in disbelief.

"Furthermore, I don't have to obey you. So, if you think you can order me around you are deluded."

Such attitude! How did this child become so disrespectful?

"Why are you even here?"

"I am here because you are too young to stay alone. Your parents told me to do whatever I thought best. That means, I make decisions for you, as they would, if they were here."

Kara laughed insolently. "You think they make decisions for me? I have been deciding what I can and can not do since I was three, and... I'm much better at it, then you will ever be."

Why that arrogant little...human! thought Sonia.

The ten-year-old turned her back, heading for the door. "And right now, I'm deciding to leave! Like it or not...bitch!"

That did it! With great effort, Sonia squelched the urge to retaliate.

She is just a child...a self- important creature, the product of peer influence, parroting what she has learned from her school chums.

But her behaviour was definitely unacceptable...especially for a dormant that would someday transform to something more deadly.

Just imagine what a hellion she could be with powers.

Normally, she would turn this responsibility over to Rhea and Jessica, but they were still in the dormant stage themselves, and it was unsafe to change that. As it stood, Great-gran was the only one capable of nipping this in the bud.

"I think you have said enough," Sonia decided. "You will not be going anywhere."

The insolent shoulders squared. The haughty head did not even turn toward her opponent, Kara was that confident.

"You can't even stop me from saying what I want," Kara sneered, reaching for the door handle. "I dare you to try and make me stay home."

To challenge this Great-gran was the worse move Kara could have made; she had even suggested the method by which that correction could be accomplished. Her matriarch almost smiled.

"You will come here, young lady," Sonia insisted firmly, but in a quietly controlled tone. "Or I will have to make you."

As she had expected, the girl considered her threat improbable, ignoring her elder.

On the first attempt, the door handle would not turn. Kara shook and rattled the offending unit, as if expecting it to obey as others did obviously perturbed at its unwillingness to comply.

But Sonia, using telekinesis, had locked it.

And now she would also deal with this obstinate juvenile.

****

"Turn around and face me, Kara," Great-gran ordered resolutely.

Kara made a face, but stubbornly refused.

That old biddy still thinks she's in control.

Her body was obeying, much to her astonishment, turning about against her will. It was as if someone or something was moving her. Even though she tried desperately to prevent it, she had no control. Her feet took the steps back, one by one, until finally she stood again in front of Sonia.

Kara faced her Great-gran, her anger rising.

She opened her mouth to argue. The lips moved, but no words issued forth. Kara attempted to swallow. Her tongue and throat were paralysed.

"Look at me!" Kara jumped involuntarily at the sound of the sudden, curt command, and abruptly obeyed.

Their eyes met; hers were level with those of her gentle matriarch. Sonia gazed back with sober eyes, the pupils so small Kara wondered if she could be seen at all.

The tiny openings began to elongate forming a widening vertical slit; the outer membrane turned from blue to purple. Kara was mesmerized.

I have always loved this shade of plum purple.

But these improbable portals seemed to swallow her.

Feline eyes...they hypnotized.

Great-gran was speaking inside her head.

"I've observed you do not use your tongue wisely. If you can not put it to better use...I might as well take it from you."

Sonia held up her hand, opened it. On the palm, a small pink tongue wriggled, as if trying to speak.

Kara panicked, tried to draw away, but her body would not cooperate. She could hear her heart pounding in her ears.

Great-gran has my tongue in her hand! How can she do that? How is it even possible?

Kara tried to lick her lips; the tongue on the hand made the same movement. The young girl screamed, but no sound came out.

No! Great-gran, no! I'll be good, Kara thought helplessly.

The minutes dragged; Sonia finally spoke again.

"If I give this back to you..." She abruptly closed her fist, the organ no longer visible. "Do you think you might show a little more respect, and...maybe be compassionate in your dealings with others?"

Trembling all over, Kara nodded vehemently.

Suddenly, she could feel her tongue in her mouth. She met her Great-gran's eyes once more, terrified.

The purple tiger-eyes swallowed her whole; she seemed to zoom into a tunnel of light and rainbow images.

Sonia was teaching her. It was as if she had been learning at her Great-gran's knees all her life.

Finally, someone is showing me how to behave.

She realized helping others had its rewards: it brought satisfaction, and caused companions to reciprocate in kind. When she gave appreciation, it helped her feel good about herself as well.

Kara noted the requirements for good conduct, and also, what came out of cruelty, selfishness, and thoughtless actions...it scarred not only others but also herself.

Kara shuddered. Then Sonia let her go deeper into her feelings.

She realized, her Great-gran was a real person just as she was, a living being with joys, memories...and hurts...

I've been so hateful, so...wounding. How can Great-gran still love me after all I have said?

Kara saw Sonia return her thought with compassion, gentleness...forgiveness; she became aware kindness and mercy was her Great-gran's very soul.

My Great-gran is the only one who can actually understand...and she is sympathetic!

Kara felt warm and cuddled, as Sonia seemed to wrap her in affection; so deeply caressed she could barely breathe. Love surrounded her, made her long to remain inside this tunnel with Great-gran, engulfed forever in her fondness.

And suddenly, jarringly, it was over. Kara sighed as Sonia released her; even moaned with regret at losing this contact with someone who understood so perfectly her needs and could adequately supply them.

Sonia's eyes turned back to blue.

I like her eyes the other way, thought Kara.

And without being told, she knew this secret between them could be told to no one else. Great-gran's safety...and that of others depended on her silence.

Sonia smiled, as if she had heard Kara's compliment.

Then Great-gran returned to seriousness again; her voice still gentle, had gone low with menace, so as to impact upon Kara the gravity of the situation.

"If I ever learn you are doing anything like this again..." And at that moment Kara recognized that she had escaped with a minor correction, that Great-gran could have seriously harmed her had she chosen that course. Sonia was that powerful. "If ever you cause hurt to another, I will be forced to punish you in the way you deserve. And count on it...today will seem nothing by comparison. Have I made myself clear?"

Tears sprang to Kara's eyes. After the care and love she had seen in Sonia's mind, her apparent displeasure cut deep. She never wanted to feel her Great-gran's anger again ...ever.

****

With great difficulty, Sonia maintained her stern demeanour. The whole episode had been a simple hallucination; she had never really held the child's tongue in her hand. Though the illusion had been necessary, and had accomplished its purpose, she had felt cruel through the process. This was not her nature, nor her usual way. The encounter had bruised Sonia as much, if not more, than her great-granddaughter.

"As for the present." Sonia realized she must verbally clarify what was expected. "You will not leave this house until that sink full of dirty dishes in the kitchen is done; your room must be tidy at all times, and I wish you to clear away all your projects from the living room before you go to have fun with your friends. From now on, you will always tell your parents...or myself, when I look after you, where you will be, how long you will be there, and what you plan to do. And...I will hold you to any such promises you make. Do you understand?"

Kara nodded, her eyes round as saucers.

"Is it possible you have something to say to me?"

The tears came then, running in great rivers down Kara's pale cheeks. "I'm so sorry Great-gran. Please, please forgive me."

"Always!" Sonia opened her arms wide, and Kara fled to them with all the abandonment of unrestrained emotion.

"I too wish to apologise for my harsh measures. I do hope you understand that I could not leave you to continue in this fashion?"

For long moments, Kara and Sonia embraced, their hug so intense and tender from both sides neither wished to break apart. The bond that was forged that day would weather the storms of life…eternally.

"I love you dearly, little one…always and ever."

"And me you, Great-gran…forever."

****

Sonia remembered with fondness that moment of total surrender. To ensure Kara was continually safe, she now monitored her constantly. Never once had the young girl betrayed her Great-gran's trust.

But Sonia worried; the human in her blood threatened Kara's safety. If she had so easily influenced the girl's mind, what would the malicious "Opposite' do with her should they become aware she existed? Even just being Sonia's great granddaughter made her vulnerable. Kara would remain the weakest link, with no power to fight back, just because she was only an eighth 'Pure'.

I could always adjust her blood balance, Sonia mused. *If the 'Pure' were a quarter…even half, her powers would intensify, her defences strengthen; even her cognition of right and wrong would be enhanced. It would all benefit the child…*

She was way too young for it to be done without risk; her development, by the species measure, was only that of age four.

Given the circumstances, with death around every corner…

Sonia shook her head. *Is there time enough?*

When it is safe to break her dormancy, I will give her the option, Sonia resolved, refusing to be negative. *Freedom to choose is always better than to force.*

After all Kara had the potential...she could be the next 'Leader Female'.

****

Another realization had come to the forefront in her dealings with Kara. The girl would not be the only one of mixed blood.

The rest of Sonia's family was already half and quarter; then throw in the new dormant they might find. People, from now on, joining their species would each have a different variation of human ethnic and 'pure' racial balance. Each person would be unique.

At present, Sonia had the power to heal, the ability to protect and guide, and the strength to emotionally shield and balance all 'Pure' individuals, but this latest breed was the beginnings of an entirely new race. She was breaking fresh ground, literally writing a new rulebook. The guidelines to heal them, protect and guide them would be quite different.

The 'Pure' education 'Keeper' had given Sonia was pertinent to Joel, Myron and herself; she had facts on 'Opposite' behaviour that was relevant to the baser side of humans, and also, knowledge was attainable regarding human physiology, mental health and emotional states. But, each person among those of her kind would require different degrees of balance. If she made a mistake in the process, it could kill them...or drive them mad. Behaviour analysis, assessment of mental stability, even healing would require expert, finely tuned ability.

And because Sonia was the only existing 'Leader Female', she would be accountable for every member of their species, responsible to heal: mental flaws, emotional disruption, and physical injury. She would need to be their moral compass, their educator, even their disciplinarian. Why? Because, according to the knowledge given her, that was the function of such a being. If she rejected or abdicated the position, or was not permitted to carry out her compunction, even behind the scenes, she would perish, the entire species going with her. The species was symbiotic. Whether others believed so, did not make it less a fact. Sonia would die. When each broke dormancy and joined the race, they bonded to her…they would also all die with her if she could not do this. It was not the way she wanted it; it was a fact of their natures.

She knew the task set before her was enormous, unending…and to her, extremely daunting, but it was her destiny to try. She had no choice.

Sonia wondered if it could be done at all…especially by this 'Pure Leader Female'…but there was no other to take her place.

CHAPTER 16

In the silence of the night, Sonia sat at her window watching the street below. Even though it was four in the morning the streetwalkers still plied their trade. Cars zoomed by, the occasional one stopping to pick up or drop off a hooker.

Every so often a lone man came by on foot. He would talk with the women, and then take off again.

Does he care about their safety, or is he just protecting his investments?

Sonia saw into the mind of one girl: this very man was the pimp responsible for breaking her spirit; he had ravished her, gotten her addicted on drugs, dependant on him, and now he expected the rewards for his labour. Only yesterday her take had been insufficient, and she had paid the price of his displeasure. There were never any bruises, but her scars were many.

He would never devalue his merchandise.

Sonia wished she dared help. She would place a mental blanket over these women so the johns could not see them. But that would do more harm than good. And tonight... she must attend to more important matters.

Rest had eluded her. Joel had not confided in her, but she was always aware of his actions. He had chosen the next days to expand their people. Starting tonight, the males he had discovered would be changed each in turn, and at least with the first few, he would need Sonia to watch his back. He had never requested his sister serve in this capacity, certain he could handle his own safety, but protection was Sonia's specialty, and even when not required, she would shield behind the scenes.

She did not need Myron's help; her action was more to include him. Sonia reached out in thought to her other brother.

Myron! His sleepy mind awoke. *What are you doing?*

I was sleeping, he replied with annoyance. *Dozing with my dog.*

He was in his cozy little cabin in the woods, as usual. Sonia longed to avoid duty as he did, but presently, she dare not enjoy life...another's existence might be snuffed out.

She already knew the answer to her questions, yet she posed them to make conversation.

What have you been doing with yourself?

His thoughts went through a video of recent events.

Well, first I cased out that enemy behind the moon, learned a lot about them... went sight-seeing...been fishing.

Where did you go sight-seeing?

Went on safari in Africa. Man! Elephants aren't as big as I thought...compared to me. I saw the Coliseum in Greece, the pyramids of Egypt...oh, yes! I was in Hawaii today. Found a girl I liked, but...she wasn't much fun. Way too small for me.

Did you let her see you?

He laughed.

Not how I really look; made myself handsome though.

Sonia chuckled. He was like a teenager with a new gadget.

You should be with Joel, she ventured. *He could really use help to watch his back right now.*

Naw, he doesn't want me around...rather do it by himself. He's on this 'I'm the big leader' kick. Want me to catch you some fish?

Not really. When you catch some, just throw them back in.

'Kay...going back to sleep now.

Joel does really need you; he just won't ask.

Ya, ya.

I love you... Sonia offered.

But Myron was not the kind to return such sentiment; he never told anyone he loved them.

****

Djura knew the instant he entered there was someone in his apartment, after all he had been working as a police investigator/enforcer for fifty some years, and over that time, his senses had become fine-tuned.

He noticed the closet door was reversed, inside out, the slider not connected to the frame. Someone stood behind it, supporting the panel.

In Mecca, especially, that spelled malicious intent.

Even at eighty Djura was still strong; he had stayed fit. His muscles bulged; his body was firm.

You never knew when a revengeful enemy might find you again.

He had always been a giant among his people, well over six feet. Though his hair had greyed some, he still cast a fearsome image as he walked among the crowds, his skin a light molasses; the large beak-like nose, and chocolate eyes that missed nothing. Even with his western dress and clean-shaven face he blended in. He preferred his hair short, his head uncovered.

Djura stood still, watching for movement. Only a second's pause, as he slipped off his sandals, then moved with lightening fleetness, running hard at the closet, planting the sole of his bare right foot jarringly against the wood and the intruder behind it.

There was an audible grunt, as air was forced from the hidden assailant at the blow to his mid-section, and both the flimsy panel and the man fell forward into the room.

Unconcerned, Djura stepped back and watched, as the intruder on the floor struggled for breath, rolled from his back to his side, gagged, and then vomited. Merciless and angry, Djura waited and watched, while the unfortunate assassin recovered enough strength to crawl, inch by inch, toward the window opposite, then rose up and ran, diving onto the balcony, and over the rail.

I will let him go...this time.

Djura slammed the outside door, pulled the chain across, and turned the dead bolt.

****

Joel had witnessed the encounter from beginning to end. When he had arrived, he had remained invisible because he realized there was another present behind the closet door. After what he had just seen, he was hesitant to even show himself now.

Djura pondered the room, puzzlement mirrored on his face, as well as in his mind. It was as if he sensed someone else was still left in the apartment.

Amazingly, the mind of the Arabian was gentle; deep within his subconscious, he had chosen to allow kindness to rule.

Perhaps the best approach is simply to touch him, and begin the change immediately?

The man started violently at his grip, and would have fought, but Joel was already breaking the exterior barrier of Djura's dormancy.

In seconds, it was over.

The process had not changed the man much. He turned younger; approximately forty, taller: near eight feet; the eyes remained brown with the usual black slit; the hair was curly, short and dark. But he appeared...even more formidable.

"I am Joel."

"I know this..." Djura responded.

The knowledge transferred so easily! Is this man that sharp and quick witted?

Joel was surprised at the man's ability to process. And thought-to-thought communication with him was effortless after that.

****

139

Mid-afternoon found Sonia still watching Joel's progress. To relax, she turned her mind to thoughts less challenging...contemplating the plight of her building's residents.

In here lived the poor of the city, many without family, or abandoned by them. They were the cast-offs of society, seldom acknowledged by those younger, wealthier, or more vital, and if at some point they were noticed, the encounter often brought negative reaction.

Sonia called them the 'forgotten ones'. Governments pretended they were non-existent; adolescents viewed their experience and knowledge as obsolete; the working class considered them a drain on the economy, and a burden that needed to be eliminated.

When Sonia was human-like, this had been her place in the community, her lot. It saddened her to realize she could not relieve all the other unfortunates...that responsibility went to their own kind.

Because these beings were the rejects of their peoples, Sonia could now easily hide away among them safe and undetected. But the surroundings and the evident situations were depressing...increasing an already morbid state to increase in Sonia.

She was aware it had been weeks since anyone from the complex had seen her, yet none noticed she failed to appear. Not one even missed her! She had not one friend that would care that Sonia was different now, that she was the last lone 'Pure' female in the universe.

As Joel was searching for the men, Sonia had also travelled by speed of light across the globe, probing every feminine human, infant to senior. Save for her offspring and herself, the males were all that remained of the species.

This made Sonia was extremely down heartened.

Until it is safe to break my children from dormancy, I will be alone among these men.

Past experience caused Sonia to view this as a potential to be dominated. Men had a tendency to overlook a woman's aptitude, proficiency, and expertise alongside their own accomplishments...at least that was her sense of human society.

The new men could deny her any rights save those of procreation of the species. Just as the physically stronger had ruled in her old world, Sonia expected to be the lesser in the new.

How could her future companions prove different, when raised by humanity's standards and principals? She greatly feared the future.

****

Chi Cho stood at a south-facing window in his top floor penthouse. Below stretched Taipei, darkness cloaking it, though the city itself never slept.

This had been one of those nights Chi could not rest. More and more as he aged, this was his norm. Today he had just turned eighty-five.

Now that he was nearing the end of his days, his harshest regret was that he had never married. He had made no time for a woman; business had always come first.

At present I own half of Taipei. I will always be alone without an heir, so what good are my billions? What have all my efforts gained me?

From the beginning, success had been phenomenal. Though an orphaned infant left on the doorstep of the aged grandmother, he had risen from the streets, worked his way through an American business major, then returned to Taiwan. The stock market had been in his favour, providing his fortune, so that to date his real estate holdings, corporate businesses and banking assets marked him among the top twelve riches people in the world.

I would give it all away, to simply be part of a family.

He watched their reflections mirrored in the window glass, as the two giants materialized behind him. They each had feline eyes, one pair in brown, the other of silver.

Why am I not alarmed by their presence?

His desire for family was uppermost in his thoughts. It was as if he had been awaiting the arrival of these men to fulfill it.

Could these unusual beings in fact bring to realization his deepest craving?

Unhurried, he did not turn about immediately. Instead, he watched the sunrise.

To his left, an ever-widening strip spread from east to west, bringing brilliance, inch by inch, across the panoramic view of the 'Roof of Taiwan'. At the centre of these eleven peaks stood Yushan, or Jade Mountain, its elevation near four thousand meters above sea level. And as light kissed the hoary head, the drifted slopes turned from dark stainless Jade to pale emerald, and finally stood before the world, the ragged crags white with illumination, the world beneath its feet still shadowed.

Chi sighed, as if expecting this would be the last time he would ever see this sight.

When the silver-eyed man touched his shoulder, all regrets vanished. With the rising of the sun over Taipei, Chi Cho got his wish. He found new life...he discovered he had kin.

And family was his haven in this merciless world from then on.

CHAPTER 17

The sun was again going down on her side of the world. Sonia had been vigilant for more than twenty-four hours, but rest was a luxury she could not afford.

Joel's efforts remained solitary, even though the males now numbered four. Without Myron to help, Joel proceeded alone. He had sent the two newest members to break out others on their own. It was a means to shorten the process.

Sonia had begun this chain of events, but from the beginning as she had viewed it, there was no other choice. She could not have left anyone to die.

She realized now these other men could be deadly. Unlike her brothers, they had no family tie or loyalty to her; these were professionals, experienced in the world... intelligent above expectation.

They could be either friend...or foe.

The recent additions were good men; their minds were quicker...perhaps because they were half human. This last was a competent administrator. If chosen, he would make an excellent leader.

Did it really matter who was in charge? It was not like she wanted to lead. Perhaps she would not make the better sovereign?

I could still work behind the scenes...if a peaceful male was selected.

But what of the other men to follow, would they be so amicable? There might be others worse than Myron.

Back in their original world 'Pure' had turned 'Opposite'; on earth good men had often turned bad, and differing agendas had caused warfare. Their planet had been female ruled; this globe had always been male dominated. Both methods had come to bloodshed ... each approach had failed at some point.

****

Sky Hawk was Navajo; it was assumed his people were unbreakable. He was not supposed to be discontent, feel inadequate, or...suffer loneliness. And up until now, he had been that stoic pillar of calm, the perfect specimen, content with his world...in the eyes of those that beheld him.

But after all these years alone, tonight he was wishing he had someone to encourage him.

Even the air about him felt empty, exposed...lost. He had never experienced such longing to belong, to be cared about, needed...and to reciprocate in kind.

What is wrong with me tonight? I feel like my life is pregnant with waiting, anticipating an event undetermined.

A feeling of unfulfilled purpose had been coming on for some time. Most times he had kept it at bay by plunging into work...but now that was impossible. They had finally severed him from his chosen profession.

Not to heal the scarred, the damaged, the broken; it had cut deeply.

The desert air around him shimmered, as cold came down with the night. He shivered, and put another log on the fire.

Sky had always taken full advantage of educational benefits available to his race. He earned scholarships, and had applied as the 'token' native in a medical training programme.

In those days, he had a mutinous wrath toward the white establishment, but he put it into gaining as much knowledge and preparation as possible from them. And he had finished at the top of his class in General, Psychiatric and Paediatric medicine. Then he had signed on to intern with the most prominent child-behaviour specialist.

It was here he discovered the flaw in the support system: the benefits were largely shallow. Upon the completion of his rotation, he was taken aside, and the situation was explained. Because of the major he had chosen, and the fact he was aboriginal, he could not be permitted to practice among the privileged white class, which ultimately contained the majority of such paying participants.

Non-pulsed, Sky switched to General practice, only to be denied access here as well to those with the income to pay him.

At last frustrated beyond measure, he gave up trying to fit into the white criterion. He left the southern states, returning to his home village in Cibolo County, New Mexico where he set up a practice among his own people. This in fact neutralized the ruling physician's board, which had worked so hard to discourage him.

His fees became produce, corn, fish and poultry, seldom if ever monetary, but from then on, Sky never went hungry, nor did he ever require transportation.

He would happily have continued in this fashion for the rest of his life, had they not finally found the way to stymie him: the trumped-up charges against him accused him of the negligent homicide of one of his patients.

The night closed down around Sky, but he was too restless and muddled in memories to sleep.

He would forever be considered guilty in the eyes of the general public, even though the trial had proven his innocence.

An owl hooted in the midnight beyond his camp. Sky shifted his position to pull out his flute. For the next hour, he went to serenading the darkness away.

When he finally set aside the instrument, and the mournful notes had fled away, the dejected native returned to his brooding.

His licence had been suspended pending the verdict, so his hospital privileges and access to pharmaceuticals had been cut off. These were never reinstated, even after the courts had set him free.

The establishment had virtually rendered him ineffective, even among his own people, but still, he had tried to carry on.

The final blow fell when his licence came up for renewal; the physician's board simply ordered him to stop practicing.

And life had been pointless ever since.

With no practice, no interaction, came too much idle time; hours to remember and dwell, bringing to light a wound far deeper: that first fracture he had ignored to this point ...the past loss...of the love of his life.

Now that he was finally facing it full on, the injury felt so devastating, so profound, it was as though it had just happened yesterday, yet it had occurred as he was graduating university.

How many years ago has that been? I am eighty-three; they died when I was in my mid-twenties. Fifty-eight years!

Tonight, the weight seemed heavier...because this day was the anniversary. And, he was not sure he could spend another day alone.

****

The drunken white woman had lost control of her vehicle, mowing down his pregnant wife. Kanara had gone into early labour, given birth, only to die of internal haemorrhage.

But it was not enough to destroy his most treasured companion, his consistent supporter, and the sweetheart of his childhood. No, they also had to take the last living connection to her.

He had caught the arrogant nurse smothering his newborn infant.

She had adamantly insisted the baby was stillborn, and her word was believed above his. But Sky would always know and believe differently.

He had vowed to avenge them anyway he could. But nearly six decades later, the fight had gone out of him. No amount of vengeance would ever bring them back.

****

The bluff above him slowly materialized as pre-dawn approached; the breeze stood still in expectation. Sky Hawk drew in an uncertain breath.

What am I sensing? It is as if something is about to happen.

They appeared like a vision on the far side of his dying campfire: an Asian and an Arabian, yet unlike any others he had seen before. Each had eyes like a cougar: brown gold with a dark vertical slit, the lids of the one with the oriental slant giving an aspect of sleepy disregard to their owner. He estimated their ages to be in the forties; they were fit men, muscular…and gigantic.

The Arabian remained at a distance, as if standing watch, while the Asian with the dark pigtail down his back, the flat nose, thin pointed goatee, and burnt umber skin approached him. Sky made no effort to rise.

Are these an apparition? Have I finally gone over the edge?

The Asian dropped to one knee; gently, carefully, he placed a hand on the thigh of the native, and Sky's world forever changed.

****

Days later Joel finally materialized in Sonia's apartment. He looked frazzled, totally worn out.

Sonia was not surprised he had come to her as soon as his task was finished. She still was his sounding board.

"Would you like to have breakfast with me?"

"Sure." Joel took a seat at the table next to the window. He knew he was not visible to humans, so he did not worry about changing into their likeness.

Sonia placed a plate of bacon and eggs in front of him. She did not feel hungry herself, so she sat to keep him company, watching him eat.

Finally refreshed, he pushed the empty platter away.

"I have found only ten surviving males on all this planet," he acknowledged, sighing sadly. "Not much of a species left."

"I found no females at all," Sonia ventured.

Joel shook his head, dejected.

After a time, he added. "Those I found seem good men...not like Myron, anyway."

She understood him to mean, they had all been cooperative.

"They range from twenty-four to eighty-five...in earth years."

"That's twelve to forty-three by the species' reckoning."

Joel nodded. "We have three above eighty (forty by our aging), another two are sixty and sixty-one (actually in their thirties), two fiftieth (mid-twenties by our maturity), and the last three are twenty-five and under...makes them twelve and thirteen. Only two are related, a pair of twins from Ethiopia, Asa and Chad."

"Those two will be special; twins work especially well in sync... They are the youngest?"

"Second youngest."

"Thirteen then?"

"I guess. Just boys really…"

"It is so sad we have no females…"

"One of the last three could always choose Nadia as a mate…or even Kara, someday."

"All these men are half-human?"

"Yep."

Sonia went to thinking. "Do you realize, in order for the last three to be half-human there were other 'Pure' still alive twenty-four earth years ago? When the 'Opposites' came here, they probably killed them…"

"I know," Joel admitted regretfully. "If you could have just broken dormancy a little sooner…"

"You are assuming these were female. Maybe the India 'Pure' where the youngest was born, and the one from Africa actually died at childbirth," Sonia suggested. "Or they could have been male, even predeceased the birth of the boys."

Brother and sister went quiet, reflecting, regretting…

"Unity is our only survival method, Joel," Sonia observed.

He agreed.

"We should bring everyone together," she suggested. "We need to discuss a course of action…and pick a leader everyone will follow. The other men have a right to a say in the matter.'

"I know. We all need to be on the same page. I'll set it up…maybe I can find an abandoned warehouse that'll serve the purpose? Tomorrow, about noon, be okay for you?"

"I'll meet you at your place just before."

CHAPTER 18

When Joel, Myron and Sonia materialized in the old deserted warehouse, some of the men were already there. All heads turned, each pair of eyes alighting on the only female. Sonia saw appreciation in the mind of each, but for once, no thoughts were lustful. Out of respect for women, these men kept their contemplations clean. It was a refreshing disclosure giving her much needed reassurance.

Appearing before them, by Joel's transference, a table and three chairs faced the centre of the room. The three 'Pure' took their places; Joel the middle seat, Sonia to his right.

She realized quickly why some of the men were delayed. Those on the dark side of the world were taking a great risk just coming at this time. They would need to jump from lighted building to building continually, just to remain safe.

As they awaited the arrival of these last few, Sonia observed the other males, noting they also appraised her...except it appeared, for one.

The Navajo appeared emotionless, stoic, standing in a relaxed posture, his hands behind his back. He did not stand out because of his stature, was an average giant male of the species, approximately seven foot two, not the tallest by far, that was Djura, nor the smallest. His skin was darkly tanned and he wore his jet-black hair in two braids.

It was his eyes that drew your attention; they were the only pair of that colour: a deep cerulean blue, turquoise shadowed sea depth, with the slit a rust brown.

Such beautiful eyes, yet...they appear so unfriendly toward me.

Because of this, save for surface conversation, Sonia closed her mind to the men, her fear returning. She kept her eyes downcast from then on whenever possible.

****

The twins from Ethiopia appeared, together with Ram of India. All were handsome, with dark skin and hair and brown eyes, each taller than Sonia. They were teenagers, their bodies gangly, in the beginnings of muscular development.

Sonia met their eyes, and felt they cherished her as a mother. The respect she found in their thoughts pleased her, and gave her the courage to look again at the group in general.

Each man stood proudly, now that the whole assembly was present, every one of them over seven feet tall, save for the three youngest. The men had the builds of athletes, the handsome looks of Olympic gods. None had scars, malformed limbs, or lacked function of any organ; neither speech, nor sight, nor hearing was impaired. Transformation had healed all.

A perfect race, one to be reckoned with...without females to ensure the species continued. Sonia both marvelled and was mournful. Their enemy had near decimated their kind, and perhaps could still annihilate all. The future depended upon the choices made here today.

****

Joel cleared his throat to gain attention; all eyes shifted his way.

"All of you have agreed to come here to join forces; it has been explained to you that we have a common enemy hunting us and we are safer as a group. In order to work together, make decisions, I believe we need to first elect a leader. I will act as chairman until that person is chosen. But...as we don't know each other well, I will now open the floor to discussion."

First to speak was a man approaching thirty; Eric was from Finland. His slight build, short-cropped auburn curls and brown eyes gave him the appearance of a bookish intellectual, which in fact he was. Sonia could picture him before his change sporting thick-lensed glasses.

"Do we have any records for our species?" he asked.

Myron's grievance was still sore. "The 'Keeper' gave those to Sonia. It's all in her head!"

All eyes focused on the lone female. Eric asked the next question.

"And do these say anything about how the race was governed? I wish for the lady to answer, please?"

Sonia replied shyly. "Our people were female ruled. It was not a democracy."

"But we are starting over fresh here," Joel quickly interrupted. "We have no need to follow antiquated laws that do not apply to us. We have freedom to choose our own path, elect our own representatives."

Ignoring Joel, Djura also addressed his question to Sonia. "Was there a specific reason they choose a female?"

Sonia took a deep breath, and went into a teacher mode.

"Every one thousand years, according to the history, a 'Leader Female' is born. It was not through selective breeding, nor a planned happening, but a natural phenomenon of the species." Gaining confidence from their rapt attention, Sonia added. "I wish to point out, because of human DNA introduction this process may adjust or be altered."

Sonia realized the men expected her to elaborate. "At her birth, the matriarch presently ruling would begin the child's preparation, but only upon the leader's death did the younger female assume command. The 'Leader Female' is born with powerful mental protection abilities…"

A murmur ran through the men, as they understood the implication.

Djura quickly clarified. "I gather this female somehow protects the species?"

Sonia nodded.

"And these beings were always completely 'Pure'? asked Eric.

Again, Sonia affirmed.

"As circumstances stand now, most of us are a human mix," observed Djura. "Is it possible for such a female to do this with us?"

Sonia hesitated. "I can not answer that; it has yet to be tested."

Chi spoke up for the first time. "Honourable Lady, would you please explain in more detail how this process worked?"

Joel objected indignantly. "Why bother? It's not like we have one available to us. We are getting way off track here!"

Annoyance registered in the oriental mind, to be quickly subdued by its owner. "Please, honourable sir…humour us."

Joel sighed, giving way to the older Asian.

And Sonia knew instinctively, she could not avoid what was coming next.

"It is impossible for me to describe the full capabilities of a 'Leader Female' so that you will understand; I could much easier show you…"

Her three inquisitors were immediately interested.

"If you wish, I will mind-link everyone; all records on this subject will then be projected to all."

A murmur of assent went out from the group.

"However…" Sonia hesitated, uncertain whether to point out the fact. "Some will not process every detail; they may be unable to comprehend, because…they lack mental maturity."

"You refer to the youngest?" probed Chi.

"Age is not a factor. Some minds develop more slowly…"

"Why is that?"

"Our people are governed by emotion; sometimes negative sentiment blocks mental maturity."

"That's baloney," Myron broke in. "She just doesn't want some of us to understand."

A wave of shocked disbelief passed through the minds of the other men.

"Myron!" Joel hissed. "Behave!"

Myron went resentfully silent.

Chi was the first to recover, but his mind contained an extreme and instant dislike of Sonia's brother. "Will the three youngest understand sufficiently?" he asked.

"At least four or five will fail to comprehend some things," Sonia admitted. "Please do not ask who they are."

Sonia waited a moment; the men were expecting her to initiate.

The blanket rapid video lesson took very little effort on her part.

When she closed off access, there was a stunned silence.

****

"Well," Joel finally interjected. "Can we now get back to the matter at hand?"

"I have one more question, honourable sir," Chi pointedly declared. "May I speak?"

Joel sighed in resignation. "Very well. Just one more, then we vote."

Chi made his thoughts clear to all. "Amethyst eyes are the exclusive mark of a 'Leader Female', are they not Honourable Lady?"

Sonia dropped her eyes. Joel appeared shocked, having assumed all female eye colouring the same. It was as if somehow the information just displayed had failed to register.

Myron simply appeared puzzled, more as a child failing to assimilate all that was transpiring.

And Sonia knew Chi had done it on purpose, for the benefit of those who had not picked up the information.

"Now, we are ready to vote," Chi agreed.

****

Joel ignored what had just happened. "Any names to put forth?"

In a chorus the others answered, "No need."

"Very well. If a name gets less than half the votes, that man is automatically dropped. We continue until someone has at least seven votes. We close our minds so we can't influence each other...that is, except to give our votes to the counter. Any one volunteer to do that?"

"I will," Djura offered.

"Let's do it then."

****

Oldest to youngest voted by turn; it took fifteen minutes silent communication. Finally, Djura revealed the results.

"One abstain; two for Joel...ten for Sonia."

Pleasure registered on all the men's faces except for Myron and Joel. Joel had a wounded look, but quickly swallowed his pride.

"Sonia it is then. I hope we don't regret this…it's in your ball park, sis."

Sonia had been the one to abstain; it was apparent both her brothers had voted for Joel. What equally thrilled and frightened her was that the other men had all been unanimously for her.

CHAPTER 19

Sonia waited a moment to give them time to adjust. Then she assumed full command.

"By your vote, I presume you also wish to follow the established ways of our people?"

As one the ten assented.

"Contrary to what history has shown you, a 'Leader Female' does not work alone. Her balance is her support system; she delegates. She is only as strong as the foundation up lifting her; one dissenter can render her powerless. That said, I intend to indeed…give each of you a commission.

"In the past, assignments were given according to expertise in the field in question. Each appointment was for the life span of the individual, and only upon his death did it transfer to another. There is only one other means of severance: if they were to turn…'Opposite'."

A shudder ran across the group; it was obvious all understood how the enemy formed.

"Chi Cho…" The oriental came instantly alert. "Will you volunteer as the male overseer?"

"Willingly, Honourable Lady." He bowed slightly from the waist to honour her. "And my fortune is at your disposal, as well."

"Thank you. When I have appointed the other positions, we will cover some of your duties."

Sonia turned to the Arabian.

"Djura you have been in law enforcement for how many years? Would you be willing to serve as our enforcer?"

He nodded curtly, almost smiling. His mind told her he was delighted by her personal knowledge of his life.

"Our guidelines will not be so harsh as those you are used to. Security, protection and correction will be your responsibility."

Sonia addressed one of the few men not yet introduced, a sturdy man with a blond crew cut. "Ihor you are from Holland. How long have you been in Market gardening?"

Ihor's grin was huge. "Since I was born, my lady, fifty-four earth years." He laughed heartily. "And now I am again twenty-seven with a healthy body to work long hours in the sun once more."

Sonia returned his smile; she liked this jolly giant. "Will you be our gardener?" He nodded agreeably. "Our production of food and distribution might prove challenging. We will need fruit trees, game…a vegetable patch…"

"May I add flowers, my lady?"

"What would life be without flowers," she agreed. "And they would attract bees. With hives of our own, we could have honey."

Sonia was beginning to enjoy this. Since she first started appointing positions, Joel had sat slack jawed with surprise. He had not realized she was analyzing everyone as she encountered them. The men still awaiting commitments also appeared stunned by her aptitude at matching function to recipient. Some were amused by her familiarity, others astounded she evaluated so well. Mostly, she had gained the trust and approval of all.

"Ryan from Italy, you have worked in utilities for forty earth years. Do you think you could set up a good water system for us, inside as well as outside?"

He was a young thirty again, and raring to go. "My lady, after the streets of my city, that task should be a breeze. Do you want waste management, as well?"

"Probably a good idea…work with Ihor on that. Gardens need fertilizer."

Next Sonia sought out the eyes of a burly man from Greece. "Marcel, stone work is your specialty, but up until now, your talents have not been taxed too heavily; apartments and businesses are somewhat inartistic. Using manipulation, do you think you could form a sanctuary for us from granite and marble?"

"Such a project would greatly please me, lady," the sixty-year-old, now turned thirty again, agreed. "I will make it a feast to the eyes of the beholder."

"Then indeed that shall be your task."

At last, Sonia came to Eric, her first bold challenger. "Eric, you were teaching robotics. Are you as expert as they say?" The professor grinned delightedly, nodding. "I have been unable to programme a 'Keeper' to protect a human. And my son-in-law and granddaughter's husband need such protection. My brother Joel is more into computers, but will you work with him as my technical staff. Your duties will also include repair and surveillance. You can help my brother search the heavens for a permanent new home planet, as well."

"I would be honoured, my lady."

In Joel's mind Sonia saw he did not like the idea of sharing, but he nodded acknowledgement also.

"Now, I realize some here do not have a specific duty. You are either still too young for leadership, or have no special training in a trade. That does not mean you have no purpose...you too will be given duties. But first...back to Chi Cho...What will be required of you?"

Eric hesitantly ventured, "Sky Hawk has been missed."

"I know of him," Sonia reassured. "I did not miss him. It is a given, he operates in his chosen profession. He has the most important duty of all, and I am certain everyone will agree he does not need to be asked to do it. It is part of his nature...automatic." Sonia did not meet the eyes of the Navajo, nor did she invade his thoughts. Another time she would deal with the aversion in his heart.

"Now Chi, you will administer finances, as they were yours to begin with, and if at any time you choose not to share, I am certain everyone will understand. Should anyone else wish to contribute they are to work out details with Chi.

"I also wish you to organize work duties, sleep schedules, and...the guardian duty. This will be the most important function of our male population, and comes first above any other work detail. Every man is to serve in this capacity."

Sonia paused for emphasis.

"Each of our dormant must have a guardian at all times. That includes their spouses, should they not be together at some point.

"A second man will serve as back up and partner, should anyone come under attack. All must stay continually alert. The second man's assistance is vital. We are too few to be negligent."

Chi nodded, agreeing with all she had said.

"Honourable Lady, if I may be so bold as to make a suggestion?"

With a slight drop of her chin, Sonia gave him permission to put his idea forth.

"I would recommend that a guardian be placed on each 'Pure' as well. You especially should have our strongest man."

"I am agreeable to that. Eric is already working with Joel; they will be protection for each other.

"Also, a word of caution Chi, when appointing guardian duty to the twins, please split them up. They will be safer with an older male. The same goes for Ram."

"Understood. Honourable Lady...about your own guardian appointments...do you have a preference?"

It was like the whole room held its breath with anticipation. Each man was hoping to be chosen.

"Before I address that," Sonia stalled, waiting for calm among the men. "I wish for my brothers not to be excluded from other guardian duty."

"They will be included in the schedule," Chi agreed.

"As for my preference regarding my choice guardian…Djura is your strongest physically."

A murmur of approval came from the other males.

"He is acceptable as my guardian. As a group, the men may choose his partner." Sonia paused, wondering if she was being wise as she pointed out the next fact. "To be considered…Sky Hawk is the most mentally stable."

Shock registered in the Navajo's mind, but he schooled his features immediately, successfully hiding it from the rest.

"Sometimes…a 'Leader Female' can be injured too badly to heal herself. Sky Hawk not only is a qualified physician, he also possesses the most potent male healing power among us."

"These two shall be your guardians then," Chi decided, all the minds around him in full agreement.

Sonia suddenly felt drained, both relieved and fearful all at once.

Myron finally voiced a complaint he had been nursing since the subject had come up.

"I don't need no bodyguard."

Sonia drew in a sharp breath. She knew how she handled him would be crucial.

"We only have twelve men, Myron. For the sake of the odd man out, please, I'd like you to consider serving as another man's guard, and he yours. Please."

Myron shrugged. "Guess I could do that…but he only comes when I call…if I need him."

"Okay." Sonia made a point to meet Chi's eyes. "The matter is in your hands."

"We note his preference," Chi acknowledged.

Sonia paused, looking around at those that made up her kind. These were good men…all of them.

****

"I believe we have covered what is most important. Does anyone have questions?"

The group went silent, each man pondering what had transpired in the privacy of their own thoughts. The younger boys came nearer to Sonia, dropped down to sit cross-legged around her chair, the twin's short nappy heads together in private communication, the straight-haired Ram adoringly watching her.

In a voice that cracked unexpectedly, like the nervous twelve-year-old he was, Ram finally ventured a query.

"My lady, are the laws of our race different from earth?"

Sonia smiled at their youngest male.

"They differ drastically," she responded softly. "We are intimately, emotionally and mentally joined. Because of this…" Sonia puzzled how best to present it. "An example: if someone is angry, we all know it."

Even the older heads nodded agreement. Joel went rigid, as if caught at something he wished to hide; he had not realized their sense of empathy.

"Most of our ways are a logical result of this ability. If we injure another by thoughtless communication or action, we must right it

167

immediately or...it will spread negative reaction like a festering sore through the entire community...and that would cause impairment...physical first, then mentally. Our quality of life will suffer; our defences will break down; the unity will be severed. Our powers are governed by our mental, emotional and physical well-being. Respect and forgiveness must always be our number one law, toward each other...and even...toward humans. Forget the past! Our future depends on it."

Myron grunted, as if he had been struck in the chest. For once he was listening, and clearly understanding.

"If someone refuses to obey this law, our only recourse is to block ourselves away from the one suffering the 'Opposite' emotion. This is both painful to the guilty as well as the innocent. Our emotions are so inter-linked we feel each person's pain, or... pleasure."

Sonia became aware Sky Hawk's thoughts had shifted to his dead wife. For the first time since arriving he projected a thought comment, before he realized how his question would sound.

"How would a mated pair ever have privacy?"

More than one of the men grinned, following easily his reasoning. Sonia realized it was up to her to cushion his embarrassment.

She grinned up at him, and he dropped his eyes self-consciously.

"I presume you asked that with a physician's concern."

The Italian, Ryan stifled a laugh. But it was obvious the group wished an answer.

"This was why 'Keepers' were first invented," Sonia disclosed. "Couples would use them to block their feelings from other members in the household; it works much like a closed door for the children of earth. The 'Keeper' also protected the family while the parents were otherwise occupied."

A ripple of amused humour covered the group; the explanation was satisfactory.

"This brings to mind a point I wish to put out to you. I ask that those guardians assigned to my married dormant relatives close off their empathic sense when they see intimacy coming. If a man will not do this, they are not to be given such duty...Chi?"

"Understood."

"Now, this gives introduction to our second basic law. Because we are so intimately connected, nothing is a secret. Also, this is why the rule was strictly enforced. Abstinence was practiced as a way of life. First, intimacy was only allowed for mated pairs. Secondly, a mated pair was considered one male, one female. As I said, we differ greatly from Earth."

Sonia watched the minds around her as they processed these facts. None seemed to object to the harshness of the reality. They were simply puzzled as to what came next.

"As our population is mostly male, and you are part human this rule may be difficult to follow. It also presents a problem as to the continuance of our species... perhaps, when we are safer...those who wish, may seek a partner among...human kind."

Hope was kindled by her words. She had each man's attention and loyalty again.

"I only add this," Sonia quietly informed the men. "I intend to follow these rules. If any man can not ...he is free to return to his old life. Say so now, and I will make it possible."

"You are able to return a man to dormancy?" Djura remarked, surprised.

"Our ancestors did it, why should I not be able to?"

Djura saw the sense in that.

"He would have no memory of what has taken place, when I have finished." To test the man's commitment, Sonia pointedly asked Djura. "Do you wish this done?"

Shocked, the Arabian quickly retorted, "Never!" And added as certainly. "My course is stayed!"

Sonia turned to the others. "If any man desires not to go on, you may come to me in private."

Thoughts spun around her, as each man realized what dormancy meant: inferior, defenceless, sickness, early death...but most of all...oblivion. None wanted separation again; and none doubted she would do it if they asked.

But...not to know or remember...the Lady, that was the ultimate curse! All... for a moment of fleshly gratification, the price was just too high!

In unison, each raised their fist in the air. The ten declared. "We are for Sonia! We will abide by these rules!"

It took her breath away. She had been hard on them, but they had taken it well.

Sonia dismissed the men.

****

As the others gathered about Chi Cho awaiting their orders, Joel leaned into Sonia, and hissed in her ear.

"Had fun, did we?"

At first, she thought he was joking, but soon realized, her brother was deadly serious. He was angry and jealous, and had covered it well.

"Joel…"

"Let's get out of here."

Sonia wilted.

****

Chi, Djura and Sky Hawk stood together; they had been watching the trio at a distance. As the three 'Pure' vanished, Djura turned to the other two.

His eyes narrowed in disapproval.

"Who will protect her against those two?" he hissed.

The Oriental bristled. "I believe that is your duty."

For seconds they stared at each other, Arabian to Asian. Djura knew Chi was right in reproving him, but his temper had always been his weakness. Even now it was not easily checked.

171

"From this moment," Chi ordered venomously. "You will never leave her side… until the other relieves you. It is your choice who takes first watch."

Djura shook his head as if he had just been pistol-whipped. The distain emanating from Chi Cho hurt, and he realized though he was enforcer, he answered to this overseer…and that was good.

He turned to Sky Hawk, a little less belligerent.

"Will you take first turn?"

Sky raised a questioning brow.

"I fear, at the moment…I am still too angry. I might just put that Joel in his place."

Sky grinned, understanding completely where Djura was coming from.

****

Sonia was trembling when she dropped into her favourite chair upon her arrival in her living room.

I have become what I was meant to be, but at what cost? Now both my brothers are in rebellion.

Covering her face with her hands, she surrendered to tears.

****

Above, on the rooftop of the building, Sky Hawk silently closed his mind, giving her the space she deserved.

Even though she reminded him of a certain white woman, with her cream complexion and blond hair, he found what Joel was doing to her exceptionally cruel.

Sky would much rather be anywhere else, than to sit here …and watch this powerful woman cry like a lost infant. He had never liked to watch a woman weep.

But now, in this new empathy, it hurt way too much.

CHAPTER 20

Joel's living room had become Technical Centre. Computers, printers, and numerous monitors connected to satellite feeds performed behind the drawn blinds. A 'Keeper' insured the safety of those stationed there, and muted sound.

As Joel rolled his office chair from one unit to another observing the planet surface and outer space, Eric was occupied developing a programme for a 'Keeper', which would provide the needed defence of a fully human spouse.

At Chi's suggestion, he had moved into the spare bedroom, but Eric knew Joel was not happy about it. His private space had been invaded. That was why Eric was keeping low profile.

Joel was also still angry about the way things had developed at the meeting. Though he tried to block those negative emotions, Eric could not ignore them completely. Joel had become vocal about it.

"You know, Sonia has only grade ten," he blurted out suddenly. "With such a limited education, how was it possible for her to come up with all this? Surely that stupid mechanical contraption didn't give her the information."

"On a chip, data can be hidden behind surface info, only becoming available with the right code. Sonia must have had the trigger in her DNA. These devices are quite sophisticated. A 'Keeper' is capable of immense storage."

Joel just wanted to let off steam; he did not desire a debate at this point. Continuing as if no one had spoken, he proceeded to argue his case.

"Sonia's little world has been very narrow, revolving around family, housekeeping, gardening, that sort of thing. She has only general experiences, no knowledge of politics or business. How can she hope to lead a bunch of men?"

"That is why she appointed the qualified ones to their stations. You still see her as she was before when her mind was in sleeper mode. She will be more proficient than previously. The 'Keeper' prepared her..."

Joel finally acknowledged someone else was in the room. He grunted with annoyance.

"Prepared her!" he retorted sarcastically. "How can a bunch of memories, records of past rules and laws, prepare her? In case you haven't noticed our progenitors were annihilated. That old way failed!"

"It was not their system that failed them. That was not faulty."

"Oh, but it was flawed! You can't fight a battle without killing some of your enemy. The passive approach never wins. They lost because they wouldn't be aggressive enough."

"Did you not understand what Sonia projected at the meeting? Did you see the power we have? One male can blow away an entire world when empowered by the 'Leader Female'. We are invincible in battle when protected and unified. She protects; we defend!"

"We do not need to kill!" Eric added. "We can wipe memories, confuse orders; she can send them to the far reaches of the universe."

"What purpose does it serve by not killing your enemy?" Joel demanded. "Using this method, the enemy just returns to haunt you again."

"The reasoning is: give him a second chance to get it right...to change."

"That's stupid! If this were all possible, why did the entire species die?"

"Because one man betrayed them! One person was a weak link. He attacked from within; he hurt the 'Leader Female' beyond healing."

"And you don't think that can happen again?"

"I hope Sonia has learned from it, and we can keep her balanced this time."

Eric perceived the sudden jealousy form in Joel's mind. The fact that Eric cared more for his sister than her own brothers at the moment, made Joel even angrier.

"Sonia can't do this!" he declared pointedly. "She doesn't have such power."

What is with this man that he is such a doubter?

Eric went silent, puzzling. The men two returned to their duties and after a time, Eric thought Joel had cooled down. But shortly, as if their discussion had never taken place, Joel came back with his original complaint.

"Wouldn't it have been more sensible to elect a man for the position of leader? After all, most of us are men. At least, I think a 'Pure' male should have at least been appointed to one of the important positions?"

Eric knew here was the real root of the problem. Joel wanted a place in leadership. He felt he had been slighted, overlooked.

It was like both Sonia's brothers had a blind spot, and their pride would not let them be bettered by a female. "You have an important position well suited to you."

Joel chose to ignore the remark.

The males of our species cannot afford self-importance, Eric thought. *Every other man had realized that, even the youngest ones. What is wrong with these two men?*

"I cannot understand why they would pick the only woman to direct them? What training do they think she has that would equip her to govern well? She knows nothing about the demands of the office...about the needs of such a group."

Eric grinned. "Really? From the beginning of time, women have been looking after families, filling the needs of men since each was conceived in a womb. Sonia has been a daughter, a wife...a mother...a grandmother...a great grandmother. And you think she is unfamiliar with the needs of the men. In my book, she is adequately qualified to execute this office.'

"But this is not a family!"

"And why not? How better to be unified?"

"We are each individual, each unique."

"True," Eric conceded. "Each man adds his special quality to the whole. When we work in sync, we create a powerful, unconquerable security."

"What is wrong with being your own man…separate?"

"Therein lies a weakness of a society; so many ideas, diverse opinions. Some are self-serving; others seek to dominate; many are simply self-absorbed. No one but they have the truth. With one set of guidelines and all following such, a fusion of minds and emotions develops, with a unity in which there is less chance of a man going rogue."

"But it's impossible to be that connected."

"With Sonia we are," Eric declared firmly.

Joel laughed sarcastically. "And the first chance she gets, she makes the proclamation …she demands you be celibate? I call that really understanding a man."

Eric's eyes narrowed. "Indeed, man has that one great weakness…and she knows it."

But Joel was on a roll. He thought he had won the debate.

"She will never hold you guys in check."

"It is we who will control this base vulnerability…to our own benefit…and for the wholeness of all," Eric defended vehemently. "Sonia made the ruling; it is the best possible judgement. We obey Sonia!"

"Why? Just because she says so?"

"Yes!"

"Just because she says, we are so connected that we can feel what another man is doing. Hog wash!"

Eric's temper flared, and because of that, he at first missed the subtle implication.

"Indeed!" he returned hotly. "If you were with the woman you loved would you wish the whole world to feel, listen and watch?'

Joel laughed. "They do it all the time in videos, on television."

"That only proves my case. Look where it has taken the human race."

Suddenly Joel realized his adversary was right. But he was not about to let Eric get the upper hand.

"Do you know what really bugs me? It's like the lot of you think this is actually possible. Sonia's put you under some sort of spell, hypnotized the whole group…"

That brought Eric to his senses. Something in the way Joel had been phrasing things all along gave him pause. It was like the man was an observer, viewing from outside reality. He frowned.

Eric turned to look directly into Joel's eyes. "You did not bond with the group, did you?" he demanded incredulously. "Have you bonded to Sonia?" Eric shook his head in disbelief, as he realized the bothers had not. "But you and Myron are her brothers!"

"What the devil are you babbling about? We've known her all our lives?"

"But you haven't bonded, you've dominated!"

"Who are you to judge?"

"Are you…complete?"

Joel huffed. "You're not making much sense, man."

Eric sat back in his chair. He would not have believed it possible.

These 'Pure' brothers have chosen to remain separate when the normal species amalgamated. Perhaps…somehow…it was not of their own volition?

"If you do not know how…I can not help you…"

"You know," Joel returned angrily. "This is getting really old. I'm tired of being told I'm stupid."

Eric was beginning to pity him.

If in fact he is not stubbornly disbelieving, what else could cause this malady?

There seemed no imbalance in his physical or mental, only his obstinate refusal to accept his sister as this potent being.

Eric decided to listen rather than to judge. Perhaps in time, Joel could be helped.

As Eric had not saw fit to answer, the man continued to expand on his cause.

"How many times during that meeting, did Sonia blatantly disregard Myron's and my feelings?"

"If she did, I am certain it was unintentional."

"She was constantly embarrassing us both."

Eric tried his best not to smile. "She embarrassed you?" He narrowed his eyes and looked straight at the 'Pure'. "Be honest. I thought you both did a pretty good job of doing that without any help from her."

Joel turned red.

"Well…she didn't exactly help the matter much by constantly pointing out we didn't understand everything."

"Was she referring to you?" Eric asked innocently.

Joel grunted, annoyed.

"And why exactly did you not understand?"

"She only lets me see what she wants. I can't get past her barrier."

He is blaming Sonia?

"Why do you suppose she does that?"

Joel shrugged.

"Could it be because she thinks you might hurt her?"

"Why would I do that?"

"Maybe if you think a little on it, you will come up with an answer."

Joel apparently did not like the implication. "I would never hurt my sister!"

"Are you not doing that right now by your judgements?"

The man looked shocked. Eric decided to let it go, and returned to the former topic. "So, in other words, you think Sonia deliberately kept you in ignorance, as Myron suggested."

"Well, I certainly didn't get all the data as the rest of you did...obviously."

"After what I have learn today, I rather doubt that was her doing."

"Personally..." Joel's ire had risen to its limit. "I care less and less what you believe!" And he turned angrily back to his workstation.

Eric tried to work on his project as well, but after the sullen silence had continued for the better part of an hour, he knew he had to make peace.

"Joel...can we agree to disagree? I am sorry for making you angry...I realize I was insensitive. I apologize."

There was only silence from the opposite corner.

What would help the man?

It is cruel to provoke him farther, but it seems the only thing that works.

"I realize it bruised your ego to take second place to your sister, but...it does not make you less a man."

Joel looked up, anger in his eyes.

"Before, Sonia always came to me; she expected I'd always have the answer. I was considered the brains of the family, and when I didn't have the answer, I found it for her. She let me lead; she never objected. Was she just humouring me all those years?"

He took a deep breath, but Eric knew he was far from finished. He was just getting started. Joel needed to get it all out.

So, the professor just let him talk.

"Now, she chooses strangers...I'm supposed to be 'Pure'! That doesn't count for anything?"

Eric knew whatever he said would be the wrong thing right now.

"I feel like I was just indulged; her man servant! It's humiliating! It was 'go find the men'...'we can't let anyone die'. Now it's done, and I'm to sit at her feet."

Eric considered it pointless to remind him, he had played the loner, not allowing Sonia to help him.

"None of you would be here if it wasn't for me!"

That too is wrong; if Sonia had not watched his back, he would not have been able to do what he did.

Eric searched his mind for a way to distract Joel from this tirade. "But she gave you a job you are good at. Why is that not enough?"

Again, ignoring the comment, Joel switched direction. "She scares me right out of my skin! I don't recognize her anymore. And I sure as hell don't want to follow her to la-la land!"

Eric ignored the implied insult. "You love your sister..."

"That thing is not my sister! My sister was this dependant; weak, insecure... with a mind so naive...she used to be innocent! That woman..."

"Used to be your confidant," Eric finished for him. "Your leaning-post...your sounding board."

"Never again!"

"She cared enough to make you the first she broke out."

183

"I wish she had left me dormant!"

"You do not mean that," Eric pleaded. "She gave you the chance to undo that," he reminded quietly. "You could still be a dormant, should you choose."

Ignoring the choice presented, Joel chose a more vicious attack. Rolling his chair closer, until he was eye to eye with Eric, he hissed in a whisper. "I wish she had stayed dormant."

He turned to stare desolately at the monitor next to Eric's table, his eyes distant and unseeing. "Nothing will ever be the same again," he declared remorsefully. "It's like my sister has died."

Eric reached over and gently placed his hand on Joel's shoulder. "You need to get past what has just happened, see her vulnerability again, then your protective instinct will surface and you will find the sister you have always loved."

"She can not do this, Eric! She is only Sonia."

"She is doing a fine job so far," Eric reasoned.

"It won't be enough. There's a long road ahead."

"Will you not look into the minds of the other men?" pleaded Eric.

Joel shrugged. "I prefer to keep my thoughts private, and I'll treat others with the same respect."

"But, they could and would encourage you...you would gain strength from them."

"Ya, right! And they could more easily influence my thinking. No." Joel shook his head dejectedly. "I have enough problems of my own without borrowing from the minds of others around me."

That saddened Eric, for Joel had just rejected the male bond that could help him from his dark aloneness.

****

Sonia was delusional; Joel well knew that. It ran in the family. Myron was a good example of that.

What Joel had not expected was that all these men would be unbalanced as well.

Is it some sort of weakness when the blood is mixed with human DNA?

Then why did it affect Myron, and...Dad? It is like being alone drove father mad.

Maybe I am the one out of step?

But no, I am the only one with a level head here. I know by instinct what is right. Without being taught, I can do the things these half-humans will still have to learn. I am Sonia's 'Pure' brother...just as 'Pure' as she is!

What right does this professor have to correct or judge me?

Joel was getting nowhere with his work; he could not even remember what he had been doing. This all made him so angry.

I released Eric from his dormant, impotent life, and this is the thanks I get!

Joel rolled to another console, pretending to search for data. But his annoyance did not cool.

The man seemed so stable at first. Why did Eric turn on me? Why have they all turned against me?

Joel sat back in his chair, placed his head in his hands.

185

How will I ever convince any of them that to place their trust in Sonia is foolish? She is not this mighty powerful being, the one she had shown them all.

How is Sonia able to do all of that then?

Joel raised his head.

That was it! Something else had control of her! Perhaps, it is one of those 'Opposites'?

Where did she come up with a name like that? Where did she get any of this?

It is pure unadulterated fantasy!

****

Later in the day, a message went by thought from Sonia to all guardians:

"Djura, discipline rules will be such:

"Minor infractions will be dealt with by amiable co-workers.

"Serious transgressions only, will be brought to me. At the offender's appearance, that person will suggest two appropriate penalties, and I will choose between them the correction to be implemented. An assistant will then be appointed, and you and he will execute the judgement.

"As you carry out these guidelines remember: to humiliate in correction defeats the purpose; vengeance is self-destructive, and anger has no place in teaching. The inexperienced deserve our compassion and mercy. Be gentle with each other.

"One other matter needs addressing: As you stand watch over you charges, some may notice what seems to them to be mistreatment. Interference will be permitted only if serious injury is eminent. You are not meant to police their lives. Let my warriors be defensive only."

Joel and Myron did not believe this message was meant for them.

CHAPTER 21

Sky liked it here on the roof of the building. It was like being on the top of a majestic mountain and viewing the valley below. At such a place you felt small, insignificant and outside the measurement of time. Unseen, he could watch the people and the street below, while he guarded Sonia.

He liked it best when he had night duty; to watch the lady sleep was soothing. She looked like any other woman at that time, peacefully relaxed, delicate and beautiful... not some force to be reckoned with, a deadly weapon that could destroy the universe if she chose. In sleep Sonia looked helpless, breakable...vulnerable. And his was the duty to protect her.

At night to look at her did not make him angry. But in daylight as now, when she moved about, it did. As he looked at her, he was reminded of the white nurse who had killed his child, with her busy walk and preoccupied manner.

He had no real reason to dislike Sonia. She was no more Caucasian than Chi. It was just that she looked white with her translucent cream complexion and short blond wavy hair.

The woman who had killed his child was more sour of face with straighter hair, and now that he thought of it, Sonia's figure was far different, and her walk did not resemble the other woman at all.

What am I thinking equating my leader in this fashion?

He knew it was transference; his medical training warned him of that.

Physician, heal thyself! But...how?

Sonia was moving about the kitchen, cooking. The aroma of the stew she was preparing became agonizing, causing his stomach to cramp and growl. Sky was hungry.

All day he had been watching, as first she prepared and baked sour dough bread. Her way was unusual, when she began the stew. Cutting steak into chunks, she browned them, then left them to bubble invitingly while she added stock, spices, barley and vegetables.

It was driving him insane with craving.

Now she was setting the table by the window, a placement of two.

Is she expecting a visitor? I did not hear her call anyone.

"Sky..." The Navajo started. "Come. Please?"

She wants me in her quarters?

"Are you not hungry?"

Sky was shocked. *She wants me to eat with her?*

"I'm waiting."

Obediently, he transported to the living room.

He pretended ignorance. "My lady wishes me to attend her?"

"I wish you to join me. I know you need nourishment. Come, sit."

Uncomfortable, Sky took a place at the table. Sonia went to the kitchen, and brought back a platter of bread. Then returned, and carrying two steaming bowls of stew, placed one in front of him, dropping into the second chair.

She is serving me!

"And why not?" Sonia asked. "I am just Sonia."

It almost brought tears to his eyes, as he considered how he had viewed her.

"Eat...please." She picked up a slice of bread from the plate, tore it in half, and proceeded to butter it.

"I just love sour dough with stew...makes my mouth water."

He could not help himself; he chuckled. And from there on the meal went easy.

****

"Tell me about yourself," Sonia suggested after a time. "Where were you born? Tell me of your parents."

"I was raised in a village in Cibolo County, New Mexico. My mother was Navajo. I thought my father white, but now know differently."

"We have all come to that realization," Sonia sympathized. "Do you know anything about your father?"

She knew his every thought, could delve the depth of his mind if she cared to, yet here she was asking him to tell her in words. It both humbled him and honoured him that she took this personal interest. Sky realized she did not view him as her servant, but as an equal...and a friend.

"My father was a rancher in the badlands, and died before my birth. I always assumed our money came from him. When mother passed away, I found the house and lands were all in her name. Somehow, at his death, it was all transferred to her, but I failed to find any records. We never lacked for finances... If she was his servant, she never spoke of it to me. I wish she were alive now, so I could fill in the missing gaps from her mind."

"And no 'Keeper' records either..."

"If there ever was a 'Keeper', it was destroyed, and my history with it."

Sonia thought a moment. "Your unusual eye colouring is not a human trait," she revealed. "According to 'Pure' history, the blue and rust was evidence of great healing ability."

He raised his eyebrows in surprise. "That is how you knew!"

"Yes," Sonia smiled with delight. "After all, I have the records. Would you like to know more?"

He nodded.

"Well...each eye colouring has significance: Brown/black is administration, labour or warrior. Some may have more than one talent. Silver/rust has technical expertise; Amethyst/black, you already know. Generally, a female is blue/black, but sometimes we get a blue/amethyst combination with the black slit. Such a female is related to or can produce offspring of 'Leader Female' ability. Then sometimes we also get males of blue/black. They have 'Leader Warrior' skills. Their powers are stronger than those of regular warriors. And lastly, we have the brown/gold female…very musically inclined."

Sky was amazed. "So many variations. Now, I understand how you were able to appoint stations so well."

"No real feat involved," Sonia admitted modestly.

He laughed. "But you also researched their history?"

"Umm, a little. I analyse everyone. It's a weakness of mine."

"Never a failing, my lady."

"Tell me," Sonia returned to the original topic. "Did you have family of your own?"

Sky hesitated. "I had a wife… It was a long time ago…"

She had slipped into his mind before he was aware, the cancerous, festering wound tender to her mental touch. She viewed with him the chain of events that had caused it, and somehow, the reliving was less hurtful when she was sharing it with him.

There were tears in her eyes when she let go. Sky decided, Sonia was nothing like the nurse, and he would never view her in that context again.

"The sadness seems even greater," Sonia observed. "When we realize, your baby daughter would have been a female of our species had she lived. Such a treasure lost…"

That thought had not registered with Sky until now. His offspring would have been a grown woman, perhaps with a child of her own, and…he would have been a grandfather.

He shook away the renewed anger that brought, choosing to concentrate on the present instead.

"You have children, my lady," he probed, attempting to divert the topic. "The guardians say there are six females. Are there other males as well?'

"I have two daughters...which are now protected by guardians; two granddaughters... Oh, perhaps I should begin with the youngest of my children...

"Zane is fifty-two...in earth years."

Sky nodded, his interest truly peaked now.

They are older than I realized.

"That will make him twenty-six when he breaks. Do we protect him, also?"

"Joel and Eric have been assigned that post."

Sky frowned. Sonia quickly followed his thought.

"It does not matter. Eric keeps track from a distance, even if Joel is unconcerned with the welfare of my son."

"Anyway," Sonia returned to her disclosure. "Zane never married, spent his life, so far, under the thumb of the military."

Sky smiled at the way she had put that. It was obvious she disliked the establishment, and she would not have chosen it for Zane, if it had been her choice.

"Then there is Rhea...married to Ivan."

"We know of Ivan. Eric has managed to develop a 'Keeper' to protect him." This fact slipped out before it registered in Sky's mind that Sonia would already know that.

"Rhea and Ivan have three children. Jessica their oldest is married to Wade, and they...have given me my first great granddaughter, Kara!"

She said it with such pride; he knew beyond a doubt, Kara was special to Sonia.

"And my grandsons are Tyler and Shawn."

So, do the males number fifteen? Or is there another son also?

"And, what of your other child?" he probed; knowing by process of elimination there was at least another female.

"There is Jade...and one other...Lance."

Abruptly, Sonia closed her mind to him. Staying hidden, she dwelt on something she feared he would judge, but he had already seen the hurt hidden there.

For the first time, Sky realized his leader feared men. The male tendency toward retribution frightened her, and she expected he was no less aggressive.

"My lady, we would never hurt you."

Sonia looked startled.

"Ah, I should have expected this... You are more astute then I bargained."

She looked away, outside to the street. Finally, Sonia returned to the conversation, but deflected away from the deeper agony. Instead, she spoke of the daughter.

"Jade was in a car accident when her daughter Nadia was only fourteen. Isaiah, Jade's husband, was driving. He was killed; Jade crippled for life, and Nadia became the caregiver and bread winner."

The shock registered on his face, for Sonia came back quickly. "But soon we will fix that!"

"Jade has no...partner then?"

Sonia grinned, leaned forward conspiratorially, and added. "The one who guards her is just the right age."

"And who is it?" Sky joined in, amused by her attempt at pairing the two.

"Ryan...but then, there is also Marcel," she added as an afterthought.

Sky laughed. "You are playing match-maker, my lady."

"I do not appoint the guardians," she returned innocently.

He grinned. "And what of your oldest child, Lance?"

Sky wished immediately, he had never asked the question. Sonia went from bubbly joy to instant fear and dejection.

"My lady?" He almost reached out to touch her in his concern, but remembered just in time, the reflex action of a 'Leader Female'. Sky knew, the safer approach would be to change the subject.

"And...these children... What became of their father?"

Her face softened, and Sonia came back at his wise approach. For the first time, Sky saw cherished memories mirrored in her mind.

"I was married to a gentle man. He loved the land...a farmer. He would never have struck anyone, least of all me. He never forced or dominated. We worked together."

Her thoughts went to a time of pleasant fellowship, and Sky followed, entering her mind as she had done with him, aware it was a time of private reliving, but wanting to cushion as she had done with him, through his hard time memories.

And while inside... He found the hidden thorn.

Now, if I can only find a way to extract the beastly splinter...the way she did for me.

Suddenly, sensing his intrusion, Sonia abruptly closed away the deeper memories, and went verbal, as if to speak aloud made her statements more potent.

Still she sidetracked from the dagger wound keeping it still hidden, and told instead of the lesser hurt...the loss of her spouse.

"My lover died of Cancer," Sonia stated quietly. "It was just before Zane was born."

Sky saw the view she implied. And she was right.

Her loss is equal to mine.

He rerouted the conversation.

"You raised the children all alone," he marvelled.

Sonia nodded. "To remarry seemed a disrespect. I have never found a human man who could come close to his stature."

Sky fully understood her statement. It was also so, concerning his Kanara.

CHAPTER 22

In the silence, Sonia noticed his empty plate. "May I get you some more stew?"

Sky looked down surprised. He had forgotten they were eating.

"The meal was very good, but I should return to my post."

"Djura came to relieve you an hour ago. You were busy, so he has shut his mind to give us privacy."

"He must think I have over stepped my bounds," Sky worried disconcertedly.

"No. He knows I asked you to join me. There are no secrets, remember?"

Embarrassed, the Navajo made an annoyed observation. "If a man did wish to court a female, the whole species would know."

Sonia wrinkled her nose, as if she too found that thought unpleasant as well.

"Anyway." She came back quickly. "Come sit on the sofa…so we might talk a little more."

When he arose to comply, the empty dishes vanished from the table, as did the uneaten bread. Sonia joined him, taking the recliner.

"You are lonely, my lady," Sky observed.

"Yes," she agreed. "Being leader is…isolating."

She had a way of striking at the core of an issue which he found refreshing. But he also realized her statement to be only half the truth.

"Things are different now," Sonia added. "My family always has been busy. They include me in major events, but the majority of the time, I am left to myself. Before, Myron and Joel filled the gap; we talked much by telephone. But now…"

Sky knew whom to blame for that.

"Joel would like to be leader; sometimes I wish he was… It has caused a separation between us." Sonia sighed, and hurried on. "I do not blame him. He is afraid of me now… And it is true; he has more knowledge of this world than I…and he is more amicable with people. He probably would make the better leader."

Sky shook his head, vehemently disagreeing, but Sonia quickly made it apparent she did not want an opinion.

"I am too emotional… Joel says, a leader rules with his head, not his heart… as I do."

Sky's temper surfaced. "My lady, you are female. We picked you for your compassion, your heart-rule. Your warmth is what makes you special. Do not try to contain your feelings; to deny them will scar you! He is wrong! We do not all feel as he does."

Sonia looked away, as if his words could not possibly be true. Her eyes were bright with unshed moisture when her gaze returned.

"The female is the emotional balance to the more practical male…they compliment and equalize each other. It is so in every race, especially in our species. The males of our kind are meant to be counter balanced by the emotional 'Leader Female'.

Your powers come from your emotions. We, your 'Protector Guardians' are to balance you!"

"I know that is the way it is supposed to work," Sonia admitted sadly. "But right now...that balance does not feel right. Something is still missing. "

I know what is missing...her brothers. And the dormant need to be awake to correct the imbalance.

"You may all want me to lead, but...I am still only Sonia."

It angered Sky that Joel would not take his place that he had made her this uncertain. She had been so confident at the assembly meeting, but now she was weakening more by the moment.

What can I possibly say to encourage her?

"In my mother's culture, mature women are all considered leaders. They do not need to be elected as such; they just are. Each such woman is given the respect and honour due her, without refute. No one ever questions their rightful place!"

"These men are not Navajo; at least half have come from cultures and customs where the female is subjugated."

"Our 'Pure' blood mixture has over ruled this."

"You hope..."

Sky sighed. "Time will be the test, my lady."

"May I show you something I have realized though our...becoming?" Sonia asked quietly. "I would like to indulge in a little...discussion."

"Indeed." Sky smiled.

She has shifted focus; balanced her own emotional. That is good.

"Do you remember what you were feeling just before they came to help you break?"

Sky frowned. *I was at the very brink, unable to go on.*

"Hold that thought," Sonia requested, reading his memory. "I remember where I was, something I said the night I changed. Just before I fell asleep, I cried out in anguish for help…"

Sky was suddenly very interested.

"When I awoke the next morning, I was as I am today…"

"The 'Keeper' helped you?"

"'Keeper' had just been destroyed."

"Then who…"

"Do you believe in the spirit gods of your people?"

Sky sighed, somehow disappointed by what he thought was coming. "My mother named me for the blue sky, because of the colour of my eyes. Secondly, she gave me the name Hawk. The bird was meant to be my life spirit guide, but experience has taught me, it is counterproductive to expect the spectre of an animal, fish or bird to help in times of trouble. Nature is both breath taking and savage, but in my opinion, it is foolish to worship it."

Sonia nodded, fully agreeing. "And what of something greater than nature…and man?"

"You mean an All Mighty Creator being?"

"Exactly."

"Now that being would be worth my veneration."

"As I see it, the one who created the cosmos would be powerful indeed."

"And do you think such a being exists?"

Sonia narrowed her eyes in thought; when she answered, she chose to reply indirectly.

"Do you realize how many billions of galaxies there are in space? And each is composed of many star suns, each with countless planets circling them. Do you not find it amazing that with all those planets to choose from our ancestors picked Earth…the one sphere upon which there was life with which we could successfully interbreed, ensuring the survival of the species? Do you think they had time to search through the universe, considering their circumstances at the time, before they left our parents here?"

Sky was seeing her reasoning. *Chance and luck seem a great stretch of the imagination. Is there a larger plan, a greater mastermind behind all this?*

"Let me give you another fact to ponder. Each one of us, just before the moment of breaking dormancy, had reached a point of inability to continue with life. Could that be just coincidental?"

Sonia sighed. "I guess what I am saying is this…and you may consider it fact or not. That is your choice. But I believe this to be so: Not only is it impossible for all these galaxies and stars to just happen, as here on Earth it is claimed…their 'Big Bang' theory, but our chances of being here, now at this precise moment with all conditions favourable, is phenomenal. If there is not an Almighty Being in charge ordering time, space etc… one with far, far more power than it has given me, how could we…by chance, exist at all?"

She leaned forward to emphasize her point. "We survived because it was planned, and not by our people. One greater, stronger, more knowledgeable and powerful than we are orchestrated it. So why should I worry about the future? Our destiny is not in our hands; it was drafted at the beginning of time…and even though I can see ahead with a vision others call 'second sight', even I can not see how it will end."

"Suppose you are right," Sky wondered. "Why would this being create us with such incredible abilities? Why give you the power to destroy what it designed?"

"Perhaps to test us?" Sonia decided. "It wants to see if we can be merciful… to use these gifts with tenderness and pardon."

"Here on Earth most don't even believe in the power of an Almighty Creator, or even that it exists."

"Humm," Sonia observed. "Remind you of a parallel? Joel and Myron refuse to believe I have power. So also, this entity: many reject it because in their eyes its guidelines set up eons ago are antiquated. Perhaps, as I do, all it wants is to protect, to love and be loved? I can't help feeling empathy with it: I did not create our species, but think how it would be if I had."

"I am certain you know exactly how our Creator would feel. If you had not made the first step, and made certain Joel and the rest of us were protected as we released the others…we would not have a species."

"Mark my words, Sky. I cannot, nor did I, create us…and we did not happen by chance. It took me a while to realize it was not only on my shoulders, but this is the conclusion I have come to in the end…

"And now, that I have expounded so unwisely on the matter…"

Sky shook his head disagreeing with her statement of being unwise.

Sonia continued. "I believe it is time to return to my original purpose in asking you to join me. I confess I had an ulterior motive…two actually."

Sky did not need to ask her first purpose; it was to correct his emotional imbalance, as indeed she had.

When the physician cannot heal himself, my 'Leader Female' is my medical balance.

"I need a favour of you, "Sonia revealed. "I would like it if you would teach me."

He looked at her astonished.

What can she possibly learn from me?

"I have noticed your exceptional external control. I want to learn to be… stoic."

He almost laughed at her innocent seriousness, but he steeled his features quickly. She was way too appealing just now, breaking down his guard.

"My lady?" he questioned in a puzzled tone.

"There! That is exactly what I mean. I need to be able to do what you just did."

Astounded, he did finally laugh.

"I do that without thinking…"

"I know!" she exclaimed in frustration. "But…how?"

"And why…do you wish this…ability?"

She sighed resolutely. "In public…I do not need to…break down."

He understood completely. Even with Sonia, it was important not to show weakness.

"How might I teach you this?" he asked.

She moved to the sofa to sit directly beside him and cautiously took his hands. At her nearness, Sky became aware she had a special delicate scent, one of vanilla… faintly mixed with cinnamon.

Something deep inside, long forgotten, stirred.

If she was aware of her effect on him, she mercifully gave no inkling.

"Let yourself be angry, then control it. I will watch in your mind as you do it."

That will be difficult. She has just softened that festering sore. To let the demon arise again is completely undesirable.

Never the less, he obeyed. Sky remembered the injustices, the anguish he had felt at his wife's death, let the emotion overpower him.

Sonia slipped in; she was gentle in his mind, soothing the hurts as he progressed through the memories. He had never imagined a white woman for a soul mate, but this one understood. He suddenly realized he was thinking of Sonia as such, and reprimanded himself. Not since Kanara had he felt this connection.

Sky dwelt on all the anger involved with the deaths, the bitterness toward the white race. And Sonia was suddenly never a part of the term. She had become Kanara, the lost injured loved one, and he wanted to avenge her.

Because of this, his anger grew unreasonably, and it was harder than ever before to control himself, to let it go. The bitterness finally turned to forgiveness, and he was able to find the strength to think of a better memory. Control ruled once again.

His features hardened, freezing, steeling to that stoic gaze.

And Sonia watched it all.

"I understand," she proclaimed softly. "Now, I will try."

He slipped into her mind as she had his, watching.

She let him see the images of her dying lover, all the pain and suffering mirrored on his face, the hurt she felt at seeing it there, watching him slowly leave his shell. He saw the mother's love, and the broken heart. She focused on her loneliness, let depression overwhelm her, then quickly used more pleasant thoughts to calm herself, closing away the deeper hurts.

Sky marvelled. *She has learned so quickly what took me a lifetime.*

They stayed in each other's minds, both comfortable together, neither wishing to sever the connection. Finally, it was Sky who broke away first.

Sonia released his hands with an embarrassed shiver. "I fear we forgot ourselves," she marvelled shyly.

"My lady…" he sighed deeply. "Forgive me."

"You did nothing…inappropriate," Sonia reassured. "I am as much to blame as you."

"I…I must return to my post…"

"Thank you for teaching me, Sky." She whispered timidly.

CHAPTER 23

Sky joined Djura on the roof. It was already dark but the Arabian had the mental barrier up around the building so they could not be seen or heard. The Navajo slipped his feet over the edge and sat down beside his partner.

"She has healed you of your sorrow, friend," observed Djura. "Your anger is gone."

"Yes, the wound does not fester any longer. I was not even aware how much it hampered. Her mental touch is so gentle..."

"Do you wish to stay? It is my shift, but I could relinquish to you..."

"No, I will go...in a bit. I think I need distance from her for a while."

Djura understood. "She gets under your skin. A man can not fail to see her vulnerability..."

They sat watching the traffic below, each man deep in his own thoughts.

"What I can not fathom, "Sky remarked after a time. "Is Joel's behaviour? How can he deliberately deprive her of their emotional connection?"

"Joel is blind and deaf," observed Djura. "He may be educated, but that makes him dense. And what he can not understand, he fears."

"It is still no excuse. His real problem is pride."

"Can anything be done about that?"

"Not at present."

Djura nodded, understanding the unspoken implication: Sonia was not in favour of retribution. "We are not meant to police their lives," he observed, quoting her decree.

Sky agreed sadly. "Yet, I am her physician, "he decided. "I am ultimately responsible for her emotional and mental health. And as I see it, she needs healing for a dagger-like thorn. I will need your help, if it is to be removed."

"I will do anything."

"It is far more devastating than Joel denying Sonia emotional balance..."

"What could be worse than Myron and Joel, her brothers, refusing to be her primary male balance?"

"That balance can also be supplied by sons, but if one is lost, or...missing..."

Djura looked up at Sky with renewed interest. "We are missing one?"

Sky nodded.

"You are the physician; how do we create an alternate balance? We will lose her if we can not..." Djura grew agitated. "This is not good is it? Every primary balance member is dormant or...refusing."

"Females do also balance each other."

"But, again, we have only dormant. How much good can they do? Sky...this is what destroyed the last 'Leader Female'. One man denied the 'Leader' his balance. Then the 'Opposites' killed her children, her mate...it destroyed the race! She was left... alone."

"I am well aware of 'Leader' history," Sky rebuked, annoyed.

"Is there another way to balance her, an alternative?"

"A mate…"

"Where is hers, anyway?"

"Dead."

Djura shook his head. "Will she take another?"

"She knows to court at this time would distract her desperately needed protection ability, and as a race, we are not ready…"

Djura became vehement with sudden concern; he was seeing through the eyes of defence. "This is why Sonia made the ruling; why she expects all to remain celibate. It would throw off her balance!" he stated forcefully.

"If she is off power, we all are weakened. Now definitely, I agree with her reasoning. It was correct! Without her we are defenceless!" Taking a swift breath, he expounded on the obvious, more for his own review than to inform Sky. "Lust always distracts a warrior…male or female. It would knock any celibate single female over the edge…the younger such males also; it would create a domino effect. They would go down one after another."

Djura's worry was poignant. "We need mates, Sky, but with the enemy so close, now is not the time! Conditions must be right; the proper separation possible…'Keepers' would be inadequate to protect us. They were used in peace time…"

That had been Sky's view all along. "One indiscretion, or one dissenter ..." Sky shook his head dejectedly. "Now you see our dilemma...we have two in rebellion!"

"We do not stand a chance...they could render us all powerless, helpless...totally impotent. Why this could turn us all...'Opposite'!"

"Sonia would rather struggle with the imbalance. Her mental will is stronger than ours, so she will sacrifice her emotional, mental...even her physical health so that not even one turns...'Opposite'!'

Djura narrowed his eyes in concentration. "Together we must see she stays in balance. I am the brawn, her physical protector; you are the physician, her emotional and mental monitor. Let us pledge to shield with possessive intensity!"

The two men clasped hands fiercely in agreement. "Indeed!" Sky rejoined.

"No one will hurt her on my watch!" Djura vowed.

Sky grinned at the fervour of the Arabian, then brought him back to reality. "Unless...she wills otherwise."

Djura laughed self-consciously. "Aw yes." He sobered. "But we still have the problem at hand. Sonia needs to be paired...at some point."

Sky disagreed. "With some still dormant, "he reminded. "We are unable to give her real freedom. We can not unify enough to shield and cover the group while the 'Leader Pair' go separate...not that there actually is someone she could chose..."

Djura raised an eyebrow questioningly. "Do you not realize...no, you have block that!" He laughed, enjoying the realization Sky Hawk was less than perfect.

"What?" questioned Sky, somewhat perturbed by what he was sensing.

"You...and she...the perfect 'Leader Pair'. She has the power; you are 'Healer Ultimate'!"

"Don't be foolish!" Sky retorted vehemently. "I...she would never put her needs first, never chose someone just because they would pair well. Both of us have more respect for each other than that. We both expect...a connection. There needs to be a love connection...and a choice."

"And you would not make it?"

"I would not be so...bold!"

"Then what solution do you purpose?"

Indignant, Sky returned to his original request. "You need to find our missing member!"

"Oh."

Djura thought on that, while Sky closed his mind in hurt pride. Finally, the Arabian broke the uncomfortable silence.

"Forgive me if I have offended you. I have over stepped my bounds..."

Sky returned the mind-link between them. "We are at peace; you meant me no harm. So...will you seek the lost one?"

Djura nodded. "Can Sonia not see him?"

"All she is able to determine is that he still lives. Most likely he is in a facility we are unable to penetrate, a place that confuses our thought readings, such as...among a very large, violent and perverse community."

Djura frowned. "Such a place would be very pain filled for any of us to enter. For her especially, it would be overwhelming. No wonder she can not find him."

"I thought considering your background, you would tolerate such a place easier."

"Perhaps," mused Djura. "I would not need to mind watch? It would be less unpleasant finding what I seek by other means. I still possess skills I learned when human-like; I have knowledge of methods, ways to trace him in human society. Coupled with the powers I have inherited...I can go where I could not before, view files without being seen."

"Work in your free time, and...it would be best if the other men know nothing of this until later..."

"Keep it secret? What of Sonia?"

"It should not be a problem. She has closed her mind to the possibility, no longer even seeks him...she has given up."

"Why?" questioned Djura, in astonishment.

"She believes he wants it that way, wants no further connection to her.

"Is that factual?"

Sky shrugged. "That is an unknown."

Djura frowned again. "What do we have here, another Joel? How will this help her, if that is true?"

"We can only try, and hope for the best."

"I will find him, but…if he will have nothing to do with her…we will be back where we began."

"We will cover that problem when it is handed to us."

The men went quiet in companionable silence, each buried in thoughts of their own, reflecting on the way of the future.

A little later, Djura motioned over his shoulder. "She is asleep…"

"Good!" Sky affirmed with relief. "I will leave you then."

With those words, Sky Hawk abruptly vanished.

CHAPTER 24

Chi had come to Sonia's apartment to report on the progress at the Sanctuary. He sat on the sofa clearly uncomfortable being seated in her presence, and she found his lack of ease disconcerting. Clearly his culture would always separate him.

"Please Chi, will you relax. I am not some great revered ancestor...only Sonia. You are making me nervous."

He was appalled at such a prospect. "Honourable Lady, I deeply regret it if this is so...I will try harder."

"Start with dropping the honourable. You may call me Sonia."

"Please...such familiarity is foreign to me. At least...may I use...My Lady, as do the others?"

Sonia sighed. "Very well." She frowned. "But if you do not at least smile, I... I will not listen to you."

A small smile hesitantly appeared.

"Better," Sonia approved, and the cultural barrier was no longer in their way. "Now, the men's quarters are finished?"

"Yes, honourable...ah, My Lady. Also, the garden, fruit trees and irrigation are set up."

"Tell me what was done."

"The fields were of shale, so we improvised. A thick layer of topsoil was placed over the rock bed, six feet deep. The fruit trees border each mile-long field, and by acceleration, are already in bloom."

"How wide is each section?"

"Half a mile...with irrigation hose beneath trees and down each garden row."

"Do you already have some produce?"

"Indeed. We have both vegetable and small fruits...and we have adequate ranging game fenced in, which is at our disposal when needed."

"Excellent! And this is enough to feed how many?"

"We are sufficient to support the entire population. Kitchen is operational on premises, and we have just begun on other quarters for females. Soon all will be able to move in."

"I will not move until all dormant are transformed. And conditions are not quite safe for us to do that just yet. However...as each of the male members is released, they will join the men. How many guardians have already moved to the Sanctuary?"

"All, except Joel and Eric, of course...and Myron."

Sonia sighed. "I doubt Myron will join you...but, is it possible to transfer the Technical Centre?"

"That room is also ready."

"Then move Eric and Joel, as well. Tell my brother it is required for safety.

"And are the quarters quite pleasant?" Sonia enquired.

"Marcel has done quite excellently," Chi declared proudly. "He has changed the colour of the marble from room to room. The working is...breath taking."

Sonia smiled at his attempt to describe in words a female would use.

"I see it in your mind it is beautiful! I look forward to the time when I might join you...but, that will not be without my daughters," Sonia reiterated. "When all are set free, we will join the men."

"Hon...My Lady, may I ask...how soon?"

"When there are no longer any dormant," Sonia repeated, not elaborating.

A frown wrinkled his brow. "But, My Lady...would it not be safer for you at Sanctuary?"

"I will not come now, Chi. No argument, please. Trust me...I wish to be close to my family."

Chi nodded, but was clearly in disagreement.

"I will require both my guardians together today. There is something important that needs my immediate attention! Will you see that they are informed and come as soon as possible? And...does Eric guard my son in person today?"

"Yes, My Lady." The Oriental hesitated. "Eric seems unusually closed of late..."

"I am aware of the reason for this. You also will understand soon. Please send Djura and Sky as soon as you return."

Chi Cho took this as his dismissal. "Yes, My Lady."

****

Sky Hawk and Djura appeared within minutes after Chi had departed.

"Good," Sonia declared. "Come."

They stood either side of her; she reached out her hands to grasp one of each of theirs. She was acting as guide for the jump, and neither man felt a need to question where they were headed.

Releasing their hands as soon as they had materialized, Sonia was all business, the in-control 'Leader Female'.

Both men immediately sensed the gravity of the situation. Neither guardian had been prepared for this turn of events.

"Sky will you wait in the kitchen? When I call, you come in human form. I do not wish to unduly stress him."

The Navajo obeyed without dispute.

"Djura take up post on the high rise across the street."

The Arabian vanished.

"Eric, remain close. When we need you, it will be to guard Sky in the healing. At the first, retain human-like appearance. He needs no alarm as this unfolds. For now, remain unseen."

The toilet in the nearby bathroom flushed.

Sonia changed to old lady appearance and took a seat in a padded rocker across from its identical twin.

****

Zane entered his living room from the bathroom. He felt absolutely drained, his stomach still roiling, his mouth tasting sour.

On unsteady legs, he headed to the rocker chair in the corner to rest. The hum and constant rush of water into the aquarium the only sound in the darkened room.

When did I close the drapes?

Too exhausted to get up and open them, he reached over to the table beside his chair and switched on the lamp. Only then did he notice he was not alone.

He started at sight of his company, would have bolted up, if he had had the energy. But he remained seated.

"Mom! How on earth?" His mind just was not processing. "You came all the way here and never let me know? Or did I forget…or miss a message? Why didn't you at least call me to pick you up at the airport?"

"You have enough on your plate at the moment," Sonia assuaged. "Why didn't you tell me?"

His mind was working too slowly. "About?"

"You have cancer…like your father had."

He sighed. *It doesn't matter how she found out; this will be easier.* He was too weary to argue.

"You have refused chemo?"

Zane nodded. "Mom, I watched Dad suffer. I think Chemo made his last days more miserable."

"I have brought you someone to help…"

"Mom, I'm dying; no one can help. I have only weeks."

"And when were you going to share this?"

"I only just found it out yesterday."

"Do they say what they think caused it?"

"There was a PCB spill in the warehouse; I had my hands in it before I realized what it was. It was when I was still in the military…I guess I'm paying for that now, years later."

"I have someone I think can help…"

He sighed resigned. *If it will make it easier for her…* "Okay?"

"Sky Hawk?"

From the kitchen came an old native; the man was even older than his mother.

When did she get into native remedies? Does the Aboriginal have a cure the medical world doesn't know of? Did mother and this guy travelled here together just to give me an untested herbal concoction? Why? It is already too late.

"Don't give up Zane…please?"

The other man dropped to fragile knees in front of Zane.

"I will be with Djura," Sonia silently informed.

Sky nodded.

Zane never saw his mother leave.

****

Djura was sobered. *How did we miss this? Eric obviously was privy, but Sonia must have given him orders to retain secrecy.*

We nearly lost her second son!

Sonia appeared on the rooftop at his side.

Djura felt uncomfortable, ashamed. He had failed her.

She slipped her legs, like a teen, over the edge of the flat roof, and sat down beside him.

When she laughed at his thought comparison, Djura realized his mind was wide open to her. He shut away the deep regions from her reach.

"I once followed my father up a ladder to where he was raising the roof of our home," Sonia revealed to put him at ease. "Scared my mother near out of her wits; I was two in earth years at the time."

Djura laughed as he envisioned it. That would have made her, by their counting, only a year old.

"You are uncomfortable with my sitting here like this," Sonia observed.

He had to admit it, and he attempted to excuse his behaviour. "Women of my culture rarely approach an unrelated male in this fashion." He thought for a moment, deciding whether or not to accept her implied offer of trust. "All my life I have watched as our women were forced to hide behind veils, subjugated, and used only for male pleasure. For me it was normal; we were taught a woman is man's property. When I took on western ways, I still considered the females of that culture brazen...to my reasoning, they teased men, and I did not like them."

Djura frowned, debating whether to go on. "But you are not like that. Your mind is not...flirting.

221

Your familiarity is fuelled by genuine concern for us. In your eyes we are all equal. There is no difference between the mind of a male or a female. It puzzles me. I find myself confused."

Sonia slowly smiled. "Yet you pledged to serve me? Why?"

"My lady...I am so tired of controlling the opposite sex. A female is precious! I never thought it possible to be part of a society without women. Suddenly the old ways seem...stupid."

"You have decided to be gentle, Djura," Sonia noted. "In one such as you, that is rare. Will you share with me how it came about?"

He gazed off into the distance, the hurt coming full force. "I once had a lover...but she joined the rebellion against our ways. When she was accused of being a spy, it was my duty to interrogate her. They made it a test of my loyalty to our leader..."

"And they expected you to torture her?"

"Yes...she later died...of the wounds I had inflicted."

"Did she forgive you?"

"That was the hardest part. With her dying breath, she declared I was not to blame..."

"But it is still hard to forgive yourself, isn't it?"

"It took a long time..."

"What matters is that you have."

Exonerated of his burden, Djura went on from there, to talk of more pleasant memories, Sonia giving an avid attentive ear.

****

Suddenly in mid-sentence, Sonia lost focus, totally stopping short in the middle of a word. Djura realized she was concentrating on the healing. It was becoming too difficult, and she needed to give stronger support.

Unaware she did it, Sonia reached out and took Djura's hand. He flinched, not at the unfamiliar and unsought touch, but at the unexpected result. Abruptly he was seeing through eyes not his own, plunged into the mind of this revered mother. There was such pure anguish and suffering present there, that for a second, he understood Sky's previous concerns. But she closed the past hurt away quickly, to concentrate on the desperate present and the agony of the participants. Tears of empathy rolled down Sonia's cheeks, and for the first time in his life the Arabian shared tears with a female.

Never again will I begrudge a woman the luxury of emotion. There is comfort in this!

Sky had lost focus as well; Djura understood without being the one to observe. He was in her mind only as a rider; his purpose was to replace the insufficient strength.

Sky should not be out of focus, Djura realized. *He failed to do something, and is paying enormously. And the male healer is connected to Sonia. Sensing he has by accident drained on her too much, and fearing for her welfare, Sky stopped the process. Is this man and woman already so coupled as to feel the slightest variation in the other? If that is the case, they are near pair status!*

Sky had felt her desperate need of strength, even though she was trying to hide the fact from him. Djura knew he held the balance.

The Arabian grit his teeth, summoning a furious burst of energy. Sky snapped back to the job at hand when he realized Sonia's needs were being met. The balance restored, the healing proceeded.

Djura gave her his physical strength to the point of exhaustion, which made it possible for her to supply Sky Hawk with hers. The healing completed, Sonia dropped the guardian's hand.

Both she and Djura gasp at the abrupt disconnection.

And Djura thought: *If Joel was meant to act as support as I just did, why can the man not do this?*

Djura's blood began to boil with wrath toward the 'Pure' brother.

Sonia touched his shoulder gently. "You are unbalanced. Control the anger guardian...fond thoughts of someone you once loved."

He did it without argument, knowing her evaluation would always be the correct one. Emotional equilibrium returned in enough degree to continue functioning, but physical weakness near overwhelmed him.

He marvelled as he sat waiting. *As a people, we are this connected. Never do I want to go back to my old world...even if this one might cost my life.*

"You will need to rest after we have finished here," Sonia observed.

And he felt too weak even to protest.

"Come, it is time to join them."

****

Sonia's eyes lighted first on her son as she and Djura materialized in the room. He was a healthy younger man again, his hair no longer greying but blond. Zane needed filling out, by her opinion.

"Mom!" Sonia and Zane both covered the distance between them swiftly. She returned his intense hug with the same vigour as he.

"And you talk about me keeping secrets!" Zane declared as he stepped back.

Sonia smiled shyly at his intent scrutiny.

Zane laughed. "You are beautiful, mom. You were always a good looker as far as I was concerned, but now...wow!"

"You are not so bad yourself; your eyes are blue with black. I always knew you would be a 'Leader Warrior'!"

Zane grinned. "I suppose I'm to work in defence?"

Sonia turned to Djura, but still spoke to her son. "Your commission will be 'Warrior Leader' but for now you will train under Djura...he has seniority until he says you are ready."

"It will be my honour to teach him, my lady," agreed Djura with pride. "Am I to train him to be your primary balance as well?"

"To remind you, primary male balance for a 'Leader Female' must be over thirty, by our reckoning," she added. "Rarely is it safe to use a son when in the defence of the species. 'Mother

Love' subconsciously rejects it; she would rather die than to see her young in jeopardy."

She saw in their minds, both Sky and Djura were not thinking defence, but were each viewing her as if they were her mate, worried about her personal emotional, physical and mental balance, hoping that this new member would be the equivalent of her brothers.

"Djura!" Scolding, Sonia turned also to the Navajo. "And Sky! I want you both to understand something. There is only one male who is truly capable to balance me."

Neither man could hide his interest; the hope was in their eyes.

"Only my mated pair can completely balance my nature, and only my mated pair would sacrifice his life so that I could save the species. Not that I would ever let him do so, should I have a choice. I sincerely hope that will never be the scenario. At present, I have not found that suitable match. To compensate, I use two males to fill that need, one is for extra energy, the other to keep my emotional balanced. And those two body guards, at the moment, are so physically drained, they are not thinking clearly, which creates a problem for us all..."

Eric laughed, amused by the situation; both her guardians dropped their eyes uncomfortable at her public chastisement, and Zane fought not to grin.

"Appears I have caused a little trouble in the ranks," Zane observed with a straight face.

"Time to go home, gentlemen," Sonia declared emphatically. "Eric you are strongest at the moment. You will guard; take Zane and Djura back to the sanctuary to rest. Sky will accompany me to my apartment...Eric bring Chi to me to be my substitute guardian, then you will take Sky to sanctuary also. You will rest Sky!"

"Better obey my mommy," Zane joked. "She's not one you want to cross. I should know."

The older guardians chuckled, then took their places. Zane had just become a favourite in their eyes.

CHAPTER 25

She was not out on a pleasure trip, though Sonia was at the mall in the city centre.

Jade and Nadia's two appointed guardians were Ryan and Chad. The Ethiopian boy-twin guardian was watching over Nadia at her class at University, and normally, Ryan would be with her mother Jade, but an emergency had developed at the Sanctuary quarters, so Sonia had stepped in to personally protect Jade, while the head of utilities went off to stem a flood.

Ryan hoped to return quickly.

Jade had been at a doctor's appointment, and had decided to pick up her own prescriptions while down in the mall.

Since her change Sonia was loath to remain invisible, so she had chosen to appear in disguise out in public. As far as she was concerned her senior image was getting a bit tedious as well. Besides requiring the cane and glasses, it hampered her movements. Also, this time Jade might recognize her, and if the daughter noticed her mother following her, it might prove difficult to explain. So, Sonia had taken on the likeness of a younger human woman: blond, slim, with a build and walk that caught the attention of those around her.

She had not done that on purpose, only taken on a form much like her true likeness.

Sonia knew Djura would disapprove, considering her cover flirtatious, but Sky was guardian today, so she felt safe appearing this young.

What choice do I have? And can I help it if my normal gait comes through in the process?

Anyway, in this guise, she could easily follow her daughter, cruising the aisles of the store just behind her, faking interest in something on the shelf if Jade looked her way. Sonia pretended ignorance of the thoughts of the humans about her, even acted unaware of the appreciative glances.

She had to admit, it was enjoyable to be admired, and Sonia knew if any man had lust in his mind, Sky would quickly confuse his thoughts and drive the human away. It was part of her guardian's fierce protection instinct. He took his posting very seriously.

Even now a young attractive human male was watching her.

But, though invisible at the moment, her protector's mind showed Sky was amused by the circumstances she found herself in, and exceedingly pleased, by her choice of appearance. It seemed the Navajo found her appealing in whatever form she took.

Were I ever to choose to flirt, it would be with Sky!

Half an aisle away Jade reached above her head for an article on a shelf.

What bothered Sonia most was that no one seemed to see her daughter there. Everyone noticed attractive, young Sonia, but no one acknowledged the cripple on the scooter.

Being still dormant, Jade appeared as a greying, fifty-four-year-old woman. Her legs had lost muscle, the body somewhat twisted to the left, caused by her position when the car had impacted in the accident.

Had someone actually looked into her eyes, they would have seen sadness; Jade still mourned Isaiah her dead spouse, even after all these years. And her constant pain lined her features. When Sonia gazed upon her suffering child, the knowledge of her past, brought tears to her eyes.

Sonia suddenly realized her daughter had forgotten her Reacher. However, not one person in the aisle with Jade came to her rescue.

The man between Sonia and Jade only had eyes for the good looking blond. He had decided to attempt to approach, hoping to score.

Sky intercepted, sending a text to his phone, causing the ring to distract the man from his purpose. Sonia went into action, willing the carton Jade reached for to slip from the shelf, and into her daughter's lap.

With her package firmly in hand, Jade headed the scooter toward the check-out counter. As Sonia watched annoyed, not a single shopper moved aside. Jade was forced to stop, wait, and then move on again. Sometimes she even had to find an alternate route.

At one point, a collection of trolleys blocked her way, merchandize piled high with stock, still to be put on the shelves. A child deliberately stepped into the path of the scooter, but the accompanying mother did not reprimand him. Jade turned about and retraced her way.

At last in the check-out line, Jade checked her watch. From her mind, Sonia read her daughter's thought: *I'll never make it on time.*

The lady at the till was as unhurried as the aisle customers. The line crawled forward slowly.

Fifteen minutes later, Jade arrived at the front entrance to the mall…moments too late.

The abilities bus was already out in traffic. Jade had not been waiting at her scheduled appointment pick up on time, so the driver rather than wait had hurried on to the next client.

Is it all about money; is care not a factor at all?

Sonia shook her head.

How often does this happen? Jade will be forced to use public transit now. And that is a chore even with a helper.

And Nadia is still in class…

Sonia needed to come to Jade's rescue, and she knew only one way to do it. Stepping back to the aisles of merchandise, Sonia produced a cell phone; a text message appeared on the screen, and was sent.

Will my daughter wonder why her mother would call while out shopping?

As Jade opened her phone to the text, Sonia watched. The message she had sent was: Hi Jade. What u doing?

Sonia knew her daughter found it too hard to text back; she would return the call instead.

The cell in her hand began to play; Sonia answered it.

"So, what did I catch you at?" She knew it was vital to keep up the charade.

"Believe it or not, I went for an appointment, stopped at the mall to get something, and just now, missed my ride back."

"You're not in mid-town, are you?"

"I am. Why?"

"By the front entrance?"

"Ahuh."

Sonia swept the aisles around her with her eyes as she talked. Only Sky was watching, and he was invisible. The attractive blond transformed into old lady senior, complete with glasses and cane.

"Why…" Sonia exclaimed into the phone. "I'm real close." She moved back into her daughter's range of sight. "Oh, I see you."

"Mom!" Jade's voice was filled with relief, as she closed her cell. "If you aren't a guardian angel today. What are you doing here?"

Sonia shrugged. "Even I need to get out once in a while." She let the comment settle, then suggested. "Say, why don't I help you get home by regular transit? Then we could have a visit."

"Oh, I'd love that, mom. I hate it when this happens. It's so hard…I really appreciate this."

The slow ride to Jade's house was tedious and agonizing. Now that she was in closer proximity, Sonia felt acutely the agony her daughter lived with daily. Her pain was a prickling hot numbness, a rat gnawing at her feet, as if each nerve was being pulled out slowly, wrenched inch by inch, until the rodent had satisfied its requisite for chewing... except it never was sated.

This is going to stop today! Sonia resolved.

To ignore such suffering when it was within her power to end it was irresponsible on her part, even if it did put the species at risk.

Without females there would be no race!

****

When Sonia had Jade settled safely at home on her couch, she took a seat beside her to talk.

"Honey, I have something I need to tell you...I find it hard to watch you suffer... when I know I can help you."

"You just did, mom...immensely."

"I don't mean a temporary fix, like helping you home. I could take away your pain..."

"Aw, mom... I know you mean well. The doctors have done all they can, and... I really don't want you to come live with me to make things easier. You're getting too old ..."

Sonia smiled at her daughter's ability to jump to the wrong conclusion. It was one of her failings.

Am I really that old in Jade's eyes?

"We manage just fine...and you are better off with those of your own age. I'll be okay."

"Will you please hear me out?" Sonia pleaded quietly. "Without interrupting... until I am finished."

"Okay. Yes, I will listen," her daughter agreed reluctantly. "But I'll probably disagree when you're finished."

Sonia grinned. "I rather doubt that." She turned to her right, seemingly speaking to thin air. "Ryan? You have returned?"

"Yes, my lady," Ryan admitted, in silent answer.

Jade's thought was: *Mom's finally flipped out. Now she's talking to herself.*

Sonia had difficulty keeping a straight face. "All is corrected?"

"Yes, my lady," Ryan returned, still by mental communication.

"Speak audibly."

Jade looked about the room, the thought going through her mind: *Maybe there is someone else in this room?*

"My lady?" questioned Ryan aloud.

Jade started visibly at the sound of another voice. "Mom? What's going on?"

"Where were you born, Ryan?" Sonia probed.

Ryan was beginning to catch on. Sonia was preparing Jade. "In Milan, Italy, my lady."

Sonia turned to Jade. "You see no one, right?"

Her eyes wide, her daughter nodded mutely.

"Come visible, Ryan," ordered Sonia. "Former human-like appearance, please. It will frighten her less."

A tall, slight man of about sixty came into view, drawing a gasp from Jade. His skin was olive brown, the shade of a light tan, hair straight, short and dark with silver at the temples; his eyes were mocha brown.

"You were rather handsome, Ryan," Sonia observed appreciatively.

A smile played at his lips; he liked the way the lady had introduced him.

"How did he get in here?" Jade asked astounded. "What is going on here, mom?"

For the next half hour, while Ryan stood quietly at ease nearby, Sonia gave Jade a limited version of what had transpired since the 'Alien broadcast'.

While they were thus engaged, Chi had sent Djura to guard the perimeter, anticipating what was about to take place. Sky also remained near at hand, unseen.

Sonia finally turned to Ryan.

"Since we appointed guardians to each of you, Ryan has been guarding you..."

"From these 'Opposite' creatures?"

"Yes, and any human stupid enough to try to harm you."

Ryan grinned at that. The lady knew him well, even though at that moment, she pretended ignorance of even his origins.

Suddenly, what Sonia had said actually registered, and Jade went crimson. "He's been watching me? Everything I do..."

Through her mind flashed the countless times in her frustration and pain she had lashed out; then there were the nightly tears. Lastly, Jade reviewed the idea of the utter exposure to this man.

All three: Sky, Ryan and Sonia watched the process of her mind, but it was Ryan who felt the need to react.

"Oh no!" he cried. "My lady, may I speak?"

Sonia nodded, trying to hide her amusement at his response.

"I give you ultimate privacy. I only stay near in case...should you need... assistance, when alone. I turn away always, only sense if you need help. Never! Never! would I be so crass." Ryan was as near to tears, as a male could be without giving way, and in his anguish his words were coming out all in a flood.

Sky's amusement was beginning to show in his thoughts as well.

"Most times," Ryan admitted, as he hurried on. "Our shield over you and Nadia is from a distance. But sometimes...I like to watch you sleep. You are at easy then, not in pain...I am sorry."

Sky's mind related in empathy, as similar thoughts of his charge crossed his memory, and Sonia knew it was time for her to step in and end this.

"I have longed to ease your torture," Ryan rambled on. "I would never want to cause pain to you..."

His obvious affection for Jade pleased Sonia, and she would have broken in if given the chance, but Ryan was so intent upon placating her daughter, he had forgotten he had an audience.

"After you change, I will always be here for you…if you wish to call on me… when I have duty, that is…"

His words finally faded; discomfort hung in the air. Sonia turned to her invisible guardian.

"Sky…come visible, will you? Your former appearance as well."

Jade grew uncomfortable again, and the thought that passed through her mind: *There are more of them?* made Sky appreciate Sonia's caution.

A stately Navajo elder appeared beside Sonia. His tall frame was muscular and trim, his white-grey hair in two braids one on either side of the chiselled features, the eyes a sky blue.

"This is my guardian, Sky Hawk. He was named for the colour of his eyes."

His compassion was evident in his eyes, as Sky turned his attention to Jade. He nodded curtly in recognition.

Ryan had been calmed by this interlude and now stood, his posture more in keeping with his post. Both he and Sky awaited their next instructions. Jade still displayed discomfort, so the men pretended unconcern.

****

As reality hit, sudden fear flooded Sonia, and Sky immediately sensed it.

"What is it, my lady?"

"Go non-verbal," Sonia suggested, then followed suit. "When I go down to do this, I will be unable to maintain the blanket protection over the entire group."

"Then allow me to do the healing. I did it for Zane."

"A single male must not break a female. It creates a love-bond. A father could safely do it, but…"

Sky nodded, understanding that the only other alternative was Ryan, and she would not make that choice for him. "It would be unwise to create a love-connection at this time," he agreed.

"This is why I haven't broken the females. We have not the male/female numbers balance needed for such healing. I hope the men will each be strong enough to maintain separate shields over their charges…or we will all be exposed and vulnerable to the enemy."

Yet Sonia knew she could put this off no longer. "Djura, come to the room, but remain unseen. Chi, take his place. Is Shawn with his mother?"

Chi acknowledgement came back positive.

Sonia felt her second guardian immediately beside her, as these two obeyed.

She returned to communication with Sky. "When I need strength for the healing, Djura must supply it. He does not need to touch me; also, he may go down, if I drain too much. Watch him carefully, but do not worry, he will come around as I heal back."

Invisible at her side, Djura understood exactly what she implied, remembering the last healing.

"Sky you will be 'Ultimate Healer', concentrate on me alone. For now, you will merely monitor as I heal. Do not worry if I do not come back quickly; give me time. Do not touch me unless absolutely necessary.

"Do we have double guardians where all possible?"

Sky shook his head. "Chi informs the others are spread too far apart, but at least one is present with each dormant, plus a 'Keeper'."

"This must be done; if not now, then at another time. It would be the same should we wait. Preferably, night when everyone is resting would be better, but that time frame puts us at greater risk. Our enemy can see us clearly in the dark. Okay…Ryan, you are Jade's guardian protector; if an enemy shows, defend at all cost…to the death!"

Ryan nodded gravely.

To Jade, it had appeared her mother was silently thinking. Had she realized the risk all were taking on her behalf, perhaps she would have objected strongly.

Sonia sank to her knees in front of her daughter, and took both her hands in her own.

Ski, Djura and Ryan moved back, and turned away, their backs to the two women to give the needed privacy to Jade.

Mid-point Djura dropped to one knee panting, but he did not fall, nor become visible.

Sky knew the man was still functional and would defend with his last breath should it be required.

****

An hour later both women were recovered and well.

"You may turn, gentlemen," Sonia said. "And remain visible, in true form."

As the three transformed, Jade's face was priceless.

Whew…big, she thought, and all males grinned as one.

"I might warn you, honey," Sonia cautioned. "They hear what you think if you don't close off." She patted her daughter's knee. "You will pick it up quickly. Gentlemen, give her some leeway while she's learning."

"We understand." Sky spoke for the others. "It is hard for females among so many of us. We will try to be…as unobtrusive as possible."

"Okay." Sonia took command once more. "It seems our men were strong enough. The shields held, and…I am able again to control protection."

"Your orders then, my lady," probed Sky, not willing to make the mistake he had at Zane's change.

"I will remain for a while with my daughter and Ryan. Take Djura to Sanctuary, then return for me. Chi is relieved as well."

Sky stepped to Djura. The Arabian appeared wiped, yet had continued to create the illusion of ready strength to this point. He reached out a trembling hand to Sky, and both men vanished.

Sonia turned to Ryan. "Will you take up position at a distance?" He was gone immediately.

"Wow!" Jade exclaimed. "They obey without question."

Sonia wrinkled her nose. "I have to get used to that." She laughed. "Now, what do you say we go jogging at the river tomorrow morning?"

"It's winter!" queried Jade.

"Well, first," Sonia admitted. "Unless we allow them to see, we aren't visible to humans, and…we can generate a hot or cool field around our bodies. It doesn't matter what the temperature is outside; we are always comfortable…even in shorts in the snow."

"I haven't jogged in ten years," Jade proclaimed in awe.

"Well, we also are able to run quite fast. I look forward to a race."

"Sounds like fun. Can our body guards keep up?"

Sonia grinned mischievously. "Don't know; never tried it before."

Jade laughed delighted, then sobered. "Mom, I have a question…"

"I know dear, you will have many questions. And they will all be answered in due time."

"But this one is important. We heal by transference? You took on my injuries? I saw…you were paralysed for at least half an hour, and I couldn't even move to assist you."

"Better you didn't try. To touch me at such a time would have killed us both."

"Could you…feel my pain?"

"What do you think? But…it's not such a bad thing when you love the person you are healing. Even you will someday be willing to do the same…when you see a loved one hurting."

Jade realized Sonia spoke of Nadia.

Sky appeared.

"Well, my escort is back," Sonia observed. "I hate to leave…"

"My lady," Sky dared to challenge. "You need to rest."

"True," she agreed. "So, we'll see you in the morning after Nadia leaves for school. Do you intend to continue living here?"

"Yes. Until it's safe to do Nadia, I'll hide in disguise as you do."

Sonia stood, took Sky's hand, and they vanished together.

****

"Ryan? Are you still there?" Jade ventured softly.

"Always. Fear not, new one." After a pause in which Jade felt his affection flood over her, he continued. "I will give you privacy, but you only need to call out silently, and I will be at your side instantly."

Reassured, Jade changed form: the green eyes turned blue; the black vertical slit became a small round pupil. And the tall, shapely blond was a handicapped older woman once again.

The outer door opened and Nadia stepped in, plunked her book bag on the table in the entry, and entered the living room.

"I thought I heard you talking to someone," Nadia claimed, gazing about the room. "You taken to talking to yourself now, mom?"

Jade just smiled. *Think how much I will have to tell my daughter when it is time.* She could hardly contain the secret.

CHAPTER 26

Sonia was dreaming: She was on a battlefield at night, was the mother fleeing with a small child. There was a flash of light...and their lives ended, forever.

She awoke with a sharp cry; Djura came alert.

Sonia sighed. *It is just a residual memory...from the recorded mind of an ancestor.*

Ever since Jade's healing, she had been having nightmares...as if she was being warned. She sensed a tragic event in the near future, something she could not completely focus on...just beyond her second sight. It filled her with foreboding.

Above, Sky joined Djura on the roof. It was shift change.

****

"She does not rest well since she healed Jade," Djura observed to Sky. "It worries me."

"I know."

"Be especially vigilant; high alert. I think she sees something by future-sense..."

Sky nodded.

Sonia drifted back to slumber.

****

When he left Sky, Djura did not go to rest; as he often did, he took up the search for the missing one.

****

The man was quietly weeping when Djura came upon him. Locked in a dark cell, with no access to sunlight, the fifty-five-year-old had given in to despair. He was emaciated, filthy, humiliated, and... had recently been violated.

Bullying inmates had cornered him in the meal room. After, when the guards searched him, they found the planted plastic shiv in his pocket. It was against the rules to have anything resembling a weapon in your possession.

They increased his sentence...once again. And put him back in solitary. His constant circumstances had turned the man numb with resignation.

Djura saw immediately this prisoner resembled Sonia in personality, except... he had given up faith that his life could get better. He would die in here if the Arabian left him so.

Djura found no hate against his mother in this son's mind. The guardian saw he posed no threat to Sonia, or to the species for that matter. His spirit was already too defeated.

The Arabian waited until exhaustion took its toll. When sleep had overcome the man, Djura approached, dropped to his knees and took the battered hands in his own. Risking exposure of himself, the Arab proceeded to heal, breaking the dormancy of Sonia's eldest son.

How can I do otherwise? Sonia has given me new life. I owe her!

****

Djura sat on the filthy floor, his back against the cold concrete wall, recovering. It was minutes before he realized they were no longer alone. Zane stood at the bars of the cell, his back to the older guardian, standing watch.

Djura used thought transfer to communicate, so as not to wake the young man on the cot.

"How did you come to be here?" he demanded displeased. "We did not wish Sonia to be burdened with this yet."

Zane turned. "My mother is completely unaware," he answered. "Her sense of us is weakened. Right now, she still struggles to recover from healing Jade."

Djura understood; he had seen Sonia's weakness first hand, just not realized others sensed how the curing had depleted her. He had assumed only her guardian pair would be aware it was so.

"Who else knows?"

"Only I. My brother is family; I felt him through you."

"You took a great risk not giving someone your where abouts...coming here alone."

"And you did not...healing unaided? You needed protection. Master, your pride could have gotten you killed..."

Djura shook his head annoyed. He knew the younger man right to reprimand him.

"I am not your master," he stated meekly. "Teacher, maybe. You are son of Sonia..."

"Teacher, then...we will say no more of this," Zane decided. "I have come as your support. Accept it."

Djura did just that, and was thankful.

Zane stood watching his brother as Lance slept the sleep of one exhausted with life.

"My brother will be a special leader after of this," he observed. "This teaches compassion..."

"What a gruesome way to train a man." Djura got to his feet. "He will not soon trust a human...if he ever does."

"Indeed," Zane agreed. "He will need our help with emotional balance for a long time to come."

"Come let us take him from this hell hole before he wakes. They can wonder how he escaped, for all I care. They will never know what became of him; I will see they never find where he went!"

Each man slipped an arm under the shoulder of the inert man, and lifted.

"He will experience freedom unbelievable," Zane predicted.

The two men jumped with their burden to Sanctuary.

****

It was the middle of the day, but Sonia sat dozing in her chair before the window. Sensing someone near, she started awake.

An unfamiliar guardian stood before her. He was approximately seven feet, in his late thirties, very thin, blond with blue eyes and the black vertical slit of the race. When she saw into his mind, the shock made her go cold.

This beaten spirit...is my long-lost son!

When she realized who it was, Sonia burst into tears.

"Lance!"

With arms open in welcome, she shot from her chair and they met mid-way, running into each other's arms. As Sonia folded her son in a fierce hug, the world disappeared. He held her so tightly, and she returned with equal force, an embrace that had waited far too long. Each was in tears, and both wished they could stay enfolded forever.

"I'm so sorry, mom. I never meant the last words I said to you; I was lashing out ...and you were the only one there to take my blows..." His voice faded in brokenness.

Quietly, Sky who had brought the boy began to back from the room to give them privacy. This gift had been satisfactory, and he was content with that.

But Sonia noticed him.

"Sky, wait."

"Yes, my lady?" He turned about.

"Please...go to Sanctuary, both you and Djura. Lance will guard me for now."

"Yes, my lady."

****

Sky Hawk and Chi sat resting together. The Asian had waited patiently, as Sky remained, his thoughts hidden and far away. At last, the Oriental voiced the question plaguing him.

"Will you tell...what is the story of young Lance? The lady does not let us all see from her mind. You are closer. Has she confided in you?"

Sky nodded abruptly, and reluctantly agreed to disclose.

"I saw a short time ago by accident the thorn she was living with. I never dream it was this bad…"

Chi waited patiently, as Sky escaped again in his mind, hiding the full horror.

With a sigh, Sky finally came rallied, and began his tale. "Lance was rather wild and rebellious in his youth…one of his common-law partners had with a girl child in her teens. Attempting to discipline her one day, he lost his temper and smashed the computer he had given her. He had been drinking, and when she verbally defied him, he struck her. Her mother called the police, and Lance was taken to jail, charged with assault."

Chi made no comment, so Sky continued.

"His young lawyer was inexperienced with the court system; he advised Lance to plead guilty, told him it would go easier on him if he did, as it was a first offence."

Chi nodded, seeing the logic of such an action.

"But while Lance was in jail, the women saw an opportunity. Their greed got the better of them. They could walk away with his property if he remained behind bars. The charge turned to one of rape, and as the young female was still a minor… Well, Lance not aware of the new charges, pled guilty as his attorney had suggested."

"He had not touched her?" Sky shook his head. "How long has he been in prison?" wondered Chi astounded.

"Ten years," Sky revealed. "It did not end there. When it came before the judge, he changed the charge to incest. He decided because Lance had been a father figure to the girl, even though unrelated, the charge was warranted. Lance was given eight years in a Federal prison."

Chi's anger flared. "Where was the defence by his public defender?"

"Lance had pled guilty; the courts allows no defence in such a case. But the worst happened when he entered the prison system. There is only one law while in there; the guards have total control."

"What happened?" asked Chi with foreboding.

"A man charged with incest is considered more vile than any murderer, even worse than a serial killer, by the inmates; and the guards would rather throw away the key than protect such a man."

Chi shook his head in disgust. "Criminals! There is no explaining their reasoning. What did they do to him?"

"When the prisoners found out his charge, he was beaten senseless. Upon recovery, he was placed in a cell with a genuine sex offender..."

Sky hesitated. "He was...sodomized...repeatedly."

"This is civilized justice?" exploded Chi.

"He was finally placed in isolation...at times he was allowed back into the general population, only to be recharged due to some trumped up offence and his sentence increased...by the time Djura came upon him, he had given up hope."

"Does Sonia realize all this?"

"With who she is...what do you think?"

"How can she endure this? She must desire revenge, to retaliate against these humans…I do!"

"As she would say, 'it will not change what happened' and 'all humans are not the same'. Her nature is mercy and…forgiveness. So is his."

Chi shook his head. "This I have a hard time with."

"We also…"

"Why did she not know where he was?"

"The prison administration took away his privileges for one of the earlier infractions, never reinstated them. Her letters were returned undelivered; phone calls denied…they deliberately lost him in the system. Then the family was told he had escaped, took his own life in some hotel room while outside…but they were never given a body to bury."

And, the Lady believed this?"

"No. But because their last telephone conversation was one of anger, she thought he had broken the connection."

"This must have torn at her very soul…how did she endure it?"

"Sonia is a strong lady…she has seen all our stories…and seeks only to alleviate our suffering."

"Because she has seen much of her own. Do you ever see her…weaken?"

Sky pondered his friend for some moments before answering.

"If I were to reveal what I witness, would I not be betraying her confidence? Would I be fit as a guardian…let alone her guardian?"

Chi nodded, understanding what he implied.

"You grow too fond of her Sky," he cautioned. "That road is the most difficult you can travel."

Sky sighed. "A new race, a new life…why not a new love?"

Chi shook his head, and grinned.

"Guard her well, my friend," he admonished, with a fond pat to the shoulder of the Navajo. Then he left for his own shift to guard Rhea and Shawn.

****

"Sky! Come."

The guardian was at Sonia's side within seconds. Lance clasp hands with him in farewell, just before he vanished from the room.

Scowling, Sonia rebuked Sky in mock severity. "And what possessed my guardian to allow someone to get this close to me without warning? What if Lance had been an 'Opposite'?"

He saw through her attempted ruse, and grinned.

Sonia melted. "Thank you, Sky," she said softly. "I will never forget this gift… nor this day."

She was happy, balanced, as he had never seen her previously.

He felt a need to kiss her, but…

Wisely went to his roof post instead.

CHAPTER 27

It was after one AM and Ivan was finally heading home in his small battered quarter-ton pick-up. Today would be his and Rhea's thirty-third wedding anniversary, and he actually had remembered it. He was proud of himself.

Before work, he had picked up a dozen red roses, and a big box of chocolates, both of which now sat beside him on the seat. Rhea would be so pleased and surprised. He was anticipating her gratitude, looking forward to his reward.

Those high beams are too dim again, he thought. *I will have to have a look at the headlights after I get some sleep.*

****

In the shadows ahead, the two 'Opposites' watched the road from the bushes.

"Look!" Etah gestured toward the oncoming vehicle with a claw. "Above its roof top...I saw a flash of light. That is either a guardian or a 'Keeper'."

His companion Diputs grunted. "A guardian would be protecting a female. Are you able to see better with the enlarger?"

Etah raised a viewfinder-like instrument to his eyes. "A male drives. No passengers. He appears human."

"A dormant! Good! You stay hidden. I will eliminate this one."

The large buck came out of nowhere, and Ivan had no time to react. He had been speeding, and…he was not wearing a seat belt.

With crunching force truck and animal found each other; the brutal impact resounding in the blackness of the country setting, audible for miles.

Metal screeched; small and large paper-thin pieces tore away from the chassis and went flying, spreading across ditches and the yards of pavement ahead and behind. Roses and chocolates splayed across the seat, some coming to rest outside on the hood. The man behind the steering wheel shot through the shattering windshield to land in an odd posture, face down on the inflexible highway.

And the huge buck limped away to the ditch, where it became a lizard-like creature once again. Though its shoulder gaped with a raw bleeding tear, it stood there laughing at the carnage it had just caused.

A 'Keeper' appeared, firing a beam of blue light, its defensive shot annihilating Diputs. Simultaneously, a red beam from Etah exploded the sphere before it could turn.

Summoned by the 'Keeper' just before its destruction, Asa abandoning Tyler whom he was guarding, materialized off to the side, seconds too late.

He never even realized there was a second 'Opposite'; all Asa saw was the mangled corpse upon the road.

This is Rhea's husband, Myron's charge!

Asa cried out angrily to Myron to come to his aid; his partner should have been here guarding Ivan.

Callously, the older man, thinking the boy's call mere attention getting, ignored him. Mumbling, 'Keeper's' on it', he rolled over and went back to sleep.

A red-hot beam pierced the darkness, and…Asa ceased to exist.

The 'Opposite' laughed.

A good night's work, thought Etah, while transferring back to the ship behind the moon.

****

Sonia let out a yell of anguish, and Sky from the roof turned to look at her. He had felt it too.

A tearing away…

Each instantly knew, they had just lost one of the twins.

****

"Myron!" The angry, panicked last cry of his twin registered even in sleep; Chad was jarred awake, then started screaming, wailing as though his world had just ended.

The males in the sleep quarters immediately reached out to cushion him, surrounding Chad in a blanket of love.

****

"Chi!" It was a mental shout from Sky the Oriental could not ignore.

"I am already on scene, Sky!" Then to the guardian group, Chi gave these thought commands.

"All guardians double together on females. No one sleeps tonight!

"Marcel, Ram. Are Jessica and Kara together?"

"Yes, and Wade is with them also. We are now on pair shift."

"Good. Ryan and Jade, you will need to work as a pair to protect Nadia. Chad cannot function as her protector. Eric, Lance, Zane…see to Chad's needs."

"What of Shawn?" asked Lance.

"He is with his mother."

"Tyler is unguarded," Sky reminded Chi. "He was Asa's charge."

"Eric. I will need you on him instead."

Chi gave one final order, before closing their joint communication.

"Djura! Let no one near the Lady! Sky. You are her emotional balance."

"What of Joel?" asked Sky. "He should balance her…"

"Neither brother even senses what has just happened," Chi returned with disgust. "They are useless! We will tell them when we get to it, after they awaken."

CHAPTER 28

It was three weeks later, and Sonia still felt that instant rupture; relived in her dreams the gruesome accident scene.

Why did I not listen to the warning?

I never expected the enemy to target a human partner!

And I was distracted...too ecstatic over Lance's return.

Never, never again will I let my guard down like that!

****

Asa's memorial was agonizing. There had been no body. Chad had no means to say goodbye to his twin.

Ihor created a sunken garden in the centre of Sanctuary in memory of the boy guardian, and Marcel formed an exact likeness of him in black marble, placing it on a pedestal at the convergence of three paths. On the plaque beneath, written in the language of their ancestors, were these words: 'In loving memory of Asa, twin to Chad. Missed by all. He died a valiant warrior.'

Chad still grieved; they all did. But the thirteen-year-old had turned his empty aloneness into guarding with possessive abandon.

Nadia had always been his charge; now he could scarcely be torn from his post. It seemed he feared she too would be taken from him, or killed, if he were to sleep.

The young man had replaced his twin connection with an almost 'love bond' to the mixed-race daughter of Jade.

They all worried for Chad. Nadia when she broke dormancy would be only eleven, but what if she did not feel a love connection to Chad? What if she refused to be his 'bonded pair' when the two were older? Would they lose the second twin as well, to madness?

****

And Rhea was equally devastated. Sonia had never felt this helpless. To be aware of her daughter's agony, and not be able to remove or cushion it was excruciating. If Rhea had not been dormant, Sonia would have softened the memory, but as it was, the picture of Ivan's battered body was raw and poignant in Rhea's mind. She had been the only one available to identify the remains.

Through the funeral service Rhea had sat rigid, her eyes puffy from crying but the tears depleted, as if the reservoir had gone dry. At the lunch after, she remained functional though mechanical, going through the motions required of her. Ihor her guardian had been nearest her, invisible but feeling her misery tormentingly. It had taken their all to balance him.

Rhea's brothers and sister, appearing human-like were equally affected by the grief of their sister; Jade remembering a past funeral of her own, but having to experience the depth of feeling all the species were enduring at that moment, it made it a new and fresh wound.

And because of all this agony, everyone had closed off feelings, retreating to their separate quarters, to lick their wounds. The devastation tore away at their intimacy.

Fear and pain in her guardians and family was more crippling then if the 'Opposites' had actually planned it so. Sonia had to somehow reunite them all again.

****

Today Sonia sat by the window of her apartment, watching the snow lightly falling on the street below, thinking and planning.

"Chi Cho," she called out mentally. "Will you come here, please?"

Chi had long since gotten over his discomfort in her presence. He appeared now, and stood quietly awaiting her orders.

"Sit, please." Sonia gestured to the chair opposite at the table by the window. "We will have tea."

The cups appeared; a teapot, steaming. Sonia served him. This also, Chi had grown to accept.

It was Sonia's way, showing a gentle unpretentious affection.

As they partook, he waited with Oriental politeness for her to reveal his purpose for being there.

"We are going to do something very dangerous," the Lady revealed presently. "But if we do not do it, we will lose our amalgamation...and the species' unity will cease to exist."

Chi nodded, having realized himself that was happening.

"We all need this...especially Rhea."

"You know, my Lady," Chi ventured. "We would carry out your wishes no matter the cost."

Sonia acknowledged that. "Jessica has suggested we go ice-skating on Christmas Eve…"

Chi raised one eyebrow questioningly.

Sonia laughed. "She is still dormant, unaware we are other than human. Of course, she does not expect her gran to do other than be there, and cheer from the side lines."

"She does not know this grandmother as well as she could."

Sonia chuckled. "I think it is a good idea. Just what everyone needs…fun… to turn the grieving around."

"This is planned for at night?" Sonia nodded. "And, it will be out in the open?" probed Chi.

"Yes. There is a small little-used rink at the edge of the city, near Rhea's house. There are lights strung overhead by wires; six-foot boards around the perimeter. It is a well-lit place."

"It should not be hard to cover with an invisible cloak and a silence shield; we will prevent even humans from approaching."

"Tell the guardians, this is compulsory," Sonia suggested. "Laughter and the joy of it will lift their spirits."

"And maybe, their empathy will be healed in the process.'

"That is my hope. Put the guardians all around the inside of the fence. The natural lighting will disguise their heat signature, even from the ship above."

Chi agreed. "Who of the family will be there?"

"Lance and Zane can remain unseen with the guardians. It will make it less complicated. Jade, in human form on the sidelines...I know that will be hard for her, but better not rock Rhea's world more than it is. Nadia will bring her mother. Tyler is away, policing for that night. Eric has been pretty stable, so put him on Tyler. Jessica, Wade and Kara will probably be there the earliest. And I want Sky with me as escort in human guise."

Chi raised a questioning eyebrow. "You are letting him...come out?"

"Jessica never said Gran could not bring someone. This will make things easier; as well, it will explain my sudden and uncomplicated arrival.

"Also, I will need my personal guardians after," Sonia added. "Perhaps, you can manipulate Shawn...just for this once. Keep him busy, both before and after. We do not need our rogue young man going off on his own, or showing up at an inopportune time."

The word rogue had brought the 'Pure' brothers to Chi's mind. "And will Myron and Joel be joining us?"

"Put Joel in Technical Centre for the night. If trouble is coming, perhaps he will at least warn us."

Chi was doubtful. "And Myron?"

Sonia sighed. "He would normally not be invited. He was no friend to Ivan...or Rhea for that matter."

"I will prepare...in two days then."

****

The evening was cold and crisp. Jessica had coaxed Rhea out onto the rink and they were trio skating with Kara between them when Sonia and Sky came upon the scene. Nadia was skating by herself off by the edge, and Sonia could see Chad, like a shadow, at her side. Fortunately, those who were dormant could not see the guardians any better than other humans would. Shawn sat by himself on a bench, scowling.

When everyone on the ice was turned away, Sonia by telekinesis replaced her boots with ice-skates, and slid on to the smooth surface.

Sky made to follow her. "Maybe, stay here for now," she suggested. "We need to let her notice you first."

He grinned, then swiftly schooled his features to become the stoic Navajo standing on the sidelines.

Sonia snuck up behind her daughter and granddaughter.

Rhea noticed her first. "Mom!" she screamed. "What are you doing on skates?"

Sonia laughed. "What do you think?"

"Momma, if you fall and break a hip you'll never walk again! Do you want that?"

"I won't fall, honey. You come hold me up."

Jessica took off with Kara, both laughing, and Rhea slipped an arm about Sonia.

"What ever possessed you? You're too old to be skating."

"Then why am I here?" Sonia asked innocently. "I thought I was invited?"

"That's a given, mom. But this is not good for you. You might fall. You and Jade can watch."

"Jade is not just watching, why should I? Look at her and Nadia."

In the centre of the rink, Nadia was skating in circles with her mother in her wheelchair. Nadia was laughing, Jade squealing with each sudden turn.

"But that's different. She's safe; Nadia has her."

"I am safer than you realize."

Rhea decided not to argue, changing the subject. "Did you bring a date, mom? Who's the guy with you?"

Sonia smiled amused. "His name is Sky Hawk…he's a doctor."

"Hummm," Rhea mused. "He's good looking…for an older guy. I never thought you'd go for a…"

"Navajo? Anyway, I thought you were in mourning?'

"Doesn't mean, I'm blind…or stupid! Where'd you find him?"

"I'll tell you about it later." Sonia gave Sky the mental command to join them, and he came skating smoothly across the ice toward them. When he had reached them, Sonia introduced them.

"This is Sky. Sky Hawk, this is my daughter Rhea."

"Pleased," Sky returned, with a dignified nod.

Rhea giggled, bent close to her mother's ear and whispered. "Don't let this one get away; you've been alone far too long." Then yelling to her daughter, she skated away after them.

Sky was laughing. "She is a child in a woman's body," he observed.

"Yes. You picked up on that impish mature too, did you? Let's take a turn together."

He slipped his arm about her, and she took his free hand.

"I did not realize you could skate," Sonia stated.

"I was unable before coming, but it is amazing what our joined minds can offer. I received the benefit of a quick lesson."

Sonia smiled. "We should do this again…at another time…when we are safer."

"We could build a pond at Sanctuary," he suggested.

"A marvellous thought! Better still, we should make it a roller rink, or… we could do both."

He grinned.

Across the ice Rhea, Jessica and Nadia were skating rapidly in a crack-the-whip formation with Kara excited, yet squealing fearfully none the less, at the farthest end. The group ran into Shawn skating by himself, and he lost his footing.

Sonia gasped and went rigid for a second, as he hit the ice.

"He is okay," reassured Sky. "Amazing what these young bodies can tolerate."

All along the fence the guardians were grinning, enjoying the entertainment as much as those involved.

"The guardians have opened themselves to unification once more," Sky observed. "You were right; this was what we all needed...to see the reason for our very existence."

"Even Joel co-operates. He blinds the eyes of the enemy."

Sky sighed, suddenly reminded of her brothers.

"How long will you allow these two malcontents to continue as they do?"

"There is good in them, Sky. To force would only turn them further away."

****

"I'm sorry, you guys," Jessica kept saying over and over. "I never meant to leave the cleaning up for you to do, but we really have to get going. Wade has to be at work in an hour, and I still have baking to do for a function tomorrow."

"Go...go!" ordered Rhea. "We'll manage."

When Jessica and family had departed Nadia offered, "I'll do the dishes. You guys visit," and headed off behind the counters stacked with plates and dirty mugs. She closed the door, so they could not follow.

Immediately, Chad took up an invisible post in front of the entry, blanketing the kitchen in a silencing shield so Nadia could not hear what would transpire.

"I'm going to my room to watch TV," Shawn stated sullenly. "Don't want to be part of a ladies gab-fest."

"Okay honey," Rhea acknowledged pleasantly.

As Rhea's youngest shut himself away, Lance and Zane took up duty outside his chamber, creating the same barrier to sound as had Chad, their presence still unseen and unknown to their sister.

Sky, next to the window, turned his back, as if he were examining the darkness outside.

In silent communication, he made known to both Sonia and Jade, "The guardians are back at Sanctuary. They should be able to take over the species shield-cover any time. Djura and Chi have our perimeter covered."

Rhea, though watching Sky, had heard nothing. She nodded toward the Navajo, and whispered, "He acts like he was hired to protect you."

Sonia laughed, and took her daughter's hands. Jade wheeled in closer.

"Ready everyone?" Sonia asked.

"For what?" wondered Rhea, but the words died on her tongue.

****

When Rhea next opened her eyes, the sight of Jade whole and standing made her burst into tears. Her own memories became distant and less raw, as Jade embraced her, and gently let her cry.

When her sister released her, Rhea exclaimed, "I can't believe you can walk again. Momma did that!"

Sonia still sat, eyes closed, her head resting against the sofa back.

"Is mom alright?"

"After a healing," Sky volunteered. "We always need recovery time. But it was easier for her this time...compared to Jade."

Rhea's tears threatened to return. So much sacrifice and pain; So many facts to take in.

"You can heal also." Sonia opened her eyes, but her voice remained weak. "And... you will."

"You have purple eyes!" Rhea marvelled.

Sonia chuckled, and turned to her eldest daughter. "You tell her Jade."

But Zane beat his sister to it. "You've got one purple eye yourself," he teased. "Now that's a weird combination."

"Don't make fun of her. I like your eyes," Jade defended. "She always was special, and it stands to reason. The amethyst eye means the "Leader Female' gene is passed through your line."

"You mean I really do have two different colour eyes?"

"Like Christmas lights," Zane taunted. "One blue, the other purple, goes well with those auburn curls."

"Stop it, Zane," Sonia reprimanded softly, then added to Rhea, "I have someone I want to introduce to you...before Nadia returns and we must return to our old images. Ihor, why are you still invisible? Come..."

The biggest man Rhea had ever seen came visible beside her. A short blond crew cut stood out against the tanned face; his eyes were brown, the vertical slit black. The chest and abdomen were tightly firm; his muscles bulged. And, his legs were thicker around than her head.

But his voice was soft as he answered her mother. "I did not wish to intrude, my lady."

Rhea gasped with shocked apprehension, but then…he grinned mischievously at her.

Why he is gentle! Nothing but a big, protective…jolly giant.

"Thanks," he said amicably.

Rhea blushed, realizing he had heard her thought.

"This is Ihor," Sonia interrupted. "Any questions, he will fill you in. Oh yes, and he is your guardian."

"Nadia comes," Chad cautioned.

The room immediately returned to pre-change status: Jade in the wheelchair; Sonia and Sky once again elderly, and Rhea went from twenty-seven back to fifty-four. Lance, Zane, Chad and Ihor disappeared.

"Well mom, you ready to head out?" asked Nadia entering the room. "Sure, was quiet in here; I thought you'd all fallen asleep."

The others tried not to smile.

CHAPTER 29

Three weeks later Rhea joined Sonia for lunch. The world outside the window was now early January.

"I've sold the house," Rhea told her mother. "But I never realized we were in such debt. The sale hardly paid half of it off."

"Have you talked to Chi about it?" Sonia inquired.

"Yes," Rhea declared delighted. "He gave me the extra money, and the guardians have been helping sort and dispose of all Ivan's junk."

"Excellent." Sonia was glad it was going so well. "Soon you will be out of there. Have you decided where you will go?'

Rhea frowned. "Mom, I don't want to move to Sanctuary just yet."

"I never expected you would," Sonia admitted. "I'm sure Jade would welcome you into her home."

But Rhea was thinking of Shawn. "Mom, why won't you let us break the children?"

Sonia sighed. "We are only strong enough to break the dormant one at a time."

Rhea had noticed her mother was still weary from the healing change, and it puzzled her. "Mom, why does it take so much out of you to heal? You are supposed to have untold power ability; is it easier on the men because they are larger and physically stronger?"

"Partly." Sonia smiled, warmed by her daughter's concern for her. "But it is actually, because there are more of them."

"Why should that matter?"

Sonia realized it was time to give Rhea a lesson on the healing process. "You know female must heal female, and male heal male?"

Rhea nodded.

"Only the 'Leader Female' is able to do it differently, as long as she has the proper balance."

"What do you mean by balance?"

"When we heal, we use a secondary female for physical and emotional balance…a guideline to come back to. All unified females lend their strength to the procedure, if needed. The support female channels the energy of the others by degrees, a very little from each so its loss is unnoticeable to the donor, and supplies it to the healing female; the secondary female can also step in and join in the healing should something go wrong, but…she in turn needs a male counter balance, preferably her pair or a relative, and he channels from the male side should the combined female strength be insufficient."

Rhea acknowledged she followed the explanation well enough, so Sonia continued. "When a male heals, the procedure is the same, only there the secondary is male, and counter balance must be…"

"Female."

"Right. The more of the main balance, the easier it is to heal." Sonia repeated for emphasis. "When healing female, the females are main balance, the pair male, counter balance. When healing male, the males are main balance with a paired female for counter balance."

"But we have no mated pairs."

"Remember I said, the 'Leader Female' can do differently?" Rhea nodded. "If there is no paired female, the 'Leader Female' must step in. I can heal either male or female, and do it without being paired. And that is why it has been so hard on me."

"Why?"

"Because I am the only female who can presently counter balance the male side, to channel female strength to them, and…I am the only female healer available to channel male energy to our side."

"Okay. But what about when you are the healer doing the healing of a female? Did you use a male in place of the secondary female?"

"No. A man can not be used without the counter balance of a mated pair."

"So, what did you do? Doesn't that mean the male energy is not available to you when you heal? Can you heal without it?"

"It is available but only through me. When I heal alone, because I am a 'Leader Female' I can sometimes access the strongest male and use his energy. I must be at a very low energy level to do it…it happens automatically when I reach death plateau."

"Ho! You're joking! That's dangerous!"

"Tell me about it! Now you see why the drain is on me, and why I can only allow one to be done at a time. When Sky healed Zane, your brother was near death. Sky refused to use the other guardians, because that would leave those still dormant unprotected; he tried to heal without their help...we've been learning and adjusting this process since we started. As Sky's counter balance, I didn't realize he had no secondary until it was almost too late. So, when he needed support, I was caught unprepared. I did not have enough strength of my own, and when I reached the death plateau, I drained from the strongest male without consciously meaning to. It nearly killed all three of us ...we learned the hard way that day. It unbalanced the men considerably."

The memory of that day made Sonia cringe. *We came so close to losing everyone involved.*

"When I was the only non-dormant female," she continued. "We had no female balance side at all. After I healed Jade, it was extremely difficult to recover my physical on my own, but the real problem was the emotional balance. This was out of sync until Lance joined us; I can't truly explain this, but somehow, the knowledge that I had both my sons back well and safe, caused me to go back to balance normal again. And when I healed you Rhea..."

"You had only Jade. Still not enough female strength..."

"I've got to admit, it has been weakening me more each time. But it should get easier as we get more women, though...the females from now on will all be younger... not sufficiently developed mentally..."

"I heard Sky is male 'Healer Ultimate'. Can he heal you or the other females?"

"He can not heal a female unless she is related or his pair. When a female is too badly injured, or cannot heal-back, only her mated pair can heal her...that is why we only use mated pairs to counter balance. You see, females have this defence reflex when at low energy, which kills any non-compatible male when he touches her, zaps him with enough voltage to explode every cell in his body. The weaker the female becomes, the stronger the reflex...it is neither purposeful nor preventable. This is her last safeguard-defence to attack. And...a 'Leader Female's' reflex is ten times that of the average female." Sonia hesitated, but decided to reveal her one weakness anyway. "The only thing that shorts out the reflex energy of a 'Leader Female' is if she is depressed."

Sonia gave her daughter no time to process this information. She continued. "So, Sky can monitor and give me energy; he can even balance my emotions to a certain degree, but he can not fully heal me, unless...he becomes my 'mated pair'. If he is not my 'pair compatible', and he tries to heal me, he will lose his life before he can do it."

Rhea missed the solution in Sonia's last statement; she directly applied the facts to the over-all female population.

"So as far as Sky's healing power is concerned, he is no good to the females?"

"He can help me, and I can heal the females, but unless he were to become my 'Bonded Pair', no, he is little help in regards to the females."

"You mentioned a relative. What about uncle Joel or Myron? Could they act as counter balance to any of the women; we are all family."

"So far they have refused to be 'complete' with us, and you need that to enter into the full healing process...they can break a male dormant, but are unable to help in a situation with a female. Even with the male, they need my outside counter balance. Maybe someday...in the future...Joel and Myron will change their minds and unify with us. Their willing touch of me for the purpose of bonding would join us all instantly."

"Until then, we can not use the male strength...except through you?"

Sonia nodded, regret mirrored in her eyes.

"Do the males have trouble healing themselves?"

"At present, they seldom need our counter balance. But if we were forced into a battle that would change quickly."

Rhea shook her head dejectedly. "What ever happened to the females being the stronger healers?"

"We still and always will be the stronger healers...when there are many of us. And...we must be well ourselves to heal. Without enough main balance females, or access to male strength for support, we cannot heal even each other properly. The 'Opposites' target the females for this very reason."

"Then their attempt to remove females from our population is not about our procreation," Rhea observed. "It's to weaken us, thereby destroying the species."

Sonia agreed. "Females are able to balance each other emotionally; also, they balance their men. Without sufficient females: the women die in childbirth because there is no support female for strength; they cannot keep mental equilibrium so they go mad. The worst is there is no counter strength balance for the male healer, so the men cannot heal each other either. The sooner the 'Opposites' get rid of all females, the quicker the species dies."

Sonia sighed with deep regret. "We have power beyond comprehension," she bemoaned. "If our females were numerous, we would be unstoppable...why even our own males do not realize the full potential of a female, it has been so long since we were many."

"So, let's say for argument's sake, we get mated pairs for some of those males now in the species, could the men then help the females to heal each other?"

"Males can do only so much for us."

Sonia thought a moment, then came back with this observation.

"It is not the healing that is the problem; it is the coming back. In repairing after healing we need to gain our strength from our support. When that is limited, we must use counter balance. It is never good when we need to go that far!

"You see, with the male counter balance we are able only to drain his strength; his emotions are useless to balance the emotional side. Their emotions are so foreign to our make-up...well, this is my observation: the male is more instant adrenalin, physically based; we, on the other hand, are more roller-coaster emotion...and affection based. The two kinds do not mix well. They are like fire and oil; sometimes you can create a great blaze; applied with the wrong mixture or at an inappropriate moment and you have an explosion."

Rhea smiled at the picture her mother presented. *It is so true even of the human race I am still part of.*

"We need more females," Sonia observed sadly. "It is equally hard at present for our male 'Healer Ultimate'. With no pairs, it means Sky is the only unifier to the men; he operates on a minor scale much like a 'Leader Female'. Always, he must function either as support or as the primary healer, and that is very draining should there be many injured males."

"Like as in a battle?"

"Or if we are breaking the dormancy of more than one male at once."

"Like my boys?"

"Yes. But I can also support the 'Healer Ultimate' while he breaks the male..."

"The only males left to break are my boys, aren't they?"

"Thank goodness! But again, it boils down to the female strength. Sky must always act as my back up, because he is 'Healer Ultimate' and I am always his counter balance. This happens automatic, even at a distance; we cannot prevent it. If our 'Healer Ultimate' gets too weak: the men will not be able to heal; their protection guard over us then goes down; the 'Leader Female' can not be balanced emotionally, or mentally, for that matter, and her protection and abilities are nullified, which leaves us totally at the mercy of the enemy: helpless, hopeless...half mad. The swiftest and most painful secondary way to kill our species."

"What is the first?"

Sonia shook her head. "That secret will remain mine alone for now. Only one thing I will say: the function of the 'Healer Ultimate' is such, that someday, the survival of the species will eventually rest with him."

"So, we have to be careful not to exhaust either the 'Leader Female' or the 'Healer Ultimate'? So, what about breaking out the girls? Can Jade and I at least do that?"

"For that, I also am your support female, and as well, be acting as opposite balance channel to the men, with Sky monitoring. But bear in mind, when the boys are broken, I am also counter balance to Sky. You have to give us the time to recover between each dormant breaking; our healings need to be spaced or the whole race will go down. Will you be patient, and let me be the judge of when it is safe?"

Rhea sighed. "I guess you are right; it is best for the children to remain dormant... until you say differently," she agreed sadly. "I just had hoped...for Shawn..."

She let the thought go unfinished. After a moment, she came back with another question. "What if we were to stop healing altogether, and just used conventional medicine? Would that be the key to our survival?"

"I'm afraid not," Sonia admitted. "You see, healing is part of our general balance; just like breathing, eating and sleeping; we need to do it. We are compelled to heal. It is impossible for us to be aware of suffering and not alleviate it. If we fail to oblige this instinct, it results in madness."

"Oh, wonderful. It seems it doesn't matter how we turn this, does it?" Rhea shook her head in exasperation. "If we just had a mated pair...guess it's up to Jade or me."

Her mother exploded. "Don't you dare pair for that reason!"

Rhea sighed. "Don't worry, mom. I still...love Ivan."

Sonia touched her hand in gentle comfort.

"Well, we couldn't make babies fast enough anyway," observed Rhea.

As if the world were resting on her shoulders, she sighed again. "Isn't there something that can be done, mom?"

"There is one thing..."

Rhea shot her mother a questioning look.

"The men must find human females, and...we must change them, heal their blood balance until they are only half human, as are our males."

Rhea made a face. "No human woman would agree to that!"

"You never know. Love is strange sometimes."

Rhea's thoughts went to her son-in-law. "Could you change the blood balance of a human male?"

"The process would be extremely painful."

Rhea sighed again.

"He would have to request it before I would even consider putting Wade through that."

"You realize what that means, mom?" Rhea quizzed. "Jessica will stay young, and …watch him die."

"I know. I've truly wondered if I shouldn't just leave her dormant…until after he is gone."

"Oh! Mom! Don't say that! Think of Kara."

Sonia turned away, and changed the subject.

****

"How is Shawn doing?"

Rhea's composure collapsed. "Oh, mom," she moaned. "It's not been good. I don't know what to do with him."

"I thought as much," Sonia empathized. "Tell me. I've felt your avoidance of this subject since you first entered."

"He claims the house was his inheritance; that I was wrong to sell it. We've had such battles."

Rhea's eyes brimmed with tears. "Ever since Ivan died, Shawn has been so mean. His thoughts tell me, he thinks he's now man of the house; he's to take his father's place. There is such anger in him, such hate. I can hardly bear to be in the same room with him. He orders, manipulates, demands…his tongue is so vicious toward me."

"He grieves for his father, as you do, but…he has no comfort support."

"I know that. It's what keeps me from just…Mom, if I were to show him what I look like…if I were to use the powers I have now against him. I could pulverize him! He'd cease to be! But I still love him; And he's a dormant!"

Tears traced down her cheeks. "What can I do to help my son, mom? What if I lose control? I could hurt my own son! I don't think I can keep control much longer. I had hoped we could break him, but that hope is lost...for now."

"You must learn to draw emotional balance from the rest of us."

"How come I don't know how to do that, mom?" Rhea declared angrily. "It seems I'm deficient somehow. You are different; you have greater power!"

"No," Sonia disagreed. "Your power isn't in question here. You must learn to use what you have. My knowledge is greater, and your bi-species condition diminishes your powers of knowing...I know without being taught; you must be trained. That is the difference. Have Ihor show you how."

Rhea shook her head. "He is a good man, but...we drive even him away some days. He goes distant to keep from reacting himself. I fear, he will someday interfere and take my boy to task..."

Sonia frowned. "My guardians know the guidelines!" she declared firmly. "Ihor, are you near?"

The gardener materialized before them, his manner stoic and solemn. "My Lady?"

"Oh, mom," Rhea pleaded. "I didn't mean to get him into trouble. Please?"

Sonia ignored her daughter.

"Show me what you have witnessed, guardian," Sonia requested quietly.

As Ihor transferred and played his memories to Sonia, Rhea hid her face in shame.

"I'm so sorry, Ihor. It was wrong of me to include you."

Ihor knew better than to react to Rhea's emotion. Though his impulse was to comfort her, his first loyalty must be to Sonia. He also knew the Lady was not asking as a reprimand to him. Rhea, however, was unfamiliar with her mother's method of rule. He could not correct that at the moment, so he did not try.

"No one is in trouble, Rhea," Sonia placated. "I simply need the facts from a second source."

She nodded to Ihor. "Thank you, guardian. Please go distant."

Obeying immediately, Ihor vanished.

When he was gone, Sonia turned to Rhea. "How would you like to visit your sister while I take care of this? I will wait for Shawn to return at your house."

Rhea knew her going was not up for negotiation. "Mom, please," she begged. "Don't hurt my son. He doesn't know any better."

"It is Shawn's time." Sonia stated. "Whether he is hurt in the process depends upon his choices. I love him also, Rhea. I love both of you, and this cannot continue. It is time!

"Please do as I ask," Sonia pleaded softly. "I will be as gentle as I am able."

Rhea agreed, reluctantly vanishing, tears in her eyes as she fled.

Knowing her own plans, Sonia realized it would be harder on Rhea if she were present at this awakening. It had not been easy on Sonia either, to send Rhea away.

CHAPTER 30

Sonia transmitted a mental request to her men. "I am in need of a guardian willing to be injured during punishment duty."

Lance, her oldest son replied. "If it is for young Shawn, I volunteer. The boy has been on my heart, and I wish to be his guardian and teacher."

"You need not be the one," Sonia objected. "Chi is his usual guardian. Are you certain you are balanced sufficiently?"

"If I am not, you will be my balance mother. I trust you."

"So be it. Come, Djura, Sky and Chi, also. Attend me at Rhea's house."

****

Sonia was seated on Rhea's sofa; the four men stood before her.

"Chi will you take the perimeter? Let me know when Shawn arrives."

Chi vanished.

"Djura, you will act guardian within the room. If Lance or I need strength you will be support to supply it." Djura nodded. "Remain unseen unless needed."

Djura moved to a corner and disappeared.

"Lance, I'm sorry, this is not going to be pleasant for you."

"I've had worse done to me," Lance admitted. "It will be worth it in the end. Just let me know, what you want and when."

"Silent communication, unless I say otherwise, invisible for now."

Lance stepped away, and faded.

"Sky, what do you think? Is what I plan too drastic?"

"My lady, his violence needs to be stopped in infancy."

Sonia shook her head; not liking what must be done in the next hours. "He will be very emotional…"

"I will be monitoring him…and you. Chi will be Djura's balance."

"Let him also be balance for Lance, if I am unable," Sonia decided. "I wish my son was not the one who had volunteered."

"He does it for the sake of the boy. Who better? He has been where Shawn is now."

Sonia nodded. "When I heal Lance, you are my balance centre."

"Agreed."

"He comes," Chi informed them, and Sky went invisible.

****

"What you doing here?" asked Shawn when he entered the room and saw his grandmother. "Where's mom?"

"She went to visit your aunt Jade," Sonia answered quietly. "I'm here because we need to have a talk."

"What about?"

Deliberately, he stood towering over the fragile old lady, just to intimidate.

"Your behaviour toward your mother," stated Sonia.

Shawn laughed humourlessly. "What business is it of yours?" He tossed his backpack on the couch next to Sonia. "I know whose side you'll take. You've always been on her side. You know, I doubt you've ever really liked me."

Sonia felt remorse that he had come to that conclusion. "I have always loved you dearly, Shawn. You are and always will be...my sunshine boy."

"Don't call me that! I ain't a kid any more."

"I know that. That's why we are talking adult to adult."

He made a rude sound, as if he totally doubted such a possibility.

"I hate you!" Shawn hissed.

Sonia winced, and that encouraged him.

"I hate my mom! I hate the whole family!"

"I don't believe that's true," Sonia disagreed. "You are feeling heart breaking grief at the loss of your father, and you don't know how to rid yourself of it. You feel alone with no one to turn to."

Shawn exploded. "Grief!" he thundered. "Why should I care that the man is gone? I won't miss him! He was an idiot! He never treated me like a person; I was just someone to do chores, someone to boss around. His main purpose in life was to keep me busy, to make my life miserable! Why should he be important to me? I never meant anything to him!"

The twenty-six-year-old began to pace the living room in pent-up anger. Sonia chose to let him rant.

"What a stupid way to die! No seat belt on...just like he lived! Careless! Driving too fast; killed by a deer!"

"You still loved him, Shawn," Sonia reminded softly. "Even with all his faults."

"What would you know about it?" He spun to face her, tears brightening his eyes. "You didn't even like him!"

"I admit I had a hard time watching what went on. He was not an easy man to get along with, but over the years I learned to regard him as a son...a son who sometimes chose a path that I thought was harsh...and often wrong, but my other children were never perfect either, and I still loved them with a mother's heart...as I do you."

"Ya, right! If you all loved him so much, how come it's so easy to forget him? Mom's selling everything! She throws away his treasures into the garbage, all without a second thought. Nobody cares if I might want some of it. He hasn't even been dead a month!"

"She has debts to pay, Shawn..."

The young man did not hear; his mind had switched again to the accident. "Stupid man! Killed by an animal!" he raved. "What do I do with that? At least if it was a man I could go out and shoot him. How do I pay a deer back for killing him?'

"Will revenge bring your father back?"

"It would sure make me feel better!"

"I don't believe it would…it is likely to make you feel worse."

He clenched his fists, his body trembling with suppressed rage. He did not dare strike his grandmother…but he needed to strike out at something.

Sonia felt and saw his distress. "Calm down, Shawn. I have something I want you to watch with me."

"Why?" he asked rebelliously.

Sonia pointed the remote at the VCR and a video complete with sound began to play on the big screen TV.

Shawn turned to watch despite himself, but remained standing. He was not sitting down in surrender beside his grandmother!

"This is a recording of your father's accident…before and after."

"No way," Shawn declared in disbelief. But he did not question how she had come by the footage.

The memory screen played through just as it had taken place. Shawn turned away at the last, unable to endure the sight of his father lying exposed in such a fashion.

When the video had run its course, silence filled the room.

"What was that thing?" asked Shawn coldly.

"Your real enemy."

"Are they the aliens from TV?"

"Yes."

Suddenly, it was as if he trusted his grandmother had all the answers.

"How do I kill it?"

He has transferred his anger. Good. Now to teach him violence is not the answer.

"Now!" Sonia ordered silently.

The 'Opposite' appeared almost next to Shawn, and he did not question its reality, nor the possibility it would single him out. He spun toward it at the sound, fearful.

Lance had the imitation down perfectly, right to the noisy breathing apparatus. He growled deep in his throat.

Shawn was of warrior stock, and he proved it that day. Sonia had expected he would. With quick thinking, the young man caught up a nearby metal bat that had suddenly appeared propped against the wall. Whether he was thinking to defend his grandmother or just destroy his enemy did not matter for now.

He swung, connecting hard with a crack that resounded through the room. Lance grabbed the weapon fiercely and sent it spinning from Shawn's hand. But that did not deter the younger man.

Shawn had lost his fear, and his temper had taken over.

Pounding with his weight behind his fists, and Shawn was no lightweight, he landed blow upon blow to the back of the beast until it stumbled to the floor.

"Allow him to feel your pain," ordered Sonia silently.

At each continued blow, for Shawn was still pounding his victim even though it was prostrate; he gasped with pain, feeling the force of his own punch, his mind puzzled by the result, yet unable to determine the source of the second enemy.

"Change," Sonia ordered silently.

Now sight deceived as well. The alien had become his father, battered and bloody. But Shawn could not stop himself; his anger controlled him. With fists that were bruised and bloody, he continued, as if the offending members had a mind of their own. And still each blow he struck gave the young man more pain than his adversary.

Panting, Shawn finally dropped his hands. He now knelt over his opponent.

"Change," Sonia ordered silently.

Ivan became Shawn.

The boy stared blankly at the beaten man, then began to scream. His voice hoarse, his shriek became a wail of anguish. The pain still wracked his body; the sight of his bleeding twin lying inert before him assaulted the tired mind, and Shawn began to rock insanely back and forth upon his knees.

He is nearing madness, but it will soon be over.

The howl became a sob, and Shawn gave way to tears of shame and remorse. "I'm sorry; I'm sorry..." As the Shawn on the floor again became Ivan, the boy leaned forward and gathered him into his arms. "I'm sorry dad, so sorry...I love you, dad...I love you..." Seated on the floor, holding his bloody parent, Shawn cried like the broken child he was.

"Enough," Sonia cried aloud.

Sonia ran to her grandson, enfolding him in her embrace, cloaking him in her emotions of love. And as she held him, she was healing both Shawn and Lance, the first emotionally, the second of his gruesome physical wounds.

When at last Shawn lay against her quiet, Sonia looked up at the men around her. Sky, Djura and Lance all had tears in their eyes.

Lance rose to his feet.

"He is yours now," she silently told her guardians. "Djura, you may have the honour of breaking his dormancy. Chi will take me home."

Sonia made the jump to Chi's location, then together they transported back to her apartment.

"Rhea, come," she called, as soon as she materialized. "Take the perimeter, Chi, until Ihor comes. Then help Djura return to Sanctuary."

Chi disappeared obediently.

****

Exhausted, Sonia was near asleep in the recliner when Sky, Lance and her grandson appeared in the apartment. Rhea was quietly waiting on the sofa.

The copper-blond giant immediately dropped to one knee beside his grandmother's chair, and took her hand. "Grandma, I am sooo sorry. I never meant to hurt you...or anyone. I was sooo angry...I never want to harm another being...ever again."

He was blue eyed, and thirteen once again, and had totally lost his former animosity; all the anger and resentment was healed away, but the inner revulsion at what he was capable of still lingered.

He turned toward his mother, including her in his apology. "Forgive me, mom." The tears glistened in his eyes.

Rhea left her seat immediately, dropping to the floor beside him, hugging him with all her might. Their embrace lasted many, many minutes.

Sonia finally sighed, finding it difficult to maintain the image of composure for much longer. Sky noticing her fatigue, broke in on the emotional reunion.

"Sonia is in need of rest..."

"Yes," Sonia waved her hand dismissively. "By all means, go home...please!"

The others laughed at her apparent callousness, understanding she had reached her limit, and Sonia feeling a little guilty, added, "When Shawn is ready...move him to Sanctuary."

Her grandson rose, and joined his uncle, and Ihor who had just appeared. Shawn had one last thing to say, just before the three disappeared with Jade between them.

"Thanks for what you just taught me, and...I always knew you were... extraordinary."

Sonia smiled at the compliment, and waved good-naturedly. "Go…"

When they were gone, she melted in exhaustion.

"Are you okay?" Sky asked with concern.

But Sonia had already dropped into an unnatural sleep.

****

Breaking the dormancy of her family is slowly killing her, Sky realized. *Yet… she is compelled. It is a mother's love creating this urge, and nothing I can do will stop it.*

I am helpless to mend her should she grow too weak to heal-back. What will happen then?

And how many more secrets does she keep to herself, which she had yet to disclose?

Sky lifted her gently from the recliner, carrying her to the bedroom. After covering her with a blanket, he sat down in a nearby chair.

That night, he did not go to the rooftop look out. Instead he sat beside Sonia, until he was certain she had healed-back enough to be safe.

CHAPTER 31

Joel materialized suddenly in Sonia's apartment living room. Instantly two guardians towered over him, standing threateningly between him and his sister.

Djura and Sky were both aware of Joel's anger.

"Stand down, guardians!" Sonia ordered forcefully. "He is my brother!"

For a moment, it seemed the two men would disobey. Sky finally relaxed, but Djura remained vigilant, though he did step away.

"Djura, go back to perimeter; Sky will remain inside."

Djura hesitated.

"I can defend myself."

At that Djura reluctantly disappeared.

Sky stepped to Sonia, still staying between sister and brother.

"Can't even have a private conversation with you any more," Joel hissed petulantly. "Why do you need a bodyguard against me?"

Sonia chose not to answer.

"Sky, will you move across the room...please?"

The guardian transferred obediently to a corner.

"Why so angry, Joel?" Sonia asked quietly.

"How long are you going to let Myron remain rogue?"

Sonia said nothing.

"He's self-indulgent, lazy…I at least work with you guys! You're supposed to be leader, remember? You made that stupid decree about punishment. How long are you going to wait? Because of him two men were killed."

"If I punish him, should I do the same with you?"

"What have I done?" he exploded.

"It's what you don't do…"

"And that is punishable?"

"It can also cost the lives of others," Sonia returned gently. "Why don't you sit down, so we can discuss this?"

"No, I won't! I demand you take action!"

"About what? Will punishing Myron bring those we love back?"

"No, but it'll get him to toe the line."

"You need his help?"

"No," he said indignantly. "What's the matter with you? You're not much of a leader if you don't carry out your own edicts."

"A leader may choose to be merciful…"

"Figures," he returned sarcastically. "I knew you didn't have it in you to handle the hard stuff…to handle these men."

In the corner, Sky bristled, but outwardly remained stoic.

"Your own rules require you to punish him."

"That is true," Sonia agreed reluctantly. "But when I do…you will not be present to watch it!"

"Just as long as you do it," Joel agreed. "And…it better be soon."

Sonia narrowed her eyes. "Leave me, Joel!" she ordered curtly.

It took a moment for the brother to realize he had gone too far, and Sky was prepared to forcefully send him from their presence, but Joel's mind at least showed regret.

Abruptly, the 'Pure' male vanished.

****

The silence in the room was deafening. At last, Sonia spoke.

"Have Chi and Djura bring Myron to me."

"Yes, my lady."

Sky jumped to Djura's post.

"You heard?"

Djura nodded, then vanished.

Neither guardian liked the thought of what was coming.

****

Myron was still struggling against his captors when the three men appeared in the room. Sky swiftly followed, without being summoned.

"Release him," Sonia said to Djura and Chi, then spoke curtly to her brother. "Don't try to teleport. I will prevent you."

Myron shook himself away, when the guardians relinquished their hold.

"What is this?" Myron asked indignantly. "Some sort of monkey court?"

"You know the rules, Myron." Sonia turned to the guardians. "I will not need all of you. Chi will you take perimeter?"

The Asian nodded, and vanished.

Sonia turned to Sky and Djura.

"Please, give us space?"

The two guardians moved to opposite ends of the room, like a pair of sentries preventing escape.

Sonia returned her gaze to Myron. "A complaint has been raised against you..."

"Ya right! That Joel again. He should mind his own business...he's always picking a fight..."

Sonia remained quiet; she did not wish to play referee, no matter what had happened between them.

Myron grew uncomfortable.

"Are you not even remorseful at what has happened?"

"Wasn't my fault," Myron defended, referring to the disagreement with Joel.

"Don't play dense," Sonia returned, perturbed. "And it decidedly was your fault."

Myron now knew she spoke of the accident.

"He was no loss, just another abusive human."

"Ivan was my son-in-law, and...Rhea loved him!"

"She's better off without him." He saw Sonia's eyes narrow, and quickly back tracked. "I didn't kill him."

"No," Sonia agreed. "But because you were not at your post, he died. And not just Ivan was lost!"

"The kid, you mean? He was just a pesty nigger."

"Myron!" Sonia exploded.

The brother's mind cowered under his sister's display of temper.

The guardians looked down, having difficulty keeping a straight face.

"He had a twin," Sonia reprimanded, quickly calming herself. "Because of Asa's death, Chad is now emotionally...unsettled."

"So, give him a woman. He's nuts over Nadia."

"She's only eleven! That's your solution to everything, isn't it? Follow your base carnal appetite."

Myron shrugged.

After the silence had dragged on too long for his comfort, he finally asked, "So, what do you want from me?"

Sonia shook her head exasperated.

"I had hoped some remorse... According to our rules, when a complaint has been brought forward, I have to act...I have to discipline you."

She let that sink in for a moment, then went on. "You must choose two punishments..."

He stood up straighter, and his eyes narrowed.

"I never wanted any part of this group," he reminded her. "What if I choose to be separate...by myself...not a part of you guys?"

"That can only happen if you were...banished."

"Then I choose that!"

"As your punishment?" Sonia clarified.

"Ya."

"And your second choice?"

Myron's temper flared.

"I don't have to obey you!" he yelled. "And you can't make me!"

"I won't," Sonia agreed softly. "Free will works better."

"Well, I choose to follow a man! Me! Myself!"

Myron's yelling would have brought the police down on them, had it not been for Chi's silence cloak.

"I'll never follow a weak woman! You're nothing but a whore!"

Tears filled Sonia's eyes.

Both guardians clenched their fists at Myron's harsh words, but Sonia shook her head warning them not to interfere.

"So?" Sonia quietly returned to the business at hand. "You will not choose a second less severe punishment?'

"I make my own rules! I'll never submit to a woman's rule. I'd rather be banished."

"When you make your own rules, you cause the death of others...our kind is hunted..."

"I don't care about your kind!"

"I know," Sonia observed sadly. "You are already more 'Opposite'..."

Sky almost registered his shock, surprised at Sonia's harsh assessment. Though Myron angered him also, he would never have gone so far as to make such a judgement. He hoped Sonia would not regret the words she had just spoken.

Myron was still in fight mode. His retort was just as unkind, quick and nasty.

"Maybe it's the way I was raised," he hissed venomously, implying unfairly to the fact she had been his older example. "You made me what I am!"

Sonia's eyes shown with unshed moisture. "You are banished, Myron," she proclaimed in a quiet, level tone.

Without another word, Myron escape her presence, vanishing.

Neither guardian made a move to go after him.

"Leave my presence," Sonia ordered disconsolately. "I wish to be alone."

CHAPTER 32

She had simply agreed!

I never expected her to follow through, to just exclude me without a moment's thought. She should have...could have, argued against it, fought with me...like I wanted all along.

She didn't even try to dissuade me! It is like she doesn't care. My sister is just like every other bitch I've had to deal with. You can't trust a one of them!

Never mind that we are blood; our history together means nothing.

Sister and brother? Ya, right!

I could make nice again...I've done it before. She always comes around if I wait long enough. I can shape her to supply my needs; it always works...like a charm.

But somehow, he knew this time was different.

She has the other men on her side now. I can't manipulate all of them.

It made Myron so angry. The sentence felt so...final. He could hide away in his cabin, but that did not make a difference somehow. The finality of it didn't go away.

It did not feel like freedom anymore. Somehow, she had taken away the pleasure. She had called him on his dare.

He still could not figure what he had done that was so wrong. They had given him a partner; a pair guardian, she called him. He had only ignored him.

Maybe I shouldn't have done that?

Myron knew he was supposed to mentor the young twerp, but could he help it if the dumb fart had gotten himself killed before he could do that?

If I had been there, I would be the one biting the dust now!

What is wrong with them anyway?

Frustrated, Myron banged his fist against the wall. His sleeping puppy woke with a start, then cringed as he realized his master was angry.

Even the darn dog is afraid of me!

Myron dropped down on his cot, then lay flat. Placing his arms behind his head, he stared unseeingly at the ceiling.

What was he going to do?

Now that he was purposely cast out, he wanted nothing more than to be a part of the whole.

The longing was overwhelming.

Moisture clouded his vision.

Men did not cry! For years he had managed to never show weakness. He wiped at the offending wetness beneath his eyes, and went on brooding.

I will never let them see how badly they have hurt me!

The dog whimpered.

"Shut up! Stupid!"

The animal cowed, and went silent.

I just want Sonia to be proud of me, to praise me. Is that too much to ask? After today, will that ever happen? All thanks to Joel!

Even if I go back, and say I'm sorry...I looked in her mind, she was willing to forgive me...but even then, it won't work.

I can never do it right. I will never fit in. I cannot be that high-fluting 'Pure' like they expect me to be.

A Royal!

I cannot be a guardian either. Even with my mind healed, I will never be as smart as Joel.

If I could just undo my mistakes, find a way to make up for what happened.

She is my big sister! The younger always fights elder domination. It is a rite of passage.

It doesn't mean I don't love her...or desire to protect her.

If there is anything I ever wanted, it is to take care of my sister and her kids; to see her happy. Sure, I like to get a rise out of her, but deep down inside, I would give anything to shield her from her struggles. I would give her all the money in the world...if I had enough of it.

But what does it matter now? She has all that; they are giving her everything she needs. There is nothing left for me to give.

Myron sighed.

I really did not mean all those things I said to her.

Liquid dribbled down the side of his cheek, rolling into his ear. Angrily, he brushed at his treasonous eyes.

Why won't they stop leaking?

She is a good leader. Even I can see that!

But I won't ever tell her that! She is a woman; the compliment would go to her head!

A spider crawled across the ceiling above his head; he reached up and squashed it into nothingness.

Just like everyone else, that arachnid does not realize the power over life and death I possess.

Sometimes, he thought. *Sonia is good to me. If only I could repair the damage to our relationship, and get back in her good graces.*

But that means I have to eat crow...

That makes me subordinate; subservient to a woman...that means she is the more exemplary person.

Never! Never! I am the male!

Men are superior, tougher, meant to be in command! They are supposed to have the last word!

But what can I possibly say that would matter?

I am no longer needed. She has all kinds of protection. I failed to measure up to her expectations.

There is only one thing left for me to be...I can make that ultimate sacrifice.

That time I was in her mind, I learned first off, how to hide my thoughts from the telepaths; I learned that well. Even Sonia cannot see into the depth of my mind...or maybe, all along...she really doesn't want to see my thoughts.

That's okay too. It makes it possible to hide from her now.

And the second thing I learned just before she shut me out of her mind: there is more than one way to conquer your enemy.

I can slip behind the moon...as long as they do not detect me too soon, before I can complete the task...then like a suicide bomber...

Myron grinned; he had his solution!

I will fix this! And in the act...I will make her sorry...make them all sorry they ever banished me.

Everyone that has hurt me will pay...Sonia most of all! She will not be able to stop it...nor her reaction to it.

CHAPTER 33

They all felt it the minute it happened; even those still dormant suffered from sudden depression upon sensing it. Joel went down, as if a clay brick had hit him.

Shaken, and numb with shock, Sonia still managed to reach out with her mind, more by reflex than anything else, to steady the moon as it rocked from the blast, and block the resulting shockwave when it hit the atmosphere. Otherwise Earth would have been sent spinning through space.

Myron had gone Nova...taking everyone on the alien ship with him!

How did he even learn how to do that? When did he see? Had he known the repercussions such an act would perpetrate?

On Earth, NASA picked up the explosion and failed to realize how close mankind had just come to extinction. They assumed a drifting asteroid chunk had collided with the visiting spacecraft exploding it upon impact. They felt no grief for loss of creatures they had not known. As far as they were concerned, the threat to them had just been eliminated and their worries were now over.

Once the world and the region of space around it had steadied, Sonia went down, not only dropping the shield of protection around her people, but her own personal mental block as well. Within seconds, guardians knew who had been lost and that the 'Pure' of their species had been dealt a deathblow…it would cost, cause irreparable damage…perhaps even annihilate their kind.

Then Sonia, choosing to suffer alone, closed her mind to the rest of the race, dropped to her knees, and gave way to deep, agonized moans of grief.

Sky was immediately at her side.

"Keep away from me!" she screamed at her protector. "Keep away! It is not safe to be near me! I am deadly to all right now!"

He could not comprehend why. Unsure of what to do next, Sky stood indecisive. He could not ever imagine her dangerous to them.

But this time he was wrong.

Sonia turned angry. "Get out of here! Go away! There is no longer a need to protect me. The enemy is not a threat any longer. Go away!" Her hands covered her face in utter despair. "Go away. Go away. Leave me alone! Give me my privacy!"

Sky left as she requested.

And in her overwhelming grief, she failed to sense where he went.

Steaming hot water…as hot as I can get it, that will short circuit the reflex…

If not…by accident, I will destroy this small planet, eliminating everything and everyone with my grief…go super Nova as Myron did.

As she stepped into the steaming bath, Sonia could hold back no longer. The tears came from heart deep, sobs so soul wrenching, body wracking, so controlling, it took her breath away. Giant drops spilled, rolled down her cheeks, melding with the vapour of the water.

****

It was the one and only time Sky disobeyed Sonia. He took up station on the roof to watch her.

Maybe she no longer needs protection from our mortal enemy, and maybe there is nothing I can do to help, but I will not leave her alone. Not at a time like this. Not now! Not ever!

Sky's control almost broke as he watched. Not to go to her in this state with comfort was to him like a physical injury, torturous. It was extremely difficult to admit he the physician was useless to her, but more so as someone who cared, he was experiencing the very depth of her agony and sorrow.

The scene below was surreal. It was like an electrical storm hung over her bath; the spit of current zapped back and forth from Sonia to the liquid in colours of hot white and cold blue, like the negative and positive were battling it out. And through it all, the impotent, helpless creature at its centre sobbed ceaselessly, totally out of balance both physically and emotionally.

Did Myron's death do this to her?

Could Joel be of help? He is now the only 'Pure' male. Where is he?

But the minds of the other guardians told him the brother had gone down also. It was as if the three had been joined physically, no matter that the males had refused amalgamation...this was something more.

We assumed Joel and Myron, being separate, were not connected to Sonia. They were apart from the general population, but is there a special junction between 'Pure'...one that is not governed by will?

If so the two remaining are dying because Myron has gone Nova...unless, somehow, Sonia can balance again.

Why does she always have to shoulder the burdens? Where is it written that the 'Leader Female' must exclusively achieve stability by her own efforts? Is there no way to carry the troubles together?

Did Myron know this would happen? Had he done this on purpose?

And is the balance of the species also at stake here? What about the planet that houses us...the universe beyond? Are all at risk?

Sky chided himself. *I know too little about the 'Pure' side of the species, and little to nothing of the 'Leader Female' balance control power...if this result comes out favourably, I must remedy that. My past training is useless...ineffective here.*

The physician in him was certain of only one thing: *Myron's death has caused this... it is not simple grief!*

Powerless to stop what was happening, Sky watched as the balance of life rocked

… And he waited.

That was all there was left to do.

If there is an Almighty Being, thought Sky. *It is time to leave this in its hands.*

CHAPTER 34

Three days later her mind returned to reality. Sonia rolled over in her bed, and opened swollen eyes.

At first, it was only Sky she was conscious of, sitting on the roof, still watching over her. She could smell his scent from where she lay: a faint essence of almonds with just a mild hint of sage beneath. The almond fragrance, as her vanilla, was the aroma of the healer.

His presence was comforting.

And then it all came pressing back: Myron was dead! He had executed a suicide pact against the 'Opposites'…and the effect upon her had nearly destroyed all their kind.

Regret was unproductive, and she knew she must go on, like it or not.

As Sonia washed and dressed, she gave no inkling she knew Sky was there, but she was acutely aware of his bone-weary state. He had never left her side, even though Djura had tried repeatedly to take his place, to coax the Navajo from his vigil. Finally abandoning the effort, the Assyrian simply brought him food.

The 'Opposite' enemy was no longer present as a threat; human kind might still be, but most were oblivious to their species. Yet Sky ever the physician had stayed with her.

Perhaps his bond has become more than is required? I have not the energy to deal with that just now.

Without taking nourishment, Sonia made the jump to Sanctuary. Sky followed.

Her senses were more keenly alert now; Sonia was aware of everything when she materialized: the beauty of her surroundings, marble walls, the rainbow hues changing room by room; Jade and Rhea with Ryan and Ihor in the supply gardens; Joel far away sitting desolate before the plaque for Myron in the sunken memorial garden.

She walked to where she was going, through the many marble halls. Sky followed wearily behind, like a faithful companion mastiff that though fatigued was still loyal.

Suddenly Sonia turned about.

"Sky, go rest," she ordered gently. "I am all right."

He came visible, his face so lined with the long hours of worry, it brought tears to her eyes.

"Go, please..." she pleaded. "My balance is coming back."

He nodded, and obeyed. Sonia turned about to resume her journey.

Five minutes later, without looking behind her, she knew Djura had taken the Navajo's place. The Assyrian's scent was faint, like gunpowder: the essence of powerful defence. The man remained alert, but invisible. Even here, he would not let his guard down.

Sonia sighed. *I do not deserve such allegiance. I nearly killed them all.*

At last, she entered the sunken garden. At any other time, it would have been breathtaking...but her eyes searched for Joel alone.

When she approached, he did not turn to look at her, nor did he make room for her on the bench.

"It's your fault he's dead," he stated coldly, when at last he acknowledged her. "You had to banish him."

The words cut deep, but she refused to take all the blame; she had been there and back a dozen times.

"You wanted him punished; he chose banishment...he also made the choice to take his own life."

"You had the power to stop him."

Sonia shook her head in disbelief. "So, now you chose to believe in what I can do?"

He looked up at her as she stood over him. "It doesn't mean I accept your leadership!"

"Joel, please," Sonia begged. "Let me touch you...we need each other..."

"I can smell your lackey is with us you know. Send him away, so we can have some privacy for a change."

"Leave us, Djura...please."

They both knew when the guardian was gone.

The garden was suddenly filled with a strong odour much like chilli pepper... the 'Pure' male scent of domination...Joel's scent. Sonia realized it had always been there even in dormancy, only less invasive. It was so strong now, Sonia could feel his dislike of her imbedded deeply in its very essence."

Does he hate me that much?

"Why do you really want to touch me? Joel asked suspiciously.

Sonia knew he would reject the explanation, but she repeated it anyway. "We need each other's comfort…and balance."

"But that's not all, is it? With my strength you get the power over life and death."

"No Joel!" she disagreed. "You have it wrong! That happens because you are not joined to us."

"I'm not letting you drain my strength!"

"We go down because I must use an incompatible stamina source…"

He laughed bitterly. "So, you're saying, inevitably, the life of this species rests with me?'

"Together we are their life source…without you I am…destructive."

"Then stop doing what you're doing!"

"I can not," Sonia returned softly. "It is…like breathing…"

"And if you don't do it you go mad…or die. Oh, I know all your excuses, and here's what I say to them: So, what! We would be well rid of your control, your lies! We lived without your protection while you were down!"

She tried to correct his errant presumptions. "The enemy was no longer a threat, and the men were shielding…"

But he cut her off. "We could take care of ourselves if you would let us. When you are dead, they will come to reason," he hissed viciously. "Next time you will die."

In horror Sonia realized this brother also plotted her demise. Tears formed in her eyes.

"You would die with me," she whispered softly.

"No! I wouldn't!" he declared assuredly. "Because I will remain separate! I refuse the full joining. And when you are gone, I will start the species over, and be my own…"

He did not complete the sentence. Yet Sonia was not willing to give up on him.

"Someday, you will join us."

"It would take something real drastic for me to change my thinking."

"Someday…the balance will be in your hands, and then, you will understand."

He assumed she meant he would gain leadership, but that had not been what she meant. She referred to life itself.

"Good. Until then, I will do the work you have given me…I have nothing else left. And I'll even give you this concession: I will obey you, so we won't make waves, but…I will never be a part of your…commune."

"You really don't understand, Joel. You don't have such control. You have no idea what you are setting in motion."

"It is you who do it all! You insist on healing, breaking out more dormant…"

"Yes, and I will continue…even without your help. They have a right to a full life."

"They were just fine the way they were."

"Were you?"

Joel went silent, remembering conditions before his change, suddenly realizing without what she had done for him he would probably not even be walking on his own.

But he was not going to allow her the last word. When next he spoke, he referred to the plaque the men had put up in Myron's honour.

"They think that metal plate will bring respect for him, make-up for their lack of inclusion…"

Sonia narrowed her eyes in disagreement. Myron had rejected them, not the other way around.

"They give him credit," Joel continued. "When you and I both know all he wanted was to get even…to kill us all!"

Sonia remained silent, tears forming in her eyes. Finally, she turned and, through a film of moisture, read the small bronze sheet on the brick garden wall. It said:

In memory of the warrior Myron,
Brother to Sonia and Joel.
A loss great to their souls.
How true that is!

Without another word, Sonia transported directly from the garden back to her apartment. Djura followed shortly, taking up post upon the roof.

****

"Zane, Lance, will you come to me, please?"

Sonia's sons joined her in her apartment living room. She had spent one more night of rest; Sky was also refreshed. It was time to move forward.

"Are you better now, mom?" asked Lance with concern, and Sonia nodded.

"I want you, Zane," she said to her youngest. "To break Tyler."

"Good! About time!" Zane agreed vigorously. Tyler was still serving with the RCMP. "I hate what that boy has been exposed to in his line of work."

"Lance, you will guard while he does this."

Her eldest agreed.

"Do it at his residence rather than at the more public police station. It will be easiest that way, and...when you are finished, erase all memory of Tyler in employment records and human minds."

"That will be my pleasure," agreed Lance. "I am not particularly enamoured to cops..."

Sonia smiled, amused by his statement, understanding where it had come from. "You may use Sky as your support; I believe he is strong enough, and I of course will be his back up from here. When you are finished, bring my grandson to me."

****

Tyler was a boy again, fourteen, one year older than his brother Shawn. Like his mother, he had always been reserved, thoughtful and caring. He was a person who was there for his family when they needed help; careful at choosing friends…he would be a real benefit to the species, and now with his RCMP training he would make an excellent guardian.

Long and lean Tyler stood before Sonia, his eyes more silver than blue. His grandmother appointed Zane as his companion guardian and mentor.

After, the last and newest male member to break talked long and intimately with his cherished matriarch about many things near and dear to their hearts.

CHAPTER 35

"Grandma, how on earth did you get here all by yourself?" Jessica demanded, upon opening her door.

Sonia smiled. *By the time I leave here, Jessica will have an answer she has never bargained on.*

"Come in; sit down. I just have to take my cake out of the oven."

And by the end of today...will you even care about such things?

Sonia took a seat, waiting.

Jessica rushed back a few minutes later. "There! All done! To what do I owe this pleasant surprise?"

"Come sit," Sonia pleaded, patting the seat beside her. "I have something very important to discuss with you and I need your undivided attention."

"Okay." Jessica sat down beside her grandmother. "Kara is away at school; Wade is on an errand. I have at least an hour..."

"This will take the rest of your life..."

"Pardon me?" Jessica frowned. *Has grandma finally gone senile?* went through her mind.

Sonia almost laughed.

"I am not senile, honey," she reproved softly. "Just...this will take longer than you expect. It is very serious."

"Has something happened? Are you sick?"

"Yes...and no."

Jessica sat patiently waiting, and for her to be still was out of the ordinary.

"Do you remember that 'Alien advertising' on TV a while back?"

"Oh, that silly thing," Jessica admonished with relief. "You need not worry. They said that was all a hoax."

"It wasn't," Sonia stated bluntly. "I am one of the children they were seeking, and …you are another."

"Oh grandma," laughed Jessica. "You do let your imagination get the better of you."

"Really? Are you certain?"

Uncomfortable now, the young woman became serious. "Well, if you are, you sure don't look very alien to me."

Sonia knew her granddaughter; she was usually pretty level headed. So she took a chance.

"Sky will you show yourself?"

"Sky Hawk is with you? Oh, that's how you got here…"

The words died on her tongue as the Navajo became solid before her very eyes. Jessica gasped.

"Your true appearance, please," Sonia suggested.

Sky metamorphed from his aged human-like form, to his younger appearance, complete with the cat-like eyes.

To give her credit, Jessica did not scream; her jaw simply went slack in speechless wonderment. Finally, after staring for several seconds at the man, she turned to her grandmother.

"Either my own imagination's gotten the better of me, or you really are…" She shook her head. "Ever since dad died, and that skating party, I've wondered…I just knew something was going on."

Sonia grinned. "And that Sky is why Kara is what she is!"

Sky who was following her train of thought easily, nodded agreement.

"So, if he looks like that," asked Jessica. "What do you look like grandma?"

Sonia laughed with pleasure, and abruptly changed.

For a moment Jessica just sat silent considering Sonia.

"That bad, eh?"

"Oh, grandma!" Jessica laughed. "You are so…beautiful!" she marvelled.

After another adoring silence, she finally asked, "How come I can't do that?"

"You are dormant. That's why I've come. But we have things to discuss before we do that."

Sky interrupted. "My lady, if it is okay, I will go distant to give you privacy."

Sonia agreed silently, and he vanished.

It took half an hour to bring Jessica up to the present.

"And now, you have decisions to make," stated Sonia. "Firstly…you are married to a human. Do you want to remain dormant, or…live in disguise until he dies?"

Jessica pulled in a sharp breath, and thought about it for a while. At last, she began asking questions.

"Could we make him...like us?'

"Yes, it can be done...partly. Sky is half human. Wade could be blood healed to be the same, but..."

Jessica waited intently.

"The process is very painful...and must be his choice...not coerced."

Jessica nodded. "And what about Kara?"

"Kara is only an eighth, she will need some blood healing...brought up to at least a quarter, or half preferably...for her own safety. I believe...she is like me, a 'Leader Female'."

"You are a Leader?" she marvelled.

"Not important right now," Sonia decided, dismissing the subject. "But if you remain dormant, so must Kara."

"I can't do that to her."

"I expected that reaction."

"Grandma, does...mom know?"

"Your mother is already changed..."

"She is!" exclaimed her granddaughter excitedly. "And I never even suspected. For how long?"

"Since the night of the skating party."

"Oh! My! And aunty Jade?"

"Even before that."

Excitedly, Jessica proclaimed, "Me too!"

"Are you certain? You will have to hide it from Wade, and Kara must remain dormant for the time being."

"Anyway, you want it grandma…please?"

"Okay, give me your hands…"

****

Fifteen minutes later the species had another female: a blond with long straight hair, a great figure, and eyes one amethyst, the other blue, just like her mother. But now Jessica was only fifteen.

"I wouldn't let Wade see you like this," cautioned Sonia.

"Oh, I know. I know…but I wish I could…"

"Jessica…it is imperative he makes his own decision…"

Jessica shook her head, almost in tears. "What if he'd rather not be married to an alien, grandma?"

"I can not dictate in this. Your life together is your responsibility. But, know this, I see in his mind an undying love for you…"

"Oh, grandma. I couldn't bear it if he stopped loving me."

"Give him privacy, honey. Try not to look into his thoughts…"

Jessica sighed. "I should have realized…thought this through more."

"I can reverse it, if you wish?"

Her granddaughter re-examined the facts both possible and probable, then shook her head determinedly. "No, grandma, that would leave Kara in limbo…until after we die. I can't do that to her."

Sonia nodded.

"So…now! Go surprise your momma!"

Jessica giggled, and jumped to her feet, laughing excitedly, then stopped.

"You sure you're all right, gran?" she asked in concern.

"I'll just sit here a while. Sky will be with me."

Jessica vanished immediately.

Sonia laid her head against the sofa in relief, closing her eyes.

Sky came visible. "This one was easier?"

Sonia just smiled, without opening her eyes.

"Two more to go," she proclaimed pleasantly.

CHAPTER 36

Ihor and Ryan were helping Rhea move into Jade's home. Sonia found the four resting and chatting amiably over soft drinks in the living room.

"Hi mom," Jade greeted, even before Sonia came visible.

Sonia smiled at her daughter's sense of her presence before she made herself known. She found it refreshing that both women were so relaxed.

Ihor stood up to give Sonia his seat; so did Ryan.

"All settled in?" Sonia asked, dropping between her girls.

Rhea immediately reprimanded herself. "I don't know why I'm even moving here? If it wasn't for Nadia, we could all be at Sanctuary."

"The guys are always here anyway," Jade agreed.

"Perhaps, we could do something about that today," offered Sonia.

Jade's excitement was evident. "Really, mom?"

Perturbed, Rhea commented. "Well! Then we did all that work for nothing."

"It will be simple to transfer from here," Ihor reassured. "The work was never hard."

"Let's not get ahead of ourselves," cautioned Sonia. "Will you three men please give me a moment alone with my daughters?"

Sky, Ryan and Ihor vanished, but Sonia knew none would go far.

Once the men were gone, Sonia came right to the point. "We only have two more dormant to break." She turned to her oldest. "Jade, I was thinking, as soon as Nadia gets home this afternoon, you and Rhea could do it."

"She should be here within the hour," Jade offered. "Are you sure it's not too soon, mom? You only just did Jessica."

"Believe me, I would wait a little longer if we had time. But it is urgent we do this now."

Sky's unexpected thought warning interrupted abruptly. "Joel comes!"

"Make no effort to intercept him, Sky," Sonia returned in equal silent communiqué. She then turned to her daughters.

"We will have to continue this later…"

Before she could say more, Joel appeared in the doorway.

"Girls will you give us a moment, please?"

"Sure." Both women jumped up in willing agreement. "We'll just go outside, and visit the guys."

From the bench-swing on the front porch, Ryan watched the road. When Jade formed quietly beside him, he turned. She looked at him making a face of disapproval, and he shook his head in evident agreement with her thoughts. Both were dreading what was about to happen inside.

Gently, the guardian placed his arm about his female, preparing to wait out the storm brewing between brother and sister.

****

Ihor stood leaning against the house wall in the back yard. Rhea joined him. As she slipped beneath his arm, he encircled her shoulders. They stood there, quietly comfortable with each other, gazing at the beauty of newly budding tulips and open daffodils.

****

Above, on the roof peak, one leg on either side of the ridge, Sky observed those below, then finally raised his eyes to scan the houses in the distance.

The four below are already coupling, he thought. *At least that is something good to look forward to. Considering Joel's unscheduled appearance, it does not bode well for the future. Joel never seeks Sonia unless he has a grievance.*

Sky had studied the 'Pure' male since his brother had died, and noted his animosity toward his sister. Even though Joel pretended to be at peace with Sonia, even now as he seemed amiable, their being together made the room zap with opposing energy.

Despite Sonia's brave front, and the fact she went on with the tasks at hand on her own, it was sensed by all, these two were not as they should be. They were in obvious disagreement.

Sky realized that was not good for either the brother or the sister. They needed to be in unity to be whole. This was not even beneficial to the overall group. He feared it would all end in another death...maybe even the demise of the species itself.

As he waited for the 'Pure' male to leave, his foreboding increased, became almost palpable.

Something bad is about to happen.

****

"What, no guardian to stop me?" sneered Joel, when they found themselves unattended. "Since when are you ready to be alone with me?"

"Your sarcasm is unwarranted, Joel," Sonia returned quietly. "I thought you promised you would be nice?"

Her comment caused Joel to rethink his attitude, to make more of an effort at civility. "I came to warn you," he said as if in apology. "More of the enemy has come."

Sonia acknowledged with a slight nod, and he continued. "I guess, there must have been a second ship out beyond the solar system. When Myron exploded the first craft, the second moved in to investigate. It just took up station behind Earth's moon."

"I know," Sonia bluntly admitted. "I was aware of it before your sensors picked it up."

"You knew this before I did?" he exploded angrily. "Just what purpose do I serve then?"

Sonia ignored the outburst. "I've suspected there must be others, so I've kept an eye out…"

"Well, seeing as you're so well informed, I suggest you get your defences back up, and put the men on duty again!"

Sonia sighed, as if dealing with a petulant child. "Joel, the guardians have always been at their posts. It would be stupid to ever let our guard down. There are always more 'Opposite'. We've never lowered our guard…"

She looked at him with pity in her eyes, and gently rebuked, "If you were complete, you would know that…and you too would see before your sensors do."

****

Without another word, Joel turned angrily, and vanished. But he did not return to Technical Centre, instead he teleported to Myron's cabin in the woods.

Here, where no one could hear him but the wild life around him, he screamed out his fury, scattered and broke lamps and furnishings, until the poor puppy hid beneath the cot.

At this moment, he hated his sister with all that was within him, and knew that if he had been present with her right now, he would have gone Nova deliberately as Myron had.

But he was not ready to end his own life. He would someday take the reins of government by another means.

Two days later, when he joined Eric, the man immediately realized he had gone viral. But Joel no longer cared.

****

Aunt Rhea must have moved in, thought Nadia as she opened the door. She could hear them talking.

The young black set her books on the table in the foyer, got herself a glass of milk and a cookie from the kitchen, then went to join the women.

327

Life should be different with aunt Rhea here; maybe she will share the workload, mused Nadia. *And maybe I could finally have some alone time...a real life! Perhaps, I could even have a boyfriend, though at present there isn't much hope of that. Even my gran has better luck with men than I do!*

Entering the living room, the young lady was surprised to find the very person she had been thinking about.

"Oh! Grandma! You are here too!" And without considering how it might sound, Nadia spoke her thoughts aloud. "Did your boyfriend bring you?"

Sonia laughed delighted, not in the least offended.

"Come, sit down with us, honey..." She patted the seat of the couch between Jade and herself.

Nadia set her glass on the coffee table, stuffed the last of her cookie in her mouth, and made to take the empty end space.

"Oh, not there," Sonia objected. "Here, beside your mom. Between us."

Nadia knew better than to argue with gran. She obediently dropped into the middle seat.

"Your mother has something to show you..."

Nadia turned to Jade, who immediately took her hands in her own...

****

When the change was complete, Sonia quietly gave an order. "Sky, tell their guardians it is safe to return."

Nadia quickly rose to her feet, backing toward the corner of the room, suddenly extremely shy. She had grown up with very little male influence, and the fact that these men were coming to view her overwhelmed and filled her with trepidation.

Will the men be gentle like Wade...or rough and commanding as Uncle Ivan, who never took kindly to my personality?

She just wanted to hide away in some wall.

Sky grew solid before their eyes, a much younger looking man than the one she had seen previously. And with him were three other giants; their names were immediately supplied to her mind: Ryan, whom she had seen often with her mother, though definitely younger, taller and more handsome; then Ihor, aunt Rhea's guardian...but the smaller one, Chad...

Immediate attraction caused her body shiver as Nadia viewed the Ethiopian teen for the first time. She knew instantly she was meant for him. The future was filled with promise: she would never again be the only black at the family gatherings.

And he likes me, too!

✳✳✳✳

Thirteen-year-old Chad's mind had gone blank at the sight of this breath-taking beauty: tall and slim, with silken caramel skin, long glossy spiral black curls down her back, and eyes of chocolate with a slit in gold.

She was beautiful before, the boy marvelled. *But now...*

He would love her to his dying day...now, he just had to convince her he was the only one for her.

Nadia had the eyes of the musical genius breed, and…the eleven-year-old gave off the most captivating strawberry scent when she was fearful.

His male protective instinct overwhelmed the young man.

****

No longer would Chad's grief for his missing twin be worrisome. It had ceased to be a factor.

CHAPTER 37

Sonia was preoccupied, her eyes closed, as she rested in the recliner. It would appear to any human, were they to observe her, that she was dozing, but her guardian on the flat roof of the building knew differently. She was watching the enemy, considering and analyzing their every move, intent on finding the weakness in their defences.

"My Lady?" Sonia came alert at Sky's enquiry. "Wade intends to see you. He is at the front door of the building at this very moment."

"Let him through, Sky. He means me no harm, and...something good will come of this. Remain at the perimeter, but I may need you later. Alert Djura to join you."

"Yes, my Lady."

When the phone rang, Sonia buzzed Jessica's husband in, meeting him at her suite door in her old lady guise.

"Well, to what do I owe this unexpected visit?" asked Sonia of Wade. "Come sit down."

Wade made his way to the sofa obviously upset. "Grandma..." Sonia smiled at his use of the term, as if she was blood to him as she was to her granddaughter. He had always been considerate. "Jessica won't tell me anything, but I know...something's wrong!"

Sonia sat down beside him on the sofa.

"And...I've got this feeling you're the only one who will tell me what it is." Wade rushed on. "It was after your last visit, she started acting so strange."

Sonia came bluntly to the point. "Do you love her?"

"With all my heart," he declared with fervour, tears in his eyes. "What's wrong with her grandma?"

"Would you love her if she was not…as she is now? Would you do anything to remain with her?"

"Definitely! Oh, don't tell me she wants to leave me…"

Sonia shook her head. "She loves you with all her heart."

"Then what's wrong?" he wailed. "Is she sick? I've tried everything to get her to talk. She starts crying all the time, and leaves the house. She spends more and more time away."

Sonia smiled. *This is getting out of hand. As I expected it would be, the secret is too hard for Jessica to keep. But she has done well to last this long.*

"If you really must know, I will show you what is wrong, and what is…required."

Sonia knew if he rejected, she could always erase the memory again.

Gently she reached out and touched Wade's arm. Her eyes went purple and for a second shock ·registered in the man's eyes, but he steeled himself as if expecting the worst, yet prepared himself to pay the cost. "See…" Sonia offered softly.

****

In an instant the human had all the facts. Sonia moved her hand back to her lap and let him process what she had transferred to his mind. Wade had a decision to make, and she was not going to rush him or force.

"I am not afraid to go through the pain," he said at last. "I meant what I said. I will do anything to stay with my wife and daughter. I could not bear to watch them suffer when I can stop it so easily."

"Are you certain? This is a great sacrifice for you. You will not be the way you were born, no contact with humans will be the same…"

"I can't say I won't miss it but my life is in my wife…my child. To realize she would make the sacrifice to live in a lesser state, just for me…" He came near to breaking down. "I am as sure that I want this as I know that I love Jessica. What I know now only increases my fondness for her. How do we do this?"

"You want me to do it now? You don't wish to consider longer?"

"If I think too deeply, I might lose courage. I'm not brave with pain. Please do it now."

Sonia nodded sadly. "I would never allow your suffering…the pain is for me…"

He frowned. "I understood it would hurt me."

"No, I will prevent that…"

"I want it done, but…not at your expense…"

"Good." As she reached for his hands, Wade's last thought was wonder, and Sonia smiled.

He will make a good guardian. Well worth the extreme agony.

∗∗∗∗

Upon awakening the new sixteen-year-old knew exactly how much it had cost Sonia...had drained from all of the species, and he cringed at the thought of the self-sacrifice paid to include him in their race.

How will I ever repay them?

Fifteen-year-old Jessica appeared at Wade's elbow. He slipped his arm about her shoulders as she cuddled beneath his arm. Wade dropped his head; Jessica raised her face toward his. Their lips met.

The aroma of fresh baking filled the air...the combined 'pair scent' of the species' first couple.

∗∗∗∗

His eyes are blue, his hair blond, and he stands just a few inches taller than Jessica, but he is adorable, thought Sonia, *even if he is the shortest of my guardians.*

Although he still might grow; after all he is only sixteen.

Our first pair of the species is sooo very young...

Even Jessica and Wade realize self-denial will be called for now that they are in the amalgamation. They are considerate of the well-being and stability of the others, intend abstinence until complete safety is a guarantee.

CHAPTER 38

Wade and Jessica were waiting for Sonia when she materialized with her guardians Sky and Djura. They had remained in human-like appearance even in their home for Kara's sake, until Sonia recovered and...for her to give the word. It had been two long, hard weeks.

But the waiting would be over presently, and that was all that mattered.

Sonia sat down on the sofa. The two guardians remained invisible.

"Call Kara," Sonia suggested.

****

The young lady in question had recently arrived home from school. In her room, Kara had just put away all her books and papers. For some unknown reason she suspected never to return to classes and had decided not to bother with the homework.

Feeling both dejected and excited, she now lay on her bed expectantly waiting for something to happen.

"Kara, will you come out here?" Jessica called.

When Kara entered the family room and saw Sonia, the young girl was the first to speak.

"I know what's going to happen, and I'm not afraid."

Jessica looked surprised; Sonia smiled softly.

"I know what my great-gran is. We are already connected." Jessica's jaw dropped in shock.

335

"You've thought you were hiding for weeks, but I've known something was up all along. Did you think I wouldn't notice a difference?"

Wade shook his head, and grinned.

"I know great-gran loves me and would never do anything to hurt me. I know she can do amazing things...I'm not afraid to...transform."

Sonia laughed. "Come here, dear." She held out her hands.

****

"She will probably have little memory of her time as a dormant," Jessica reasoned, underestimating her own offspring. "After all, she is so very young."

The little girl on the sofa opened her eyes. The last thing she recalled was falling asleep as Sonia said, "I'll just cause drowsiness first. It will be easiest for her."

There is suddenly an enormous amount of information in my brain, more knowledge than I can immediately sort out, plus twenty other people's thoughts are all rattling around in there as well.

Instinctively, Kara closed out all but the surface thoughts of those present in the room. It wasn't really that hard; it came naturally.

"I haven't lost any memories," she stated bluntly, and all eyes turned her way. "Just because I'm only five, doesn't mean I don't remember! I can still see the time when great-gran was holding my tongue in her hand."

"She's unbalanced!" Jessica declared in horror.

Sonia laughed. "Now, that's an encounter that will be immortalized forever, right Kara?"

Suddenly great-gran let them all see the humiliating episode, and Kara's cheeks went bright pink.

Kara sat up, and swung her feet over the sofa edge. "I thought you said not to tell, great-gran?" Kara reproved indignantly. "I'm…ashamed. I was so bad!"

Sonia grinned. "We will all help you…be better. Okay?"

The five-year-old bounced up from the couch excitedly. "Now, can we all go to Sanctuary?"

"As soon as everything can be transported," Sonia agreed.

Kara turned amethyst eyes toward her mother, her long straight blond hair swaying behind her. "Can I go before that?"

Behind her back, Sonia nodded approval.

"Your guardian will take you," Jessica agreed.

That was when Ram appeared. Kara turned to survey him.

He stood two and a half feet taller than her four feet, his skin like a dark tan, with jet black, straight hair. His eyes were a chocolate brown with a black slit that could hardly be seen unless you looked closer.

Kara did not mind going with him at all.

Now he is protection!

CHAPTER 39

Sanctuary had been built inside two connecting mountains with the fields in the valley between, all under a dome of 'Keeper' security. Only their species and those with them could transport in or out...unless, of course, that vanguard was disabled.

When Sonia arrived in her new home, new sights, scents and feelings bombarded her senses. The marvels of the complex would have to wait however. Sonia was so used to keeping track of everyone, her main concern now was that all in her care were safe.

With her heightened mental awareness, she located each individual: Nadia sat with Chad in the sunken garden; Kara was playing chess with Ram in the common room. Marcel was forming stone serving plates, while Wade and Jessica artistically arranged fruit upon each as he made them.

Of course, where but in the kitchens would my granddaughter be the most comfortable?

Lance and Zane were playing baseball with Shawn and Tyler. Ihor and Ryan had joined in, while Rhea and Jade shouted encouragement from lawn chairs on the sidelines. The ball field lay somewhere in the valley surrounded by fence to keep at bay animal intrusion.

Eric was with Joel in Technical Centre, always monitoring for trouble, and somewhere way off, Chi and Djura were standing in a hallway discussing a security failure.

No one seemed to have noticed Sonia had finally put in an appearance.

Beside her, Sky chuckled. "It appears they all are too busy to greet their illustrious leader," he observed with amusement.

"Perhaps it is better that way," Sonia decided. "I've never wanted special treatment. I just want to be treated like any other."

In view of that, Sky queried, "Would you prefer I leave you on your own then?"

Sonia considered a moment. "Yes, you go," she agreed. "Allow me time to explore on my own."

"Your quarters are to the left, up ahead."

Even though she had made the choice herself, the moment Sky vanished, for a second Sonia felt abandoned. This was the first time since the meeting that had began it all that she was without a guardian. She had grown used to it.

Now, being alone felt...disconcerting.

But the lack of companionship soon became a non-issue. Her first pleasant surprise was her own private apartments.

A dim light filled the space as she entered, glowing from ceiling and the onyx walls. These were of cream marbled with mauve. Walking through the bed chamber, Sonia noted the sleeping couch: long and wide; soft and inviting, covered by a silken coverlet of cream with pink and mauve carnations and green leaves patterned across the flat surface, layers of ruffles hanging in tiers at the sides. The temptation was strong to use it immediately.

But Sonia gazed about to take in the rest of the room instead. The guardians had disposed of any unnecessary furnishings while moving her, but many of her treasured mementos and knick-knacks were on inset stone shelves along the walls.

She turned to the room beyond, where the floor dropped six inches leading in a stepped gradual slope to a huge sunken marble tub. Even now, it flowed with bubbling water piped directly from hot springs deep beneath the caverns.

The bath water looked so inviting Sonia immediately shed her clothing and stepped into it, her exploring totally forgotten for the moment.

The cares of the past months soon washed away as she lay soaking in the suds. An hour later, she sighed regretfully when the water having cooled, the tub began to empty on its own.

She dressed by mere thought: choosing a pair of jeans and a blue blouse, with ruffles about the neck and as sleeves. The clothing appeared on her body as she willed it.

Once again, out in the grey marble hallways, each sectioned panel took on the familiar light-glow, illuminating her path as she walked.

Sonia soon found the different rooms: Jade's was emerald green; Rhea's blue; Nadia's quarters turquoise, each owner's chamber done in their favourite colour, the shelves lined with personal cherished memories: dried flowers, ornate boxes, pictures.

The next chamber was larger and of pink quartz. Jessica and Wade had been given a family unit with a small anti-room for Kara.

Their bedroom was 'Keeper' insulated which meant the couple could go separate from the completeness of the species and go private, should they choose.

Her great granddaughter's room was done in Jade marble and the inset ledges were lined with trinkets, porcelain ethnic human dolls, and...one in the likeness of their species.

Ram made that one for her!

Every chamber she had visited had been prepared lovingly for its owner by their guardian, decorated in suitable colours and the chosen treasures carefully placed upon the shelves.

The last one was no exception.

Joel's rooms were in travertine, a dark rust stone, and upon his shelves were his bowling trophies, framed honour awards and old family portraits: one of their parents on their wedding day, another of Sonia as a baby, and...one of Myron as a young boy, holding a treasured fire truck.

Sonia turned away near to tears at the sight of that picture, the long-forgotten memory it evoked slamming home the loss once again.

He was so proud of his gift that Christmas!

Rather than let grief take over, Sonia hurriedly returned to the outer corridor.

Some distance farther on she found a monstrous cavern. This was the men's dorm.

A hallway, some four feet wide and about one hundred sixty long, stretched alongside smaller rooms on either side, seven cells to a side, each twenty feet square. In the empty wall between the

341

two farther most cubicles, she could see a doorway, which she realized led to the male showers.

She did not go into the huge enclosure, so as not to invade the men's privacy, but from where she stood, Sonia could see each chamber was fashioned much the same as those she had already viewed, with the owner's favourite coloured stone, and the display shelves holding mementoes, and a comfortable sleeping cot. She could only see into the cell nearest: Djura's walls were of marbled grey and black granite.

Sonia turned and continued on in her exploration. Proceeding at last through one final door, the only one with a door, she emerged into sunlight.

And immediately realized she had come out at the wrong end of the complex.

****

Before her lay the whole valley, and the rope bridge in front of her led down across the river and over to the far side gardens.

On her side, fields stretched for miles: barley, oats, wheat, corn, and sugar beets, running parallel with the bridge, and way at the farther most end were what appeared to be small spice plots swaying in the wind, down in the shadow of a second mountain. A tiny stone bridge could be seen from this distance, spanning the space between the two peaks, and Sonia knew that was where she should have been.

A thundering waterfall dropped from the face of that far mountain, part of which disappeared inside the rocky wall at one point reappearing just above and to the right of the bridge, then descending in lesser force to a fish filled lake at its foot. Eventually, this body of water became a river that meandered her direction through the length of the valley and under the rope bridge at her side.

On the opposite bank a path led from this bridge through small pools of Chinese vegetables and rice paddies, then disappeared into the first of four vegetable patches, each surrounded on three sides by trees of every kind of fruit and nuts imaginable. At the farther most distance on that side was the baseball diamond, empty now, surrounded completely by fields of flowers, dotted here and there with small beehives.

Ihor got his wish!

And at the outer limits behind all this on all sides, back against the two joined mountains, the gardens and the fields were the fenced pastures, divided to keep wild and domestic apart. In one area Sonia could see milk cows; one area held poultry; another pig barns.

All this is 'Keeper' maintained. And it is a good thing, too. My guardians would work themselves to death if they were required to do all this.

Rather than traverse the path all the way back, Sonia simply chose to teleport to the stone bridge beside the waterfall. Behind the rushing sheet of water, she discovered the entrance to the second set of mountain caverns.

****

Once inside again, she found a short hall; a few steps and she was in the common room. The ceiling glowed when Sonia entered, just as it had in the many bedrooms and the corridors.

The chamber was empty, Ram and Kara having vacated the premises ages ago.

As Sonia gazed about, it took her breath away.

Marcel you are a genius! she thought, as she studied the water scene.

Against the back wall was the vanishing waterfall, gently cascading over the vertical marble obstacle, the spray causing rainbows in the air near the ceiling as it found its way through to the outside world.

Of course, there is an unseen barrier between it and the rest of the room, to prevent moisture damage to the treasures it contains.

Still the water-cooled the air considerably, making the space almost like an air-conditioned room.

Sonia turned to take in the rest of the common area. Across from the picturesque fall, on all three of the other mint green marble walls, ledges were inset from floor to the twenty-foot high ceiling. They held an extensive library: thousands of books in many languages and genres, the collections saved by the diverse and multi-cultural residents now residing here. Some had even belonged to Sonia; cherished works she had collected over the years.

Beneath this vast compilation, lamps stood on tables of black granite, beside invitingly comfortable darker green chairs and benches of cream and rust marbled onyx. On a stand to the right of the doorway she had entered by, stood a black and cream onyx chess set, sitting on a stone board of rust and cream squares, just inviting you to play. In another corner near the feature wall, stood exercise equipment.

The space is multi-purpose, Sonia decided. *It is designed to suit everyone.*

She felt remorse as she left the beckoning rest area.

Sonia continued through a door to her right, and entered a different corridor. That was when she discovered they had prepared a supplementary entertainment: a roller rink.

Sonia chuckled to herself.

When she entered the doorway, she saw a space resembling that of an open-air roller coaster pathway minus the tracks, its descending and rising course travelling all around the circular centre court, which held a revolving carousel of benches. Overhead lights blinked in multi-colours causing the appearance of stars on the subjects partaking of the past time.

Sonia could visualize the enclosure also as an ice rink, should anyone be inclined to transform the stone floor.

Sky too has gotten his wish!

Leaving that amusement plausibility behind, she moved on, and came upon a large banquet hall. Here at last she found evidence someone else was actually in this dream residence.

As with the other rooms, the ceiling once again began to glow at her entrance, but this one was surreal, presenting a likeness to the midnight sky. Tiny lights resembling stars winked back at her.

Turning to the left of the door, Sonia noticed the walls were all done in mini-murals depicting the history of the species. The first panel was set so you saw it the moment you stepped in.

Set against a blue-black star-studded background, it was a battle scene above a planet where enemy ships hovered over the surface shooting streaks of blue, white and red toward adults fleeing with babes in their arms.

Upon seeing this, no human would understand the significance...

But it brought tears to Sonia's eyes.

So real! The terror on the faces could almost be felt!

Who is this artist? Marcel? It's as if he was there!

Almost reverently, Sonia moved on around the walls.

Each scene was encased in a five-foot circle set against the blue-black wall: here was Sky at a campfire before his change; there Ihor in the market gardens of his childhood, and here a tiny girl was climbing a ladder up to a shingled roof top, the space between lower story and roof opened to the air, the child seemingly suspended in the space between.

Sonia gasped.

That is me!

She had told Djura...

Did all the guardians have a part to play in this memorial?

Here was one of Sky on the flat roof of her apartment building; Zane's healing was in another frame; and a different one showed Jade in a wheel chair. One was of the skating party at Christmas; all brought back poignant memories.

They have made a 'Memory Wall'!

The last wall, and the space to the right of the entrance door was empty...waiting for the future events to be recorded.

Sonia looked away her eyes bright with unshed tears. Sighing she took in the furnishings in the room. Against the farther most wall stood a huge black granite table shaped like an inverted horseshoe. Place settings were already set out, ten on the long side against the wall behind, six on the inside, the smaller side.

Across the open end of the main table sat a second small straight table of the same black granite; it had been placed at such a position as to block quick entry from the hall. On this were the remaining five place settings. The backs of those sitting there would be to the door leading out into the corridor, but that did not mean they would be unaware if an intruder entered.

I know what this set up is; it is called the 'protection circle'! Our species has done it this way since the beginnings of our existence.

The inner circle was meant for the females; in the far past there had been enough to fill all the inside seats, but as it stood now, Sonia would be seated in the direct centre of the larger table, the youngest females beside her: Kara at her right; Nadia to the left. And beside Nadia would be her mother, Jade; while next to Kara would be her grandmother Rhea and Jessica her mother. Across from each would normally be their pairs, but in this case their

347

guardians would be seated opposite them. At each end of the male side would be the sons and grandsons, in this case Shawn and Tyler would place next to Jessica's pair, Wade, and Zane and Lance would be seated at the opposite end. If they had been paired their partners would have been across from them on the female side.

By the entry at the straight table, would be the early defence should the enemy surprise at a meal: Djura, Marcel, and Joel at centre here, being the only 'Pure' male, then Eric and Chi. Having no pairs either, they also would eat the meal alone, and out of courtesy to the 'Leader Female' would face into the room.

This way had there been a full compliment of females, males would surround them all. Even should an invader transport into the centre, the guardians by the door would be aware first and defend. All the most treasured women and children were secure; thus, it was considered a 'Protection Shield'.

****

It suddenly dawned on Sonia she had happened upon a secret; she had spoiled a surprise. This room was decorated beyond the norm, not simply set up for a common meal.

The tables had centrepieces of beautiful flower arrangements; napkins were placed beneath the eating utensils; above, the upper walls were bedecked with colourful ribbons of streamers, and in each corner hung triple silver Chinese lanterns, each descending one smaller than the one above.

Wisely, Sonia quickly vacated the chamber should someone discover she had been there or come upon her early. It was silly, yes; with the common mind between the species they would soon realize anyway…but for now, she would try to let them surprise her.

As she continued down the passageway, and rounded a corner, she came upon a fork, finally recognizing a place she had been before.

She had travelled this way the time she had come to talk with Joel. The corridor to the left led to the kitchens, the one on the right to the sunken garden. Her tour was complete.

It had been so pleasant to wander in unattended safety, without fear of attack, relieved even of concern for the well-being of the others…all cares forgotten. This indeed was a Sanctuary…even for her.

She came at the last into the memorial garden, stepped down to the nearest of the three intersecting paths, moved past Asa's statue, making her way to the cast iron bench across from the short brick memorial wall that held her brother's plaque.

It was here Sky found her resting a half hour later, contemplating the past…as well as a future yet to unfold.

****

"My lady?" The guardian's voice was hesitant, as if he was reluctant to break into her reflections.

Sonia looked up.

"The feast is near prepared. They will soon expect you."

She sighed.

"I suppose I should change and freshen up? Perhaps, if you can give me fifteen minutes?"

"I will come for you at that time."

"Guardian protection is no longer needed as we are within Sanctuary," Sonia reminded. "Are you perhaps volunteering as escort without being obliged?"

"Indeed, my Lady." He chuckled. "May I accompany as a friend, and…trusted confidant?"

"I would like that."

CHAPTER 40

True to his word, Sky appeared at her chambers some fifteen minutes later.

Sonia was ready. She had arranged her curls back from her face, taking special care to leave slim spirals just front of each ear and another dropping across the forehead on the left.

Choosing a floor length gown of chiffon with a shaped fit, a halter neckline, and a tiered ruffled skirt in two shades of dusty rose; she had accented it with a simple small pendant of gold with a mauve stone, and matching drop earrings. Her feet were shod in flat rose-coloured slippers.

Sonia greeted her escort at the door. Sky too had donned festive apparel: soft tan deerskin leggings and matching over shirt that came just below the hips, with a beaded belt at his waist. He also wore mid-calf moccasins.

At seven foot plus, he appeared pure Navajo; formidable at any other time, but Sonia knew his spirit to be gentle. His eyes always gave him away.

She smiled.

He too was appraising her. His attention strayed to the curves accentuated by the dress. The cerulean eyes lifted; the rust brown slit narrowed.

Suddenly shy, uncertain at his scrutiny, Sonia needed reassurance.

"Is my attire… appropriate?"

He grinned. "Indeed," Sky proclaimed in a low, husky voice. "You are breathtaking, as always, Sonia."

His daring familiarity caught her off guard; it was unlike him.

"Only one thing is missing," he added.

Sonia frowned, puzzled.

What have I missed?

Sky reached out to touch her hair, and she permitted it. Then she felt what he was doing there.

A wreath of dusty rose carnations formed just back behind her ears and across the crown of her head.

The sensual act made her body tingle.

"There," he said softly. "Now, you are perfect."

Sonia dropped her eyes, blushing.

The male guardian held out his arm. "Shall we?"

When she accepted his offer, she was trembling; he pretended not to notice.

****

They materialized in the direct centre of the tables. Chi was the first-person Sonia noticed, at the edge of the doorway table. He also had dressed in ethnic costume, wearing a maroon Hanfu, the traditional Chinese silk robe, with white socks and black cloth shoes. He too was proud of his mixed-race heritage.

Sky slowly turned Sonia, as if formally presenting her to all guests. The guardians of the back table Eric, Joel, Marcel and Djura were all smiling as if the honour of her presence were a special occasion. Amazingly, even Joel had pride and approval in his eyes.

They turned one last step, to face forward.

Like a colourful rainbow, standing sideways to meet her Sonia's daughters, granddaughters and great granddaughter stood in soft shades: Jade, with eyes the colour of her name, in shimmering silver grey, her daughter Nadia, the dark beauty of the family, in wine. An empty chair waited in the middle, and beside it, fair young Kara in canary yellow, her grandmother Rhea, with the copper tresses, in pale emerald green, and blond Jessica, her mother, in cerulean blue at the end. Beyond these were their guardians, Sonia's sons and her grandson's; all males were in formal or traditional attire as well.

Sky seated Sonia almost reverently, then made his way to the back of the table and sat down opposite her as the rest of the community took their seats.

Sonia sighed in relief. *Perhaps now that pomp and ceremony is over, I can relax.*

The room filled with fond soft chuckles, as her subjects read the unguarded thought.

Nadia, beside her, comforted. "I understand grandma. I don't like the centre of attention either."

After that, formality disappeared, and they were all like one big family.

****

Bowls of fruit, platters of meats and delicacies from the various countries represented, passed to you when you wished. No one served them; willed thought was all that was required, and conversation flowed as freely as the food and drink. With the dark ceiling above and the stars winking from it, they felt like they picnicked beneath the night skies.

For so long their species had been hunted by night, forced to hide during the hours of darkness because the glimmer of their presence was more evident with the absence of sunlight. Here inside, they were safe even in a darkened room, and though it was only an illusion, they seemed free.

Sonia gazed about. Their being all together like this made the evidence more obvious; each member was gleaming…literally. A shadow of light-glow surrounded each figure. No wonder in the light, they were not visible to humans!

Little Kara turned to her great grandmother. "Great-gran you hold our memory history," she stated, as if it were not already common knowledge. "Do we…our species have a name?"

Sonia laughed. "Of course we do, little one. The Greeks of Earth had a special name for us."

Marcel came alert. "We were seen on the Earth back in the past?"

Sonia turned slightly in her chair to answer him, as he sat behind by the door. "Our species used to visit, but they were only actually visible by night."

"And their name for us?" he quizzed.

"It was 'Aopato Auta'."

"Ah!" Marcel exclaimed in wonder. "That means 'Invisible ones'! I have heard legends…"

"Great-gran?" interrupted Kara in puzzlement. "We can only see each other?"

Sonia turned back to the young girl. "When I first changed, I thought it strange when the humans acted as if I wasn't there. I quickly discovered that I had to make them see me…but it is wisest to not let them see your real eyes. For some reason they are very frightened by their unusual appearance."

"Because they think of cats," Kara reasoned. "Are we not deceiving them? You said to always be honest."

"True," Sonia agreed. "But, when we do it so as not to harm them, it is different."

"So that's okay? What about when we go about disguised?"

"We do that for our safety. It is my belief their fear would cause them to harm us. We are so much taller than most of them."

"Have they harmed our kind in the past?" asked Tyler.

"They have misunderstood our intentions, viewed what we have done as a threat rather than helpful, and yes…they did do us a great deal of harm."

"How?" Wade was the one posing this question. "What weapon could humanity possibly have that could harm or kill us?"

"We are not invincible, Wade," Sonia stated with sadness. "They attacked when our people were most vulnerable, as they were healing. To touch us at such a time throws us off balance; it is deadly."

"Maybe, they didn't mean to hurt us," Kara defended in a small frightened voice.

"The first time was accidental, but when they discovered they could kill us that way…they purposely used it like a weapon against those who were healing their injuries."

"Is that why we erased all memories of us?" Kara asked.

Sonia nodded solemnly. "Now we heal in secret…and always with pair balance and a guardian protector."

****

Some time later, when everyone had eaten their fill, and the tables had cleared of food and dishes, they remained talking in easy conversation. Sonia was feeling relaxed, happy, and content. Her family was about her, everyone safe.

Then a question from Zane changed all that. "So, mom, what do we do next?"

The room around them went silent; everyone wanted that answer, and awaited her response.

But before she could give it, a sudden, unexpected flash-forward vision shocked Sonia into absolute dread. Her emotions rocked, then plummeted; depression flood over her.

Foreboding invaded the room, as the others sensed the rapid threatening change in their leader. Like an infection, it spread to them all.

Sonia knew she must not let them see what she had just received…she must not permit them access to the terror it instilled in her…the knowledge had been for her alone. She only must bear it.

Being together like this is too close proximity. Each individual feels the other. I dropped my guard in my comfort, and it went far too low. I could not

356

close my mind quickly enough...and now Kara too has sensed something.

****

Fortunately, Kara was still too innocent to realize the full import of her vision. To her credit, the young girl kept her head. The only thing she was certain of, was that her great-gran had gone emotionally unstable; Sonia needed balance. Kara's instinct was pure reflex action.

In this case, close quarters became a benefit.

Little Kara reached out and touched her great-grandmother gently, actually merely to reassure. But that simple act caused an effect that was phenomenal.

A balance beam of pure blue light zapped across the two 'Leader Females', then from there went both ways to the females: from Sonia to Nadia and Jade on the one side; from Kara to Rhea, then Jessica on the other. When the spark hit the paired couple, it turned to a white light as it arced across to the male side through Wade, again travelling both directions: Wade to Shawn and Tyler, and the opposite direction to Ihor, Ram, Sky, Chad, Ryan, Zane and ending at Lance. Here at both ends of the large table of males, the white static jumped across straight to the back table by the door: from Tyler to Chi, to Eric; on the other end from Lance to Djura and Marcel. Both lines stopped at Joel as if he had refused it.

****

The 'Pure' brother knew what had just happened, even though this had never happened before. The emotional balance had been set right purely by accident, by the contact of the two 'Leader

357

Females'. In an instant, support had been given to all because of their unity. The 'Leader Female' in waiting even though she was still so young, in conjunction with the serving 'Leader Female', had corrected the cascading unbalance, giving comfort to all. It was instinctive even in an untrained such female, the first evidence of Kara's budding power.

But Joel wanted no part in such unity. He had excluded himself by choice, stopped the energy. Refused it.

I will not be a part of their joining!

The 'Pure' brother was still choosing to remain separate.

Yet, he could not ignore the evidence; their unity had just gone visible...and had obviously been beneficial...and he was shut out from that asset.

Everyone had returned to stable pleasant status, while he sat trembling, as he attempted to balance on his own. Being apart was damaging to even his physical body.

****

Sonia released the hand of the child at her side. The room went silent, less brilliant. Ignoring what had just happened, as if all had simply taken a refreshing drink from a communal cup, she sighed in resignation, and answered the question Zane had posed before their unbalance had begun.

Speaking in resolute tones, Sonia stated firmly. "We do battle...with those who insist on acting as though we are enemies."

Still fighting depression, Joel challenged sarcastically from behind her. "Haven't the 'Opposites" always been our enemies?"

Sonia did not even turn her head to acknowledge him. "Not in my eyes! They are those of our species who have gone errant; they were once of our own kind. It is wrong to kill...let alone eliminate any of our own race. To me that is like killing my own... brother."

The room went deadly quiet. The guardians had never heard this cool anger in her tone before. Even Joel did not dispute further.

Risking his mother's wrath, Zane quietly reminded Sonia. "You did say...do battle? And you also say we are to be defensive only. Which is it?"

For a moment, Sonia's mind seemed preoccupied, as if she were seeing something far away, which they were not privy to. This began to worry certain more experienced guardians.

Sky and Djura shot each a meaningful mental warning. Only once before had they seen Sonia like this, and because she had failed to take her foreknowledge seriously enough then, two men had died. It was obvious; she was choosing the opposite path this time.

The 'Leader Female' steeled herself. "We will do battle and still be non-aggressive, defensive only. We will initiate...strike the first blow."

All male heads snapped up in shock. Had they heard right?

Lance was the first to recover. "That's not defence only..."

"If we strike at their equipment, their weapons, is that not defending? They attack us with those weapons..."

Djura actually laughed, delighted at the prospect. "You are brilliant, my Lady!" he stated appreciatively. "Without their weapons, we are on even footing..."

"Do not take such pleasure in the bringing down of another," warned Sonia.

Djura's excitement died within him as she turned sideways to face him. To her, this was not a triumph, nor did she feel pleasure in the prospect of battle.

Her security chief dropped his eyes, to listen quietly.

"Until now our species' one rule was to wait for slaughter, for the 'Opposites' to attack, yet our ancestors had superior power to knock out their systems. Why do you suppose they chose that method? They were not unintelligent..."

No one came back with an answer; they knew one was not required.

"They went to their deaths, an entire race perished, all still hoping their brothers ...once their friends, would choose...and change...come back to them again, whole."

The mood in the room shifted. Everyone in the room felt the agony of the past... even Joel felt shame, realizing he was repeating the sins of his kind.

"We are only different now because some of us are part human, and...we have seen the result of friends and loved ones turned enemy..."

Djura dropped his head, feeling the sheer impact of that statement.

"We...I still hope, still want to give the 'Opposites' the chance...to come back. I believe they can."

The sadness of her heart had spread to her guardians. They were feeling ashamed.

"But...it is obvious, our methods must change. To allow things to go on as they have is unwise; to allow ourselves to be massacred is...foolishness. The 'Opposite' are so used to us doing nothing, they expect it. We are a new generation different totally yet still much the same. I have learned from the past...some of it shows wisdom, other times... stupidity."

Her audience held its breath, waiting for her next words.

"I am so very, very tired of being hunted, of living in fear. NO MORE! We will start this encounter...and it will be finished before they know what hit them."

"The 'Opposites' will not be expecting the first blow to come from us," observed Djura.

"Exactly," Sonia agreed. "And...I anticipate they will fight back when they realize we have changed tactics. As all cannot be accomplished in an instant, we will no doubt be in a skirmish for our lives. We will take casualties. However, we will still... always, maintain our non-violent approach. No 'Opposite' is to be killed or maimed."

"We seek only to eliminate the threat?" clarified Djura. "How do we do that?"

"Leave that to me?"

"And...when will we do this, my Lady?"

"I will let you know…when we are ready."

****

When the others retired, Joel did not return to his quarters. Once again, he retreated to Myron's cabin.

From a distance, he stood surveying the structure in seething wrath.

So, she would do battle, would she? She degrades these men with her very words, and they simply take it.

If I were in charge, the battle would be for real. Non-violent! That just isn't possible!

He would watch as she destroyed her own credibility.

As if the log cabin were his adversary, his sister, with all the force of his anger, he willed it to explode. Then, as early dawn broke above the trees, he watched the blaze burn.

All through the day, the hot flames licked at the logs. They crackled, fell in on themselves, and blazed higher again.

Then the rain came, cooling the steaming embers, and with that his fury.

What have I just done? Is my sister a mere animal? I once loved her!

A chastened, subdued Joel, repulsed by his own act, hunted through the rubble, found the charred remains, and buried the innocent, half-grown puppy whose only crime in life had been to be chosen. And thought of his sister as he did.

Eric said nothing, when Joel returned to his computers. But the minute he entered the other guardian knew beyond a doubt what had transpired.

Joel told himself he did not much care…yet deep down inside, the black hole was slowly swallowing his sense of reason.

CHAPTER 41

Sonia knew it would not be long now before it all began. She sat in a secluded spot, an alcove-like ledge of her own making just above the waterfall. Here she was hidden, out of the way, private. The thundering curtain of water was muffled; even bird song could be heard above it. Here time stood still, and recollection could be warded off.

She knew Sky followed her everywhere now, worried by the fact she had seen into the future again, expecting the worst. He was right to be concerned. This time these visions had rattled her beyond measure, shaken her to the very core.

There is no way to prevent the inevitable.

Sky and Djura thought they could. They had made another pact, hoping if they kept her guarded, they could prevent a repeat of last time.

How impossible that is. This will be far, far worse.

Even now, Sky sat above her and to the left on a ledge of his own, thinking her unaware of him because she was still and appeared unseeing. He waited, as she did, not for the arrival of the enemy, as he had countless times during her sojourn in senior housing, but for the future events he was yet to be made privy to.

"There you are!" Jade came visible on the log beside her.

Sonia tensed.

So, this is how it is to begin.

****

Jade sat beside her mother for long moments, looking out over the fields and gardens. The view from here was spectacular, but her mother appeared unaware, far away somewhere else in thought, and the daughter could not penetrate the mental barrier she had put in place.

Why is she so distant?

Finally, tired of being ignored, Jade broke into Sonia's reverie.

"What is wrong with you?" she asked petulantly. "Are you mad at us? Didn't you like the banquet in your honour?"

Sonia at last looked at her daughter. "The banquet was a pleasure. Sometimes, I see things I must hide from you. It does not mean, I am angry."

"So, you've seen something bad? Can you at least share it with me?"

"You will begin it…"

Jade pondered that a moment. "Well…don't hold it against me, when I haven't done it yet. I might act differently than you expect, and…what you see could be… wrong."

"I hope so."

Silence cloaked them again. Finally, Jade spoke. "What do you see, mom?"

Sonia sighed. "My death…"

****

On the ledge above, Sky came alert. Though usually considerate and deliberately inattentive, he knew this time it was necessary to eavesdrop.

365

"Are you afraid to die?" probed Jade.

"No…I am fearful of…killing."

What is this? wondered Sky.

"What on earth, mom?" Jade's annoyance was evident in her tone. "This is what has you bothered, that you'll kill some of them. I don't think anyone will blame you if one of the 'Opposites' is killed in that battle."

Sky read Sonia's unguarded thought. *Just like Jade to jump to a conclusion unthought of to this point.* Sonia glared at her daughter.

"What? Do I have to agree with your every opinion?"

"No."

"But you are leader; I know I have to obey you. And we have to do it your way."

"You have a free will. I am not going to make you."

"Aw, mom. Okay, I know what you're saying is best. All right?" Jade sighed. "But, there's something else wrong. You've been so closed up since you had this vision. Do we lose the battle? Is that what you saw?"

Sonia shook her head. "I believe we win the battle…"

"Then why are you so troubled? Something is obviously not right here. Just what exactly did you see?"

"I see the before…and beyond. I see betrayal…and our death."

Above, Sky winced.

"Our death?" Jade repeated. "But if we win the battle...death will be a long time in the future...hopefully."

"Not really... It will be...right after."

"Mom, I know your powers of precognition reach farther than my own, but...you can really see to your death?"

Sonia nodded, her attitude regretful.

Jade sat thinking, then came back with the obvious. "Well, you have to prepare Kara to replace you."

Shocked by the cold calculation of her daughter's words, Sonia made the next comment without considering the consequences.

"But...you will die also."

"I know that, mom," Jade reproached in exasperation. "But there is time for the rest of us. You are older."

"My age is not a factor in our death."

"Stop saying our! If you die, we would get past it. We would carry on."

"No, you would not! We are all interlinked as a species. When one is weakened, it affects us all!"

"We got over Myron's death," argued Jade.

"Did we? Like Chad got over the loss of his twin?"

Jade went silent. Even she had felt the empty space in Chad.

"When a leader of our species dies, it is quite different," Sonia asserted softly. "And for me to die at this time is deadly…Kara is too young to carry…"

"Okay. Then we just pick someone else."

"You fail to understand. It must be a 'Leader Female'!"

"Why? Enlighten me; you're forever keeping things from us!"

"I keep things to myself because it is too complicated to explain to you. Experience is the only means to fully comprehend."

"You are saying we aren't as smart as you?'

"No! No! But there are things beyond your abilities…and sometimes people refuse to believe what they have not had exposure to."

"So, how does this have anything to do with your death?"

"It comes too soon…I never realized other factors could bring us down this way…"

"Aw mom, you're making no sense at all. You worry too much. This is years in the future."

Sonia disagreed, and made to say so, but Jade rushing on, cut her off.

"Even if you do die, the rest of us will still continue on for a while. You act like it's the end of the species when you pass."

"It is!" Sonia stated bluntly. "The present species began with me; it also dies with me!"

Above, Sky went cold inside, suddenly understanding.

"Don't be silly," Jade reprimanded harshly.

Sonia took a deep breath, and made a more valiant attempt to make herself understood. "We are an interconnected species...symbiotic...amalgamated."

"What does that mean?" yelled Jade. She was not simply annoyed now, rebellion lurked in her tone coloured by a hint of foreboding premonition. "What are you really saying?"

Sonia narrowed her eyes in concentration. "Because you are all connected to me, unless there is another 'Leader Female' available who is able to support everyone... you will all die with me!"

Shocked, Jade stared back at her mother.

"I...I thought we were just joined by feelings...and mentally...that we simply sense each other..."

"And how do you think that is accomplished? I join us physically...the connection is maintained by the 'Leader Female'; no one else is capable of it."

"Mind, emotions...physical...like arms or legs?"

Sonia nodded. "Symbiotic! Organisms living together as one, in a beneficial relationship...our condition goes beyond any description available."

Jade blinked stupidly, then horror flooded her features. "We are really going to die when you do?" But still she made one last attempt to refute Sonia's revelation.

"But...when you cut off an arm or a leg the whole person doesn't die."

"If you cut out the heart or remove the brain…"

"Can't you set us free? You are saying when you die, you will kill us all!"

Tears formed in Sonia's eyes. "That's what I've been saying; I don't want that. But I can't release you…"

Jade's voice rose to anger pitch. "Why didn't you tell us this before we were changed? You did this to control us! You did it on purpose!"

"No," Sonia objected vehemently. "It is an automatic condition of the species. I have no control over the start of it."

"It wasn't necessary!" Jade yelled. "Uncle Joel is separate. Didn't we have a choice also?"

"You became a part of me…before you were born. Uncle Joel is 'Pure'; you are not."

'So, we had no choice? I don't believe that!"

"The nature of it can not be denied."

"When we were dormant, we wouldn't have died with you?"

"No. But now the process can not be reversed."

Beside herself at what she had learned, Jade stood up to pace the small rock shelf. Suddenly, she turned on her mother again.

"The guardians were not a part of you…Wade wasn't a part of you!"

"They each made a personal choice to join…and when they did, they willingly were amalgamated…became a part of the whole."

"But did they understand what they were getting into; did they realize it was only for the duration of your life?"

"Some did. But normally, I would have passed you all on to Kara...she is too young still to support everyone...I thought there would be more time..."

"Did the men know about Kara?"

"We did not know for certain that she was a 'Leader Female'..."

"You could have prevented this, mother! You betrayed them too!"

Sky watched Sonia's thoughts as she wavered in self-doubt. *Maybe, subconsciously, I did want only the power? I did let them down!*

"You know, with all your knowledge, mom, you are so smart you're stupid sometimes! You made this happen!"

Sonia shook her head in denial. "I didn't mean to hurt you. This is a condition of our species. I wanted to help, to save all of you!"

"Yeah, right! You sure did, didn't you?"

Jade went back to pacing. "This can't be right!" she told herself. "Somehow, you've gotten this all misconstrued. There has to be a way out of this!"

Turning venomously on her mother, Jade screamed with frustrated fear. "You're killing your grandchildren and great-granddaughter; did you think of that?"

Sonia's eyes filled with tears; quietly she closed her mind from them all, but not quickly enough to block out Jade's last insult.

"Who made you god, anyway?"

Jade vanished from the ledge; anger, rebellion and fear hung in the air behind her.

On the shelf above, Sky did not dare move. He was too outraged and shaken by what had just transpired, but he wanted to yell after the female, to defend this good woman whose only crime was protecting her family.

Then he remembered Sonia's first words, when asked what she had seen: 'I see the before…and beyond. I see betrayal…'

And unexpectedly, the words made perfect sense to him now.

****

Sky was witnessing it everywhere; every mind in doubt, in turmoil: the men, Sonia's sons, even her grandchildren. Ever since Sonia had revealed their symbiotic nature to Jade, the word had spread like wild fire, and along with it fear, discontent and mistrust.

Some of the men were simply agreeing with the women, too cowardly to brave an argument, preferring peace with those they had grown fond of. But others outright doubted Sonia's leadership ability, going along with Joel's thought as he had often previously pointed out. Also, because Joel had safely remained separate, the sons and grandsons also wondered why they could not also break away to save themselves. It was as if the malady affecting Joel had spread across the species to everyone else, and the 'Pure' brother was not hesitant to take full advantage of the situation.

All had previously been raised as independent individuals, taught that their welfare depended upon their own actions. To find their lives were hinged upon, interlinked so closely with the life force of another, was not only disconcerting, but seemed to go against the collective giant ego.

Sky could not believe how disloyal they had all become; their trust had gone out the window. It tore at his very emotional fibre.

Why is this concept so hard to accept? How can they all forget where they were just months before, the hurts of their before-life? With great personal suffering, Sonia healed many of them, yet they have seemingly forgotten. What does it matter now, that she holds our lives bonded to hers as a result?

Their dislike of the reality would not make it less a fact.

As Sky walked through halls, he heard Jade begin many a choleric discussion. Her lead in question was always the same: "Who put mom in charge, anyway?" But instead of the replies of defence that should have been, there was evasion. And Jade's come back, if there was resistance, was ever the same: "I never had a vote!"

What happened to the love for their mother, where the fondness for the dotting grandmother? Is it only bestowed when she brings blessing?

If all would simply protect her, up hold her, life would continue...and be a blessing.

In retrospect the celebratory banquet now seemed an insult. No wonder Sonia had plummeted emotionally that night upon foreseeing the coming events.

And Sky had no doubt that had been what she had seen.

Only young Kara, the infant of the species, was steadfast.

"No matter what you say," she remonstrated to her parents and other elders. "I will not turn against my great-gran. I will be loyal to her, regardless what the rest of you do."

Staunchly, she faced her grandmother Rhea's sister Jade. "I will forever believe my great-gran meant only good will. She would never cause injury willingly!" Brashly, she added, "You, on the other hand, are the one doing us harm!"

Sky, and a very select few, fully agreed with the child.

****

"Do you realize what everyone is saying?" asked Joel, when he cornered Sonia one morning outside her chambers. "I told them all at the election meeting, you would not make a good leader. Now they see I was right. Here we have enemies on all sides: humans, 'Opposites' and we are at odds among ourselves...too bad we can't just erase the memory of all this, and everyone return to the way they were."

"I can do that, if that's what you all wish," Sonia challenged quietly. "But it would not make any difference in the end."

"Oh, I bet you just could! Now, they are connected...whether dormant or not?"

Sonia nodded to acknowledge his half-question.

"Man! When you make a mess, you sure do it grandly."

Sonia looked back at him with reproach in her eyes. "You don't have to worry. You were never connected to them, anyway."

"Sure glad I held out too! Well, here's something else for you to chew on," Joel hissed in her face. "If your selfishness gets any one of these people killed, you'll have me to answer to, do you hear me?"

From behind Joel, Sky watched as Sonia's eyes filled with tears. That had been the last straw!

When Joel vanished from beside her, Sonia closed her mind, and escaped into her apartments.

Sky slipped down to sit against the passageway wall, determined to guard Sonia against any farther unnecessary harassment by her subjects.

If I have to, I will do combat with her brother should he return!

CHAPTER 42

Sky was a stoic individual, seldom rattled under pressure. He was uncomfortable with all the tension in the air, and even he would have liked to flee it, but he did not expect what happened next.

Oh yes, he should have, but then he thought like a male.

And Sonia's reactions were pure emotional female.

That was why it rattled him so...and also, because he had allowed himself to become far too attached to her.

At first Sonia simply hid away in her chambers. He would never step beyond the door-less entry. No one did that to anyone, though all entries to the apartments were so. Each portal was sentry guarded, and only the owner of the rooms could physically or verbally admit you. And only they could jump in or out...unless the machine was programmed to allow someone else to enter.

Sky suspected Sonia's 'Keeper' was set to permit him, but out of courtesy, he would never take that liberty.

So, he spent his days seated against the wall outside waiting...and warding off Joel, if he came to battle his beleaguered sister again, or any other with like intent. At nights Djura took his place.

Like a beloved pet that might crawl away to die alone to spare its owner grief, Sonia had shut everyone out. The trouble was there was a difference here: she was no longer treasured, and no one made an effort to coax her back.

The situation both bothered and angered Sky.

He was not concerned by the fact the species would die all at once if Sonia had interpreted the visions correctly, nor was he worried about his own welfare. He feared most for Sonia, her mental and emotional state. His heart agonized at the suffering these circumstances were incurring.

And now that he could not find her, for the first time in decades, he felt uncertain and fearful.

She had finally come to the entry seeking his assistance. Sending him to bring her food, she had slipped away as soon as he left her presence. He should have realized she was side tracking him. She could easily materialize her own sustenance right there in her quarters, but his concern for her condition had made him dim witted, and she had used it to her advantage.

He should have realized, in her emotional state she would do anything to be left alone. Sky did not blame her; she was not thinking clearly.

But in his eyes, he had failed her.

Panic filled the Navajo as he frantically searched through all her favourite spots in Sanctuary: at the shelf above the waterfall, the sunken garden, the common room and the kitchens. But he found no trace anywhere. He knew he should at the very least be aware of her vanilla-cinnamon scent even if she stayed invisible. Usually he could sense her anywhere in the complex. But not today.

Where is she?

At last, desperate and beside himself, Sky went to wake Djura to elicit his assistance.

"How could she just vanish?" worried Sky, never realizing the absurdity of those words. If Sonia chose, she could hide from the world invisible to everyone for as long as she desired.

Analytical, clear thinking Djura always came right to the point. "She is not dead, Sky!" he reassured bluntly. "She stated we all die with her, remember? And that is to happen after the battle, which has not yet been fought."

Sometimes, Sky hated the calculated way the Arabian thought things through.

That is not a comfort the way he said it!

"She has obviously left Sanctuary," reasoned Djura. "In my experience all fugitives do basically the same thing. They return to old haunts, places where they felt safe and comfortable…where they would be unnoticed…"

His words triggered an idea in Sky's mind. "I think I know now where she might have gone."

"Good. Then let us go there."

Sky raised a questioning eyebrow.

The man has had little rest, and he wants to join me?

Somewhat self-consciously, Djura answered his mind thought.

"I come along to…watch your back, as they say…while you deal with this, ah… crisis."

Sky grinned, feeling grateful.

At least I am not the only one who cares.

****

He found her at her old, empty apartment seated by the window, looking dejectedly out at the street below.

The rooms were stripped, empty and barren looking. The owners had either not rented the rooms to another, or the next tenant had not yet moved in.

Sonia will no longer be able to come here once these rooms became occupied, Sky reasoned. *Her old world will be gone soon, with no retreat to past fond memories. She is being severed on all sides. It isn't good.*

Sky stood in the doorway simply observing her. She had been crying.

Her spirit is so bleak...

"You stick to me like glue," she stated without turning, her tone lacking emotion.

"I am your guardian."

"And why would you guard something that no longer has value?"

He realized she had reverted back to her old lady image: the grey hair, the useless glasses that hid her eyes...her pre-change form. It gave him an insight into just how low she had dropped: to consider her past appearance more desirable, safer to be, than the perfect beauty she had become.

He desperately wished he could embrace her.

"Come back to Sanctuary," he entreated. "There your guardians will keep you safe."

"My guardians no longer care if I am safe."

379

"I care…right at this moment, Djura protects us from the roof top. And Chi…he still holds you in great esteem."

"But they no longer trust me. They doubt my word…even you doubt…"

That is true, but to say so will not encourage her.

"Come back," Sky pleaded. "We need you!"

Great monster tears filled the swollen eyes. She turned away to hide them.

"I just wanted to be loved," she stated dispiritedly. "Like I used to be…that's all I ever asked for. Was that too much?"

Sky entered the room, approaching her chair, standing near enough, but not too close, so as not to intimidate her.

Sonia shook her head dejectedly. "I can't do this anymore…"

Tears spilled over, tracking down the wrinkled cheeks.

"Tell Joel…" She took a deep breath. "He can lead."

Sky's temper flared for the first time since his change.

"Joel can not lead!" he exploded. "We will not let him!"

She did not even notice his outburst, and that filled Sky with foreboding. It also quieted the rage that had just raised its ugly head.

Her despairing thoughts made him fear she was giving up.

"Please, my Lady," he begged. "Don't cease to hope…"

Tears began to flow, following each other down lined cheeks. "I need…just one person to believe in me…" She gulped at air, attempting to breathe through passages that had suddenly become too clogged. "To love me…without question…not for what I am …" She gasped for another ragged breath to sustain her. She was crying so hard now, her voice came out rasping. "Not because I am 'Leader Female'…but because…I am a person…who needs it!"

Sighing deeply, tiredly, she closed her eyes and moaned from deep inside her very being.

Sky could not bear to see her like this: so broken, so defeated. It ripped his heart from his chest, severed his very spirit.

"I love you!"

He dropped to one knee before her chair, trembling with the intensity of his emotions. "I will always love you." Tears formed in his eyes. "It doesn't matter to me what powers you possess…or if you are right or wrong. I do not care what appearance you chose to take…don't you know, my love, you are more to me than just my leader?"

Sonia dropped her head dejectedly, covered her face with her hands, and let the despairing tears take over. Buried in her own misery, beyond hearing any words he might say, her mind closed out any further communication.

Sky wondered *did she hear anything I said?*

I cannot leave her like this!

Sky knew the risk, but he took it anyway. Carefully, he reached out, touching her hair, lovingly smoothing it back behind her ear. The reflex shock static he expected from her never came; it was non-existent.

Is her emotional state so low as to nullify her defences? Has her depression gone that deep?

And the females had withdrawn their balance from her. Her daughters should have given that normally, but it was obviously missing.

Do these women realize they are fulfilling her prophecy by refusing to balance her?

Sky did the only thing left for him to do. He reached around, and folded her into his arms. She slumped loosely against his shoulder, limp to the point of exhaustion. Sonia had given up!

He felt it, as she slowly absorbed his energy, endured the drawing to the point of excruciating pain. Hope leached from him to her.

Sky had known a male was not supposed to attempt to balance the 'Leader Female'. Only her pair could do that. He knew it would bond them or cost his life...but, he was beyond caring.

He felt the futile, despondent, desolate emotions pass from her into him. Being male, his reaction was wrongly opposite from her needs: the anger returned full force; the injustice of his past fed his unbalance.

Sonia started to attention, suddenly changed to her real image: the slight, younger, taller figure, the golden hair and purple eyes. With a gasp, she realized he was trying to balance her.

"No! Sky! Not like this!" She pushed at him forcefully.

He sat back on his heels, releasing her; he was panting from the experience, the exertion.

Sky watched as her emotions righted; she was doing it on her own, fired by the prospect of his losing his life because of her. It gave him reason to fight also. His own equilibrium began to return.

"I could have killed you!" she reprimanded. "Why? Why, would you try that? Did you realize the risk you took?"

"I was willing to pay such a price."

Sonia shook her head in violent disagreement. "Never! Guardian...never." On the last word her voice softened. "I would never want such a sacrifice..."

Two tears slipped over the rims beneath those amethyst eyes, travelled slowly down the smooth cheeks.

"I could not bear it," she whispered softly. "If I had killed you so that I might live ...I could not go on...without you."

Reaching out, he dared to brush away another tear as it threatened to fall, and...she did not shock him.

A shudder ran through her; she drew a deep breath, and let it out in a soft sigh.

He stood, and backed away. She rose to her feet.

Reaching out one hand toward him, she allowed him to enclose it in both of his.

'Let's go home, guardian."

They jumped to Sanctuary together.

CHAPTER 43

Two days later, Sonia was standing in the doorway to her suite when Sky came to relieve Djura. After the other guardian had left for his sleep break, Sonia turned to the Navajo.

"Will you come with me to the lookout ledge?"

He nodded. She had never asked before, simply made the jump and he would follow. This time she placed her hand in his.

A moment later, they were seated together on the log above the waterfall.

"You are well rested?" Sonia asked, her hands comfortably in her lap.

"Yes, my Lady."

He waited, knowing there was something more.

Sonia scanned across the fields, her gaze taking in the scenic gardens, the rope walking bridge in the distance, the river. Sky's eyes were on her, expectantly waiting.

But when she at last spoke, it was not of what had transpired between them. It was as if it had never happened.

Without taking her eyes from the spectacular view, Sonia dropped her revelation. "It is time to do battle!"

Sky's jaw went slack. "Now?"

"Yes, now," Sonia returned quietly.

"Will our people even come when you call?" he asked incredulously. "Nothing has changed."

Sonia smiled softly, then turned to meet his eyes. "It will."

He marvelled. She was no longer afraid.

Had she seen more?

Sonia answered his thought. "It will be all right, Sky. I now know the solution. Trust me."

I always will.

His leader returned her eyes to the distant garden, and added, "I will miss this beautiful place."

Puzzlement flooded through him. Had she not just said, everything would be all right?

But then it dawned on him she had not said everything.

Sky opened his mouth to question, but Sonia spoke first.

"Give Djura a few hours rest, before you call the meeting," she suggested quietly. "Then both of you come and get me."

"The battle will begin...when?"

"Before the day is over it will be finished. We proceed right after the meeting."

Sky waited.

Sonia added, "It is safe to leave me alone. Please?" He still had the nagging fear she might bolt. "Go guardian...I need to be alone to think...to prepare."

Still, Sky hesitated.

"Sky!" Her voice had gone annoyed. "You said you trusted me. Please…" Her voice softened. "Be my obedient guardian again…for just a little longer." Her tone dropped to a whisper. "I can not explain…it would be too hard for you."

What could be harder than this? He felt like she was rejecting him.

Suddenly he understood perfectly how Chad had felt over Nadia.

"Where is my stoic Navajo?" Sonia pleaded softly.

That rekindled hope, and brought him to his senses. There must be a good reason.

Sky rose from the log. "Forgive my hesitation, my Lady."

Sonia smiled. "I will await you…here."

He nodded, and left to do her bidding.

****

In the dark regions of the mountain Marcel had created an enormous meeting room, large enough to accommodate at least a hundred large men. Lit as the other rooms, the glow came from the black granite walls and ceiling.

When Sonia appeared with her two guardians the space was filled with the murmur of agitated conversation. Everyone had come, but no one turned toward Sonia to give her honour when she arrived. Apparently curious, they would obey the summons, but would no longer accept on blind faith.

Perhaps it is better this way, mused Sonia.

She materialized her own chair, then sat down to wait. Sky and Djura stood uncomfortable on either side of her, each embarrassed at the disregard for their leader.

Sonia continued to wait quietly. Chi stood in a corner, an unusual show of irritation on his features, and for the customarily dignified Oriental to display that much spoke volumes. He was indeed extremely vexed at the attitudes about him.

Joel smirked just behind the Overseer, watching Sonia with an 'I told you so' look. Sonia calmly stared back…and waited.

The room filled with discomfort; unease spread, and slowly conversations dropped off, group by group. All eyes finally faced the front.

Sonia allowed the silence to linger just a moment longer to give those present the experience, and disregard they had been inflicting upon her. Their eyes dropped as one, ashamed.

At last she spoke, her voice calm and quiet, yet clearly understood by all. "Each of you men have a choice to make today; I expect the same from my daughters and granddaughters. You are welcome to serve…or to go. Only hear me out first. We have a common adversary. It will hunt you whether you are with me or against. The perfect moment to initiate a battle is today. Who will help me do that?"

The room was deathly still; there was a moment of hesitation where no one moved. Then Chi stepped forward, followed by Eric and Marcel.

A second passed.

Ram left Kara's side, and after a moment, Chad joined him. The rest remained unmoving, though none left the room. Not even Joel.

Sonia continued to wait, until the silence became uncomfortable again.

Sky cleared his throat. Sonia looked up at him.

"May I speak to them, my Lady?"

She hesitated long seconds before finally giving an agreeable nod.

Sky took a step forward.

"When we first came together, as we became aware of the things we could do, and we discovered that we were not merely human but more, you chose this Lady to lead you. She has taught you all you know; how to live as a species, unified and complete; often she protected you even when you were unaware…"

Sky turned angry eyes toward Joel, and the 'Pure' man dropped his own in shame.

"I have watched this Lady go through agony to make you whole…"

His eyes found Zane, Shawn, then Jade. Each dropped their eyes in shame.

"She has comforted you in sorrow…" Rhea hung her head. "Sonia nearly died with her own grief when her brother died. Did you know that? Who comforted her?"

Humiliation was spreading like a plague.

"And you Lance, was your life so good before your change, that you have forgotten what it is like

389

to face death undeserving?" A moan of anguish escaped from Sonia's eldest.

Sky turned to the two guardians still standing back. "Perhaps, your life was better before…" Ryan and Ihor could not meet his accusatory gaze. Sky's found Wade. "Your wife was so important you willingly gave up being human…"

He scanned the group with reproach in his eyes. "I know you all feel betrayed. Why? Your loyalty has faltered. How has she failed you? When did she hold back her care?"

Most were now studying the floor, their images fading with embarrassment. None could refute what he said.

"As far as I am concerned, if Sonia had not given me this better life, I would not have one today. And if my life ends with hers…the time I have known her was well spent. No matter how short…this life with her was the best for me!"

"And for me also," seconded Djura from behind him.

"If you can not do this for Sonia," Sky finished. "At least do it for those you do love."

Sky stepped back, returning to his guardian stance.

It was Chi who spoke in the silence that ensued. "Let those who are not with us, leave."

No one turned to step from the room…not even Joel.

Sonia rose to her feet; her chair vanished. All eyes were on her, awaiting instructions.

"The battle begins now!" she stated succinctly.

CHAPTER 44

"How do we do this?" asked Djura.

"I maintain your outer shield, and...I am your core energy source."

"Therefore, you must be protected at all costs, or we will all go down?"

"Yes. Usually the 'Leader Female' is direct centre, then the females next in a circle about her; males outer limits, interspaced, also in a circle.

"I will first drop our defences over Sanctuary. That will pull enemy eyes toward us and they will be able to see us because I will allow them to see our heat signature. I will then knock out their systems, draining their power and converting it for our own use. Then they will come to us."

Everyone was listening intently, but Wade appeared puzzled.

"Ah, would you mind explaining how a guardian actually defends?" he pleaded. "I'm not familiar with the process. Seems I haven't learned how just yet."

Sonia turned to explain. "Your weapon is in the eyes. A beam shoots by your will operated from the slit centre."

"I will teach him quickly," Djura offered, touching Wade's shoulder to make the knowledge transfer.

The lesson was instantaneous. "Oh, now I understand," Wade remarked. "Man! It's a good thing I wasn't called upon to fight before this."

"The outer guardian edge is only for protection," Sonia corrected. "I am your real weapon. As each enemy comes visible, I will deal with it. Only if too many come at once, will a guardian need to use his beam, and then you are only to distract. Never use it at full force power; not only will that kill, but it also drains strength from whatever I must do. You need only misdirect the 'Opposite' long enough until I am able to get to each."

Sonia turned back to the overall group. "I also am your protection. The only way my protection will fail you is if you refuse to accept it, or if someone else prevents it from covering you."

"Who would wilfully do that to another?" Djura demanded in indignation.

Sonia ignored the comment, continuing her instruction.

"Remember, you females are the inner protection circle. If an enemy injures a man, you are to surround him with your own shield. Each woman will protect the man of her choice. I will do it for those who remain."

"Isn't that a lot for you to do?" asked Wade. "I mean, you maintain the outer shield; you are the energy we draw from, and the inner shield for extra males, plus you do the actual damage...whatever that is that you plan to do to this enemy. Is it even possible for you to be strong enough to do all that?"

"I guess, that remains to be seen," Sonia reasoned bluntly, knowing full well, they were beginning to doubt again. She turned once more to the females.

"The women are vital to the male vanguard. The men hide in your glow. Brighten your image as hard as you can behind them, so the adversary is blinded and cannot see into the circle. The 'Opposite' then fails to detect your man. The glow of a guardian decreases just before he sends his defence beam. Usually that warns his opponent, but this way, all it sees is your brightness; it eliminates that weakness."

Suddenly, the women realized their importance. They were not simply there to be protected, but they had an essential role in this engagement.

"Grandma?" queried Nadia. "What happens when our energy gets too weak? If the battle goes on a long time...there are a lot of 'Opposite' in those ships."

"That is why our life-forces were joined in the beginning. Like a circle with no ending, we cannot be broken through when we remain in unity. The energy will not drain completely unless we disconnect."

"As long as we keep them from attacking the centre where our power source is located," Djura finished for her.

All eyes turned to Sonia. At last they realized the true reason for being joined to her. It had nothing to do with control over them, and everything to do with...their very survival!

"We must protect our centre...at all costs!" reiterated Djura. "At all costs!"

Sonia sighed. "Let's do this," she directed.

****

The meeting room became the battle zone. The defences over Sanctuary went down.

Sonia reached out with her mind to the enemy battle cruisers, and indeed there now were many. She knocked out all larger weapons aboard them, and the equipment powering them. The enemy suddenly saw where they were.

****

"Their barrier just went down!" yelled an excited technician aboard the lead ship. "We can get at them!"

But dejection coloured the next statement. "We've just lost all weapon's systems… Then, now we have no power."

"They attack us?" quizzed the astounded commander.

"Yes sir."

"We still have our belt devices," the irate leader screamed. "Do direct battle! Attack their queen. She is the source of their power!"

"Complete annihilation of their complex?" asked his second. "How do we do that without ship weapons?"

"Fools! Fools! Never mind their surroundings. Transport directly to their location! Kill them! You must get at their queen!"

"Kill them! Kill them!" The war cry went up from his warrior fighters. "Kill their queen!"

****

The first 'Opposite' appeared quite suddenly. Up close they were extremely ugly, lizard-like, their skin scaly and dark green, their eyes yellow with the black slit centre. The breathing apparatus they wore was noisy; the odours from them fowl, leaving a taste upon your tongue of dying things. But they stood much smaller than any guardian.

Yet Sonia's warrior men were filled with sudden fear. The apprehension spread into the inner circle.

Sonia turned her mind to past pleasurable moments: her children's devotion, her guardians' former loyalty. She was filled with affection for all of them.

Each warrior felt inundated with her forgiving love; it went out from the 'Leader Female' in a visible wave of light, passed over all, and through them all. It humbled each woman and man, and as each struck out at the creature in his sight, they emanated the same feelings with such force it became the defensive beam. The 'Opposite' felt loved. And that confused it, for such an emotion was foreign to it, had been for centuries.

The foremost 'Opposite' fired with a laser-like weapon, which was part of its glove; at a section of the circle he felt appeared weak. It could not see its adversary, only painful, brilliant camouflage. But he fired to rip out an opening. He must get through to the centre; that was all he cared about.

Sonia froze its movement, wiped clear all conscious thought and its memory, then sent the being through space to a far distant star system placing the unfortunate creature on the smallest, most inaccessible area of a planet. To begin life over. Perhaps at last to realize the error of its ways.

Each 'Opposite' met the same fate, each was sent to a separate star, each threat eliminated. The battle raged about her, but Sonia was so concentrated she was not aware of any one specific person. She carried out her function as was needed.

It was hours before the hideous creatures ceased to come, and Sonia was already dealing with the empty ships, imploding each into itself far beyond Earth's atmosphere. All at once the room around them was again unexpectedly filled with another wave of attackers. Somehow, they had hidden themselves, either on the surface of the moon or on Earth, then transported in from there.

Once more the battle raged, but this time, as if they sensed her weakest point, the enemy was concentrating on breaking through where Eric and Joel were situated. Earlier on Sonia had realized her brother was the crack in her armour. He fought only sporadically, and would not accept her protective cover. Because he stood in the direct path to Eric, she also could not shield that guardian.

One by one, Sonia dealt with the new intruders. She was aware at the edge of her sight, when Eric fell. Because of his blocked status, she was unable to place a protective shield about him, and repeatedly the beams hit him. And her exposed brother stood indecisive.

Sonia froze the beam that would have certainly ended Joel's life.

The end was near now; the last creature to be vanquished was the one standing over her brother. She sent it as far away as she could master.

When it was over, Sonia sank to her knees in exhaustion. Her mind found it difficult to ignore this latest betrayal, but all about her the thoughts of others mirrored humility, shame and regret. It eased the last injury, gave her reason to go on. Her subjects were emanating such desperate need for her forgiveness as they broke ranks, she could only respond by giving the gift they ask for.

Most had fought well...even the females. Their support for her had been good. With her last burst of energy, Sonia reached out in compassion and comfort, encompassing them in pardon and love.

The battle was won! But Sonia sat back on her heels trembling. It had taken every last ounce of her strength.

Jade made for her. "Mother!"

"Do not touch me," Sonia warned weakly. "It is not safe for us to touch at this moment."

"What can we do to help?" Jade begged.

"Just love me," Sonia moaned. "I must rest...come back...recover...on my own."

"I am so sorry, momma," Jade cried, tears slipping down her cheeks. "I was so very wrong...I will never doubt you again!"

Sonia nodded wearily. "It is forgotten...forgiven...forever. I love you... forgiveness...will always be here...in my heart...for you. No matter what..."

Jade was sobbing openly. She dropped to her knees just inches away, a place that was extremely dangerous to her to be. But she stretched out her hand toward Sonia, palm upward. "I wish I could touch you…"

"Later…okay?" Sonia gasped.

Jade nodded, and obediently withdrew her hand.

Sonia jumped to her chambers with her last once of energy. She collapsed upon the soft covers of her sleep couch, and knew nothing more.

It was days before the others were aware of her consciousness again.

Only Sky dared enter her suites during the long painful heal back, and each time he did, Sonia seemed to sleep. He would breathe a sigh of relief each occasion, and go away reassured.

At least she still lives! he told himself each time.

CHAPTER 45

The almond-sage scent was ever so light but Sonia was aware of it as she sat above the falls soaking in the evening sun, watching the busy gardens below. The girls and their guardians were manually picking fruit.

"I know you are there, Sky," she said softly.

He chuckled, coming visible beside her on the log. His arm went around her shoulders, and she lay back gratefully against his chest.

"You are still very weak," he observed.

It was her first time up; she had been longing to see the sun. Sonia sighed. "This too shall pass..."

"I brought you something." A peach appeared in his hand.

She took it, examined the fuzzy ripe fruit, and bit into it, the juice dribbling from the corner of her mouth. With his free hand, Sky reached across and tenderly wiped the moisture from her chin.

"Want a bite?" Sonia offered the half eaten fleshy orb.

He shook his head, and she continued, enjoying his offering. When she finished, Sonia tossed the pit into the falls, licked her fingers, and lay back against his shoulders again.

Sky grinned, amused.

"What?"

"You don't act like any royal I know of."

Sonia wrinkled her nose, and he laughed.

They sat comfortably together watching the activity below. The brief harvest was coming to an end, and some of those involved were already disappearing with their baskets.

"You do not mention Eric?" she probed.

Sky sighed. "I don't know what to do. I've tried time and again to heal him, but his wounds are as raw when I step back as they were to begin with. He grows weaker with each day."

"How long has it been?"

"Ten days. Why can't I heal him, Sonia? The male support side is sufficient; even the female side should be stronger now, but something prevents it. Have I lost my ability to heal?"

"You still have your power, but...do you remember when Myron died?"

Sky frowned. "It's effect on you?"

"Yes. Tell me, at that time, did either of us have control over the situation?"

"No. To be honest, sometimes, I believe we are not in control at all."

"We aren't!" Sonia said with conviction. "I did not balance myself then; the reaction simply stopped. And before the battle, when I went so low...you did not balance me, did you? You were going down with me."

Sky thought about that. "What are you saying?"

"I have only so much ability, Sky...after that something else takes over..."

He smiled understanding. "Your Almighty Creator theory?"

Sonia nodded. "It is my belief we are at another such vulnerable time... We do not control... What I saw...I do not make happen...I know what needs to be done, but the outcome is not in my hands. Someday, when the time is right...you also will know what must be done. It will come...naturally."

Puzzled, Sky wondered if they spoke of the same things. He knew Sonia would only reveal what he was able to handle. Also, she was usually right. Every one of them had learned that painful lesson by not trusting her.

"So...what of Eric?"

"He was wounded because I could not shield him. Even that was not by chance... It all has to do with our becoming whole."

"And even I know, we are definitely not all complete."

"Because I failed Eric, I need to be the one to heal him."

"You are not sufficiently recovered," objected Sky.

"We may not believe so...but perhaps the Almighty Creator has a different plan? We must proceed on the course set for us."

He knew better than to argue against this.

"I will try the healing...tomorrow. Set up a bed for Eric in the meeting room, and ...those who wish may come to...watch."

Sky did not like what was coming. He still had her prediction in the back of his mind, but he hesitated to ask, for fear their course was set for destruction and she would confirm that fact.

Their attention eventually returned to the orchards below.

"They are no longer angry with me," Sonia observed.

He laughed softly. "I hope we have all learned not to doubt your word…or question your purpose."

In view of what she had just told him, Sky was having difficulty practicing this trust himself.

"Funny how it takes experience to convince…"

Sky sighed in surrender. "Even for me," he admitted. "Forgive me."

"Sky, remember, what ever happens…it will be okay in the end."

He gently eased her head back against his chest. After a moment of silence, he added, "Marcel has put up a motto on the memory wall…so we will never question your motives again."

Sonia made no comment. Below the orchard was quiet, the shades of night beginning. The last stragglers had gone in; old habits died hard. They still went inside as darkness descended.

Sky's mind had not left what Marcel had created.

"The inscription reads: 'Remember out failing, that we may do it no more.'"

Still Sonia said nothing, so Sky let it go, and just watched the sun as it sank beyond the horizon. The stars came out, one by one. For tonight, they were safe in the open air…all because of her.

What more can I ask?

After a time, her even breathing told him she was asleep. When he felt she was deeply enough into slumber, he slipped her completely on to his lap, lifted her into his arms, and stood. From there, he jumped to her quarters.

Gently, he placed her on the bed and tenderly covered her with the mauve and cream coverlet.

Then Sky left her chambers. He was humming as he walked, a tune he had once played upon his flute. He realized, he had not played that flute in a very long time. Perhaps, it was time to do so?

I will have to bring it out, and play it for Sonia, he resolved.

****

True to her word, Sonia came the next morning to the meeting room. Most of her people had already gathered inside for the healing.

As Sky caught up to her, Sonia turned to give instruction. They moved around a nearby corner for privacy.

"I know you will not agree or like what I am about to ask of you today," Sonia stated in a low tone. "But I require your absolute obedience today. Will you promise to follow my wishes without question or deviation?"

Sky was suddenly wary. "I will gladly act as balance," he offered.

"Do I have your promise?"

"I will not deviate from your instructions."

She then dropped her bombshell.

"Joel will be my balance today."

Sky was perplexed. "But he…"

"I know he has not connected to the overall unit, but this is the way it must be done. You are 'Ultimate Healer' and it is imperative that you remain separate while I heal today. Trust me on this. The survival of this species will ultimately rest with you. You must remain apart!"

Sky was disconcerted, but he nodded reluctantly.

"Now, if Joel does not give me of his strength, Djura is not to touch me. Is that understood?"

She is tying our hands on all sides!

"We will probably have to restrain him," he objected.

"Then do so!" Sonia fired back with forcefulness.

Sky nodded, his objection mirroring on his face. "Do you intend to heal on your own, if Joel does refuse?"

"If that must be the way, yes!"

"Let me be your support," Sky pleaded, trying to reason with her.

"Only my brother, or…my pair may support this time."

Hope jumped into his thoughts.

"In my heart, I am already…"

"Don't say it, Sky," Sonia begged softly. "Both must be willing…"

He looked at her in shock. "You reject?"

Sonia knew what he was offering. "No…" she answered quietly. "I hold back… because…to be the pair to a 'Leader Female' is…a weighty responsibility."

"One I would willingly take on."

"You are not ready! I will not let you…not like this…not yet…the time is not right…such an action must be taken with much deliberation beforehand, not spur-of-the- moment!"

"But Joel…will fail you. Without the proper support…" In a last-ditch effort, he appealed to her protective instinct. "We will all suffer the consequences."

"I am aware of that. But we will never be whole without Joel. He has a lesson to be learned here. It must be he who is my balance…no matter the consequence."

"You risk us all for the life of one man?"

"For two. And, I would do the same for anyone of you, were it you instead of Joel. It is so that we all might be whole in the end." Sonia sighed. "I told you this would not be to your liking."

Sky turned away frustrated.

"You promised…"

"At that time, I did not realize exactly what you planned."

"The promise was…without question or deviation, Sky!"

"I did agree to that," he admitted in surrender. "I will do as you say...it doesn't mean I will enjoy standing back..."

"Sky..." she said tenderly. "If you did, I would not...trust you."

He dropped his eyes, the fight gone out of him.

"Without deviation?" she reiterated.

He nodded.

"And do not try to heal me afterward."

His head came up with this final blow.

He sighed. *Even that she will deny me!*

"Trust me...it will be okay."

He hoped she was right.

****

Sonia almost cried when she saw Eric. Great gaping slashes marred his arms and upper body; half his face had been blown away. The wounds she could see were infected.

What unseen injuries lay beneath the sheet that covers his lower extremities?

Sonia turned to those standing around; these had come to help and observe.

"Joel, will be my only support." To her sibling, she added, "Come, stand next to me."

For once her brother obeyed without objection.

Sonia continued. "No one else is to interfere. Especially do not touch me."

She moved to the sleeping couch, sat down on the stone floor beside the stricken man. Leaning with her shoulder against the draped bed, she faced sideways, so that those present could see her face. Joel stood towering over her, to her right.

With her left-hand Sonia made the connection, clasping Eric's limp right hand in her own.

The glow around her enlarged, moving over and encompassing the wounded guardian until they were both enclosed in a blanket of light. Next the field about them turned grey.

Like a visible virus, the man's injuries began spreading to her, down her arm, across her face, to the opposite arm.

Joel gasped with revulsion, and moved away in fear.

Has he never seen a healing? Sonia supposed not. *That is why he must see it now; to experience just what is involved.*

They all need to see this!

The injuries grew painful; her face felt raw. Her breathing became laboured.

Eric was growing a new face. The raw festering slashes were healing and disappearing. Finally, he was whole.

Sonia felt suddenly so weary. She dropped Eric's hand. Reaching out for Joel, needing help, the extra energy and strength only he could provide, she pleaded with him through dimming eyes.

But Joel moved back instead. He refused to take her hand.

In silent pleading, Sonia weakly raised her hand a second time toward her hesitating brother.

This time he shook his head determinedly.

Sonia closed her eyes. Went limp.

****

A moan ran through those who watched, but Sonia no longer heard.

Sky flinched. He had expected this.

Djura surged forward. Sky whirled.

"Prevent him! Restrain him!" he ordered. "Only Joel may touch her!"

Joel turned in anger, and rapidly strode from the room.

****

Chi and Marcel held his arms. Djura struggled desperately.

"I would rather die!" he screamed wrathfully.

Why will Sky not allow me this honour? I need to go to the Lady's aid! Has the man turned traitor as well? Is he 'Opposite' that he is so callous?

"Those were her wishes," Sky answered remorsefully.

The room filled with groans as all realized what that meant: Sonia must heal back on her own!

Djura struggled violently against the enforcers.

"Let me give my life!" he yelled.

Ryan grabbed him from behind, and the Arabian fought harder.

"She does not desire your life, Djura," Sky tried to reason. "She wants to kill no one."

"I would rather die…than watch her lose her life!"

"You will only do her harm if you were to touch her now, Djura."

At those words, Djura went limp in surrender. He dropped to his knees as the other men released him. He began to sob openly.

All I want is to give her my strength. I've done it before! Why is it different now?

But...if Sky said it will harm her... That I will never do willingly!

He might be the brawn, the strongest male in the race, but Djura was not stupid. He realized what was taking place: their greatest fear was coming to pass, and he had to stand back and watch it happen.

Sonia is dying!

'One dissenter can render us powerless', she had said so long ago. That moment had come.

Djura knew it!

They all knew it!

Yet Sky seemed not to have given up...

Maybe this is not hopeless after all?

****

Sky turned back to watch Sonia...he waited for some sign of her recovery.

Her glow had gone very dim.

He dropped to his knees the better to wait patiently, to endure the long vigil ahead.

Around the room, others followed his example; some sitting against the walls, others standing slack, but still all remained, attentive and hopeful...because he was.

Benches materialized, and the room became like the waiting room of a hospital.

At times, some paced during the hours that passed. At one point, Kara began to cry softly against her mother's shoulder.

Jade's face was a mirror of terrified concern, not for herself, but in fear for her mother. Rhea squeezed her hand to give reassurance.

All seemingly held their breath, keeping their breathing to a minimum as if that would help the sufferer.

****

Eric sat up. When he realized who had healed him, and what had transpired, he cried out in anguish.

"Why did you allow it? I would gladly have made the sacrifice. My life means nothing…compared to hers!"

Sky merely cautioned. "Do not touch her guardian. Be careful when you move away, or you will do her other harm."

Carefully, Eric stepped off the cot, and around Sonia's battered form, to join the others…to wait and watch…and to trust this would end in life and not death.

Without touching her, from where he was, Sky raised her broken body by telekinesis, and placed Sonia carefully on the cot vacated by Eric.

The hours passed…yet there was no sign of recovery.

****

Sky puzzled over the words she had spoken at the lookout ledge on the mountain.

What did she mean?

She saw the future, was privy to results he could not yet see.

He knew one thing for certain: Sonia did not wish him to usurp Joel's role.

But if I cannot touch her...how am I to give that final balance?

'When the time comes you will know...it will come...naturally', she had said.

But I do not know the how...at least not yet.

Her come back from the battle has taken ten days, Sky reassured himself. *Perhaps...*

Hopefully, this time, his balance would not be needed

CHAPTER 46

The Navajo sat cross-legged four feet from the sleeping couch. Sky had kept vigil all day, as had everyone else. Not a one had left the chamber...not even Eric, who was still weakened.

Sky had the nagging feeling the next step was his to make, but he could not for the life of him think what he was to do. Sonia had tied his hands!

I promised; she gave the order: 'you are not to try to heal me afterward'...I am not to give her energy strength either. And she was explicit! No one must touch her! What is there left to do?

Now that Eric was obviously healed, could she still not be touched? Had she meant, until she again opened her eyes and sat up?

She was not healing back! Every female, every guardian that waited could see that!

Little Kara slipped from her mother's lap, and approached. She stood beside Sky, as if wishing his comfort, so he reached over, slipped his arm around her, and drew her on to his lap.

"Great-grandpa? Sky?" she whispered softly, cuddling against him. "Why can't I help great-gran?"

The very fact she called him that name made shivers go down his spine. Kara had an increased sense of precognition, just like Sonia.

Is this a prediction...or an unintentional directive?

When Sky did not immediately answer, the young girl continued her plea. "I will be 'Leader Female' someday…"

Sky closed his eyes to keep back the tears. It was like tearing open afresh a wound he did not know he had acquired: to think of the time when Kara would take over; that would mean Sonia would be dead. He could not bear to think of such an occasion.

When he had control again, Sky opened his eyes and looked directly at the intent, diminutive would-be benefactor. "You are not ready, little one. You are neither prepared enough…and you are much too young."

Tears formed in the miniature amethyst eyes, so like Sonia's. "Ah…great-grandpa; she will die…"

Sky closed his eyes again, and pulled her close against him. "You are too young to carry such a burden…leave it to adults to find a solution…"

She raised her head hopefully, making direct eye contact with him, as if she were trying to communicate some hidden message.

"You will work it out, Sky," Kara proclaimed softly. "I know you will not fail her."

Then she slipped from his lap, and fled to her mother.

There it is again, Sky thought. *Like she knows what I have to do.*

It's just the way Sonia gives me little bits of information, probing me along.

If he could just unravel the puzzle!

'The survival of the species ultimately rests with you'. He could still hear Sonia's words in his mind.

What is the next step? What am I to do?

Sonia could no longer tell him.

****

Darkness was swallowing her whole, enveloping. All Sonia could feel was Joel's anger, but he was angry at his own failure. He felt useless, helpless, self-loathing regret.

He was taking the blame for everything...right back to the loss of Myron. His guilt felt overwhelming.

Joel hated his sister for being what she was, for putting him in that position. He wanted her dead!

And yes, her brother's emotions were killing her, making it impossible to heal back. Joel was killing them all...destroying them from within.

He needed her forgiveness...yet she had not the energy to project it.

****

Sky had risen to pace, both to relieve leg cramps and to think more clearly. He was remembering a conversation last winter between Sonia and Rhea, when their 'Leader Female' had been schooling her daughter on healing.

"Only her pair can heal the severely injured female..."

Sky stopped short in his tracks; he stood staring unseeingly across the room at Djura.

Is that the answer?

****

The first evidence that something was very wrong began with Djura. At first Sky wondered if somehow, he had been responsible.

Djura suddenly just slumped to the floor.

He was Sonia's last source of strength energy, and she could access him without touching!

Sky whirled to look at Sonia, foreboding climbing through his spirit, freezing his thoughts...and literally his heart.

Her life glow had vanished!

With horror and dread, Sky turned to look at Kara. She abruptly dropped into slumber.

That sleep is not natural!

Sky shivered. *It is too late! I've waited too long!*

Chad dropped to the bench next to Nadia; she slumped against him. Ram dropped at Kara and Jessica's feet. Jessica leaned into Wade and they both fell against the wall behind. Tyler and Shawn dropped in their tracks, as if shot by a weapon. Lance and Zane followed.

The youngest and the females are going down first. Can I stop this? It is happening so fast!

Ihor dropped with Rhea; Ryan just before Jade. The other guardians were dropping like birds wounded in flight. One by one they fell: Eric, Marcel, and last of all Chi Cho.

Why am I still standing? wondered Sky. *Because I am 'Ultimate Healer'!*

He understood fully now why she had insisted he keep separate.

But we have run out of time…haven't we?

I love Sonia! Why have I waited this long? A lifetime together would have been no sacrifice at all!

Why have I been hesitant?

I held back…because I promised! Is the timing important?

And now he was the last one standing…left behind to watch as they all died.

What if I was her pair? Is there a time when her partner should choose her welfare over her orders?

He wished now that he had done that.

Is that the mark of true love?

Sky sighed, and moved forward as if in a dream.

If he must be the last to die, he knew there was only one place he wanted to be.

****

His steps slow, yet unfaltering, Sky Hawk crossed the room. He stood beside the white draped bed looking down at the mangled creature upon it…and saw only her former beauty. To another she was no longer appealing but ugly: the half-melted face, the lovely amethyst eyes closed, covered by long lashed lids that swept her cheeks. Sky saw the sun-gold hair fanned across the pillow, remembered the rhythmic walk and curving figure, the small delicate feet.

And he wept.

You would not allow it in life, but I will be you pair in death! he resolved.

Gently, Sky lay down beside Sonia, his face against her good cheek; his arm carefully circled her waist.

His mind climbed into hers...to stay there, forever.

The cloying aroma of almonds and sage filled the room. It lingered long moments, then gradually dissipated.

Was that a faint essence of vanilla and cinnamon just beneath?

And Sky gave her...his energy.

The second fragrance increased in potency, mingling with the first, as it too began to gain strength. Suddenly both scents were gone, replaced by a third: a rain fresh meadow with a suggestion of expended lightning.

What is this? The bouquet of death...or did it perhaps...give hope of new life?

The room slowly, gradually dimmed. At last it went dark.

****

Joel had been alone all day. He had seen no one even enter the halls, or the kitchen, when he went to fix himself something to eat.

No one called him.

What is happening with Sonia? Is she dead?

His curiosity finally got the better of him, and he went to sneak a look. Carefully, he peered around the door jamb of the meeting room.

They were still visible, but each lay where they had fallen: Kara in Jessica's arms; both appeared dead; Jade and Rhea on either side of them; Nadia beside her mother. Many of the guardians were crumpled against the walls, Lance, Zane, Tyler and Shawn among them.

Joel looked toward the bed. It was not Eric that lay there. Side by side, his arm around her, Sky lay with Sonia.

He watched as the last light glow over them died…and the room itself suddenly went empty…then dark.

Joel turned with a scream, and ran, through darkened corridors, past yawning black doorways, and the sunken garden now absent of lighting. At last reaching his chambers, he found them in darkness as well, and producing one tiny candle by thought, he sat down on his bed, placing the luminous wax beacon on his bedside table.

Joel was shivering with fright.

I am alone!

****

Minutes passed…an hour. The silence in the meeting room was deafening.

From the bed came a tiny glimmer. The faint glow began at Sonia's heart. It grew, and expanded…

Then the lights in the walls came on…

Was that minute spark real or imagined?

CHAPTER 47

Joel sat on his sleeping couch in the pitch-black room. The candle had long since burned down, sputtering to nothing, and too depressed, he had not bothered to materialize another.

His mind was filled with thoughts of suicide. *But how do our kind do that? Go nova like Myron?*

No, that is too easy!

Joel felt repulsive, unloved, unneeded…a traitor!

Because of my stubbornness, my need to be right, a whole species has died.

Oh sure, I can start it over, but… Without Sonia the companionship is gone…the knowledge, the abilities. Everything will have to be learned over. And…there will never be another 'Pure'…never be another…'Leader Female'. There will never be the union she brought about.

Without Sonia, I cannot even correct my own emotional downslide.

Why did I remain separate? Is my pride that important?

It had not been worth it. He had gained nothing by it. And now…his madness was growing.

Sonia was right from the start!

He had been so very, very wrong…so arrogant! The most dimwitted of the species…

And I can't even tell her I'm sorry.

Joel wished he could just die, maybe simply decide to and stop breathing. He wanted punishment; he required torture.

I could turn 'Opposite'; that would be the life of hell I deserve!

But rather than be like the enemy, he would much prefer just to rot away, inch by inch.

That's what I will do!

Joel thought of Eric's face, how Sonia had healed it and taken the deformity into herself.

Maybe, it can be done in reverse?

As he wished for it, his hands began to swell, then burst into ugly festering blisters.

He cried out in his misery.

Angry welts travelled up his arms, turned ulcerous and burst open.

Joel began to sob. It was not merely the pain. But the sheer hopelessness of his situation…the loneliness and grief overwhelmed him.

****

She appeared like a spectre in the darkness of the room. Sonia stood before Joel whole, completely well; the picture of vibrant health.

He cried out in anguish, tears streaming down his face.

"I'm sorry, so sorry," he moaned brokenly. "Don't haunt me now, too."

The room flooded with illumination. The lights had come on!

And Sonia still stood there.

****

"Oh Joel! Baby brother," Sonia reproached softly. "What have you done?"

I am three times her size, yet she still calls me her baby brother. Is this really my sister?

Sonia sank to the floor at his knees.

"Don't touch me!" he cried dejectedly, trying to back into the wall behind him. "Don't heal me! I've done too much harm already. Just let me go!"

"But you are sorry now," she whispered gently.

"You can heal yourself..." Sonia suggested.

"I...don't...want...to!" he admitted between remorseful sobs. "I deserve this!"

"No." Sonia disagreed quietly. "You are forgiven."

He cried harder at that.

"Be one of us, Joel," Sonia pleaded.

He gulped for breath. "Are you real?" he rasped.

"As real as you."

"Oh, sis. Why would anyone want me back?"

"Because we love you." Sonia held out her hand. "Let me touch you."

No longer hesitant, Joel allowed her arms to go about him, and as brother and sister embraced, he was suddenly pain free, unmarred, and...complete.

****

Sky sat on the empty couch in the meeting room watching. Sonia had left him there, wanting to go alone. He was to wait and watch the others.

Kara sat up first, stretched lazily, and yarned as if awakening from a pleasant sleep.

Sky chuckled. *Of course, she will be foremost. She is a 'Leader Female' to the core.*

Jade opened her eyes, then Rhea, followed by Jessica and Nadia. The men began to rise, first Lance and Zane, then Tyler and Shawn. The guardians also were recovering one by one.

It thrilled Sky. It was like a resurrection!

Joel has completed us! The energy balance is corrected!

As he had been the first to fall, so also Djura was the last to rise.

Djura was grinning as he approached Sky. "You are 'Leader paired'!"

Sky smiled awkwardly, and gave an almost imperceptible nod of acknowledgement.

CHAPTER 48

Sonia was playing chess with Kara; Sky sat reading, every so often peering over the top of his book to see who was winning. The common room was a popular place today and most of their members were present. It was raining in the valley.

Eric rushed excitedly into the room, Joel close at his heels. Though the 'Pure' brother stood taller than his co-worker partner, his posture was one of insecurity still. His shoulders stooped forward ever so slightly. His attitude emanated shame and embarrassment whenever he joined in with the others of the species.

But they were all working on that, giving encouragement to bring him back to a complete balance. However, his own self-reproach would take time to lessen.

Sonia looked up. "Yes, Eric? What has got you so stirred up?"

"My Lady!" exclaimed the professor exuberantly. "We have found a habitable planet!"

Sonia feigned disinterest.

"Sooo..." she wondered in a teasing tone. "You want us to leave this beautiful, safe place we have created?"

Sky chuckled. Eric frowned.

"Nooo..." the guardian answered uncertain. "I...we thought...you still wanted..."

Sonia laughed, breaking his discomfort. "That is wonderful news! Tell us about it."

Relieved, Eric launched into a description of their purposed future home.

"It is much like Earth...but will suite our energy needs much better, also hide our heat signature easily..."

"And what about other life forms upon it?"

"Animals, oceans teeming with life, birds, vegetation...and mountains of granite, marble and onyx."

"Sounds good. But what of a higher life form?"

"None. Intelligence is primitive...it's like it's been waiting for us."

Sonia smiled, as if she had expected there to be a home waiting out there in space for them. "So, there is no threat there to us?'

"None we are aware of."

The room about them began to buzz with excited conversation. When Sonia spoke again, all went quiet.

"It is obvious, we cannot continue to burden Earth with a second dominant species. It will not be good for humans...or us. I believe it is time we formed our own world."

Chi put forward a suggestion. "We could send out guardians ahead to scout it out, and they could begin settlement set up."

"No," Sonia disagreed. "That is too unsafe. Without females they have no balance, and the range is too great to connect with those remaining behind."

"Then what is best to do?" asked Joel.

"We must all go together..." Seeing Joel flinch, Sonia pointedly added. "Even you, Joel. Don't think of remaining behind. You are one of us now."

There were murmurs of agreement with her statement; heads nodded approvingly. Joel dropped his eyes, uncomfortable.

"We do want you along, great-uncle Joel!" Kara declared firmly. "Please say you will join us."

He gave a slight nod. "I obey Sonia...always...from now on," he promised softly.

A pleased pride at his answer emanated from those present; then the buzz of excited planning took over.

"One more thing," Sonia cautioned quietly. The room hushed around her.

"We can take nothing with us." Moans greeted that statement. "The distance is much too far for us to carry our mementoes."

"The memories we will leave behind..." Rhea lamented, thinking of Ivan.

Thoughts of regret spread from one to another. They had become attached to Sanctuary. But still, none chose disobedience.

"Your cherished treasures can be recreated at the other end," Sonia comforted.

"When do we go?" asked Sky.

Sonia looked around at each of them. "Unless there is an objection, we leave tomorrow night."

All minds gave assent; not one considered delaying. Like pioneers, they were to set out for a new life. What they left behind was the prospect of discovery, and danger from human beings.

There was simply no comparison.

"It is not like we cannot return some day," Kara offered hopefully. "Just to visit..."

Everyone smiled at that prospect.

Epilogue:

They left from the stone bridge above the waterfall. Chi and Djura were now the 'Leader Pair's' guardians, but they did not lead. Joel was permitted that honour, to operate as point.

"Does everyone know how to transport through space?" he questioned. Eager, but serious faces nodded all about him. "We protect the core at all cost. There may still be 'Opposites' out there, stragglers from the original fleet. We must never let our guard down." Joel turned to Chi Cho. "It is your function to order the guardians, therefore, I leave it to you."

Chi stepped forward solemnly. "Inner most core is Sonia, circled by her pair and appointed personal guardians, equally spaced. Sky is point, Djura, left; I am on the right."

He turned to the females. "Second circle is as in battle defence; the women around the inner guardian core this time. Jade is point forward, slightly left of Sky, Nadia behind her to the left, Rhea to her right. Behind Rhea, is Jessica. Kara you are at the very back to the left of your mother and behind Sonia completing the ring."

Chi turned to the 'Leader Female's' male family. "Lance is point in third circle, Tyler right of him, Zane left. Shawn is behind Zane, Wade behind Tyler; you Wade guard your pair."

At last Chi turned to the remaining single guardians. "You are the outer protection. Joel is forward-most point, the leader for this migration.

He knows where we are headed. Should anything happen to him, Eric will be to his right. He would take point, as he also knows our destination. We sincerely hope he will not be needed to serve in that capacity."

The other five guardians waited patiently for placement. "Ryan to Joel's left, in front and to the side of Jade, behind him Chad is opposite Nadia, next Ram behind Kara to her left, Marcel across to the right of Ram. These last two are rear guard for special protection to Kara. And Ihor you are behind Eric, Tyler to your front right with Rhea being inner opposite to him and to your far upper right. Ihor you are Rhea's guardian protector first and foremost."

Chi asked one more question. "Are these placements understood by all?"

Affirming nods of admiration greeted Chi. His expertise was evident. He had set them up in an egg-shaped four-layer defence system not only surrounding all females and the guardian core with males, but had also managed to place each personal guardian across from the female he was responsible to protect. This was no easy feat. As they were set up, there would be no getting past their tight defence system into the treasured females, and especially not to the inner core where their 'Leader Female' was harboured.

"We are ready, my Lady."

Sonia turned to take one last look over the valley. "I will miss this beautiful place," she admitted regretfully.

Sky took her hand and squeezed it. "It will be 'Keeper' guarded…and maintained," he reassured. "We will be back."

Sonia nodded, then took his hand. "Let us do this!" she ordered.

****

All the world below saw that night were streaks of light heading into outer space. Like an unscheduled meteor shower going the wrong direction, instead of falling to earth twenty-one bright lines rose into the ebony darkness.

The 'Aopato' were finally free, leaving the place where they had been birthed.

###

About the Author:

Margaret Afseth, a Canadian novelist, lives in Saskatoon, Saskatchewan. She is a widow with four grown children, and five grandchildren.

An avid reader and clandestine writer since her late teens, she only recently stepped to the publishing stage. Though she has training in both art and as a freelance writer, she is self-taught, her expertise gained mostly from observation and life experience.

From an error in judgement early on, she learned a hard lesson. A narrow-minded counsellor burnt the only copy of her first novel. Perhaps this man did Margaret a service, as when one of the manuscripts destroyed was later rewritten, a single novel became the trilogy she now offers for your enjoyment.

Discover other titles by Margaret Afseth at
Amazon.com
Remedy
Turn Back

If you enjoyed this book here is a sample of the second in the series:
Remedy
By Margaret Afseth

The city had received an unusual amount of rainfall these past three months, and the tributary was dangerously high and swift as it flowed past the concrete wall on which Chrystal was perched. Heedless to her dangerous position, arms wrapped around her chest, her legs suspended over the edge of the barrier, the twenty-five-year-old rocked back and forth in agitation. The tears blinded her eyes, flowing in rapid succession down her cheeks.

"You going to jump?" a male voice bluntly asked.

Starting violently, Chrystal lost her balance and would certainly have fallen were it not for the strong arm of her inquisitor, as he hastily reached out and circled her slim waist wrenching her to safety.

He plunked her down unceremoniously, on the opposite side of the barricade, with her back to the cement, then sat down next to her.

While she caught her breath, Chrystal took note of the man. He was not much more than a year or two older than she, with copper-blond hair that was straight and fell to his shoulders ending with a slight curl at the ends. His body was strong and fit; the eyes blue.

"Whatever possessed you to sit like that?" he asked annoyed. "You trying to off yourself?"

Chrystal was trembling. "No," she admitted sheepishly. "I...forgot where I was."

"You're disking me!" he retorted with amazement. "What's got you so bothered you forgot you're on a barricade hanging over a fast-flowing, deadly river?"

The doll-like face turned to a mask of despondency; the blue eyes flooded, and the sunshine head dropped into her delicate hands. Chrystal gave way again to shuddering sobs.

"Ah...come on...don't cry," he pleaded awkwardly. "It can't be that bad..."

He sat quietly, not attempting to touch or comfort her further, just giving her time.

After a while when she was calmer, she drew in a steeling breath, wiped her cheeks with the sleeve of her sweatshirt, and sheepishly looked up.

"I'm sorry."

Her chin still quivered, the eyes threatened to spill moisture again, and her voice had gone hoarse, but Chrystal made a staunch effort to steady her grief.

"I...I guess I should say...thank you."

"You don't have to, if you don't want to." He held out his hand. "I'm Shawn."

She clasped it without much enthusiasm, limply, revealing her own name, then dropped his hand abruptly.

"You must think the worst of me..."

"Naw," he laughed. "I've got a sister. I know how emotional females can get."

That almost made her cry again.

"Ah, I'm sorry. I'm good at saying the wrong thing...still learning to be a nice guy..."

"No...no. It's me. It's not one of my better days."

He let her sit silent for a time, just waiting her out.

Man, he's patient! she thought. *That is rare in a guy.*

"Care to talk about it?" asked Shawn.

Chrystal shook her head.

"Sometimes, it helps to talk to someone. I find strangers listen pretty good, and they don't judge because they know nothing about your past behaviour; most never see you again."

She smiled dejectedly, but still said nothing.

"Maybe I could actually help?" he offered.

"Not unless you know where I can find work," she allowed finally. "And…a place to live…and give me a new family," Chrystal added, as an afterthought.

He grinned at that. "That's a tall order. What kind of work do you do?"

"Until today, I was a teacher," she declared with venom. "That was until they decided I was too…intimate with the kids."

"You mean…like listening to their problems, touching hands, hugging them to comfort?"

"You got it! Apparently, that's no longer permitted!"

"Ummm…I always say, a teacher's no good when they're not genuine; can't keep the kid's attention."

"My thoughts exactly!" Encouraged by his apparent empathy, Chrystal found bravery. "I got fired at work, and I guess that old adage was on my back today…'bad luck happens in threes'. When I got home, I was locked out of my basement suite. The landlady tells me, my cheque bounced, and she already has a renter to replace me…"

"Whoa!" Shawn declared in sympathy. "You said, three?"

"Yes…it is the third strike." Her voice dipped, trembling on the verge of tears again. Her eyes lowered to take in her hands. "Last month, my mom suffered a heart attack and died instantly."

"Ah...I'm soo sorry. What about your dad...your siblings, can't you go to them?"

"It's been just me and my mom since before I turned twelve. Dad died in an industrial accident."

"Sorry to hear that..."

"I don't know what I'm going to do...now..."

Shawn sat thinking. "Well," he said after a time. "I can't bring back your mom, but...I might know a possibility of work..."

"You do? Where? Oh, but...likely they won't be any different. They'll look at my record, and never consider me for a teaching position...I'm also a pretty fair artist..."

He smiled at her hope, the unconscious boast; let it pass. Suddenly she was embarrassed again.

"Sorry...what kind of a job? I kinda jumped to conclusions."

"I know where there is a need for a companion-nanny, teacher type, and I have an in with those hiring...I could put in a good word for you."

"You would do that?"

"Sure."

"Where do I apply?"

"Where are you staying for the night?"

Sheepishly she looked at her shoes again. "I guess at a women's shelter...the landlady seized all my stuff as payment for the missed rent."

"Do you have money to buy a newspaper? Or can you get to a computer and go on line?"

Chrystal looked at her watch. "The library closes in an hour, but if I hurry, I can use a computer there. They let you use the Internet for free."

"Okay...here's what you do. At the very end of the classifieds: work available is an add. It will begin like this: 'Required: Companions for younger and elder family members of visiting sovereign...' Just follow the instructions at the bottom. They'll answer back, and tell you where to go for an interview, but...you'll have to wait at that terminal until they E-mail back the location and time of your appointment. If you miss it, it won't come again."

"Then, I'd better get a move on, or I won't have enough time."

"I'll tell them to rush the answer."

He rose to his feet, offered her a hand and helped her to rise. They stood uncomfortable for a second.

"I suggest you wash your face before you go into a public place like that," he offered hesitantly. "Maybe, you can find a service station on the way..."

She lifted her hands to her face, chagrined.

"Oh...yeah. Guess I must look a mess..."

"You look beautiful...just a little wet." He moved to pass behind her. "I'll see you around...after you get the job."

It dawned on her then, he did not know her last name, but when she turned, he had already disappeared.

All that lingered was a faint scent of ginger.

How odd. He smells of ginger, Chrystal thought. *I did not notice that before. And man! He must be able to walk fast to disappear that quickly!*

PLEASE GO TO AMAZON.COM TO
PURCHASE THE REST OF THE BOOK.